MIDNIGHT AND BEX

HEATHER VAN FLEET

WISE WOLF
BOOKS

WISE WOLF BOOKS
An Imprint of Wolfpack Publishing
wisewolfbooks.com

Cover design by Wise Wolf Books

ISBN 978-1-953944-30-6 (paperback)
ISBN 978-1-953944-31-3 (hardcover)
ISBN 978-1-953944-29-0 (ebook)
LCCN

To Jess.
My friend, my confidant.
You keep me going. xx

MIDNIGHT AND BEX

NOTE FOR READERS

The scenarios in *Midnight and Bex* are entirely fictional and not based on any one place, situation, or person. The religious content believed by those in The Children of His Mercy stems purely from a tyrannical power rather than actual beliefs and practices in Christianity or Catholicism. I mean no offense to any particular religion or religious experience. By and large, this is a romance between two teenagers—one who has been through a very *fictional*, traumatizing experience at the hands of an evil leader.

Content warnings include: physical/psychological/emotional abuse, misogyny, and grooming. Mentions of past sexual abuse as well.

Midnight hour, death awaits.
Heartbreak comes to those who wait.
Losing limbs and eyes and veins, break me down with no escape.
I'm lost to you, to us, to me—I'm lost to those who can't roam free.
Follow me, breathe me, complete me.
My sin, your loss.
Our time concludes.

CHAPTER 1: MIDNIGHT

APRIL 2020

IT WAS HAPPENING AGAIN. This time in the middle of the night.

"We gotta go, Midnight. Now."

Mom flicked on the light in my bedroom. I jumped awake, covering my eyes with an arm.

"What the hell?"

"Pack the essentials." She tossed my duffel onto the edge of the mattress. "We'll be taking the bus."

"But you said we were done running." It was why I'd settled in, started making friends. Things guys my age would be doing already if they hadn't been running their whole lives from nonexistent ghosts.

"I know what I said." Darkness filled her blue eyes as she stared me down. "It doesn't mean anything now."

I frowned, glanced at the plastic crate on the floor beside my bed. A half-empty glass of Coke and my alarm clock flashing *1:15* sat on top.

"Did the power go out sometime?" I yawned.

"Don't know." She pointed to my duffle. "Now, get your things together and let's go."

Running a hand through my hair, I watched her panicked gaze move around the room. There'd be no talking her down. Not this time. *Run* was in her eyes, followed by *hide*. My two least favorite words.

Questions weren't allowed when she got like this. I just did what I was told, otherwise I'd wind up locked in a closet for hours until she finally realized we were good. I'd learned my lesson the hard way on that—a few too many times to count. And even though I was twice her size in weight and height now, I wouldn't disobey. If I did, she'd break down.

"I have a right to know what's changed at least." Unhurried, I got up and walked to my dresser. I yanked out socks and a hoodie, pretending to pack.

"Unless you wanna get knifed up, you'll do what I say and not question me."

"Knifed up by who?" I asked.

Either she didn't hear me or didn't care because she moved in front of my closet next and yanked a box down from the top. Inside sat fake IDs, some other paperwork I hadn't seen in a while. That wasn't a good sign.

"Mom, what's..." Then I heard it. Three knocks on the front door of our apartment.

I froze.

"No." Mom dropped the box, pressed both hands to her mouth, and backed toward the closet. "No, no, no. Midnight, *noooo*." A second later, she collapsed on the floor with a sob.

Goose bumps covered my arms when they knocked again. Faster and sharper—angrier, to the point where I knew this person wasn't just an early morning delivery boy.

"Cora," a guy said from the hall. "I know you are in

there, sweet lamb. Just open the door, and we'll make this easy on you."

The tightness in my chest eased. My mom's name was April, not Cora.

Breathing unsteady, I crouched down in front of her. "Just stay here. They've got the wrong apartment."

Her chin started to shake, and tears filled her eyes when she looked at me.

"Cora," the voice in the hall growled out again. Louder. More impatient. "Open the door—now!"

Mom grabbed my ankle when I stood. "No." She shook her head, strands of brown hair sticking to her tear-stained cheeks.

"No what?"

"Window," she whispered. "Go to the window, Midnight. Jump. But do not, I repeat *do not* answer that door."

"I'm not jumping." I pulled my leg back.

Ignoring me, she leapt to her feet and headed toward the window, yanked on the wood, and pounded on the glass when it didn't budge.

"This isn't happening," she cried. "It can't be."

"Stop," I said. "You're gonna break it." We didn't have the money to pay for broken windows, and the landlord was a dick. Already we were three months behind on rent, and destruction of property would get us kicked out.

Ignoring me, she grabbed the baseball bat I kept hidden between the head of my bed and the wall, then slammed it against the window. Glass shattered in seconds, spreading on the floor like rain.

I stood there, gaping.

"Go." Mom threw the bat outside, and the wood clattered on the sidewalk somewhere below.

I went to yell at her but stopped when I saw the blood. Her palms were covered in it, wrists too. It dripped down to her elbows when she lifted her hands, then coated the sleeve of her pajama shirt.

"You're bleeding." I swiped a T-shirt off the floor to clean her up with, but she ripped it from my fingers and tossed it to the floor.

"Go. Right now. Jump." She grabbed my wrists and dug her nails into my skin.

"Are you kidding?" I jerked my head back. "We're two floors up and it's raining."

Ignoring me, she shoved me toward the window. I tripped over my feet, fell back against the crate and everything on top of it toppled over.

Mom wrapped her fingers through my hair and yanked. "Get up. Now. Go before it's too late."

"Stop. That hurts." I shoved her hand away, wincing.

They pounded on the front door again. "Open the damn door."

I looked up at Mom, ready to tell her it was gonna be fine. To chill. But her gaze had grown empty, focused on her hands—more so the clump of my black hair that sat in her palm. She whimpered, dropped it, then refocused on my face. Tears dripped down her cheeks even faster than before.

"I'm fine." I rubbed at my scalp, reassuring her.

She licked her lips. Looked at the window, then the hall, and finally me again. "I'm sorry, Midnight," she whispered, backing toward the window. "I'm so sorry, baby. I just...I can't go through this again."

My insides grew cold. "No," I said. "Please, Mom, I..."

The front door slammed open, distracting me.

"Cooooraaaa," the voice cooed. "I warned you once about disobeying me."

Unrushed, heavy footsteps thudded through the apartment. With no time to waste, I grabbed a piece of glass on the floor and wrapped my hand around it. Seconds before I could run into the hall and slam it through the dude's skull, a scream echoed from behind me, and I turned, eyes widening.

Mom was gone.

"No!" I rushed over, looked outside, scanned the common ground between the apartment buildings. But instead of a body I saw footprints in the mud and heard the wind carrying her cries as she ran away.

I froze, the lump in my throat choking me the longer I looked outside for her.

My head pounded in my ears. The room spun. Mom was gone. She'd jumped. She'd run.

She'd *left me*.

I leaned my forehead against the wood of the window frame, trying to breathe. My chest heaved and my heart raced faster than my mind.

A dog barked somewhere in the distance, and I jumped.

Maybe she was waiting for me. Maybe she was down there, hiding, calling my name and—

"Look at me, boy," the same voice growled from directly behind me now.

Closing my eyes, I sat on the edge of my bed, shut the curtains on my window. I could scream for help. I could jump. But deep down I knew it was too late.

"I said, *look at me*." Fingers grabbed the neck of my T-shirt, yanked me across the mattress.

I landed on the floor with a thump, ass grazing broken pieces of the window. I winced, reached beneath me to pull some out of my shorts—still holding tight to the glass shard in my other hand, despite the fact that it tore into my skin.

"I-I called the cops," I sputtered.

He said nothing.

I sat up to face him, flinching when our eyes locked. He was huge. Six foot five, at least, with a short, dark beard and dark hair that sat on his shoulders, gray at the temples. He was thirty-five, maybe forty years old. Closer to Mom's age. His eyes scared me the most. They looked like pale blue storm clouds.

"You look nothing like her." The man clicked his tongue against the roof of his mouth.

Seconds later, two other men rushed into my room from behind him.

"Please, man." I got to my feet, the glass shard still in my grip behind my back still. "I-I don't know what you want, but—"

"Enough," he barked. "You speak only when spoken to from here on out, understood?"

I slammed my mouth shut. Nodded.

I wasn't the guy who'd be first to a knife fight. I was the dude who'd sit in the car, hide in the back seat, and lock the doors. Mom had taught me flight, not fight, but something told me her ideas wouldn't work with these three. Not if I wanted to stay alive.

"This him?" one of the other men asked, lifting his chin. He wore a black tee, no coat, had greasy brown hair that hit his chin. He wasn't as young as the blond dude beside him, but he looked like he'd been through some shit.

I shuddered and looked away.

"Yes. It's him." The leader nodded.

"What's the plan, Prophet?" The blond man put a hand on the leader's shoulder.

"Cora's gone," the greasy haired one said. "Kid ain't worth our time."

"There's nobody named Cora here," I told the leader guy. The *prophet*. "Y-you got the wrong apartment."

"Oh, no. It's you who is wrong." Slowly, the guy pulled out his wallet—more specifically a square picture torn at the edges. He flashed it my way, shook it once, encouraging me to take it. "I gave her that name myself, you see. It means *maiden* in Greek."

My stomach churned when I took it from his fingers. It *was* my mom—fifteen to twenty years younger—but her all the same. She was asleep or passed out, I couldn't tell, wearing a T-shirt, a pair of ripped jeans. The thing that had me wanting to puke was the fact that her hands were tied together with a brown rope on her lap.

"W-Where'd you get that?" I asked.

The prophet dude grinned, then tucked the picture back inside his wallet. "Oh, I have pictures of all my beautiful little lambs. But Cora was my favorite, so I tend to keep her close. It's why I'm so upset I missed her this evening."

I clenched my teeth.

He stroked his beard and looked me up and down. "But at least she left me a gift this time. My very own flock member." He took a step back and motioned the other men forward with his hands.

"You sure the kid's worth it?" the guy with the brown hair asked, his gaze shooting from me to his leader's profile. "Cora can't be too far from here. We could find her and—"

"Don't question me, Brother Simon. Grab the boy. It is His will now."

Blood poured down my wrist from holding the glass in my hands so tightly. I wanted to drag it across all of their faces, tear eyes out, dig it into jugulars.

The brown-haired guy—Simon—grabbed me by the elbow and yanked me toward the hall. Knowing I didn't have much time, I pulled my hand back with the glass and stabbed him in the face, just below the eye.

He cried out, then fell to the floor, taking me with him.

"Damn, kid. You got a death wish or something?" he growled, climbing on top of me. He pressed his elbow against my throat, and the glass still protruding from his cheek seemed to bleed even more.

"Please," I managed. A buzz filled my ears. My vision blurred in and out.

"Stupid," the guy muttered under his breath. "I should end you right now. Save us all the trouble." But he didn't. Instead, he let me go, sliding onto his back beside me.

I gasped for breaths, rolling over until I was on my elbows and knees.

"You wouldn't dare kill him anyway." The prophet man laughed from somewhere above. "Seeing as how he's my son."

CHAPTER 2: BEX

JANUARY 2022

I WISH I WERE INVISIBLE. Not because I want to sneak into places or eavesdrop on conversations. It's just that sometimes my life, more so the people in it, are too much and all I wanna do is disappear.

"Bex, are you listening?" My friend, Jo Donahue, twirls a lock of her platinum blonde hair around her finger.

"Uh-huh." I reach into my locker and grab my notebook and a few of the gross, sparkly pencils Mom bought for me at the beginning of the year.

"Okay, like I was saying, I ate this super nasty shrimp the other night. I think it gave me food poisoning." Jo pauses and tips her head to one side. "Have you ever gotten food poisoning before?"

"Nope. Don't think so." I close my locker and turn back to face her, along with our other two friends, Gia and Carson.

On my first day of school back in August, I was sitting alone in the lunchroom, minding my own business and reading a book, when Jo first approached me.

She took the seat beside mine, uninvited, propped her chin on her knuckles, and declared me to be the bestie she never knew she needed, before dragging me to her table.

Part of me had wondered if I was some elaborate joke to her. Let's prank the nerdy new girl and all that. But then the lunch thing became a day-to-day occurrence, and just like that, I'd unknowingly inherited a friend group for the first time.

"I think I got it once after eating at Taco Hut," Carson says, clutching her stomach. "That place is nasty."

"Oh, babe. How did I not know this?" Gia links her fingers with Carson, and the two make gaga eyes at each other. The two of them are sickly in love.

"Well," Jo says, "one time I saw this TikTok where an employee from there was walking around with his phone and recording how they store their food and stuff." She shudders. "Let's just say, I am *never* eating there again."

Gia gasps. I'm pretty sure Carson's face turns green. I cringe too, though I like to pride myself on having a tough stomach.

The three of them go off about all the places they won't eat at anymore. From restaurants to fast food, it's another weird—yet normal—conversation for us to be having while we wait for the halls to clear after school.

With over two thousand kids running the halls at Altoona High, we don't tend to rush out of here. I'd leave on my own, but the one time I'd tried to, Jo had freaked because she'd thought I was mad or something. I don't know. This whole socializing and having friends' thing, is hard to understand sometimes.

Gia's loudmouth pulls me from my thoughts. "He looks rougher than usual today."

I furrow my brows. "Who?"

"Him." She points down the hall, and my heart skips a little when I see who she's talking about.

Midnight Turner. My lab partner and sort-of-but-not-really friend who I blabber crap to, only to have him ignore me or tell me to stop talking—which only makes me talk more so I can piss him off.

"I know him." I shrug. "He's moody but cool."

Jo narrows her eyes. "You know him."

"Yeah. He's in my Chemistry class." And the reason why I am *finally* going to pass that class after having to retake it from last year. Science is not my thing. Guy's smart, if not a little antisocial. Okay, maybe he's a *lot* antisocial, but whatever. I am too.

"How did I not know you shared a class with him?" Jo asks.

"Because *I* didn't know that *you* knew him." Or cared, for that matter.

Like the rest of the girls do, I watch him move down the hallway. Slumped shoulders, head down like always. Gia's right. He *does* look moodier than usual, like someone who doesn't want to be seen. I know that look well myself because I've been wearing it since my dad died.

"Don't talk to him. Ever," Jo snaps.

"There a reason why?" I ask, continuing to watch him. More so the way his black hair sweeps across his neck and temples as though he's been running his fingers through it all day. It's long—to his shoulders, and today he's wearing a sweatshirt that's too big for his slim figure, which isn't anything new.

"He can't be trusted, that's why." Jo narrows her eyes and stares at her boots.

"Trust is a hard thing to earn when you've never talked to someone before," I say.

"Oh, I've talked to him. A shit ton of times actually." She pulls out her phone and scrolls through it.

I open my mouth to ask what exactly she's talked to him about, but Carson jumps.

"We should go," she says.

"Yeah, I gotta get home and babysit my little brother," Gia adds.

Jo tucks a hand through my arm, guiding me toward the stairs, acting like we didn't just have an almost-fight about the school's most mysterious dude.

I keep watching Midnight from the corner of my eye, though, frowning when he makes a sudden dash across the hall toward our Chem class. It's like the world's on fire beneath his feet and his entire life depends on getting inside that room. I glance at my friends, thinking I'm seeing things, but none of them seem to notice.

As we head down the steps, Jo goes on about her party this weekend—the outfit she's going to wear and the fact that she invited this new guy she's been crushing on. Meanwhile my brain's still running wild with questions about Midnight and what he's up to.

We're halfway down the second flight of steps when I finally give in to my curiosity. *It's the future journalist in you,* Dad would say. Mom, on the other hand, would call me nosy.

"Hey." I touch Jo's shoulder. "I forgot my phone in my locker."

"You want me to go back upstairs with you to get it?" She arches a brow.

I look to Gia and Carson as they round the corner on the last flight of stairs. "No, it's fine. You catch up with them."

She nods. "Text me later?"

"Yep."

I wave goodbye and head back up, stopping in front of the classroom door. I don't open it right away but instead peek through the side glass window, hoping to catch a glimpse of him.

It's dark inside. Maybe he's already gone. Regardless, I'm curious enough to wrap my hand around the knob and turn it. *Leave no stone left unturned,* my father's voice echoes inside my head.

The room is silent, other than a ticking clock above my head on the wall. The room's neat and tidy, all micro-scopes and equipment tucked away safe. It's only when I'm ready to bolt do I hear it—a soft, repetitive whisper from the next row over.

Slowly, I walk to where my and Midnight's lab table is, feet silent against the linoleum. The next thing I know, a large hand reaches out and grabs tight to my ankle.

"What the—"

"Get down," he hisses from under the table, tugging on my pant leg.

Fear captures his blue eyes, and the sight of him in the near dark has my heart racing. I open my mouth to ask what's up, but he jumps out from underneath the table and wraps an arm around my waist.

"What are you doing?" I gasp.

"Hide." Seconds later he drops to the floor again, sliding under the table and pulling me onto his lap.

"Midnight, let me go." I squirm, heart racing so fast I'm dizzy.

"Please"—he places a hand over my mouth— "don't make a sound, or he'll come for you."

I freeze against him with my back pressed to his heaving chest, wondering who he's talking to—if anyone.

He starts to whisper again, the words in a different language. "Pater obsecro. Pater obsecro. Pater obsecro."

Chills slide down my spine and my entire body shakes like a tidal wave. I'm not sure how long we stay like that—an hour, ten minutes, or five. But the longer we sit there, the more my eyes burn with unshed tears.

"Orate mecum," he says.

And that's when I feel it—hot, wet tears against my temple. *His* tears. The kind that don't slow as they crawl down from his face to mine. They drip over my chin and onto my neck, the sensation unfamiliar, not to mention strange because I have zero idea what's going on.

Another minute passes. His hold on me loosens—probably because he's shaking now too. Using that to my advantage, I yank his hand from my mouth and jab an elbow against his ribs, recalling the self-defense moves my dad tried to teach me once.

Midnight grunts, immediately letting me go. Then as fast as I can, I scoot out from between his legs, smacking my head on the underside of the table when I try to stand.

"Ugh," I groan, holding my palm to the already growing bump.

"Stop it," he hisses at me through a choking sob, grabs at my ankle again.

"Let me go!" I yank my foot back and turn over, crab-walking backward to get away. But then I make the stupid mistake of looking at him again, and what I see has me faltering.

Ears covered by hands, he rocks back and forth, looking like a scared child, not a six-foot-plus teenage boy with a bad attitude. I should get up and run while he's distracted, locate a teacher, and ask for help. But for the life of me, the only thing I can do is stare.

"I'm sorry." He bows his head and tucks it between his knees. "I'm so, so sorry."

"M-Midnight?" I stand on trembling legs. "Are you okay?"

He whips his head up, dark brows pulled together. Blinks a few times too. "W-what're you doing in here?"

The question catches me off guard, and I look around, struggling to think of an excuse.

"Answer me," he snaps, his upper lip curling.

"My, uh, *phone*. I left it in the basket." I point to where the teacher stows them away during class behind his desk.

"No, you didn't." He eyes my pocket, where it's currently lit up inside.

"Heh, right. Yeah." I clear my throat, take a step back for distance's sake.

He wipes his face with aggressive hand strokes. "You should go, Bex."

"But—"

"Go. Now." He crawls out from under the table and gets to his feet, eyes narrowing down at me. He's hella tall, yeah, but it's not his height that scares me right then. It's his wandering mind and the pieces of him I can't see.

"Why did you just..." *Freak out on me. Trap me. Cry and speak in another language?*

"Leave," he says again, losing the bite in his words. "Please just...go."

"But—"

"Never mind." He shakes his head, sliding around me to grab his bag. Then he does exactly what he asked me to do and leaves the room.

I stand there once he's gone, gaze locked on the door, then zeroing back in on the dead space beneath our table. What happened couldn't have been real...more so an out of body experience—déjà vu, even. Yet no matter how many times I try to convince myself of this, I know it's untrue. Not when I can still feel his hot tears on my neck.

CHAPTER 3: MIDNIGHT
MAY 2020

IT WAS STILL light outside when he came to my door. Three slow knocks. The guy was always punctual, always lurking, and always so damn serious. Noah was his name. The man who'd been assigned to me as my guardian while I was there. The blond guy who'd broken into our apartment a month ago. Unlike his prophet though—a man I'd come to know as Emmanuel—he was only a half-ass bastard instead of a whole.

"Brother Midnight, are you dressed?" he asked from the hall.

I shifted my head on the pillow trying to get comfortable. "No."

Warmth seeped out from beneath the bandages along my back, despite the fact I'd barely moved off my stomach all day. I should've gotten stiches. But the only doctor at this place was just as sadistic as the rest of the men here.

"There will be consequences if you're late," Noah said.

"Screw the consequences," I mumbled under my breath. Death would be a hell of a lot better than what I was going through.

Fiat voluntas Dei.

Fiat voluntas Dei.

Fiat voluntas Dei.

It is His will.

Emmanuel's words ran through my mind like a hamster wheel. I had no idea what they meant, but they'd been repeated with every strike of his wire whip across my back two nights ago.

The door creaked open. I didn't bother to look up and instead stared at the chair sitting beside my bed. It was nailed to the floor, probably so I didn't break the glass window and jump out, something I should've done with Mom.

I wasn't mad at her. Not now that I knew what she'd been running from all this time. She might not have been the best mom, but she was mine. And as her son, if taking her place in this hell hole was the only way to keep her safe, then that's what I'd do.

"It's your first Young-Men Service, Brother Midnight. You're required to attend."

"Screw your flock," I said, turning my head to look at him again.

Noah sighed, moved farther into my room, then stopped in front of me. Unlike Emmanuel, he wouldn't beat me for smarting off. I didn't know why, but he was nicer than anyone at this place.

"How is your back tonight?" he asked.

"What's it matter to you?"

"It matters because you're my Shepherd who I've been tasked to watch over and keep safe."

"Then why didn't you stop the beating? I wasn't exactly *safe* then."

"If you had obeyed him, then this wouldn't have happened in the first place."

I grunted, too tired to argue.

Noah crouched down in front of me, picked my bible up off the floor, and stared at it. "He is your Prophet, not to mention your father."

"I don't have a father." I shut my eyes.

He sighed again. "Follow his word like we all do for a path that you deserve. A happiness that will come easier if you'd embrace it with open arms."

I curled my top lip. "And what if I don't believe in *his* word?"

Noah placed my bible onto the empty chair before standing. "Then it's my blood on your hands as much as your blood will be on mine."

———

YOUNG-MEN SERVICE WAS a three-ring shit show of dudes chanting in a language I'd been told was Latin. Young boys and older guys my age, ranging from eight to eighteen, stood inside a white room in the basement of the building, holding hands as they listened to Emmanuel.

He was in the center of us all, speaking of peace and a new world, a chance to rid every one of their sins and be one man instead of a million for God.

"He has challenged us all yet pushed us down a righteous path with His never-failing word," Emmanuel said, looking around at each one of us, before stopping on me.

His gaze narrowed.

I hated that we shared the same color of eyes—a blue so light they looked clear.

"For we do His bidding as it is ours and all will be right." He raised his hands into the air. "Orem us." *Let us pray.*

Everyone dropped to their knees and set their foreheads against the ground like soldiers. Even the littlest kids. I swallowed hard, fighting the urge to yell, to tell them all to get up, that they were brainwashed SOBs who followed a freak, not some renowned holy leader.

Emmanuel stepped closer to me and folded his hands at his waist. "Midnight," he said. "Is there a reason why you're not in prayer, my son?"

"I'm not your *son*."

He lifted his eyebrows at me. "Biology has said otherwise, I'm afraid."

If it didn't hurt so badly to move, I would've flipped him off.

Like he could read my mind, Emmanuel asked, "How is your injury this evening, hm?"

I gritted my teeth. He knew exactly how it was. "Fine."

"Proverbs 12:22 says, *'The Lord detests lying lips, but he delights in people who are trustworthy.'*" He strolled around me, gaze shooting from my head to my toes. "You can be trustworthy, can't you?"

"Yes." But only because my body wouldn't survive another beating.

"Good." He pressed his fingertips together at his waist. "Now, tell me again—be honest this time. How is your injury?"

I inhaled through my nose and exhaled through my mouth before answering. "It hurts."

He hummed to himself and moved closer. "It does pain me to know you're hurting, truly." Spoiled-milk breath hit my nose the closer he got, causing my stomach to churn. "But it pains *Him* even more knowing not even an injury will keep you from sinning. From *disobeying* me. From inflicting instability on our home that you have been so graciously invited into." He put a hand on my shoulder. "Which is why I must ask you one more time to *get* on your *knees* and *pray*."

Emmanuel shoved me down and knocked my feet out from under me. I flew forward, my face—my nose—slamming against the concrete ground. Everything around me blurred.

A ringing noise filled my ears.

"You will obey me." He held a hand against the back of my head, forcing me to stay down. "You will pray. You will ask for my forgiveness. You will be the son I was gifted, the man born to lead this flock."

I moaned, tasting blood.

Without giving me a chance to move on my own, he shoved the toe of his shoe beneath me and kicked my stomach. "On your knees."

I cried out. The raw skin on my back burned as I moved. Sweat slid across my forehead and neck. Blood dripped from my nostrils to the floor, making a small *tap* noise against the tile.

"You will follow my word, Midnight."

I shook my head, the ground spinning.

He kicked my ribs again.

I grunted, elbows too weak to hold myself up.

"You will follow my word, *Midnight*."

Another kick followed. I groaned and my eyes started to water.

Reaching down, he grabbed the back of my neck and

pulled my chin from the floor, getting in my face as he spat, "You will follow. My. Word."

I blinked and then opened my mouth, caught the blood in between my lips, and spit it at his face. That was the last thing I remembered before everything went dark.

CHAPTER 4: MIDNIGHT

NOVEMBER 2020

I'D RARELY BEEN outside the walls of Children of His Mercy in seven months, other than standard exercise around the fenced-in commune and in between the tiny homes outside of the main building. The pale color of my scarred skin was proof.

Today was a special occasion, according to Emmanuel. Instead of my normal study days inside where I'd read and learn the bible, Latin, history, and occasionally math, I was sent to a different location on my own—a different hallway leading to a door that would take me outside.

At first, I thought it was a joke, until Simon showed up.

I greeted him with a nod. He curled his upper lip.

Other than the classroom, the room for Young-Men Service, the cafeteria, as well as my bedroom, I hadn't been anywhere else. Out-of-routine things here scared the hell out of me.

Since the night after my first Young-Men Service, when I'd been knocked unconscious by Emmanuel, I'd learned to do what I had to do to survive. Escaping this place wouldn't be an option, not anymore. The guards standing watch made sure of that. It sucked because everyone else here had the chance to leave if they wished. Everyone except for the son of the prophet—a title I sure as hell never asked for.

The second we stepped down a set of brick stairs leading outside, I held an arm over my eyes to block the early morning sun. It might have been late fall, but natural light wasn't something my eyes were used to, other than through a tiny window. It made me feel like a vampire, without the ability to kill with my teeth. I wouldn't have been surprised if my scarred-up exposed skin turned to ash for as pale as I was.

The others didn't seem to notice I was there. These weren't the normal guys I was used to spending time with, so maybe that's why. They were all ahead of me, talking and laughing, at least three or four years older. I wondered if they'd been out here before. If this was familiar to them.

When my vision cleared enough for me to take everything in, I dropped my arm, blinking a couple times. Everything out here seemed so normal. Like I was walking through the park that was close to Mom's and my old apartment building. In the center of the rectangular-looking courtyard sat a white fountain. It was old and split down the sides, like something out of a museum. In the middle of it was a stone man who looked dangerously close to an immortal Emmanuel.

I grimaced and looked away.

Around the brick walls of the fountain were empty wooden boxes. Noah had said they grew a lot of their own food here, so this could've been where it came from.

Either way, I was looking at some second-world shit, for sure.

Benches sat in all four corners, and in one of them was the only thing I hadn't seen since coming here. A girl. She was dressed in all white and wore a veil over her face like a bride. Her head was bowed so I couldn't see what she looked like, but her hair was the color of honey and it hung down to her waist. On her lap sat a book. An old bible, from the looks of it.

"Brother Midnight," Simon grumbled from behind. "Move before I make you."

Ah, Simon. I'd almost missed the son of a bitch.

He shoved me. Not hard, but enough to get me going. I caught up with the rest of the guys a few seconds later, finally drawing their eyes and whispers. Again, they weren't who I normally shared Service with. And they were all staring at me like a bunch of gossiping idiots.

"You deserve joy and are so close to obtaining it. Which is why I've invited you to Service with the Gentlemen."

My spine stiffened at the sound of his voice, an automatic response when it came to Emmanuel.

"You've shown great change within the last seven months," he continued. "Become a standout Shepherd among a field of bewildered sheep. That is the reason you're here this afternoon, with us."

I didn't say anything, mostly because I didn't know what *to* say.

"Come." Emmanuel grabbed the back of my elbow and steered me forward. I glanced over my shoulder to look at Simon, finding him in the same place, talking to Noah.

Swallowing, I turned back around and searched the courtyard. In the distance, on the other side of a small wood gate, was a group of houses. Beyond them sat an even taller gate made of what looked like barbed wire. It was prison-worthy, and I felt just like an inmate.

Behind the podium was a large cross with the words *Children of His Mercy* written across the wood. "You are here to prepare for what is to come," Emmanuel said.

"What's coming?"

"You'll see." He winked.

A creepy sensation tickled the back of my neck, like spiders crawling across my skin. His cryptic words freaked me out more than usual.

The girl on the bench grabbed my attention again seconds before we reached the other guys. Lost in her studying, she didn't notice us. But it didn't take Emmanuel long to notice her.

He sighed and shook his head, loud voice booming across the courtyard. "Romans 13:1-2 says those who refuse to obey the law of the land are refusing to obey God and punishment will follow."

The girl jumped in place, then stood, keeping her head bowed. "Prophet, you're here, and..." She hesitated, glancing toward the podium, the stage, the men, then me. Even though I couldn't see her face, I could tell by the way her hands tightened around her bible she was nervous.

"Come along, Midnight," Emmanuel said to me. "It is time you learn the rules while they are ripe for the teaching." He squeezed my elbow even tighter and dragged me toward the girl.

"Eve," Emmanuel *tsked* when we finally stood in front of her. "You were told not to go outside, yet here you are disobeying me again, my sweet lamb."

She bowed her head and took his outstretched hand, kissing the back of it. "Prophet," she whispered, setting her bible onto the bench behind her, before getting on her knees in front of him. "I didn't know I wasn't allowed out here. Ignosce me." *Forgive me.*

"Ah, but you did know." Emmanuel shook his head. "Which is why you will be forced to pay for this error of ways, I'm afraid."

Her shoulders stiffened, words shaky as she repeated, "Ignosce me."

Emmanuel petted the top of her head like a cat. He pulled off the veil and tossed it back onto the bench as well. I still couldn't see her face because it was pressed against the sidewalk now, but I heard her whispers. Her *prayers.*

"This is a good lesson for you, Midnight." Emmanuel looked at me from over his shoulder. "If the lambs are not birthed behind our walls, then they are to be tamed by our hands under His guidance, just like our sweet Eve here."

Tamed. Like some sort of wild animal.

Emmanuel twisted fingers into the back of the girl's hair and yanked her head up. She cried out, and I drove my nails into my palms just to keep from grabbing the back of Emmanuel's hair.

"Say it louder," he yelled, drawing eyes from the men. "Pray for my forgiveness, for your sins, for the pain this causes me having to see you on the cold, wet ground. For being out here on display for my Shepherds to lust after."

Nobody had even paid attention to Eve—or noticed her, as far as I could tell. But now that Emmanuel had drawn attention to her, the guys in the group started gathering around us. Noah was there too, along with Simon, both of their faces empty of emotions.

"I-ignosce m-me," the girl cried out again. "Please, Prophet. I didn't know. I was waiting for you, and—"

"Enough." Emmanuel bent over, getting in her face. I tried to look around him to see her, but his hair framed her head like a curtain. "You should be very thankful I saved you and brought you here. Sheltered you and gave you what you needed in a time when you were so very lost, sweet lamb. When nobody else cared, always remember I was there."

"I know. My love for you is endless," she whispered.

An angry buzz filled my ears, and it was like I'd been transported back in time inside my apartment with Mom. I wanted to beat Emmanuel's head against the concrete, watch the blood bleed out of his eyes, his nose, and his ears. He talked like a savior but behaved like a demon, and nothing about him was saintly. If he really was my father, then I'd deny it until I died.

Before I could speak out, Noah moved in next to me. He grabbed my wrist and dug nails into my skin. I glared at him. He shook his head. The guy knew I had a hot temper, but he also knew how deep my hatred toward Emmanuel ran. In his own messed up way, he was probably trying to protect me when he should've been protecting this girl.

"She is yours," he hissed in my ear.

"My what?" I growled back.

"You are to have a ceremony during Service soon. You've been gifted this. Gifted *her*."

I shook my head. "What the hell does that mean?"

"This young girl is soon to be your lamb, Brother Midnight. Your life partner."

CHAPTER 5: BEX
JANUARY 2022

EVERYTHING in the cafeteria looks duller than usual today. It's probably because of the incoming snowstorm. Gray skies angry and hiding the sun, ready to explode with white in a matter of hours. I love the snow because it's a disruption in the universe that always matches my mood. Today is no different.

"So, did you think more about my offer?" Gia asks, leaning away from the cafeteria table.

I blink when I realize she's looking at me. "What offer again?"

"My cousin." She rolls her eyes. "He said he'd be your date to Jo's party on Saturday if you want him to."

"Your cousin is in eighth grade," Jo jumps in with a huff. "Besides, if Bex wants to go solo, it's fine."

"What she said." I shrug and take a bite of my pizza.

Dates and parties mean nothing to me. Besides that, I've got other things to worry about. Like the upcoming essays I've gotta write for college apps and Netflix to binge.

"You're still coming, though, right?" Gia asks, laying her head on Carson's shoulder.

I force a smile, already plotting my way out like I did for Jo's *last* party.

"Wouldn't miss it."

Jo's family has some land way on the edge of Jillian County. I haven't been there personally, but it's supposed to be *the* place to party. The cops from our town don't cross the county line, Carson told me once. And the only cops in *Jillian County*, where the land is, tend to stay closer to the populated areas. Western Illinois is a whole other universe compared to the Chicago area—which is where I was born and mostly raised.

"Just be sure to get some sleep the night before." Gia looks me over. "Your poor eyebags look like they're carrying coal."

"G," Carson says.

"What? I'm only trying to help. Our girl here is fine as hell, but she doesn't even bother trying."

I roll my eyes, used to her insults. It doesn't bother me that Gia doesn't have a filter. If anything, truth-talkers make my life easier.

"Thanks for the compliment, but I'll be dressed for the weather. It's gonna be ice cold on Saturday."

"But if you wanna bag a lover, then take my advice." Gia leans over and pats the back of my hand. "Sleep more. Read less."

My face heats when I looked down at my book. It's from my dad's collection. I'm trying to get through his sci-fi box before spring break in April. Then when I get back to school, I can dive into his non-fic stuff.

Jo leans back in her chair and huffs. "I wish he'd just go away already."

I look to where she is, not surprised to see that the

source of her frustration is Midnight. Every time he's in the same room as her, she complains about him. It's usually rude, snide comments, and since she won't tell me what her issues are with him, I refuse to take sides.

Like every day since I first met him in August, Midnight is decked out in jeans, boots, and a black sweatshirt that's too big for him. His hands are tucked into his pockets, and his head's down, chin to chest, black hair blanketing the sides of his pale face.

"I think he's coming over here again, Jo-Jo," Gia mumbles.

"He better not be." She sneers.

"Oh, come on, Jo. It's your fault he..."

Carson nudges Gia with an elbow, then looks at Jo.

I frown, uneasy. Usually, the secrets they keep between one another don't bother me. But this does.

"Did you do something to him?" I ask Jo.

"Uh, no," she snaps but keeps her eyes on Midnight the entire time.

As nonchalantly as possible, I pull the end of my brown ponytail over my shoulder and study the dry ends. The bad part about having beautiful friends is that you tend to question things you might not have questioned before. Like boob size, butt shapes, and now, in my case, the condition of my freaking hair. Hair that's nothing in comparison to Gia's black-and-pink curls or Jo's long blonde hair or Carson's cute red pixie cut.

Life was so much easier when I was a loner back in Chicago.

It doesn't matter, I tell myself. *I don't like him like that.*

Or so I tell myself because after yesterday, all bets are on the table as far as how that boy makes me feel.

Midnight stops in front of our table, gaze focused solely on Jo. "Hey," he stutters. "Can we talk yet?"

Something green fills my chest, swollen and ugly, like I'm filled with a bottle of liquid jealousy.

"I've got nothing to say to you." Jo lifts her chin.

He leans in, hands on the edge of the table. "Just five minutes."

"I told you, no."

I let my gaze slide back and forth between them. It's hard to understand why she hates him so much. It's even harder to keep my mouth shut about it.

"Please, Jo, I don't…"

He trails off, looking around the table like he only just now senses an audience. Then he spots me, and everything else seems to fade away, as cliché as it sounds. His bright eyes focus on my face so intently that my cheeks warm, and I find myself sinking deeper into my chair. Dark circles, possibly worse than mine, sit beneath them today—circles I hadn't noticed this morning in class. It leaves me wondering what keeps him awake at night.

I rub my arms to fight the goose bumps beneath my sweater. This reaction of mine is suuuuper annoying. Not to mention unwelcome.

"For the thousandth time, leave. I don't want you anywhere around me or my friends." Jo shoos him away with her hand.

"I just thought that—"

"Maybe I wanted to hang with a freak?" She laughs, the bitter sound causing my stomach to twist. "Because you've got it wrong like always, dude. I want absolutely *nothing* to do with you, and neither do my friends. So step. The hell. Away."

Midnight spares me a quick glance, his gaze empty, before he turns and walks off.

"That was harsh, Jo," Carson says, taking a drink of water.

"I don't like him. He's trash."

Gia winces, following Midnight with her gaze. "Yeah, but he's been so—"

"I swear to God, G. If you don't stop sticking up for him, then I'll punch you in the boob." Jo pushes her tray away and stands, looking at me. "You coming? I don't wanna be late."

I blink up at her. "You shouldn't have called him that."

"Called him what?"

"A freak."

I don't usually stand up to Jo—there's never been a reason to do so, and I hate confrontation. But the way she snaps at us for no reason isn't fair.

She quirks a brow. "And why not?"

"It's bitchy."

Jo rolls her eyes. "You have zero clue about the guy. So, I suggest you don't say shit unless you understand."

"I know more than you think," I say.

I may not know him on a personal level, but on a relatable one, I know he's broken like me. That he's hurting for some reason. I know too, that he's just as lonely inside as I am. It doesn't take a rocket scientist to figure out that he has some serious emotional wounds. Wounds that have him pulling girls under lab tables and speaking words of salvation to them in Latin when he's done his very best to ignore them the entire year up to that point.

Jo takes a few steps back from the table, her jaw set. "Whatever. I'm going to class. Are you coming or not?"

Since the week I first met her, Jo and I have kept the same routine—her dragging me to Trig post lunch. Me tagging along like it's my duty. But I need a moment now. And from the anger I see in her eyes I think she does too.

"I need to go to my locker first. Go ahead without me."

"Fine." She twists her lips, turns, and walks away, leaving me with a heaviness in my belly that I'm not used to when it comes to her and me.

"Don't take it personally, Bex." Carson touches the back of my hand. "She and Midnight—"

"Carson," Gia jumps in, lowering her voice. "Watch what you say, babe."

"What?" I ask, leaning forward in my chair.

"G's right." Carson cringes. "It's not our story to tell. You'll have to ask Jo about it."

Fire burns between my ribs. The kind that has me wishing for a glass of honesty and Tums. Regardless, I can't let them see how much this bothers me, otherwise it'll ruin my reputation of not outwardly giving a shit.

"It's cool." I push my tray aside and stand. "I'll see you guys later."

I walk out of the cafeteria, then into the hall, blinking to keep my eyes from leaking. Maybe some water on my face will help the sting. Or if someone's smoking in there, I'll ask for a hit off their pen instead of mentally handing out lung cancer pamphlets.

After passing the gymnasium and a couple of empty classrooms, I round the corner that leads to J-Wing. The bathrooms down there are the farthest I can get from the cafeteria. I don't want to run the risk of seeing anyone I know—more specifically Jo again.

I keep my head down, gaze on the tile floor while I count each square. Putting numbers to things is a tool I use when I'm anxious. Even still, I can't seem to stop the ball of emotion climbing up my throat.

"One. Two. Three. Four. Five—Oomph!"

I slam headfirst into a body. Someone's side is more like it.

"Shit, I'm so sorry, I didn't..." I blink when I look up. "Oh, Midnight. Hey, I didn't see you there."

A section of his hair falls over one eye, and through it I see his brows bunching together. There's a scar running across his temple I haven't noticed before, probably because I'm always on the opposite side of him in Chemistry.

"You should be more aware of your surroundings," he tells me.

"Right." I salute him then clear my throat. "Sorry for that."

His eyes narrow a little more, until he finally looks away into his locker. He puts a hand on the metal. It's shaking, I notice, and his knuckles are practically white as he squeezes the metal. The scars on the back of his hands draw my gaze. I've never asked about them in the five months we've been Chem acquaintances, but now feels about as good a time as ever.

"Sooo..." I swing my right arm, bouncing up and down on my toes as I wait. "Did you, like, get caught up in a boxing match gone wrong or something?"

Midnight shuts his locker and faces me. "What?"

I point to his hands.

He looks at them, then tucks them into the pockets of his jeans. "No."

"Oh, well...what happened?" I hold up a finger. "I mean, you don't *have* to tell me. I was just curious is all."

"Hmm," is all he says.

One time, I asked my dad why he chose the career he

did—investigative journalist for the *Chicago Sun-Times*. He said it was because there was real meaning behind it. A chance to share some truth with the world in order to help ease the pain or fear of others. Plus, he was able to write, which was his one true love—besides me and Mom, of course.

Standing with Midnight, I truly see the appeal when it comes to Dad's career because I'm suddenly dying to know everything about the guy—even if he's not *dying* to tell me.

He lifts a brow staring at me. The dark circles under his ocean-blue eyes look even harsher up close. "You need something?"

I bite the inside of my cheek, keeping my disappointment in check. "Guess I just wanted to apologize."

"You did that already." He frowns.

"No, I mean, I wanted to say sorry for something else." I hesitate. "For what Jo said in the cafeteria. I don't understand why she, you know…"

"Hates me?" His eyes narrow a little.

I nod and look at my Converse, not wanting to say yes out loud because it doesn't feel right.

Midnight seems to take my silence as a cue to keep going. "It's fine. She's got her reasons."

"Yeah, but it's not cool of her to be a bitch like that." I look up, catching him rubbing a hand along the back of his neck. The pain in his eyes as he stares at me has my chest squeezing.

Who hurt you? I want to ask.

"It's okay," he says, his voice softening. "I deserve her hate."

"No, you don't." I squint back at him, not understanding the self-sabotage. "She's bullying you. I won't let her get away with it."

"You say that like you've experienced it."

"What?"

"Bullying."

I shrug. "Who hasn't?"

He runs a few fingers through his floppy hair. "You should go to class now, Bex."

"You should get to class too."

"I'm not going."

"Why not?"

"Because I have things I need to take care of."

"What kind of things?"

He shakes his head. Takes a good five steps back. "Didn't I tell you once that asking so many questions will get you in trouble?"

"You did." I grin. "But didn't I tell you once that I wanted to be a journalist? That means it's in my nature to be nosy."

Intending to follow him no matter what, I step forward and...trip over the toe of my stupid sneaker. I'm nose deep against his chest when one of his arms encircles my waist.

"*Adtentus,*" he whispers.

"What does that mean?" I ask.

His Adam's apple bobs. "Careful."

I nod and breathe in through my nose, taking in the smell of laundry detergent. He doesn't wear cologne, I decide, but he smells like soap again.

"I'm sorry," I finally say.

He pulls back, placing both hands on my elbows. He looks at me with furrowed brows once more and asks, "What are you sorry for this time?"

"Being cliché and falling into your arms?" I cringe.

Instead of smiling like I'd hoped, Midnight says, "*Auribus teneo lupum.*"

Instead of asking for a translation, I ask, "What language is that?"

"Latin."

My eyes widen a little. "Wow. That's a hard language to learn. How did you—"

"Church." He looks away.

"Oh." I chew my bottom lip, flex my fingers too.

I've never attended church a day in my life, not even when Dad died. It's not that I don't believe. More so I wasn't raised with a whole lot of faith.

"Are you good now?" Midnight asks.

"Yeah." I laugh, both of my cheeks on fire. "My, uh, feet and gravity don't get along."

He drops his arms from around me, steps back, and looks at the floor. "I have to go."

Seconds later, he's turned and heading down the hall.

It doesn't hit me again until he's five feet away that I didn't ask the one question I need an answer for right now.

"Did you hurt her?" I call after him.

He freezes but doesn't turn around.

I step closer, slower this time, like he's a ghost I don't want to spook. Even as I slide in front of him, he doesn't say anything.

"Did you hurt Jo?" I ask again.

"I don't want to talk about this."

"Okay, fine." I cross my arms. "If you don't want to talk about *Jo*, then let's talk about what happened after school yesterday."

He winces, then looks out the window to his left. "Can we forget that happened?"

"I have a right to know why." I lower my voice to a whisper. "Especially since you freaked out on me like you did."

He scrubs a hand down his face, clearly frustrated. "It's called having a bad day."

If that was a bad day, then I'd hate to see what an actual *terrible* day is like for the poor guy. "Look." I take a deep breath. "I won't tell anyone what happened. Nor will I bring it up again." I lower my voice. "I just want to know if you hurt Jo. That's it."

"Never." He looks at me again, his expression open and sincere for the first time since knowing him. My chest warms because of it, and if I could, I'd hug him.

"All right, then." I wave him on. When he starts walking away, so do I.

He stops. Clenches his jaw. "What now?"

"I just…" I wince. "Wanna know where you're from. That's all."

"No."

"Oh, come on. Getting to know me won't kill you, especially since we spend an hour every day together already."

He shakes his head and starts walking again. I'm right there with him though, step for step.

"You're pushy," he tells me. "I don't like it."

"There are much worse things in life to dislike than me."

"No shit."

"Wanna play a game on our way to class?"

"No."

"I'll start. Let's tell each other the things that we dislike. I'll start."

"Bex, I—"

"Peppy people, for one. They're super easy to dislike, especially when someone's in a perpetually bad mood like me." I tick more examples off on my fingers as I say them. "Then there's broccoli, cats, apple pie, and the sun." I shudder with that last one. "I really, *really* dislike the sun."

Midnight stops and narrows his eyes.

"What?"

He doesn't answer, of course.

I circle a hand in front of me. "Now's the part where you jump in and tell me what you dislike." I hold up finger. "Not *hate*—because that's different."

Midnight purses his lips. "Why are you doing this?"

"Because I love to collect data in my mind." I tap my temple. "This thing doesn't know how to shut down. It's kind of like a car that needs fuel. But instead of gas, I need useless knowledge to make it run." I take a breath. "And since you won't tell me what's going on with you and Jo or what happened yesterday *or* where you're from, then you can at least do me a favor and refuel my head with stuff that doesn't matter."

His lips twitch.

I blink, not believing what I almost just saw.

Midnight never smiles—or even looks remotely human. He's like a dying robot in need of major repairs. But I swear on everything holy that the dude just grinned.

"Well?" I lift my brows, waiting, internally fist pumping at the same time.

In a surprising turn of events, Midnight answers. "Fine. I don't like flowers."

"Yeah. Same." I curl my nose. "They're pretty for a while, but then they wilt and die like everything else in the world." It's a morbid thought. But that's my mind for ya. "You know what else I don't like?"

"What?"

"Summer," I say. "I absolutely dislike sweating, the humidity, and, again, the sun." I hold up a finger. "I also highly dislike anything that involves social niceties that are unnecessary."

"Winter," he says. "I don't like...winter."

"How is that possible?" I mock gasp, then look over his shoulder, smiling because the snow is finally falling outside. It's so fresh and clean, untouched by the world. "It's gray out when it snows, therefore you can stay in your pajamas all day, eat bad food, and watch TV when it's snowing. What's not to like about it?"

"It's cold." His ocean-blue eyes darken, and the intensity I see inside of them sends a shiver down my spine. "And bad things happen when it's cold."

"Did something bad happen to you?" I hold my breath, wondering if I can get more out of him.

He doesn't disappoint. "My world froze over."

My stomach twists. I open my mouth, then snap it shut. Instead of asking more questions, I study him, look for clues, something—anything—to tell me what's going through his mind. But other than the flexing of his fingers against his thighs, he's a force of silence.

The tips of our shoes touch, and he stiffens when my knees graze his. Still, he doesn't move away. It's like some weird, supernatural force is pulling me toward him, as if I was destined to be here, in this moment, with this very broken boy. Someone who may be worse off than I am.

"Midnight?" I whisper, pressing a hand to his forearm.

He doesn't answer. He doesn't look at me either. But I know he hears me because his chest stops rising and falling when I start to speak.

"I'm a good listener if you ever want to—"

"Jesus, there you are," Jo calls out from behind me, grabbing my arm and yanking me a few steps back. "The teacher asked me to go look for you," she says, glaring up at Midnight. "And you, asshole, I told you to stay away from my friends."

"Jo," I hiss as she drags me farther down the hall. "You're being ridiculous."

"No, I'm not. You are. I told you to stay away from him, Bex."

"And you're not my mom."

She stops, throws her head back, and blows out a deep breath before looking at me again. "Please." Tears fill her eyes. Her bottom lip trembles. "Can we just go?"

Knowing she won't stop until I listen, I nod and let her guide me away, glancing over my shoulder at Midnight. Only then does he finally look at me again.

Despair is so evident in his eyes that my throat burns with the need to call out his name. I was so close to knowing something about him—so close to solving the secret formula that consumes the pain in his heart.

"You can't be alone with him. Ever," Jo tells me the second we turn a corner.

I shake my head, still angry but mostly confused now. "Tell me why? Do you like him or something?"

She stops us in the middle of the hall, grabs me by my shoulders. The color on her cheeks now matches the strawberries I ate for breakfast. I don't know if she's angry or embarrassed.

I lower my voice and try again. "Did he hurt you?"

She winces, shakes her head. Neither move matches the other, but that doesn't stop me from digging.

"Then tell me what it is about him that pisses you off so bad?"

"He's sick in the head." She looks at the ground, drops her hands from my arms.

Her choice of words make me cringe. "That's not cool

to say about someone, especially when you don't know what's actually going on in their head."

I think about Midnight's tears from yesterday under that table—the sadness so heavy in his shoulders I could feel it weighing *me* down. I'm not an empath, but I've got a sensitivity to others' emotions. That's why my friend-less state back in Chicago had exactly one perk—it allowed me to keep my emotions intact and away from others.

"All right," she steps back, fidgets with the silver ring she's wearing on her thumb. "You really want to know?"

"Yes!" I throw my hands up. "Jesus, Jo. I wouldn't ask if I didn't want to know."

"Fine." She closes her eyes. "Midnight is a brain-washed cult member. A guy who spent a year of his life with religious, murderous *freaks* somewhere in Missouri or Arkansas, I don't know."

I blink, not expecting that. "Oh."

"Yeah," she scoffs, reopens her eyes again. "'Oh' is right." She looks down at her hands. They're shaking.

"Hey." I touch her wrist. "Talk to me." I want to know why this bugs her so much. There has to be a reason. You can't just hate someone because of a past they probably don't have a lot of control over.

She clears her throat and wipes her nose. "I'm fine. Just do me a favor and stay away from him. Midnight screws up everything and everyone he gets close to. You don't need that in your life."

"How do you know all this?"

She looks at her phone. "People."

"People." I huff, only for the last lunch bell to go off.

"Yeah, well, be thankful I told you." Jo tucks her arm through mine, completely cool again as we walk toward fourth period. "And if you're into the bad-boy types, fine. Have at it. Just as long as it's not him."

My neck warms. "It's not like that."

"Sure it's not." She snort-laughs, pausing a second before jumping in again. "He's got this way about him. Like, he sucks you in, thinking you're going to mean everything to him. Then bam, he sells your soul to the highest bidder."

I frown, wondering why I can't see that side of him.

Once we reach the outside of our classroom, she pulls me to a stop again. "So, you'll stay away, right?"

I force a smile. "Yeah. Okay."

"Good." Relief washes over her face. Seconds later, she heads into the classroom, shouting, "I found her. She was puking in the bathroom."

And it's like nothing's even happened. She's all joy and big energy. I don't even flinch at her lie, either. She's really good at it, I've noticed. I, on the other hand, struggle with lying. It's trickery in witch form, minus the magic. But when it comes to Midnight Turner and my future interactions with him, lies may soon be normalized for me too, because I can't, in fact, see myself letting him go yet.

CHAPTER 6: MIDNIGHT
NOVEMBER 2020

TWO NIGHTS after finding out who that girl was, I was left alone in my room like I'd suddenly stopped existing. Noah didn't check on me. Emmanuel stayed away too. I wasn't sure why I'd been given so much freedom, but I took advantage of it—scoping the halls whenever I left for Service or meals. I needed to find a way out of there, bottom line.

Emmanuel told me constantly that nobody was a prisoner at Children of His Mercy. That everyone came on their own free will. I knew that was a lie, though, because every exit to this place had a guard standing watch.

Voices filled the hallway. The first was Emmanuel, but he wasn't alone. My door handle moved; the door hinges creaked and then it opened.

"Good evening, Midnight," Emmanuel said, stepping inside. On one side of him was Noah, his expression empty. There was another body behind him, but I didn't look too hard to see who it was.

Playing the game I'd gotten good at, I bowed my head and replied with, "Good evening, Prophet."

"You're looking tired, my son." He stepped closer, hands clasped together at his waist, from what I could tell. I wished he'd stop calling me *son*.

"I'm fine, Prophet." If anything, all I'd done over the last three days was sleep.

"Well," he sighed, "that's very good news because for many nights to come I'm afraid you won't be getting much sleep."

I lifted my head up slowly, heart thumping faster with fear.

"Not to worry." He laughed. "There's a very good reason as to why you're going to feel exhausted." He glanced over his shoulder. "Brother Simon. Bring her in now, please."

I moved to the edge of my bed and set my feet on the floor. That was when I saw *her*.

Honey-colored hair, two braids held together at the ends with brown ribbons that matched the color and material of my uniform.

It was the girl from outside. Eve was her name.

Simon held her upper arms from behind. He stared at me from over the top of her head, and I could almost swear there was pity in his gaze—though it didn't last.

I swallowed and refocused on the girl.

"Thankfully, she's a little more well-behaved than the last time you saw her," Emmanuel continued. "We've spent the last few nights discussing what she needed to change in order to make this pairing work. Like I mentioned, she wasn't a born a lamb like most of the young girls here but someone seeking salvation from pain. Just like you were."

I clenched my teeth together. Seeking salvation my ass.

"Get to your feet." He waved me up. "Greet her."

I didn't move.

His smile fell. "Don't just sit there like a fool." He narrowed his eyes. "Stand and meet your precious lamb the proper way."

My knees shook when I finally stood. "Sorry, Prophet."

Emmanuel pulled the girl away from Simon and pushed her closer to me. "Leave, Brother Simon," he told him with a dismissive wave. "Your services are no longer needed."

The door clicked shut, and I shifted my gaze between the two men before stopping on the girl's bowed head.

"Brother Noah, bring forward the Entwinement Rope, please," Emmanuel said, no explanation, no nothing.

"Are you sure, Prophet?" Noah hesitated. "Perhaps you should wait until Gentlemen Serv—"

"There you are, questioning me again." He folded his arms. "Do we need to reevaluate your position beneath me?"

"No, Prophet." Noah lifted his chin. "I just don't want this to be frowned upon under the eyes of God."

"And you know how rare of an occasion this is," Emmanuel said through gritted teeth. "This is our vision, after all."

Vision? I frowned.

"My deepest apologies for questioning His will," Noah said. I was pretty sure he didn't question Emmanuel a lot, which was why this all didn't make sense.

"You are forgiven. Now, let's get on with it."

"W-what's going on?" I finally asked.

Noah turned to the girl, ignoring me. "Raise your arms, Eve," he told her. She did what she was told, both hands shaking. "Now, press your wrists together and intertwine your fingers." He looked at me next, nodding me closer. "Midnight, do the same with your wrists, but spread your hands apart instead of clasping them."

I did because I had a feeling if I didn't, Emmanuel would whip me again.

"Now, join together," Emmanuel said, his tone almost giddy, eyes sparkling like chandeliers.

Sweat formed in the back of my hair. It dripped under the neck of my shirt and down my spine. The sensation made me shiver. I'd never been so close to a girl before, let alone touched one. It felt wrong, made my stomach churn.

"Do it," Emmanuel said, yanking me closer by the arm. "Like this." He wrapped my fingers around her intertwined fists. Fists that shook so hard they forced mine to do the same.

"Wrap the rope," Emmanuel ordered Noah.

Noah did as he told, taking a long brown rope from the bag beside him, before tying our wrists together in a binding so tight it nearly cut the circulation off to my hands. The bristles dug deeply into my skin, making it throb, but I kept a straight face and stared at Eve. I wanted to see her without the veil and know what she was thinking, but she never lifted her chin. Either she'd been trained to keep her head down or she chose to do it.

"Gloria Patri,

et Filio,

et Spirituie Sancto.

Sicut erat in…"

Emmanuel's prayer was softer than I was used to

hearing. He wrapped his hands around ours and shut his eyes.

I didn't know what was happening, what he was saying either. And every time I tried to look at Noah, he was focused on the ground, his own eyes closed, brows pinched together like he was in pain.

An image of my mom ran through my mind then. The younger version, that picture Emmanuel had shown me the night he'd taken me from our apartment. Her hands tied in a rope that looked nearly identical to the one wrapped around ours.

I swallowed and my throat filled with a razor-blade type of pain.

"And with every day that passes…" Emmanuel paused, looked at me, then her. "You will seal the partnership until you bring forth a blessing to the community and the Lord himself. Amen."

The girl started to cry. It was silent, and I couldn't see her face—mostly because my vision kept going in and out now—but her shoulders shook. Somehow, I managed to keep myself still until the ropes were removed from our hands, but I felt like puking every second longer this went on.

When Noah pulled Eve's hands from mine, I glanced down, noting blood inside her palms. From the looks of the tiny half-moon indents, she'd cut into herself with her nails.

"You bleed for her, Midnight." Emmanuel grabbed one of my hands, smiled, and sliced my palm open. I didn't even flinch. Noah grabbed my arm away from Emmanuel and held it out, palm side up. I watched the blood drip over the sides, biting my cheek to fight a hiss.

Seconds later, Emmanuel did the same to Eve's palm, starting at the creases where her nails had been. I winced when she started to sob. She bled so much more than I did, so it had to hurt worse for her.

"Joined as one, you will now be eternal." He pressed Eve's bloody palm against mine, forcing our fingers to intertwine. "For God has given you both a gift..." he whispered, tipping the girl's head up as he finished with, "each other."

My stomach heaved when I looked at her. Pale, pink cheeks, dripping with tears, and green eyes the color of emeralds.

"Bed," Emmanuel whispered. "Go forth and create your miracle now."

I blinked. "What?"

"It is your duty."

"Placet exspectare," *please way,* the girl cried out, tears falling down her cheeks. "This isn't what you promised, Prophet. You said—"

"Do not talk back to me." Emmanuel lifted a hand as if to smack her, but she fell onto the floor on her side before he could. She pulled her knees to chest and started sobbing harder.

I curled my upper lip, bloody hands balled into fists. "Don't touch her."

Emmanuel lifted his brows at me. "What did you just say?"

"I said don't touch her."

Noah grabbed the back of my shirt, fisting the end. Either he was trying to protect me, warn me, or hold me still so Emmanuel could get a shot in.

But instead of reaching for me like I figured he would have, Emmanuel did the last thing I ever expected: he grinned.

"Consider this your one pass, my son." He shrugged.

"Aside from that, I wouldn't hurt her, even with that terrible mouth. Not when we need her healthy."

My shoulders sank in relief. I opened my mouth to say thank you, but Emmanuel held up one finger.

"But if you and your lamb do not create a blessing together within six months—"

"A blessing?" I asked, throat tightening.

"A child." He tipped his head to one side, looking at me like I had ten heads. "Children are rare at Children of His Mercy. It's quite unfortunate, I'm afraid. But you are young, as is Eve. And I feel that it is God's will, as it is mine, that together you will create a purpose for Eve's body. Just like I did with your mother's."

CHAPTER 7: BEX

JANUARY 2022

"ENJOY YOURSELF TONIGHT," Mom calls from the front door.

I look over my shoulder to say bye from the sidewalk, cringing instead when I see what she's wearing. *That* hadn't been on her body ten minutes ago.

She's wearing a red crop top, which is totally fine. Mom's rail thin and able to dress like she's twenty, not forty-three. But those bottoms are another story. They're skintight pants—the same ones Dad used to call her biker leathers. I haven't seen them in a long time—years, really. At work, Mom's a jeans kind of lady.

Raised by Harley-obsessed parents, Mom was, apparently, the epitome of biker chic when she first met my father—the Brontë-loving, Hemingway-devoted nerd with the tape on his glasses because he was too in love with the pair to get any new ones. He was in college—Chicago State University—and stopped by the bar she'd been working at with some friends. The first time he saw her wearing them, Dad was the dork who said, "Leather is stiff. I don't understand the appeal." Mom, being the alpha of the pair, had apparently "bewitched him" the next day when she bought Dad his own pair, tracked him down, and left them on the hood of his car with her number and a note that said, *If you want to experience the dark side, call me.*

They'd been inseparable from that day on.

I swallow a lump in my throat at the thought, trying not to show my embarrassment when she calls out to me, "Have a good time, sugar."

Sparing her a quick wave, I make my way to Gia's car, sliding into the back seat like it's the most purposeful place on Earth. I'm instantly bombarded with the loud sounds of Mitski, not that I mind. If anything, music erases the thoughts in my head, which is why I pretty much have my earbuds in every chance I get.

"Damn," Carson says, staring out the side window. "That your mom?"

I roll my eyes and buckle.

"She's fucking hot," Gia chimes in. "Total MILF."

"Shut up, you guys," I stare out the window, determined to ignore them. I know they're kidding, but I'm already regretting coming out to the party as is and the car's still in Park.

"Sorry, Bex," they say at the same time.

"It's fine." And it is fine. I'm just in a crap mood now and wondering what the heck Mom's up to.

It's a twenty-minute drive to get to Jo's farm. The two of them talk a bunch along the way, laughing and singing to music. They both try a few times to get me involved in the conversation, but I don't have a lot to say.

We travel down a gravel road fifteen minutes later, hitting every snow-induced pothole possible. I clutch the grab handle above my head and close my eyes, teeth rattling together like an earthquake in my brain. When we finally park, car somehow still intact, I take in the dark hills outside my window.

My friends do some bag exchanging from the trunk to the back seat, spray a bunch of perfume that clogs up my nose, then slip into their jackets, giggling about who can finish first. I open the door for some fragrance-free air and kick my legs out the side. The night's cold and frosty but doable. It's too quiet though. Even with the muted music echoing from the giant barnlike structure at the top of one of the hills, there's this emptiness with a small town and a farm like this that I'll never get used to.

With a sigh, I focus my attention on the barn—though it's not exactly the kind of barn I was expecting. It's not a rundown house for animals but, like, an Airbnb. It bothers me that I didn't know this place existed, especially since I'm supposed to be Jo's closest friend. I guess only knowing someone for five months makes it impossible to actually discover everything about them. But there's also the fact that Jo has never mentioned this place until now.

"You good?" Carson asks me from behind.

I glance at her from over my shoulder, watching as she touches up her lip gloss, using her phone camera as a mirror.

"Yeah. Fine."

She clicks off her phone and looks at me. "You haven't said a lot since we picked you up."

"Just tired." I shrug. "Been a long week."

"Jo should be here already," Gia says from the front seat, her lips shiny, her eyeliner done in that cat eye way I've never be able to achieve. Even in hoodies and jeans, they both look beautiful. "We'll find her once we get up there, 'kay?"

"Sure." I smile.

I love Gia and Carson, but the two of them know I've got this codependency thing with Jo. Whenever we go out in public as a group, I cling to her like glue, mostly so I don't have to talk to anyone else. She talks for me.

Five minutes later, we begin the trek toward the barn. It's super snowy, and the wetness keeps soaking into my boots and the two pairs of socks I'm wearing underneath. I didn't dress for style but warmth, just like I told them I would. Still, being bulked up makes it hard to move.

"Jesus, it's cold." Carson tucks her arm through both mine and Gia's. "I need warmth, bitches."

"What about me?" Gia groans.

"I'll warm you up later, G."

The two of them go on like that as we wade through the snowy fields and up the small hill to the barn. The twenty-degree wind slaps our faces and, according to my weather app, it's only going to get worse.

"Look, there's Jo." Gia points at someone by the barn doors. Bright lights and loud music fill the night, and I wince when I hear the loud laughter of people.

Jo waves wildly at us. I can tell by the way she's tipping to one side that she's either drunk or getting there.

"When did she start drinking?" I ask.

"Probably at, like, four this afternoon." Carson shrugs. "She doesn't ever do anything half ass, especially when it comes to partying."

"I'm glad she's drunk, honestly," Gia says. "She's always so stressed, especially since it's been like, over a year since everything happened."

"What's everything?" I ask.

Before anyone can reply, Jo rushes me, wrapping both arms around my waist. She rocks me back and forth, murmuring all these things I can't make out over the noise.

I pull back and take her in, grinning a little. She's wearing a hoodie over the top of her short skirt.

"You smell like grape Popsicles," she tells me.

I look down and spot a huge kiddie pool filled with a purple-looking liquid on my right. A bunch of chopped-up fruit sits inside. "Yeah, I don't think that's me."

"Oh, right." She giggles. "You want some?" She points to a table with red cups on top of it. "It's called Jungle Juice."

"No thanks. Not drinking tonight." Because *somebody's* gotta be sober to drive home.

"Whatever." She tucks an arm through mine, facing Gia and Carson, who are already scooping drinks up with their cups. It's really gross and unsanitary, not that anyone cares.

"Let's go!" Gia lifts her cups and starts dancing her way into the barn. Carson follows, and Jo tugs me in behind them. It takes all of me not to run back to the car and hide away. I can't dance. I'm sensitive to crowds. And I hate, *hate* attention of any sorts.

Why did I come here again?

"Look at this place," Carson says, twirling, her arms outstretched. "Your mom outdid herself with the remodel."

"It's magical, Jo!" Gia does the same thing as Carson, spinning until they fall against each other with giggles.

I'm not a twirler, but I do turn in a slow circle to take everything in. Everything's decorated in tea lights and fake white flowers. Chairs sit in lines toward the back, and above us are huge speakers lining the high ceiling. Music blasts from them, something hip hop.

"My parents host weddings and parties here," Jo yells

over the boom of the speakers. "Or they're going to, I should say. They just paid to have it upgraded not long ago."

I nod. Makes sense, I guess.

The room is filled with nearly half the school, and I wonder if Jo's parents know she's having a mad rager in their moneymaking barn.

Couples dance on the makeshift floor, and Gia and Carson join them. Some people sit off to the side in chairs, snuggled close, drinking and laughing and... Yeah. This isn't a place for a loner like me.

"This is intense." I rub my hands up and down both arms.

Jo grins. "Then let's go out back and hang with the chill crowd."

"There's a *back* to this place?" I ask.

"Yep."

Grinning, she takes my arm again, her blonde hair all done up in braids that circle the top of her head like a crown. When we finally make our way onto a large deck that spans the length of the barn, it's as if I've jumped into a whole other universe.

And I thought the inside of this place was fancy.

A bunch of people stand under tall, lit heaters. Hanging lamps with florescent light bulbs fill the space as well. A few fancy picnic tables line the edges, and in the middle of everything is a long rectangular fireplace with glass surrounding it that goes a good ten feet into the air. It's beautiful—mesmerizing, even.

"Whatcha think?" she asks. Her drink spills, soaking her hoodie sleeve, then landing on my hand.

I wipe it off with my own hoodie sleeve and look around again. "It's really great here, Jo."

"Thanks, though it's mostly my mom. This is her

passion project and pretty much the only thing that makes her happy anymore. Dad just funds it." Her nose curls as she says all this.

"Is your mom okay?"

She laughs and shakes her head. "Hardly."

I open my mouth to ask more questions, but Jo goes wild when she spots a group of people at the other end of the deck. She drags me toward them, saying, "You have *got* to meet my friends."

Friends. People she has outside of me, Gia, and Carson. I forget sometimes that this girl is probably the most popular person in the school. Which is why it surprises me so much that she picked me to be her new BFF. Or the corner of their four-person square, as she called it on the first day of school.

"Guys, look who's here!" She wraps an arm around my shoulder when we stand in front of them. "It's my bestie."

The looks I get aren't exactly welcoming. A few look me up and down—mostly the dudes with dates. The girls are nice, but some ignore me altogether. To them, I'm just the quiet new girl who Jo has taken on as a charity case. I'm forgettable, just the way I like it.

The group goes back to whatever they were talking about, each of them with something in their hands. Joints or glasses of the purple drink, a few cans of beer thrown in here or there. It's an endless stream of loud debauchery and laughter. They all sound like hooting owls. I hate every second of it.

After a few minutes of being forgotten about, I go in search of peace. Nobody notices. Not even Jo, who's wrapped in her date's arms. It doesn't bother me that my friends are all hooked up and happy. But it does leave me wishing I could've taken Mom's car and driven myself.

I wind up on the other side of the deck, arms propped on the railing as I stare down at something. It's a frozen pond, shining in the moonlight with the snow surrounding it like natural lanterns. There are even a few fire pits set up around it—three or so, I think—but I don't see anyone using them. It's incredibly beautiful to look at—and exactly where I need to be.

CHAPTER 8: MIDNIGHT

DECEMBER 2020

IT WAS MY BIRTHDAY. A day I should've been celebrating. Seventeen. Not yet an adult, but not really a kid either.

But instead of parties and cake, I was holding back the hair of a girl who was supposedly my life partner as she vomited into a garbage can.

"Let me get Noah," I told her. "He'll find the doctor."

She shook her head.

In the two weeks since everything had happened, Eve hadn't said three words to me. Most days she laid on the floor and cried. Then if she wasn't crying, she was praying.

I sat on the floor beside her, inhaling sweat and puke. "What if you need medicine or something?"

Not listening to me, she laid down on her side with her back to me, her whole body shaking like she was seconds from exploding. I leaned against the wall and sighed, banged my head against the drywall a few times too. I wasn't supposed to leave the room without her; that'd been implanted in my head like a chip. If I did have to leave, I had to get Noah to come stay with her. But that was only during day hours. At night, Simon was the on-call dude, and he was the last person I wanted to deal with.

Eve started to moan at the same time her teeth began chattering. I looked at the top of her blonde hair, then ran a hand down my face. If I went to the infirmary myself, I'd grab meds or something to get her through the night. But doing so meant the risk of getting caught. If I didn't go, though, I'd possibly wake up in the morning to someone dead on my floor. Then I'd get into even more trouble for not saying anything.

"Screw it."

I got up and put on a clean shirt that didn't smell like sweat and vomit. Without thinking twice, I opened the door, stepped into the hall, and slowly let it click shut behind me. I leaned back, took a huge breath, then pressed my ear to the door. It was silent. Eve wouldn't leave. Pretty sure she couldn't move to do so. The infirmary was probably locked up, but I had to try.

The hallways were lit with only one tiny light each. Made it hard to see when I needed to go in the opposite direction. I took a left, making sure to stay close to the wall. The middle of the hall squeaked a lot. So did the right side.

The infirmary was on the third floor, opposite end of the building. I'd been there once when the lash marks on my back hadn't healed right.

I took the stairs two at a time, finally reaching the top. There was no light to guide my way, so I used my hands, grabbing walls and doors to guide me. Just before I made it to the last door on the left, voices sounded from the floor below. I didn't recognize them, but I didn't wanna stay and find out who they were either.

I reached the last room, knowing this was it. For a second in time, I shot a prayer up to the Big Guy, wondering if he'd do this one favor for me. He'd not answered any of my others so far, but maybe since this was for someone else, things would turn out different.

After I slid my palm around the door handle, I twisted it and grinned. It was unlocked. Slowly, I crept inside and ran my hand along the wall, searching for a light switch. I found it within seconds but hesitated before I flipped it up. Even though I'd closed the door behind me, the light could still be seen from under the door. But if I didn't have light, I wouldn't know what I was grabbing.

I shut my eyes, tried to imagine the layout of the room when I'd been in there before. Back then, though, I'd barely been alive, so my mind was fuzzy. I took what little light I had from a nearby window and walked to the back of the room. Just barely, I made out some shadowed cupboards hanging on the wall. Hands out in front of me, I found the latch to pull them open.

I tugged.

They didn't budge.

I tugged again, rattling the glass.

Nothing.

"Damn it." I dropped my head and turned back around, leaning my back against the counter's edge to think.

Before I could do anything, I heard those same voices again, closer this time. Footsteps followed, thumps and bumps and...

The door swung open, and the light switched on.

I blinked.

It was Simon and Noah.

CHAPTER 9: BEX

JANUARY 2022

I FIND a set of stairs that leads from the back of the deck to the pond. It's lit by light posts, so my chances of tripping are minimal. Still, I'm not talented on my feet enough to speed race down, so I move slowly, releasing a breath when I reach the bottom unscathed. Thank God for salt, shovels, and shoe traction.

The crackle of the fire pits surrounding the pond draw me closer. I almost wish I had some marshmallows. The first of the three fire pits I get to sits in front of a gazebo. The sidewalk is all shoveled off, thankfully, so I sit down next to it and lean back against the white trellis that makes up the gazebo sides.

Feet kicked out, I close my eyes, relaxing. Only when I do, Dad's face pops into my head—no surprise there. He's always with me, especially when it's quiet. I never thought of him as an outdoorsy kind of guy, but this place, sitting here more specifically, feels like something that would've made him happy. The ambiance more than anything. He was a chill dude with chill tendencies. He was also an introvert like me. A lover of nature, as long as it didn't require exercise.

I laugh a little at my last thought. Dad and I had the same mentality when it came to movement. Less is best.

"Bex."

I scream at the voice, jump to my feet with fighting hands at the ready. When I see who's standing a few feet away, my heart rattles harder, but I also drop my hands.

"What the hell, Midnight? You scared me." I close the distance between us and shove him in the shoulder.

He slides both hands into his coat pockets and puts his head down. "Sorry. I saw you walk down here..." He pauses, releasing a slow sigh. "It's not safe to be alone out in the open like this."

I scrunch up my nose. "What, were you, like, watching me or something?"

"Not exactly."

"You're a bad liar."

Midnight lifts his head, hovering. "I was already down here."

"Hiding in the shadows, ready to creep up on an unsuspecting girl apparently." I roll my eyes and back away, sitting where I was. If this guy keeps sneaking up on me, I'm gonna be dead by eighteen of a heart attack.

Midnight sits on the other side of the fire pit. I'm surprised he's not running away from me like he usually does. He's quiet and contemplative, other than a bouncing left foot. I can tell he's nervous, I just don't know why.

"Sooo..." I pull both of my legs up and wrap my arms around my shins. "You good?"

He leans back, runs a hand through his hair. "Fine."

A man of few words like always. "Why are you down here if you're good?"

"It's complicated."

Those must be his two favorite words.

I get it though. Everything is complicated in some way. Life, the people in it, an entire world filled with bad things that happen to good people who don't deserve them. But *it's complicated* is different from *none of your business*. Which I'm sure is what he's really trying to say. Still, I choose to humor him rather than annoy him for once.

"I get complicated." I shrug.

"You do?"

"Why wouldn't I?" I manage.

He rubs a hand over his mouth and shakes his head. "You started at this school five months ago like me, yet it's as if you've lived in this town your whole life." He glares out at the pond. "Jo took you under her wing, no questions, when I can't even get her to even look at me anymore."

I don't miss that word. *Anymore.* As in they were friends once.

"You know it's not my fault, right?" I narrow my eyes.

"I didn't say it was." He shuts his.

"Seriously though. I can't help that her friendship fell into my lap. And I can't help it if she hates you either."

His jaw loosens, but his gaze stays on the pond. "I just don't understand is all."

"Lemme guess." I tap my lip, pretending to think. "You don't get how a girl like me—a nerdy, skinny, sweater-wearing chick with the personality of a skunk—can just be suddenly *in* with that crowd?"

He doesn't answer. Instead, he bows his head, like he's ashamed.

"I'm not in with that crowd, Midnight. Like, at all. If I

was, then I'd still be up there instead of down here, arguing with you." I flinch, not meaning to be so harsh. But he's got me riled up with his accusations. He knows nothing about me, other than the fact that I fall a lot and suck at Chemistry.

"That's not what I said," he whispers.

"But it's what you meant, isn't it?"

He doesn't respond, so I know I'm right.

"Look," I start, losing the attitude, but only a little. "Jo, like, I don't know...found me. Took me under her wing and shit." I play back that scene in my head, remembering how annoyed, yet secretly flattered, I'd been that day. "She picked me out on the first full day of school this year, who knows why." I scoff. "Then Gia and Carson came along, and honestly? I don't get it any more than you do."

"But you're always around them."

"So?" I shrug. "Doesn't mean I'm in their group." Even if they think so, I don't. Not because I don't like them but because I'm not *there* when I'm with them. At least not mentally. I just go through the motions, and that's nobody's fault but my own.

Midnight stares down at the back of his hands, flexing his fingers several times before laying them on his knees. They're so scarred it's hard to look at, even in the dark. At the same time, the jagged edges feel like clues into his past. I can't stop studying them, taking in the dark lines and ridges. My insides are screaming for me to ask what happened again, but I know he won't tell me.

"Do you think you're unworthy?" he asks.

I press my lips together. It's a weird question, but I don't expect anything different from him. "Of their friendship?"

Midnight nods.

"Nope." I lean forward, butterflying my legs. "Life's dealt me a really shitty hand, but it feels like I've got this chance to start over, ya know? Even if I'm not grabbing it by the metaphorical balls and making the best of it."

He shakes his head, and I swear there's a ghost of a smile on his lips, but it doesn't last long. *Tough crowd.*

"Why *are* you down here?" he asks, jumping topics.

"Because I don't wanna be up there." I jerk my head back in the direction of the barn. "Partying's not my thing."

His brows furrow. "But you came."

"All part of the game, Midnight."

"Hmm."

"'Hmm' what?" I tip my head to one side.

"That's still no excuse to be down here unaccompanied."

Unaccompanied. I blink a few times, trying not to laugh. He sounds like a man in the eighteen hundreds who insists that I'm *chaperoned* to protect my virtue.

"I don't know what makes you think I'm some damsel who can't protect herself, but I've been through enough in my life to know how to handle bad situations."

"But what about the bad *people*?" he whispers. "Do you know how to handle them?"

I stare at him without blinking, wondering if he dealt with those *bad* people in his cult. I don't ask though. Midnight should terrify me. But at the same time, I can't find it in me to be scared of him, not even when he throws cryptic lines at me.

"If I came across any of these *bad people*, then I'm sure I could handle my own."

He nods, pulls his knees to his chest like me. "I'm sorry," he says. "That was a dumb question."

"No question is dumb," I say. "But I gotta ask... should I be worried about something or someone?" I'm only half-joking is the thing.

"No. There's nothing to worry about. It's just a habit I have."

"Warning people about danger?"

He nods. "And I also knew someone, and she thought she was tough like you, but she wasn't, so I'm..."

"You're what?"

He sighs. "Paranoid."

I lick my lips. "So was this *she* your girlfriend?" My cheeks burn the second the words are out.

He stares at his knees. "It's complicated."

"Ugh. Not that word again." I laugh.

Midnight doesn't laugh. Instead, he pushes to his feet and says, "I should go."

"Wait." I get up and move around the fire to stand in front of him. "I'm sorry for pushing. Your past isn't my business."

He doesn't sit back down. But he also doesn't leave either. Instead, he holds my gaze, lingering, lips parted, his warm breath filling the air between us. He smells like minty toothpaste and fresh soap tonight.

Even with the distance between us, my stomach fills with tiny jumping butterflies from how close we are. It's wrong but right, and everything I shouldn't be thinking of right now.

"I should probably—"

"Bex, I—"

I laugh. His cheeks grow pink.

The two of us break eye contact at the same time. A rush of air leaves my lungs. Without asking, Midnight sits where he was, and I do the same, not ready to go after all. I don't know this guy. But it definitely says something that I'd been ready to give away my first kiss to him just seconds ago.

"So," I say, clearing my throat. "When did you get here?"

"A while ago," he says. "I come here every Saturday night to watch the sunrise."

I frown. "You said you hated the cold though."

He nods but doesn't give me an excuse.

"Do you live close?" I ask.

Another nod.

"That's cool," I say, wondering if Jo knows he comes here. I'm guessing that'd be a hard no, otherwise she would've called the cops on him by now, what with how much she hates him.

"How did you know this was here?" I ask. "The pond, I mean."

"Just do."

I roll my eyes. "You really suck at conversations."

"And you really suck at being quiet."

I wink. "Glad to hear it."

He rubs a hand over his mouth, but I swear I hear him laugh.

"Wanna know something funny?" I ask.

He lifts his head, blinks at me.

"I've lived in Altoona for months, yet I didn't have a clue that Jo's family owned this place."

"Jo's private," he says.

I study his profile. "You say that like you know her."

He licks his lips. "Hard not to."

It's on the tip of my tongue to ask again why Jo hates him so much. But I have a feeling it's a conversation he'll just blow off like the rest.

"I didn't want to come tonight," I tell him.

He leans back against the trellis, stretches his legs out. He's wearing what has to be three layers of shirts and a coat because he looks ten times bulkier than what I know he is. He's shaking too, even next to the fire.

"Why did you, then?" he asks.

"Because I promised Jo, Carson, and Gia I would."

"But you just told me you're not in their group."

"I'm a quandary, what can I say?" I wink like an absolute doofus. "Anyway, it doesn't matter. I made my appearance, and I'm guessing they wouldn't care—or even know—if I left."

"Do you always do things you don't want to do just because someone tells you to?"

"Nope." I laugh a little. "But staying home tonight would've meant hanging with my mom."

"Is that a bad thing?"

I nod. "You think I'm pushy. She will demand my entire life story told back to her like she hasn't been my mom for seventeen years."

What I really want is for my dad to be alive still and for me, him, and Mom to be back in Chicago, living our best three-family-household life on a Saturday night. Mostly ones where Mom was working, and Dad and I would watch crime documentaries all hours of the night and fall asleep until Mom got home at three.

"I say I wanna be alone but being alone really sucks." Midnight bows his head.

It's another random and out-of-the-blue statement from him. I don't mind, of course. If anything, that's the first bit of truth I've heard him say. It breaks my heart. On the other hand, he's so dejected and sad. Broken too. I hate that for him. I want to *help* him. The problem is I'm not a people fixer.

"Being alone has its perks." I press my lips together. "But I get it. Sometimes you just need people around you, even if you don't talk to them. I think that's why I keep hanging out with Jo and them."

"You think it's worth it?" he asks.

"Worth what?"

"The chance of them not being who you think they are? The chance that they could hurt you in the end?"

I consider this, tapping a finger to my lips. I've never been the type of person who has trust issues. I meet someone, see through them immediately, then decide one way or another if they're worth sticking around for or not. Maybe Midnight can't do that and it's why he's closed off.

Who hurt you? I wanna ask but don't.

I poke my tongue against the side of my mouth, thinking of something to say. "I'm going to make a promise to you."

He looks at me, his forehead wrinkling. "What kind?"

I hold up three fingers like a Girl Scout. "On my honor, I swear that I will always tell you the truth, no matter how much it hurts you."

Midnight seems to think on this, his eyes going distant as he looks around me, not at me. He zones out, disassociates, and I can tell from that alone the two of us could be friends...if he ever decides to let me in.

"Why would you promise that when you don't know me?" he eventually asks.

I lean back on my hands, kick my feet out in front of me. "Because I think everyone needs that person in their life."

"I can't be that person for you, Bex."

It's the saddest statement. Not because I'm hurt but because I hear the pain in his voice and even see it in his slumped posture. It makes me want to be someone to him that nobody else has ever been. Even if it's one-sided.

"I had someone like that already, so no worries. I'm down with non-reciprocation." I cringe, not meaning for it to come out so weirdly.

"You did?"

I breathe out, my chest aching a little. "Yep. My dad. He's dead though, so..." It's the first time I've said those words out loud. *He's dead.* It chokes me, like someone's got their hands around my neck squeezing. I'm not sure why Midnight is suddenly like my vault, but it feels good to tell someone.

"How did he die?" His voice is so low I almost don't hear it.

Tears burn the corner of my eyes, so I lean my head back against the trellis and shut them, clear my throat to make sure my voice isn't shaky before I speak. "He, uh, was run over by a car."

"I'm sorry," he whispers.

"Me too." I shrug and stare at the pond again, a lone tear dripping from my left eye. I wipe it away with my shoulder, trying to be coy. I don't know if it works or not because I feel Midnight's lingering gaze.

This got heavy fast.

After a few minutes of uncomfortable silence, I decide that maybe it's best if I did go, especially since I'm about to bawl my eyes out—something I'd prefer not to do in public.

"I should leave." I stand, study the ground as I do. "I bet my friends are looking for me." Doubtful, but it's the only good excuse I have to leave.

"No," Midnight whispers, standing too, coming

around to meet me toe to toe. It's reverse déjà vu. "Please."

I look up, hold his stare. "You don't want me to go?"

He shakes his head, then does the last thing I expect, wrapping his fingers around my pinkie—all five of them. He's like a little boy, looking for comfort as his gaze searches my face. I feel like I'm that someone he wants to hold tight to during a storm in the middle of the night. I look down, bite my bottom lip, unsure if I should shake him off or ask for a fainting couch because his touch makes my knees weak and my world spin.

"Why not?" I ask.

"Because…" He swallows so hard I can see the pull of his Adam's apple. "Because I like you. I think I wanna be your friend, Bex."

I press a hand to my throat, trying to stay cool, even though his confession has my entire body warming.

"Then I won't leave." I lift my chin and smile.

"Does that scare you?" he asks. "Me saying that?"

"Nope," I say. "Because I think I want to be your friend too."

CHAPTER 10: MIDNIGHT
DECEMBER 2020

EMMANUEL PULLED the familiar wire from his wooden box with a light gleaming in his eyes.

We were in the sanctuary where service was held. Where bonded life mates were supposed to hold hands and praise both Emmanuel and God for all the blessings they received. Little did everyone know about the blood getting ready to be spilled on the very same floor.

Not even the son was safe from the Prophet.

Simon had tied my legs to the metal chair I was currently sitting on. He'd grunted under his breath the entire time, but I couldn't understand what he was saying. I was guessing he wanted me to suffer. He'd tied my hands behind my back with a rope that wasn't much different than the binding rope used for the ceremony Eve and I had gone through. When he was finished, he stepped in front of me, eyes glued to my face with zero expression.

"Normally this wouldn't be how things would happen once you are bound to your life partner," Emmanuel said, standing next to Simon. "But in this case, with Eve being as sick as she is and neither of you bothering to tell us, I'm afraid the punishment must go to the source." He shook his head. "And that would be you, son."

My throat burned at his threat. It'd be easy to cry. But I never gave Emmanuel the satisfaction of seeing my tears. He'd like it too much.

"Noah," Emmanuel spoke to him over my shoulder. "Go get the lamb now. Sick or not, she needs to witness this so she understands that it's not okay to hide an illness from the ones who love her so dearly."

"Is that really necessary?" Noah asked. "She has pneumonia. It could be bad for her if she's with child."

I stiffened. *With child?* Shit.

Emmanuel reached down and grabbed the ends of my hair, yanking my head back like he could read my mind. I'd barely gotten Eve to look me in the eye, let alone even think about what we were supposed to do together.

"Tell me, son." Emmanuel searched my face, eyes narrowed into tiny slits. "Is there reason to believe you have put a child inside of your lamb?"

When I said nothing, Emmanuel nodded. "Get her." He hissed. "Now."

Noah's footsteps echoed from somewhere behind me. Simon followed a second later, not sparing me a glance.

When it was just me and Emmanuel, I lifted my chin, stared him dead in the eyes. "It's not her fault. She shouldn't have to come here."

"Noah tells me she's not cooperating, that you've been nothing but kind to her." He folded his hands together at his waist. "I'm afraid this is the only way we will be able to knock her out of the state she's currently in."

I tightened my jaw. It was bad enough going through

a whipping but having someone else there to see it go down was another form of humiliation.

Emmanuel tilted his head to one side. "You're a lot like your mom, Midnight." He rubbed his chin. "Tiring, overthought everything the Lord required her to do…"

My nostrils flared. Whenever he brought up my mom, I wanted to Hulk-smash his face in.

"She was spirited too. A woman with many purposes to me, which is why I didn't give up on her." He tapped his foot against the floor a few times. "After all, most of the men here are only given one life partner."

"She was just a kid," I hissed. "And you're—"

"She was eighteen. I was twenty-four. I'd hardly say there would be an age issue if that's what you're referring to." Emmanuel lifted his brows, likely daring me to keep going.

I didn't.

"You're judging me again," he said, the lines by his eyes curling with his lips. "I see it. And though I would normally punish you for that as well, I'm going to go easy on you because you, too, are going to need to stay healthy in order to create my miracle."

"I was trying to help her," I yelled. "She needed medicine, and I didn't want to wake Simon."

"By keeping her illness a secret?" He *tsked*. "I'm afraid you could've endangered her life, which cannot happen. Not when she is so valuable and precious to me."

To me. Those words didn't go unnoticed.

The door creaked open again. I jerked my head away from Emmanuel, finding Eve in a wheelchair being pushed into the room by Noah. Simon was beside him, a nasty gash under the scar I'd given him that first night.

I didn't know this girl, but I suddenly felt like I was the one person left who wanted to keep her safe. She wasn't a part of this community either. And whatever sick mind games Emmanuel had been playing to get her there gave me even more of a reason to protect her.

"She's looking better already." Emmanuel turned to face her as she was pushed up beside him. Her watery red eyes met mine, and for the first time since we'd met, I saw life in them.

"Yeah, but she scratched the hell out of my cheek." Simon cupped the gash.

"You didn't warn her that you were picking her up. You just did it," Noah spat.

"Free his hands, Brother Noah." Emmanuel ignored their arguing and pointed to me, keeping his gaze on Eve.

When Noah got close, I saw pity in his stare—an eye crinkle, a down-turned mouth. I shook my head and looked away, wishing I could smack it off his face. If he felt so bad for me, then he should've stopped Emmanuel from doing what he was about to do.

He pulled my hands free. I flexed my fingers, then my arms on my lap. It was in the back of my head to try to untie my feet and fight to get loose, but I wouldn't get far.

"Stretch your arms out, palm side down," Emmanuel ordered, running the wire's end through his fingers.

Then came the words I never wanted to hear again.

"*Misereatur vestri omnipotens Deus, et dimissis peccatis vestris, perducat vos ad vitam aeternam.*" May Almighty God have mercy on you, forgive you your sins, and bring you to everlasting life.

"*Fiat voluntas Dei.*"

The strike came hard, fast, and without warning— eating into the backs of my hands like bites from a razor-toothed monster. I gritted my teeth, held back my scream as much as I could, though my elbows gave out within seconds.

"Hold his arms in place, Noah."

"Prophet, I—"

"Hold them. Now!"

"But the lamb—"

"Brother Simon!" Emmanuel screamed, his face red and covered with a sheen of sweat. "You hold him. It's obvious Brother Noah has forgotten his calling momentarily."

Simon moved in behind me, arms coming around my waist so he could grab my elbows and hold them still.

"Don't hold your breath," he whispered. "It'll only hurt worse if you do."

Seconds later, the wired whip came crashing across my hands again. This time I couldn't stop the scream.

Sobs filled the air when another strike came.

Then another followed directly after.

My lungs rejected every breath. I grew dizzy, to the point where black spots started appearing. On the fourth strike was when it happened—Eve's pleas. I was almost too far gone to open my eyes.

"Please, Prophet. Stop. It's not his fault I'm sick. It's not his fault he left to get me medicine. I misbehaved. Ignosce me."

Somehow, I managed to see her through tunneled vision. She was standing—or at least trying to, one hand on the arm of her wheelchair. When I looked at Emmanuel, his right eye twitched. Then slowly, with his gaze still locked on my face and his lips pressed into a hard line, he dropped his wire and left the room, leaving me alone with Simon, Noah, Eve, and my newest best friend: pain.

CHAPTER 11: BEX

JANUARY 2022

MIDNIGHT DIDN'T COME to school the following week. It bugs me not knowing where he is and the fact that he can just skip out on life like that. The thing is I also don't have a right *to* know. We spent one Saturday night together, that's it. And I'm the one who'd done most of the talking while *he'd* wound up bailing on me minutes after the sunrise, zero explanation as to why.

I didn't realize how annoying it was to be the one-sided conversationalist, and I promised myself I'd do better when it came to Jo, Gia, and Carson.

Mom plops down next to me on the loveseat with a huff. I've been flipping through the preview of every Netflix show that comes up for the last hour, yet nothing interests me enough.

"What's up?" she asks. "Not hanging with your girls tonight?"

"Nope," I say, deciding it's not worth explaining that I'm having a mega-internal crisis over a boy who I'm pretty sure is more effed up than I am.

Mom sits down beside me. "That's a shame."

"Not really. I like being home."

Though *home* is a stretch here in this little box of an apartment—one that's even smaller than our old one in Chicago.

Mom kicks her feet out and sets them on the coffee table, her leather boots untied.

"You working a later shift tonight than usual?" I ask.

"Taking the eleven to three. Martha and her husband are doing an anniversary thing. Told her I'd close up."

Martha's not only her best friend but the owner of Vic's, the bar my mom works at. Martha is also the reason why Mom moved us here last summer. I think she got tired of it just being her and me. Plus, I wasn't much company when all I did was lay in my room, cry, read, or go to school.

I look at the time on my phone. It's ten-thirty. "What are you still doing here, then?"

She leans her head back against the couch, the scent of her pineapple shampoo filling the air. "I'm taking the bike tonight, so it won't take as long to get there."

"You're *what*?"

"It's fine." She waves me away. "It's only thirty degrees, and the streets are all salted."

"But Vic's is on the other side of town."

She pats my thigh. "And I'm also an expert rider."

I scowl at her hand. Mom hasn't taken the bike out in months—not since we moved here. And riding it in the middle of winter isn't smart. She knows this. Regardless, it's not my job to parent her, no matter how much I want to sometimes.

She goes super quiet. When I glance at her, I discover why that is. She's texting someone—grinning. Pink cheeks and bright eyes and...almost googly, really.

"Who are you talking to?" I ask.

She jumps a little, clears her throat and quick shuts off her phone. "Nobody."

"Mom. Your face is bright red."

"It's hot in here."

"Sure it is." I frown, staring at the goose bumps on her arms. I set down the remote and turn to face her, pulling one leg up onto the couch. "Look. If you have something you need to tell me, just do. I don't like secrets. You know this."

Her shoulders slump and only then does she look at me. In her eyes there are a million things she wants to say, but the one that comes out of her mouth rock me. "Fine. I met someone."

"Oh." My stomach twists. "What's their name?"

"It's guy." She shrugs. "And we don't need to talk details about this tonight, sugar. Just know that he's a good person." She bounces her right foot. "I can bring him over for dinner one night so you can meet him, how 'bout that?"

My face turns cold at the thought of some man—good or not—taking my dad's seat at the kitchen table we've used for fourteen years. It's not like I'm going to make a big deal out of things or throw a fit. Mom deserves to be happy again. But that doesn't mean it won't bug me.

She tucks her brown hair behind her ear. "You're mad at me."

I shake my head.

"You know I still love your dad, right?" she asks.

"I know. And I'm not *mad*. I'm just...feeling things today." I look at my hands, the hangnail on my thumb. I want to pick it to distract the ache in my chest, but I can't move.

When he died, I wanted to die for a while too.

"Sugar," Mom whispers, putting a hand to my face,

urging me to look at her with a gentle push. "I don't mean to upset you."

My eyes burn with tears, which is my cue to leave.

"It's cool," I say. "I swear. But I think I'm gonna head to..." My phone buzzes with a text. I frown when I look down at the unknown number.

"Seems I'm not the only one getting secrets texts tonight." Mom nudges my shoulder with her own.

I swipe at the screen, cheeks combusting with flames when I see what it says. Or more so *who* it's from.

Unknown Number: Pond tonight? Midnight

"Pond?" Mom asks.

I shake my head. "It's just Jo."

My hands shake when I start to type my reply. I pull it a little closer so Mom doesn't see.

Bex: How'd you get my number?

"She want to hang out?" Mom asks.

"Yeah," I say absentmindedly.

A million and a half thoughts run through my head, and I bite the inside of my cheek as I ponder each one. *He likes me. He wants to hang with me again. He wants me to come so he can lure me into the cult he's possibly still a part of.*

"Bex?" Mom nudges my knee with hers. "You're buzzing again."

I look down, blinking.

Unknown Number: Eleven.

That's twenty minutes from now.

Jo won't be there. She told me her family didn't have another wedding planned there for three months and that she's out of town with her mom. So it's not like she'd know if I went. There again, it's probably illegal to sneak onto someone else's property.

The warning label Jo's been pushing on Midnight since she caught him and me together in the halls has been weighing on me—even after we spent time together last Saturday. Still, I can't find it in me to say no because, well, I like Midnight. And I really do want to be his friend.

"Bex, do you hear me?" Mom says.

"Huh? Oh, yeah. Sorry." I stand and put my phone in my back pocket, annoyed with the fact that I'm already amped up on this strange high Midnight gives me whenever I think about him. "Change of plans. I'm gonna spend the night at Jo's."

"Then it's a good thing I'm taking my bike to work after all." Mom winks. "Car keys are by the door."

I force a smile, sliding my shoes on, then grab my jacket by the door. If anything, hanging with Midnight will help me *not* think about the fact that Mom's got a possible new boyfriend.

"Hey, sugar?"

I reach for the door handle. "Yeah?"

"Don't do anything I wouldn't."

"That's not gonna be an issue." I laugh.

Sad part is Mom would do anything and everything *I* wouldn't.

———

MY CAR DOOR SLAMS, echoing over the hilly area. An owl hoots, and the branches on trees crackle beneath the weight of ice and snow. The one light I see when I get out of Mom's car is from the street far behind me, not the barn up the hill this time. It's creepy dark, and a shudder runs through me at the thought of what I'm about to do. More specifically, *who* I'm going to do it with. Midnight makes me want to be a good girl who breaks all the rules, and it makes zero sense.

"Am I crazy?" I ask out loud, zipping up my coat, then sliding my hat and mittens on.

Nobody answers obviously, therefore I take it as a sign that I'm one hundred percent in control of whatever I'm about to do. Or maybe the voice in my head doesn't answer because she's just as freaked out about this as I am.

I take my first step up the hill to the barn, shoes crunching against the icy snow, only to hear my name being called.

"Bex," Midnight says.

I turn, finding him on a nearby sidewalk, hands in his pockets like usual.

"Oh, hey." I wave like a complete dork. "You're here." *Hello, Captain Obvious.*

"The hill's snow packed and covered in a layer of ice," he tells me. "Let's take the sidewalk and stairs."

"Right," I say, laughing—though nothing is actually funny.

Midnight approaches me with wide, curious eyes. "You came," he says.

"Why wouldn't I?"

He shrugs.

"You, uh…" He points at his elbow. "It's slick."

I stare for a moment, clueless…until I'm not. He wants me to hold on to him. Like a gentleman. Because it's slick.

"Oh, right. Thanks." I smile and latch on, all fun and games and bestie-like.

He studies me before he moves, one magnificent blue eye meeting mine through his dark hair. Midnight is trouble with a capital *T*, and if I don't do something smart, then I'll do something stupid instead.

I could get lost in this guy if I'm not careful.

Needing to play it cool—and to somehow ignore how sweaty my hands are beneath my mittens—I say, "So, what's up?"

Midnight runs a hand along the back of his neck, then leads us down the sidewalk, then around the large hill where the barn sits.

"I...don't know."

"You don't know," I deadpan.

"Can we just..." He motions his head toward the other side of the hill. "Hang out again? Like last time?"

I swallow hard, trying to keep my voice even. "At the pond?"

"Yeah." He blows out a slow breath. "There."

We don't say much as we make our way over. My nerves are too overwhelming. By the time the gazebo from last weekend comes into view, I'm a shaky mess of sweaty hands and soaking-wet shoes. But complaining will only make me look like a wimp.

"Gazebo?" I ask when we're a few feet away from it.

He nods. "I lit another fire."

Sure enough, by the time we're walking down the cement steps, I see the flames. When we reach the final step leading down to the pond, I pull my hand free from his arm.

"So," I say, "for a dude who hates the cold, you sure are in it a lot."

"It's necessary." He tucks both hands into his coat pockets.

"Aren't you afraid someone will see us down here?"

"There's nobody here tonight," he says.

I look at the barn behind me. It's dark, not a single light on inside. He's not wrong.

When we manage to make our way over, he's

standing in front of the fire, staring down at the two chairs he's set up on either side of it.

"You pick which one you want."

I take the one closest to me. He takes the other, clearing his throat at the same time.

"It's warmer tonight," he says, reaching beside him, then pulling a couple of blankets out. "But I brought these in case."

Butterflies jump in my stomach. It's more than obvious he planned this and, well...I don't know what to think about it. It's sweet yet suspicious. Tingle-inducing, but nerve-racking too.

I take the blanket he's offering and say thank you, tucking it over my knees. He does the same with his.

"So we're *not* going to get in trouble for being here?" I ask.

He bows his head. "I know Jo's dad. He, um, lets me come here whenever I want. And since I hate the cold but like to sit down here to watch the sunrise, he leaves wood and lighter fluid for me." He shrugs. "I've been coming every Saturday for months now."

"So you lied to me, then." I lean back and kick my feet up on the lounger.

"No." He looks at me. "I just said I come here on Saturday nights. He knows. Jo doesn't."

"Fair enough." I purse my lips. "How you know Jo's dad?"

"Just do."

"*How* though?"

"Bex..." he whispers, and I can instantly hear the regret in his words. I shouldn't push him. I told him I wouldn't. But I'm hoping that in time, he or Jo will tell me what their beef is.

"Sorry. I'll drop it." I hold my hands out in front of me.

"Thanks," he says, bowing his head a little.

"So can I at least ask why you like to be outside in the middle of the winter, all night, just to watch sunrises if you don't like the cold?"

"Reasons."

I ball my hands into fists, take a deep breath. "Like...?"

He's quiet, lips pressing together in a hard line. I almost wonder if I've pushed him too far again. But me asking him questions is the only way I'll be able to figure out our boundaries—what to talk about. What not to talk about. What kind of friendship this will be, most of all.

Midnight takes a deep breath, and I'm sure he's going to tell me that this is one of his no-talking points, but he surprises me.

"I do it for a friend."

I squint at him. "Can the friend not see the sunrise anymore?"

He rubs his hand over his mouth. "Something like that."

A weird thought runs through my mind. What if this *friend* was actually a girlfriend, and... "Nope," I tell myself. "Don't go there."

"What's that?" he asks.

"Nothing. I was just talking out loud to myself. I do it a lot."

Her purses his lips and narrows his eyes.

"Don't tell me you don't talk out loud to yourself," I say.

He shrugs.

I roll my eyes. "Dude. If you don't talk to yourself, then who *do* you talk to?"

Slowly, he turns his head again, and our eyes catch. It's always like this when he looks at me. Intense and curious, like he's searching my face for answers to a puzzle he can't quite solve. I get that. I'm a puzzle solver too. But what I don't count on, every time we look at each other, is the warm sizzling in my chest. How I can't help but hold my breath as I wait for him to speak.

"You," he finally tells me. "I talk to you."

I scoff. "I'm nobody."

It's Midnight's turn to squint at me. "That's not true."

I lift my eyebrows. "Um, yes? I'm the quiet-until-I-don't-wanna-be new girl who pretty much hates people but deals with them because they intrigue me. There is absolutely no reason for you to want to talk to me."

Yet here he is, eleven-thirty on a Saturday night with me.

My palms start to sweat even more, so I take off my mittens and rub my hands over my jeans. The thoughts running through my mind when I glance at him are dangerous, yeah. But my reactions to said thoughts are even worse.

"You don't give yourself enough credit," he says with the softest, sweetest smile.

My lips part as I take it in. The glory of his first ever smile for me. It's like I'm alive and buzzing—human, really, for the first time in years. Midnight is not a cure for my grief, but he's one hell of a good reprieve.

"What?" His eyes narrow a little.

"You're real," I say, knowing how stupid it sounds. Up until now, Midnight's felt more like a figment of my imagination than anything. Someone who's there but doesn't necessarily feel real until I hear him speak.

"Huh?" He furrows his brows.

"What I meant to say is you're not a monster after all."

"How do you know I'm not?" he asks.

"Monsters don't know how to smile."

"They do." He looks back at the pond. "It's just for different reasons."

"Noooo, not in that way you just smiled." I laugh. "You, Midnight Turner, are not a monster. You're a human boy with an obviously broken soul."

He stiffens. I do too. It's been okay to think that way about him, but saying it out loud makes it more real, not to mention makes him uncomfortable.

"Sorry, that wasn't—"

"Tell me more about your family," he says, cutting me off.

My stomach tightens. The buzz of happiness that'd been sitting just under my skin disappears. Either he's trying to prove a point about exposing secrets or he's just being a different version of himself. One who's trying to know me. It's an olive branch of some sort at least, and I'm gonna strangle the hell out it if it means getting him to talk.

"Well," I clear my throat. "It's just me and Mom. My dad, like I said, died."

"When?"

I look away. "Almost two years ago."

Midnight goes silent, staying that way for a while. Maybe he's rolling my words around inside his head, trying to understand them. Sometimes I don't want the condolences that come with talking about my dad, but without them, I don't know how to continue conversations.

"Anyway, it's just me and Mom," I go on. "Lived here for seven months, as you already know."

"And where is your mom right now?" he asks.

"Work."

"At eleven forty-five at night?"

"Yeah. She works at Vic's Bar, so she goes in late."

"And you're home alone every night?"

"Yep," I say. "It's a small town though. Nothing bad ever happens here."

He shakes his head and stares at the ground, not me. "It doesn't matter. Small towns, big towns, you shouldn't be staying alone at night."

"It's Altoona." I laugh. "The only thing that's gonna swipe me up is a damn cow."

"No." He jumps to his feet, anger flashing across his face. "You can't..." He squeezes his eyes shut. "You need to stay with someone. Always."

I narrow my eyes. "There are locks on my door, and I know how to shoot a gun."

We don't even have a gun, but still. Mom took me to a shooting range once after Dad died. Told me it was a good stress reliever. I'm not going to say I'm an expert, but if a gun ever fell into my lap for some reason, I wouldn't freak out. Might miss my target, but whatever.

"Things happen, Bex," he says, running a shaking hand through his hair. "Bad things when you don't expect them. I'm just... I'm trying to help you."

I shake my head, wondering if this stems back to his life in that cult.

Making a last-second decision, I stand and take my chair with me to the other side of the fire.

"What are you doing?" he asks when I set it next to

his. I like the fire, but unlike him I don't need the heat.

"This," I say, reaching out to take his hand in mine.

Surprisingly, he lets me, watching with a softening brow. The move isn't supposed to mean anything, but there's an undeniable tingle racing up my wrists that I can't ignore. Especially when I run my thumb over the scars along the back of his hand.

"Look," I say. "I appreciate the concern for my wellbeing, but I promise you, I'm gonna be okay."

His panic slides away to something more relaxed, as if he's come out of whatever messy headspace he was just in. Even so, there's a twitching by his left eye that can't be missed, and I have a strong urge to smooth it out with my thumb.

"I-I'm sorry," he tells me, shoulders slumping. "It's just that my mom…"

"Your mom what?"

"Nothing." He sits back down. Talk about whiplash. Midnight is even more complicated than I am.

I wonder if anyone's bothered to help him or talk to him, even tried to be his friend. A counselor, teachers, someone who has better insight on how to help heal trauma—that's assuming he's actually traumatized. I'm no doc. God knows I'm the last person he should be turning to for help, especially when I'm barely holding on myself some days.

Those scars on the back of his hands break my heart, yeah. But the scars he so obviously has on the inside break it even more.

"Can we talk about you more?" he asks, clenching and unclenching his fingers.

My shoulders slump in disappointment. Someday, maybe, he'll open up to me. For now, I guess it's on me to build this new bridge between us.

CHAPTER 12: MIDNIGHT

FEBRUARY 2021

IT'D BEEN four months since Eve and I had met. And despite what had happened in the beginning, she'd become a pretty important person in my life. Before her, it felt like my whole world was on fire. But every time she looked at me, the pain in me dulled into something warm and tolerable. Comfortable, most of all.

"You better get ready," she said from the other side of our shared room as she finished her second braid.

I twirled the ribbons she'd wear at the ends of her braids through my fingers. "I'd rather stay here and watch you mess up your braids all day than do anything else."

She walked over and sat on the bed beside me, bumping my shoulder with hers. "And what fun would that be?"

"Super fun." I poked her ribs with a finger. "The best fun ever." I did it again, making her giggle.

"Midnight!" She shoved my chest, only to grip the material of my shirt and pull me back in—closer this time.

Her lips parted and we both went silent. Something shifted in her stare when she glanced down at my mouth, humor to curiosity to embarrassment that had her cheeks turning red.

Two weeks ago, things between us had changed. We weren't just two people, stuck living together, stepping around one another like we were scared the other person would crack in half. We'd shifted from friends to something I couldn't describe. Not child groom and bride, but something close to a relationship that wasn't a real relationship. We hadn't kissed or anything like that. It just felt different. And it'd all started one Saturday night after we'd stayed up together and watched the sunset through the tiny window of our room.

Can we do this forever? she'd asked.

Do what?

She grabbed my wrist and squeezed, tipping her head to look at me. *Watch the sunrise on Sunday mornings like this.*

Yes, I'd told her. *I'd like that.*

From there on out, we'd been pretty much inseparable. Friends, mostly, but something more.

She turned away. "We should go."

"Yeah, you're right." I cleared my throat and stood.

Today was our first outing with the other selected pairs. The official *Shepherd and Lamb feast* where we'd get to socialize with other people, not just as singles. Normally the guys and girls were kept apart until we reached eighteen, but Emmanuel thought it'd be a good idea for me and Eve to get involved with the older group to help us feel more acclimated to the idea of being a pair.

Eve got to her feet and asked me to tie the brown ribbons around the end of her braids. My fingers shook the entire time. I brushed my knuckles against her shoulder by accident when I finished up, and she shivered. Like that, she reminded me of the sunrise.

"I'd like it if we met some of the others," she said a few seconds later, looking at the door. "You know, make friends? Like Emmanuel suggested."

I cringed. That word *friends*—sent a chill down my spine. Making *friends* would mean accepting this place and wanting to build a life here. That was the thing about Eve. Other than the first few nights with me, she seemed genuinely happy at Children of His Mercy. She was obsessed with Emmanuel's bullshit teachings and the prayers, learning Latin ten times faster than me.

"Let's get this over with, then," I said.

"Thank you, Midnight." She laced our fingers together and kissed my cheek.

I froze, not expecting either the hand-to-hand contact or her kiss. She smelled flowery—probably from whatever shampoo they gave her to wash her hair.

"Let's go." She pulled me out the door and into the hallway, practically bouncing as she spoke. I answered when she had questions, like always, and smiled a lot too. But the second we got to the last set of stairs before reaching the Service room, uneasiness filled my stomach like knots.

Tonight was a first for the both of us. And unlike Eve, I was terrified of every new thing at this place.

She did all the talking when we stepped into the room—to the girls, though, because she wasn't allowed to talk to guys, other than me and Emmanuel and occasionally Noah. I stayed quiet and didn't leave her side, while the rest of the men gathered on one side of the room. I did search the room for Noah. He was supposed to be one of the watchmen tonight, leading the initial prayer doctrine before dinner.

Since the night we met, he'd changed too. Become less talkative but somehow more attentive at the same time. Always there, always watching me. Always with angry eyes that said something I didn't understand. He wasn't mad at me. He looked at everyone that way. But every time our eyes met, he seemed like he wanted to tell me something. It was weird.

"Wow," Eve whispered. She squeezed my fingers and glanced around the room. "Midnight, this is beautiful."

I scowled, taking it all in.

The white walls were covered in gold lights. There were long tables with gold tablecloths covering them, placed above the exact location where the backs of my hands had been split open. In the center of each table were crucifixes. At every place setting, a small bible, along with dinner plates and silverware and even wine glasses sat.

Everything about this room tonight screamed wealth, and it confused me because Children of His Mercy stood for a simple life, not this crap.

"I can't believe he did this," Eve turned in a circle, her lips parted in a smile.

"Who?"

"The Prophet." She looked up at me. "H-he did this for me, Midnight." She shook her head. "For *us*. I know he did."

"What're are you talking about?" I asked, voice low.

"Nothing." She looked away. "Let's go find our seats."

She moved before I could respond, her hand in mine as she said hi to another girl. I nodded at the dude beside her but didn't recognize him. He looked older, unlike most of the younger guys I'd spent time with. Hell, everyone in this room looked older than us—guy-wise at least. The girls were all young, closer to our age. Though none looked unhappy, I had to wonder if they were, deep down.

Eve smiled and talked to everyone. She was a natural, but this also wasn't the girl I'd gotten to know. This version felt fake. Like a perfectly trained girl who'd grown up with wealth, not someone like me. Not that it mattered either way.

We got to the table, where there were also place settings and paper cards with names on them. *Shepherd Sam, Lamb Scarlett. Shepherd Jacob, Lamb Harriet.* I read each one, searching for our names, but by the time we got to the end of the table, there was only Eve's card, not mine.

"I don't see your name," she said, turning to me.

I walked around the table again, looking at each place card again. It wasn't until I got to the opposite end of the table did I see it. The empty seat with a name there that sure as hell didn't read *Shepherd Midnight.*

"I'm sure it's a mistake." Eve squeezed my arm. "We will find Noah, and—"

"It's not a mistake," I said.

She frowned. "Of course it is. Why would—"

"My flock!" A loud voice boomed from the doorway, echoing off the walls. I didn't need to look up to know it was *Emmanuel.* The one whose name was in *my* spot. "I am so happy you're all here, blessing me with your beautiful presence. What a joyous night. A beautiful occasion, as always." He lifted both hands in the air. "Oremus."

Chair legs scraped across the floor as everyone got on the ground to assume prayer position.

"Midnight?" Eve whispered, tugging on the end of my shirt when I didn't move.

"Disobeying me again, my son?" Emmanuel *tsked* as he approached us.

"No, Prophet," I said, schooling my face.

"What seems to be the problem?"

"Nothing, Prophet." I crouched down next to Eve and bowed my head. She reached for my hand and squeezed. I squeezed hers back.

Emmanuel had yet to move.

"Midnight," he said, his voice steady yet unnerving. "Stand back up, please."

Other than the soft gasp of Eve, who'd squeezed my hand even tighter, the room stayed quiet. I turned my head to face her, nodding to let her know I'd be okay.

When I got to my feet, I looked Emmanuel in the eyes, thankful I was finally as tall as he was.

You don't own me. You never will.

His nostrils flared like he could read my thoughts. But instead of another beating, or even making a comment, he motioned for me to stand behind him before taking the remaining seat at the table. The one with his name on the card across from Eve.

Emmanuel went on to pray, ending it with, "Ora pro nobis, Sancta Dei Genitrix." *Pray for us, O Holy Mother of God.*

Everyone sat back onto their chairs at his command. Everyone but Eve, who moved to stand beside me. She grabbed my hand again.

Go sit, I mouthed.

She bit her bottom lip, glanced at the table, then me again.

"Sweet lamb." Emmanuel looked over his shoulder at her. "Take your rightful chair, my love. We can begin to enjoy the delicious meal we've been graced with when you do."

"B-but Midnight doesn't have a spot to—"

"With all due respect, Eve, you have a place at this table, and I suggest you take a seat and not question me," Emmanuel snapped, his words like an invisible whip against my back.

"Go, Eve," I hissed.

Emmanuel pushed away from the table and stood, eyes on me.

Shit. I knew that look.

My hands shook. I opened my mouth to say something, stick up for her, but he was in front of us before I could get the words out, fingers on her upper arms, squeezing so tight I knew there'd be marks.

"You're hurting me, Prophet," Eve whimpered.

Instead of looking at her, Emmanuel looked at me, eyebrows lifted. "What do we do with defiant young lambs, Midnight?"

"Let her go," I said, voice shaking worse than my hands.

"No. I'm afraid that's the wrong answer." And with that, he bent over, put his shoulder against her stomach and lifted her above him.

"Prophet, please let me go," she cried out, her head hanging down his back.

I growled under my breath when I saw her white dress slide up to her waist, revealing parts of her body no one was supposed to see. Before I could rush the back of him, someone grabbed me from behind.

"He won't hurt her," Noah said. "He won't discipline her either. Not here."

I still struggled against him, trying to pull away, relaxing only when Emmanuel set her down onto her assigned chair.

"Disobey me once, shame on you." Emmanuel crouched down in front of her, hands pressed to her knees. "But disobey me twice…"

Eve's face turned white, and her chest heaved with

wild breaths. Her braids were already undone, and blonde strands fell over her eyes.

Not once, though, did she look at me.

"See?" Noah said, patting my upper arm. "She's fine."

"She's *not* fine."

"She is safe," he reiterated.

I wanted to ask what the hell was going on, but Noah was right. Fighting got me nowhere but the infirmary—and even that wasn't guaranteed.

Everyone watched as Emmanuel spoke to Eve in quiet whispers I couldn't hear. *Jealousy*, or something close to it, slid into my chest like an ugly monster and made my chest heave in and out.

It was a sick thought to have, but the way Emmanuel's hands were spread across her knees made me think this wasn't the first time he'd gotten up close and personal with her.

"Ignosce me." Eve bowed her head and reached for Emmanuel's hands, bringing them to her lips. She kissed his knuckles, while he petted the top of her head.

"Bene habet." *All is well*. Emmanuel voice boomed in the air, loud enough for everyone to hear. He stood and pushed her chair in, settled the napkin on her lap, and ran a finger down her cheek. When he finished, he walked back to his chair, stopping in front of me.

"And that's how it's done, Midnight."

CHAPTER 13: BEX
JANUARY 2022

IT'S MONDAY MORNING, 8:03. Midnight has exactly two minutes to get to class before he's considered tardy—not that I'm counting down the minutes or anything.

I put my cell phone back into my pocket and look at the empty seat beside me, thinking of Saturday night... thinking of *him* most of all.

I wonder if this is what a crush feels like. Because as much as I don't want to have one on Midnight, I think I kinda, sorta, *maybe* do. Having it be on a guy as complicated as that guy, though, is unnerving.

The bell rings and, not surprisingly, his chair stays empty. I sigh, trying to ignore the sinking disappointment in my belly as I concentrate on what I have to do today. It's lab day, unfortunately, which is always a shit thing for me. But I am woman, hear me roar and all that.

The teacher starts in, explains what we'll be doing. I'm not a scientist, but I love the unexplained, so while I suck at this stuff, it's also kind of exciting to me. It would be *more* fun if I had Midnight here to help, but beggars can't be choosers.

My teacher approaches when I've got my workstation set up. "Bex?"

"Hmm?" I stare down at the things I'll need. Test tubes, glass, paper, droppers...

"Do you know what you're doing?" he asks.

I frown at him. "What do you mean by that?"

He stuffs a pen behind his ear and motions toward my clean workstation. "You haven't started yet."

"Um, because I just literally finished getting things ready." I purse my lips and look at the instructions.

"Are you sure you can manage doing this on your own?"

"Positive, Mr. Philips." My smile is tight. His lack of confidence in me is annoying. I'm more than capable of doing one little experiment on my own. It can't be that hard.

Once he walks away, though, my mind seems to freeze up. And the longer class goes on, the more I start to struggle with measurements; what goes first, second; what should be mixed and what shouldn't. Ugh. I blame the asshole teacher for stealing my light.

At one point, water spills on the paper, making the ink I'd used run. I groan, reaching for a towel, knocking over a beaker filled with something bubbly at the same time. It drips across my workstation and flees toward the edge of my table like an escaping rat. I reach out to try and keep it from falling and wind up slamming my hand a little too hard on top of it. It breaks within seconds, tiny pieces shattering and digging into my palm.

"Gah!" I yell.

The entire class rushes to surround me, though nobody actually asks if I'm okay. This will just be another story to share with their friends at lunch today. *Glad to be your entertainment, idiots.*

"What happened?" Mr. Philips asks, running to me.

I lift my hand and show him my palm. "I broke a beaker."

"With your hand?"

I shrug, not claiming to be the brightest crayon in the box. This *is* my second time taking this class.

"*This* is why we don't work without a partner." He shakes his head and grabs some gloves.

"It was an accident," I say. "I'm sorry."

He picks out the few shards he can, then tells me to wash my hand. When the bleeding has mostly stopped, he says, "Go to the nurse."

"I'm fine. Don't you have a Band-Aid or something?"

He shoos me toward the door, ignoring my question. "It's policy, and you'll need to fill out an accident report with the nurse."

Like a puppy in trouble, I dip my chin and head to the nurse's office. When I get there, she's on the phone with someone and tells me to go to the back of the room behind the long, drawn curtain, and sit on one of the cots. I could be missing a limb and she likely still wouldn't care.

When I get there, I'm so distracted by my miserable mood that I don't see him right away—the boy sitting on the furthest cot from mine, looking out the small window.

I gasp quietly as I take him in. He's shirtless, and across his skin are layers upon layers of pink, jagged scars. It looks like he'd been whipped with something sharp.

A second later, he turns and spots me, blue eyes dead like always when they meet mine.

"Midnight?" I blink. "W-what happened to your back?"

He reaches over, grabs the hoodie on the cot next to him, and quickly slides it on.

"It's nothing." He sets his feet on the floor and bows his head.

"That didn't *look* like nothing."

He shrugs one shoulder. "It is nothing."

I get up and move to the cot beside him, releasing a slow breath when I sit. Our knees are a good foot apart, but the sparks inside of me are still there popping, as if we're connected. "Does it hurt?"

"Not anymore," he tells me.

There a few hundred things I could say in response, but I decide to keep it light. "Well, you're not gonna win any swimsuit contests anytime soon, are you?"

He lifts his head and stares at me in surprise.

"Shit, I'm sorry." I wince. "That was mean."

Seconds later, his lips start to twitch, then he does the last thing I expect.

He laughs. And it's not just an old man Santa chuckle either. It's a belly laugh that lasts a solid minute. I stare at him the entire time, not sure if this is some hysterical reaction or what. But when he finally finishes and looks at me again, it's the smile he's wearing that confirms the truth.

"You're…" He rubs a hand across his mouth.

"I'm what?" I smile back, though mine's less sure, more cautionary.

"Kinda funny," he says.

I sit up straight, smiling wider. "And thank you, I'm here every day after all Chemistry Class accidents." I turn my palm over, frowning at the marks that still bleed, though not as much.

"Shit," he says, eyes narrowing. "Are you okay? What happened?"

"Yeah. I just realized that my lab partner does the measurements for a reason now."

Fear captures his ocean eyes.

"I'm fine. Nothing a little Band-Aid can't fix."

His face goes white. "I should have been there. I'm sorry."

"It's not your fault. Seriously," I say.

Without asking, he reaches for my hand and sets it on his thigh. His palms are surprisingly soft compared to how the backs of his hands look, and I find myself relaxing instead of stiffening. Midnight makes me feel safe for some reason.

"Is this some sort of *you showed me yours, now I have to show you mine* kink?" I ask.

He snorts out loud.

I grin.

Fingers wrap around my wrist as he carefully runs his thumb in between the small cuts. I shiver a little, hoping he doesn't notice.

He lifts his head to look at me again, pulling one knee up on his cot while the other stays flat on the floor. His legs are thin, kind of like the rest of his body, but he's so tall that even sitting down he's at least five inches taller than me. And he's so close now too.

I lick my dry lips, suddenly nervous. Or maybe excited is a better word for it.

"You need medicine," he says. "Antibiotic cream or something."

"Thanks for the tip, Doctor Midnight. Mr. Phillips was kind of a dick about it, but whatever."

He narrows his eyes. "I hate him."

"We *do* have something in common, then."

He smiles a little, the left side of his mouth higher than the right.

If a person could die from beautiful things, I might be dead already because this guy is the prettiest one I've ever seen. Flushed pink cheeks, full lips, white teeth—a little crooked, but endearing at the same time.

Never have I let myself feel things for boys, mostly because I've never cared one way or another. But Midnight has me contemplating kisses I'll likely only be experiencing in dreams.

He clears his throat, and I jerk my gaze from his mouth, finding his eyes on me, a flicker of something inside as he studies my face. "A few of these may scar," he whispers.

I shrug, then release a quiet breath. "Scars are badass. They make you look sexy."

He freezes, and it takes me less than five seconds to realize what I just said.

"Shit." I yank my hand back. "I mean not *you* in particular." I cover my face with my good hand, only to look at him through my fingers. "Can we pretend I didn't just say any of that?"

He pulls my hand from my face and leans in, lowering his head to meet me at eye level. "You don't need to hide from me."

"I kind of do when I say random crap like that. It's embarrassing."

"I like your rambling." He pulls my hand onto his lap. "You're real. And I like real people. They're easier to trust."

His words hit me right in the chest, digging like he's a shovel searching for something ten feet under. It doesn't hurt, but it aches—the kind of ache where I have to put my hand over my heart because it feels like it's gonna burst.

"You trust me?" I ask.

He looks at his lap and sighs, like he hates admitting it. "Guess so."

I want to tell him that realness and trust aren't things that I give out easily. Fully trusting someone takes too much energy. Hell, I've barely scratched that surface with my friends. But Midnight is a rarity, and because of that, I've opened a part of myself that doesn't normally get shown off. Not since my dad died. I'm not saying Midnight has fixed me—I'll never be fixed—but sharing a tragedy of any kind with someone who's been through their own pain makes it easier to relate to them.

Midnight reaches into his pocket and pulls something out. It's a white tube of medicine, mostly empty by the looks of it.

"I want you to take this." He sets it on my thigh. "It's a scar cream. I don't need it anymore. Today was my last application."

I bite my lip. "That's why you were in here."

He nods. "The nurse puts it on for me."

"Oh. How come?"

"Because she's the only adult I trust to do it."

I frown at that, curious as to why he doesn't trust the people he lives with. Guess it goes to show just how little I know about him still.

Saying thank you feels too corny. But being all googly-eyed about his sweetness is even worse. So, I do what I'm best at. "You know it's illegal to share prescriptions, right?"

He scoffs. "I'll take my chances."

Our eyes hold for another long minute, neither of us looking away. We've been doing that a lot since we started talking outside of class. His eyes seem a little darker than they were seconds ago too, the ocean blue turning navy. I wrap my good hand around the medicine, fighting the urge to touch his cheek or hold his hand.

I want to ask what he's thinking—it's like my life duty to know this anymore—but I'm seeing clarity in his gaze I'm not used to. An openness that says, *I can be your friend and you can be mine*, even though all I can think about is how pink his lips are. How soft they seem too.

Normally dudes have chapped lips and scruffy cheeks that look like their covered in pubic hair, but not Midnight Turner. He's soft looking with hard angles that leave me wanting to trace each and every inch of him with my fingers.

His lips part, and soon he's looking at my mouth too. If he's thinking about kissing me, I sure as heck wouldn't push him away. But that's a super dumb thought, especially here in the nurse's office.

"*Decoris*," he whispers seconds later.

The word is so soft it sends goose bumps across my arms. It's like he's using a paintbrush to spell it out across my naked skin.

"What does that mean?" I ask.

"You'll have to figure that out on your own." He gets to his feet, hovering above me. "I should get to class."

Like clockwork, the bell rings.

"Wait." I stand too, wanting to follow him out, even though the nurse lady hasn't even bothered to check on me yet.

He wraps his fingers around the door handle.

"Please, Midnight." I touch the space between his shoulders, not realizing what I'm doing until he jerks away from me and turns back around.

He squeezes his eyes shut, like he can't stand looking at me.

"Shit. I'm so sorry," I say, yanking my hand to my side. "I shouldn't have touched your back without permission. It was stupid—"

"Not stupid," he cuts me off, lifts one hand and cups the side of my neck. With a soft shudder, he tips my head back, thumb beneath my chin as he urges my head up to meet his gaze. "And that word, Bex, means *beautiful*."

I blink up at him, cheeks so warm I feel like I'm seconds from bursting into flames. "B-beautiful?"

He nods, gripping the front of my hoodie with his free hand, like he's suddenly scared of falling. "Yes."

There are no words needed, despite the fact that I have a crap load of them running through my mind. Things are shifting so quickly between us that I can't keep my head on straight. It's the dizziest I've ever been, like I'm stuck in a tilt-a-whirl that never stops, climbed the highest mountain peaks with no way down, and all I want is to keep twirling and climbing until I've lost my focus completely. And I want to do it with Midnight by my side.

"Have lunch with me today," I blurt out.

He blinks a few times.

"We can eat outside," I rush to add. "I mean, if you're worried about Jo."

He pulls his hands back from my face and hoodie pocket. I miss the warmth of them instantly.

"She won't like it."

"Jo?" I cross my arms. "Who cares. I don't like all of her choices either, but I still deal with them."

His shoulders slump, and I'm sure he's going to make up an excuse as to why he can't, but...he doesn't.

"Okay," he says. "I'll have lunch with you."

"Really?" I bounce up and down on my toes, then rush him with a hug—a hug that I realize, too late, is probably unwanted. "Shit, sorry. I did it again." I try to drop my arms, but he stops me, wrapping *his* arms around *my* shoulders in a move I don't expect.

"I still should've asked." I bite my bottom lip and take a chance, laying my cheek against his chest. "To hug you, I mean. Consent works both ways."

He relaxes but not much, his stiffness matching his personality. Still, there's no denying what's against my ear—his heart racing like a horse at the derby, galloping his way to the finish line, both eyes on the winning roses.

I don't hug people lightly. I actually *hate* hugs. There's something about having another body pressed close to me that feels invasive. But Midnight's arms around my shoulders and his chin on top of my head feels like I'm finding a new home. One I've been missing for years. And despite the warning bells in my ears telling me how screwed I am, I can't find it in me to let him go.

CHAPTER 14: BEX
JANUARY 2022

MIDNIGHT AGREES to meet me outside the doors of the lunchroom at eleven-twenty. Since I packed a lunch for myself today it'll make this secret rendezvous of ours easier.

Three minutes into waiting, though, I get a text from Jo, thrown off my emotional high. Crap. I forgot to message her earlier and mention I won't be at lunch. At least not at lunch with her.

Jo: where you at?

Me: gonna take a test then eat in class.

I blow out a slow breath. Lying sucks, and I hate doing it. Yet if Jo was honest with me about why she hated Midnight so much, then maybe I could figure out a way to keep the friendships separate without having to keep him a secret from her.

Whatever. It's not like this lunch thing is gonna be an everyday occurrence. Midnight's probably only doing it to try and prove how much of a mistake it'll be, then come tomorrow, he'll be back at our table, begging for Jo to talk to him again.

Either that or he won't meet me at all.

Another text from Jo comes through.

Jo: oh. I was hoping we could hang

Me: after school?

Jo: ...

Me: Don't be mad

Jo: I'm not

"Like hell you aren't." I shut off my phone and tuck it away, spotting Midnight down the hall.

My heart leaps at the sight of him.

He towers over everyone else, and there's this time-lessness to him that makes the guy seem ten times older than the others around us. My belly twists and spins the closer he gets, the feeling so overwhelming I almost can't breathe.

He looks up from the ground, spotting me, and for a second, I see something that looks dangerously close to fear in his eyes. But I don't know if he's scared of me or whatever is happening between us.

Like with Jo's texts, I don't have time to contemplate what's up. We've got thirty minutes to do this lunch thing, and I want every second of it to count.

I meet him halfway, then motion toward the door leading outside. "Wanna go out there?"

He cringes. "It's snowing again."

"I keep forgetting about your aversion to the cold." I wince. "Sorry."

He doesn't nod or reply, just stares at the fresh layer of white on top of the other six or so inches already on the ground like he's trapped in a memory he can't escape.

"We don't have to eat out there," I rush to say. "We can sit in the hall outside the—"

"It's fine." He finally looks at me, blue eyes cold, mouth set in a hard line.

"Are you sure?" I ask.

He nods, then points to the one table that's under the roof overhang, as dry as can be. "There okay?"

"Absolutely—lead the way."

We head through the unlocked doors. I look to my left and right down the hallway first, careful to stay unnoticed by teachers as we exit. I'm not sure if eating outside is allowed during the winter, but it's the only place the two of us can go without being seen.

He sits across from me at the picnic table, close enough that our knees touch beneath, but so far away emotionally I wonder if he's regretting this meet-up already.

He points to my lunch. "Are you going to eat?"

"Aren't you?" I lift both brows. Unlike me, he doesn't have a bit of food in his hands.

"Not hungry."

"I can share." I pull out a peanut butter–banana sandwich, give him half. Surprisingly, he takes it. I offer carrots, but he shakes his head, looking down at the table as he takes a bite.

The two of us chew, focusing on everything but each other. I hate the awkwardness of all this. Which is why I'm the first to start the conversation like always.

"How's the rest of your day been?"

He finishes the last of his sandwich, swallows, then speaks. "Fine."

Ooookay then.

I start talking about random crap after that. Occasionally he nods or grunts, but his eyes keep flashing toward the windows, the ground—everywhere but at me it feels like. It's kind of annoying, which is why I jump to the big questions.

"So, where do you live?"

"In Altoona."

"No, smart-ass. Like, *where*? And with who?"

He hesitates, then looks inside again, sighing. "It's complicated."

"Complicated." I frown. "Like, are you actually secretly homeless or something?"

"Not homeless. It's just...my guardian isn't around right now. Won't be for a while."

"Where's he at?"

His brows furrow. I know he doesn't want to tell me, but I can't help but pry. I want to know Midnight, but he's making it difficult.

"I get that you have your secrets." I cross my arms. "But you can trust me, remember? I swear. I'm a locked vault."

He whips his head my way, scowling. "I don't *do* that, remember? I told you."

"Do what?" I seal up the bag with my uneaten carrots. "Trust people?"

"Yes," he grumbles and leans forward, setting both elbows on the table. "Look, you need to understand this about me, Bex. I don't like to spill a whole lotta shit about myself or my past. And you're not gonna come into my life and think you can just change that. You're not important to me."

I don't flinch. I'm the queen of nonchalance. And even though it feels like I've been stabbed in the chest, I keep my judgmental face off and aim for the one I need the most: unaffected. Likely he's saying what he is on purpose to push me away anyway, but it still hurts. Guess it's a good thing my skin is pretty thick.

"That's a sad life you lead, you know?" I take a bite of my sandwich this time, followed by a drink to wash the peanut butter down. "I mean, whatever happened to you in the past must've been pretty shitty for you to be so untrusting of people."

His nostrils flair, yet his words are absent.

"Buuuut," I continue, "if we're going to be friends, then you have to be honest with me about some things. You don't have to tell me everything, like I said, but if it's going to affect me at all then I deserve to know, don't you think?"

He runs a hand through his hair, glaring. "Why are you so damn determined to be my friend?"

I jerk my head back, thrown off by the question. "Um, were you not the one who just messaged me on Saturday asking to hang out?" I ask. Midnight presses his lips into a hard line. "Look, all I'm saying is, a friendship only works when both parties are putting their heart into it, and you asking me to hang out like that..." I leave the words unsaid because he knows what I'm talking about. He *has* to know.

"I asked you to come to the pond because I wanted you to see who I am."

"And I did. But if you were trying to scare me, it didn't work," I say. "We're all damaged, Midnight. It's just that some people show it more than others."

If anything, I've been seeing him from the beginning of the year. From the moment he yanked me under that table in AP chem to the nights by the pond, then this morning in the nurse's office, I've *been* seeing him clearer than anyone I've met in this town. He's showed me bits and pieces of what's beneath that broken armor he wears, showcasing a vulnerable dude with five thousand different versions of one person who I can't seem to get enough of. I'm so intrigued and so drawn to him that walking away would hurt. Even if it means keeping the trust between us one-sided.

"Then why the hell are you here with me, knowing I'm so *damaged*?" he asks. "Are you a masochist?"

I shrug one shoulder. "Maybe? Probably. I don't know."

He growls out the next words, like he's trying to scare me. "I come from trash, I've done trash things to good people, which means you need to find someone else to make over."

"Make over?" I laugh because he obviously has no idea what it means to want to be friends with someone after all.

He pushes up from the table, hovering, his hard eyes like knives twisting inside his own chest this time, not mine. He hurts. I know he does. I recognize that look in his eyes because I've been wearing it in some way, shape, or form since losing my dad.

Not wanting to give in to the fight he seems to be begging for, I stand too. If he's trying to be scary, it's not working.

"I'm here with you right now because this morning in the nurse's office I saw something in you that I know is real. Something that's so far removed from the angry act you're putting on right now."

"You saw something in me," he spits the words out like they're poisonous, his upper lip curling.

"Yes, like..." I blow out a slow breath. "Something good, ya know?"

"You are so clueless, you know that?"

"Um, excuse me, dick for brains, but I don't think you wanna talk to me like that."

"It's true!" He throws a hand in the air. "You have

this entitlement about you, despite what you think. It's like all I am to you is some problem that you want to fix to help get over your own issues of losing your dad."

My stomach drops into my feet. "That's...not cool."

He shakes his head and laughs bitterly. "You have no idea what pain is either. Not until you've had a whip made of barbwire slapped against your back seven times in a row for mouthing off to your own father. Not until you're locked in a room, forced to be with a girl until you get her pregnant. And not..."

My body goes cold, my face follows suit. I wait for him to finish, but he shuts himself down, like there's nothing left.

Dear God. Did he really have to go through all of that?

"Have you ever had your hands whipped with wire, Bex?" He gets in my face, staring down his nose at me, voice like ice.

"What did you just say?" I whisper.

"Have you ever had someone break into your house in the middle of the night, only for your mom to jump out the damn window and leave you there?"

"Midnight," I say, blinking through tears.

"Stop it," he growls, rubs the heels of his hands into his eyes and takes a step back. "Just fucking stop crying. Please. Leave me alone."

A sob breaks loose. I can't help it.

"Go!" he yells again. "Leave me alone."

I bite my bottom lip and turn to leave.

How could they do that to you?

There's a half second when I'm standing at the door, hand wrapped around the handle and shaking so badly it's numb, when I think about fighting back. Word for word, I'd turn around and allow myself to be his verbal punching bag. But in all honesty, I don't think I'm ready for more of his truths. Not until I can comprehend what he's already told me.

CHAPTER 15: MIDNIGHT
FEBRUARY 2021

"PLEASE, MIDNIGHT, TALK TO ME." Eve fell onto her knees in front of me on the bed, crying.

We'd just gotten back from the dinner. I wasn't in the mood to talk. I'd been through a lot of shit with Emmanuel, but something about tonight had hit harder. Humiliation was one thing, but to have it happen to you in front of men who were twice your age and in front of your life partner sucked.

"I'm not mad at you, Eve," I finally said. "I'm just tired."

"But I feel like you're mad." She set her hand on my shoulder.

"I'm not." I threw myself back onto the bed and crashed against my pillow.

With a shaky sigh, Eve took off her shoes, her tights after that, then undid her braids She laid down beside me, hands across her stomach. "I'm sorry," she whispered again.

"You didn't do anything wrong," I said.

"But I was so excited about going and wanting to

have fun. We should've just said I was sick or something."

"And you know what would've happened if we'd gotten caught lying."

She blew out a breath. "Emmanuel told me that this would be like a group celebration of our pairing."

I scowled. "When did he tell you this? Our pairing was four months ago."

Another shrug. Pretty sure she was deflecting.

I swallowed hard, brought back to that night. The marks, the rope, the blood... That wasn't something I wanted to celebrate, no matter how close Eve and I had become.

"That night sucked," I reminded her.

She turned on her side, facing me, her eyes locked on my face. "No, it didn't suck. It brought us together, remember?"

I studied her through the half dark, seeing the smile on her lips. She really thought that the night had been worth it. The pain, the lies, forcing two kids our age to get together and have babies just to populate a community I wanted nothing to do with... Emmanuel could create new little followers—Shepherds or Lambs, whatever the fuck he wanted. But I wouldn't.

"Do you ever think about leaving?" I brushed a hand through my hair.

She didn't answer. And the longer I waited for her to, the tighter my chest got. I'd never outright asked before, mostly because I was nervous to see what she'd say. But after tonight, I wanted to know so I could see if it was worth it to develop something further between us.

"I do," she eventually whispered, and it felt like every muscle in my body relaxed when she said those words.

"Would you leave"—I swallowed so hard my throat ached, but getting this out was important— "with me?"

Eve sat up, pulling her knees to her chest as she faced the window.

"What is it?" I asked, slowly sitting up next to her.

"I-I tried to kill myself a year ago, Midnight."

My breath got stuck in my throat. I blinked a few times too, thinking I was hearing things. "I didn't know."

"You wouldn't." She shrugged. "Only Emmanuel knows."

I hated how he knew things about her that I didn't.

"My older brother and I had gotten into a car accident," Eve continued. "It was my fault. I'd messed with his radio and was doing little things to annoy him because he was always gone and I missed him. Then he got distracted and drove off the side of the road, hit a tree and…" She sniffled, then started to cry.

I wrapped my arm around her shoulders and pulled her against my chest. "I'm sorry."

"It was my fault," she cried. "Mom and Dad were devastated, and my sister stopped talking to me because she blamed me. I was so alone."

I kissed the top of her head, holding my lips there. I'd only ever had my mom, and she was half-ass. No brothers, no sisters. It was hard to imagine how she felt. But I tried.

"His name was Luke." She shivered.

"That's a good name," I told her.

"It was."

We stayed like that for a while—her in my arms, neither of us talking. I wanted to know what had happened, how she'd tried to kill herself, when she'd tried. But I was pretty sure if I knew, I'd never be able to leave her alone for fear she'd try again.

I swallowed hard at the thought, lost in my own head.

"My parents didn't know what to do with me. I was so depressed after it happened that they sent me to my grandma's in Georgia for the summer because they thought I needed a change of scenery." Eve shrugged. "I thought they hated me and just didn't want me around anymore, so the first chance I got, I downed some sleeping pills."

I squeezed her even closer.

"Grams found me. My parents came and tried to take me home, but I refused. So they left me there, and then when I was better, my grams started forcing me to go to church with her."

"I'm so sorry, Eve."

"It's okay," she said, and I could hear a smile in her voice when she talked. "My faith got me through the pain."

What she'd said was hard for me to believe. I wasn't a nonbeliever, but if I had to choose, I'd go with people who believed in atheism versus places that had beliefs like Children of His Mercy.

"Anyway, my grams was friends with a man who was starting his own church, with longer hours and late night services... And since I didn't have much else to do, I started attending every night of the week. It was very freeing." She blew out a long breath. "There were so many different types of people there, yet we all related to one another in some way." She shrugged. "It's also where I met Emmanuel. He'd been driving through the town and had stopped by to pray. We met, and bonded.

He treated me so kindly, then told me he was starting a community where everyone was loved and accepted."

"And that's how you wound up here?"

She nodded.

My jaw locked. The way she said Emmanuel's name, like he was *her* God or something, made it feel like the scars on my back and hands weren't important to her.

Eve leaned back and stared up at me. Maybe she could hear my silent judgment. She didn't say anything, but I felt her question: *Why can't you believe too?*

"Emmanuel's a shit person," I said, pulling my hand off her back. "This cult is shit, and his followers are shit, and—"

"Don't say that." She glared at me a second, then stood up from the bed and walked to the other side of the room to stare out the window. "It's the only real thing I know now. I feel more like I belong here than I ever did at home or even with my grandma. And being a part of this place reminds me that Luke is now in a better place. And that I have no more reason to feel guilty."

"Eve..." I groaned and rubbed a hand across my head. "There are other good churches and places to believe in out there."

She swirled around to face me with narrowed eyes. "Emmanuel took care of me. Gave me new purpose. He is the *one* person who didn't abandon me when I felt my life was over."

I stood too, anger heating my face. "So, what, do you think everything he's done to me was okay, then? The scars on my back and hands from his wire?" I wanted to grab her by the shoulders and shake her. Emmanuel wasn't a hero. He was an evil, manipulating son of a bitch.

"He kidnapped me," I hissed the words out, fisting

my hands when she said nothing. "He's beaten me almost dead, Eve. How can you think he's a good person?"

"Because..." Her shoulders slumped and she bowed her head. "He told me that God intended for you to suffer so when the time came you would be happy *with* me."

"And you believe that?"

"Yes. Emmanuel wouldn't lie about something so secret like that."

I ran a hand down my face, disgusted. "This is messed up, you know that?"

"It's not messed up," she said, practically stomping her feet. "He made me believe I wasn't a failure. That it wasn't my fault Luke died. Nobody's said that before."

I paced back and forth, ran a hand through my hair. "So, what..." Saying the words felt like a knife piercing my throat. But I had to ask. "Do you love him or something?"

She stared up at me, blinking before looking down at her hands. "Yes, of course."

"That's wrong, Eve. How—"

"Don't." She put a hand over my mouth, holding my gaze. "It's a different kind of love, Midnight." She cupped my face with her other hand. "Not the kind I feel...when I'm with you."

And then she kissed me.

CHAPTER 16: BEX
JANUARY 2022

IT'S BEEN two days since Midnight and I had our fight at lunch, and I still can't shake the things he said to me. How he pushed me away most of all. He hurt my heart to the point where all I wanna do is rip it from my chest. Possibly rip my brain out too because I can't seem to shut the thing off.

I shouldn't have cared since *he* was the one who pushed me away in the first place. But I can't shake the sense that I did something wrong.

"Hey, sugar." Mom stands in my door frame wearing her black leather pants and a flashy purple tank. Her brown hair is nothing but wild curls pinned back at the sides.

"You going to work?" I ask, leaning against my headboard.

"Yeah. Martha needs me in early before the storm hits. Supposed to get a lot of truckers in town looking for places to stay till the snow stops."

Another snowstorm. Great. If I wasn't so distracted by my social life, then I'd be bouncing with excitement over the probability that I might get to have a snow day tomorrow. A snow day that would mean one more day of not facing Midnight.

"It's fine," I say, playing it cool. "I'll probably just watch TV."

"You sure you don't wanna call one of your girl-friends? See if they can hang out for the night?"

"They all have plans." It's a lie, but mostly because I'm not in the mood to hang out with anyone.

"All right, then. I left my credit card out on the table if you wanna order food."

Lowering myself onto the pillow, I pull the blanket up to my chin and reach for my remote. "Thanks."

She leans away from the door like she's leaving, then stops. "I also got a huge stack of blankets piled up in my room in case the power does go out. If it does sometime in the night, don't open the fridge much."

"Got it." I nod once.

"Okay, sugar. Love you. Probably just gonna crash at Martha's after work if it's bad. You good with that?"

"Yep."

I love my mom, but I'm not used to this overbearing, worried version of her, even two years after Dad's death. It's her new thing to be a half version of him and herself. The protector parent and the fun parent. But I know it's gotta be hard on her, likely more than it is on me, which is why I don't call her out on it.

My phone rings from the bedside table a few minutes after I hear the front-door lock engage. I don't have the desire to talk to anyone, but I don't wanna be rude either.

I swipe it up and put it to my ear without looking at the caller ID. "Hello?"

"Hey," Jo says. "How are you?"

I frown. Her voice is off. Stiffer. More formal.

"I'm good." I sit up straight and click off my TV. "What's up? You sound upset?"

Silence follows. This is far from a normal Jo call.

"Come on, Jo," I say. "Talk to me.?"

"It's nothing." She clears her throat.

"It's not nothing, otherwise you wouldn't be calling me," I tell her. "So tell me what it is so I can fix it."

"Fine." She blows out a long breath, "Have you been hanging out with Midnight?"

I swallow a lump in my throat, thinking of what to say that's not a lie but not the full truth. Sadly, I'm blanking out.

"That's what I thought," she scoffs, and I can practically hear her eyes roll. "I told you he's not good. Why can't you just listen to me?"

"It's not like that," I blurt out. "We've...just been thrown into a few weird situations together is all."

"Weird as in you skip lunch with us to go eat with him instead?" She scoffs.

"Not exactly. I—"

"Don't lie. Carson said she saw you two outside on Monday eating together."

"He's not that bad, Jo." I bite my bottom lip.

She laughs. "Because you know him soooo well now."

"He wanted to talk about our latest chemistry lab. Said something about loud crowds making it hard to concentrate." I hate lying, but this is a special circumstance.

"Damn it, Bex. He's dangerous and manipulative. I told you."

I pinch the bridge of my nose, tired of arguing about this. "Fine. I'll stay away, okay?" That won't be a problem anymore seeing as how he's already made the decision for us. Still, there's a pain in my chest from admitting it out loud.

She sighs, like she's relieved, then says, "If there's something going on between you two, you'd tell me, right?"

"One hundred percent honesty from here on out." More like, one hundred percent *I'm going to hell*.

"Thank you," she says. "That means a lot to me. You have no idea."

I want to roll my eyes—Jo keeps secrets from me, but I'm not allowed. It's kinda bullshit, honestly. I'm tired of everyone thinking I'm just some innocent girl who doesn't know how to take care of herself.

"If there's a snow day, we should hang out tomorrow afternoon. You, me, Car, and Gia," Jo says.

"Sure." There's no point in saying no. She'll come by anyway, even uninvited, wearing a grin that says *you'll never say no to me*.

"Oh, and I'm gonna have another party next weekend at the barn. You'll come to that, right? I miss you. Everything's felt off lately between us."

I wince. The "off" part is partially my fault. I've been distant, yes, but only because I've had things on my mind —people, more specifically.

"Sure. And I miss you too. Talk later?"

We say our goodbyes, and though I want to say things between us are okay, I can't. Lies suck. Lies by omission are even worse.

Even though my mind is twisted with too many thoughts for my own good, I'm able to settle back into bed and get semi-comfortable. I even order a pizza and watch a movie. Unfortunately, it was a horror movie that revolved around a cult, which has me obviously thinking about Midnight and what he's been through.

Sleep is still a bitter whore who only comes when it's convenient for her, and—surprise, surprise—tonight is one of those nights where she's too busy for me. So I lay there in the dark in my bed instead, studying the shadows from trees outside as they dance across my wall all while listening to the winter storm roll in.

Ice pings against the glass like wind chimes, and I can't help but sigh. It's a sound that's dangerous to most but soothing to me. Dad died in the summer. A hot night on the streets of downtown Chicago with too many idiots not watching where they were going.

I'd take a snowstorm over a heat wave any day.

If he were here, there's no doubt in my mind we'd still be living in Chicago, in the same crappy apartment that I claimed to hate but secretly adored. I'd be dead set on getting into Chicago State University. Dad would be so proud of me for choosing his alma mater that he—and Mom—would take me to my favorite Chinese restaurant just one block away, where the dumplings were supposedly better than sex.

I cover my face and groan, angry at myself for thinking about him when I know it'll only mess up my emotions more. Maybe I should start seeing a therapist again. I'll have to talk to my mom about it.

It's not even a minute later when I hear it. Two single knocks against my window, followed by a loud thumping on my roof.

"Great. And now I'm about to get murdered in my room."

Slowly, I sit up on the side of my bed and pull a hoodie on. It hangs to my knees when I stand, covering my underwear and lady bits. For safety, I grab an old unused baseball bat from my closet. I know I'm not very smart. I should actually call the cops. But there's this gut instinct in me that says *check first, freak out later*.

I'm glad I do in the end because when I get to the window a familiar face pops into my line of vision.

"Shit," I say, dropping the bat to the floor.

Midnight's here.

With shaking hands I shove the window up, gasping when icy pellets slice through the air and hit my face.

"What the hell are you doing?" I ask.

Midnight's on his hands and knees, hair sopping wet and hanging over his eyes. He stares blankly at me through the dark, looking as if he hasn't slept in days.

"C-can I come in?" he asks with chattering teeth.

"Jesus," I say in place of a yes.

He must take it as an okay because he slides into my room.

I step back, staring up at him. Water drips down his face and clothes once he's upright. It soaks my carpet and everything else on my floor.

"What were you thinking climbing onto my roof at one in the morning in the middle of an ice storm?"

I walk to my closet and pull out a fluffy blanket, coming back to wrap it around his shoulders like a cape.

"I wasn't," he whispers, bowing his head. "Thinking, I mean."

I inhale, taking in the mix of wetness and cinnamon gum. "You could've slipped and fallen," I say. "Plus you hate the cold."

Instead of making up an excuse, Midnight grabs me by the elbows, yanks me close, and hugs me to his chest like I'm the last thing he'll ever hold on to.

My eyes pop wide. My shirt's soaked within seconds. I leave my arms dangling at my sides, not knowing what to do with them. I hate hugs. But Midnight hugs, wet or not, might be my new favorite thing.

While I'm lost in my hugging comatose state, I don't realize at first that his shaking is getting worse instead of better.

"Hey," I whisper. "You need to get out of these wet clothes."

"N-no." He hugs me tighter.

"Why not?"

He shakes his head but doesn't answer.

"Please?" I beg. "You're going to get sick."

"I can't, Bex."

I tip my head back and squint up at him. "As in you can't or you won't?"

"C-can't." His eyes are squeezed shut like he's either too afraid to look at me or too afraid to ask for my help.

"Why not?"

He slowly reopens his eyes. "Because I'm afraid."

"Of what?" I ask.

His lips part and he searches my face, like he's just experienced some life-altering revelation. "You."

My entire upper body goes warm, but I push out a scoff, pretending not to be bothered by his insult—if it even is one. "Dude. I'm nothing, remember? Just a girl who's obnoxious and you want out of your life."

Yet here he is.

"You're not nothing. You're real." He licks his lips and searches my face.

I tip my head to one side. "Flesh and bones real, sure, but—"

"No," he growls out in frustration, his teeth no longer chattering but clenched. "You don't get it."

"Then help me understand." I throw my hands up in the air and finally take a step back. When I'm close to him, I can't think clearly. "Every time I try to get to know you, you push me away. I ask questions, you bark at me. I try to help you, you call me annoying. So excuse me if I'm a little bit frustrated by your hot-and-cold bullshi—"

"I like you, okay?" he growls out, the sound fierce like a lion.

This is the first time I have no desire to play down an intense moment with humor.

"You…like me?" I hold my breath.

"Yes. A-and if I like you and tell you what really happened to me, who I am, then I'm afraid you'll…"

"I'll what?" My stomach dips as I wait for his answer. It's like tiny roller coasters have gathered each of my emotions inside and are currently having the time of their lives inside.

"You'll walk away. Just like she did." He shakes his head. "Just like everyone else I get close to does."

It's on the tip of my tongue to ask who this *she* person is, but I know he won't tell me if I do. So I go with a confirmation of my own feelings instead.

"Midnight." I reach for his hands. "I like you too, but—"

"My name is Midnight Josiah Turner. I was…" He takes a shuddering breath, then walks backward toward the window before continuing. "Born in Ontario, Missouri, raised by m-my mom until I was sixteen. Her name is…" He shakes his head. "April." He winces and reopens his eyes. "Cora. Her name was Cora."

My breath catches, though I'm not sure what to do with all this new information he's given me. It's not even that much, but I suddenly feel like he's gifting me the world.

"It's okay." I walk to him but keep my hands by my

sides. "You don't have to explain anything to me right now."

"I want to," he says, opening his eyes. "I-I want you to know me because I trust you. More than anyone else."

I touch my lips, open my mouth, then shut it. I may never understand why he's picked me to spill his secrets with. Yes, I've bugged him about it, but I couldn't have been the only one to do so. The thing is I wasn't kidding when I told him I'm nobody. A plain Jane with a chip on her shoulder. Broody, sarcastic, and easily annoyed. It baffles me as to why he likes me at all. I mean, I'm cool in my own world, but not normally in anyone else's.

"Look," I say, taking a deep breath. "You can tell me whatever you want about who you are, your name, your past, what you eat for breakfast on a daily basis..." I put my hands behind my back, twisting my fingers together. "But you *have* to get into some dry clothes first."

"I-I don't have any."

"Well, lucky for you, I do."

Without thinking, I leave the room, not only to get the clothes but to give my brain an emotional reprieve. We're in new territory here, the unexplored. And as much as I wanted this before, I'm terrified of what I might find now that he's about to let me in.

In the bathroom across the hall, I flip the light on and grab a couple of towels, catching a glance of myself in the mirror when I stand. I'm a hot mess. My hair's greasy and my cheeks are as pale as the snow. If there was a beauty pageant happening around me, they'd kick me across the country just so I don't taint the atmosphere.

I smell my armpits, then shrug. At least I have that going for me.

Next stop is my mom's room next to mine. I know she keeps a small box of my dad's clothes in the back of her closet. She sometimes wears his sweats and long tees to bed. It feels invasive to steal them and loan them to Midnight, but it's only temporary while I dry his clothes off. Mom will never know.

When I step back into the room, I see that he's got his back to me, shirt still on as he stares out the window. His fingers are spread against the glass and shadowed by the night. He's like an angel. One who's been sent to be my demise or savior.

I clear my throat, realizing I've been staring too long. "Here you go."

He turns, heavy-lidded gaze searching my face. He does that a lot, but I don't mind.

Midnight's soul sits on his shoulders—exposed, tired, tattered, and broken. If I had the ability to sew it back inside of him, repair it with a thread and needle, I would.

"Take the towel first," I say, handing it over, then setting the clothes on my desk chair.

He glances at each item, then looks at me.

"You do know how to use a towel right?" I ask.

His lips twitch. And for a second, it feels like he's going to smile, but he doesn't.

"Thank you." He takes it from me and runs it through his hair, down his face, across his neck and arms...

My throat dries up as I watch. When he catches me staring, I quickly turn away, praying my cheeks aren't red —not that he can see.

"Um, I'll leave you to get changed." I step into the hall. "Just open the door when you're dressed."

Outside my door, I lean my head back against the wall, wishing I didn't have the urge to bust back through that door to see what he looks like naked.

"Stooop it," I tell myself. He is just a dude, not an Adonis.

The door creaks open then. "You can come in," he says.

"You're quick." I take a second to get myself together, then walk back in, expecting to see him sitting in my chair or on the edge of my bed. But that's not the case. He's at my window, looking outside again...shirtless this time.

Emotions fill my throat the second I see the marks, the slashes, the invisible pain I want to cry for. I cover my mouth, struggle to swallow, but the ache doesn't go away no matter how many times I attempt to gulp it down. Just like when I was in the nurse's office the other day, my eyes fill with tears that fall quicker than rain. It hurts me to see him like this, even though he says it doesn't hurt anymore.

I should hate this guy. Truly. I should push him back out the window and tell him to go mess up some other girl. Yet the thought of doing so makes my stomach hurt, and now that he's exposing himself to me—to something so obviously painful—the only thing I find myself wanting to do is walk up behind him and wrap my arms around his waist.

Midnight is giving me something impossible and making it probable.

It feels like a gift.

Or maybe it's a curse.

Either way, I'm gonna savor it.

"He did this t-to me because I didn't wanna pray," he says, obviously sensing my presence.

My tears fall faster, quick and unsurmountable. I don't know who this *he* is, but I know for a fact I'm going to murder him one day.

"Midnight," I whisper, fingers on my lips.

He shudders the closer I get. I don't make a move to touch him though.

"Three days," he says. "I'd been there three. Damn. Days when he did it."

"God." I shake my head, not knowing what to say. *Sorry* doesn't even begin to cross my mind because this kind of pain deserves more than a simple apology from a girl who barely knows him.

"I'm not telling you to feel sorry for me." He turns, faces me with wet eyes of his own. Our chests are inches apart, and my fingers itch to cup his face and wipe the wet droplets off his cheeks.

"Then why *are* you telling me?" I whisper.

"Because," he says, lifting a hand to brush a piece of hair from my eye. It's so tender. So unlike him. "Like I said, I like you."

He runs his finger down my cheek, and I lick my lips. When he lets it fall away, I have to curl my hands into fists just so I don't touch the spot. It burns as though he left a sparking fire behind.

I look down and study his chest instead.

Unlike his back, it's smooth and untouched. It reminds me of a fresh coloring book that nobody wants to touch for fear that the magic will fade when the crayons graze the paper. He's thin yet toned. Not six-pack, muscular, but firm. His shoulders are wide and broad but so thin I can see his collar bone. I can't help but reach out and touch it, wondering if it feels as sharp as it looks.

He shivers as I allow my hand to trace it. His Adam's apple bobs, but I don't know if he's uncomfortable by my touch or enjoying it. I've always been attracted to him, but this...this is something different. Something dangerous.

"Who was this man?" I finally get the courage to ask.

He doesn't speak but doesn't look away either. I think he's going to tell me he can't say, but he doesn't.

"I'll tell you. Everything."

"Yeah?" I hold my breath.

He nods, and the saddest question spills from his lips. "Can I stay with you tonight? I-I don't want to be alone."

I blink and immediately yank my hand back, slingshotted right back into reality.

"As in all night?"

He nods.

I look around the room, at the door, my tiny twin bed. It's a bad idea. A terrible one. If Mom came home, she would absolutely freak out. She may want me to have a social life, but I'm pretty sure that doesn't include sharing a bed with a boy all night while she's at work.

At the same time, saying no and kicking him out would shatter any of the progress we've made. So instead of speaking, I walk to the door, put a chair under the handle, and then climb into bed, pulling the other side of my comforter back behind me.

"Sorry I don't have more than one pillow." I shrug.

He doesn't move, but I can hear his breaths quickening.

I pat the mattress. "Are you just going to stand there all night and be creepy, or you gonna sleep?"

"I-I can sleep on the floor."

I roll my eyes. "Get in the bed."

Midnight still stands there, staring.

"Dude. If you don't get in the bed, then I'm gonna ask a million more questions and you're not gonna like any of them, got me?"

I lie back down, facing the window, then shut my eyes

to try to keep my heart in check. Seconds later I hear him sigh, followed by the sounds of his feet thumping as he walks around the bed to the other side of me.

My entire body shakes with anxiety. The good and bad kind. Despite my casual demeanor, this situation freaks me out. I've never even kissed a dude, let alone shared a bed with one.

The blankets move from behind me, the mattress shifts as he settles himself on top of the comforter instead of under it. I wait a few minutes, hold my breath, hoping he'll start talking or something. Maybe ask to slide under the blankets for warmth.

But when I glance at him from over my shoulder and find his lips parted and eyes shut, his bare chest slowly rising and falling, I realize there will be no awkward conversation, no truth sharing either, because Midnight has already fallen asleep.

CHAPTER 17: MIDNIGHT
FEBRUARY 2021

"HEY," I said, grabbing Eve by the shoulders when I stepped back from her kiss. My lips tingled, and her face was bright red. Still, I couldn't let this happen. Not like this. "We don't have to…"

She looked at me, big green eyes filled with something I'd never seen before on a girl. "I want you, Midnight."

I shut my eyes and settled my forehead against hers. "I don't know if it's a good idea though."

She wrapped her arms around my waist and pressed her ear to my chest. "Why not? Do you not like me like that?"

I did.

Or at least I thought I did. Everything was complicated behind these walls, and I wasn't sure if I liked her as a sister, a friend, or something more.

"I do like you. I just…don't like it here."

I thought about my mom. How Emmanuel had gotten her pregnant at this place. How she'd run her whole life from him because of what he'd done to her. But if I told

Eve that, she'd probably think I was being over dramatic or something.

She grabbed my hands and pulled them onto her lap. "If we don't do what Emmanuel wants, then he'll take me away from you."

I lifted a knee on the bed and turned to face her. "Then let's leave. We can go hide somewhere till we turn eighteen."

She bit her bottom lip. "But what if we get caught?"

"We won't."

"How do you know?"

"I just do."

She huffed. "You don't even have a plan."

"I'll come up with one."

"*Fiat voluntas Dei.*" She sighed.

"It is His will?" I frowned. "Why are you saying that? We can do this, with a little planning. I know we can."

Eve shook her head. "It's not a good idea."

"Look," I said. "I've been through a lot of things, just like you have. But do you really think we were brought together just to have babies at seventeen years old?"

"Maybe? I don't know, Midnight."

"Don't you wanna graduate high school?" I asked. "Maybe even take some classes at a college? I think I want to even join the army and—"

"Send me back home with parents who don't love me while you get to do everything you want?" She jumped up from the bed and walked to the window. "I can't go back there, Midnight. You don't understand."

I stood, staring at the back of her head. "Then help me understand. Give me other ideas because I can't do this here. But I can't leave without you either."

She started sobbing again. When life went to hell or I asked too many questions, it was what she seemed to do.

It made me sad to know she was scared of everything and everyone. But that also made me want to hold her tighter and protect her even more.

I turned her around and looked her in the eye, one hand on her upper arm, the other wiping tears from her cheek. "I'll take care of you."

"How?" She sniffed and put her hand over mine on her face. Her rosy, pink cheeks looked like two cherries had formed on them, and I leaned down to kiss her forehead.

"I'll figure it out. Swear it."

She nodded and settled her forehead against my chest, her sobs growing louder with every second. Like that, I was helpless. And no matter what I said, I couldn't get her to stop. So I squeezed her tighter and just let her get it out.

All I wanted was to leave here, start over somehow. Problem was I didn't know what to do if I did get us out. It wasn't like Mom was anywhere around, waiting to rescue us. And if Eve's parents knew she was out, then she was probably right that they'd do whatever possible to get her back home.

"We should sleep," she mumbled against my chest.

I nodded and took her hand.

We laid down on the bed, side by side with our heads touching and our hands interlocked. I stared up at the ceiling for a long time, thinking. For a first kiss, things sure as hell hadn't gone the way I'd expected. But nothing about our relationship was normal either.

"I miss my sister," she whispered out of the blue.

I let my head fall to the side to look at her, holding my breath. "Yeah?"

"Yeah. I mean, we could get in touch with her if we

left. I think she'd help. She has a savings built up, and I don't think she'd rat me out to my parents."

I frowned. "You don't *think* she would?"

She shrugged and shut her eyes, burying her face against my shoulder. "I don't know. But we could at least try, if you really want to get out of here that badly."

I squeezed her hand. "Yeah. Okay. We can do that."

The two of us fell asleep like that, tangled close, breathing in sync. It was the best I'd slept in forever. Probably because we finally had a goal to reach for that went beyond this place.

CHAPTER 18: BEX
JANUARY 2022

I WAKE EARLY in the morning with frozen toes. Blinking so I can clear my vision, I notice that the window is cracked a little. I try to sit up so I can go shut it, but an arm snakes around my waist and yanks me back against a warm chest.

"Don't leave me," Midnight whispers, clearly still asleep.

I'd almost forgotten he'd stayed all night.

Knowing I need to check the time and see if my mom texted, I slowly slide my hand around the bed until I can feel my phone beneath my pillow. I click the power button, seeing one lone text message.

Mom: Power's out at the bar and the streets are covered. Gonna stay with Martha for a while. School's canceled already. Love you.

That was twenty minutes ago, according to the time on my phone. Makes sense as to why all my LED lights are off. The heat too if I had to guess. I type out a quick message back.

Me: Love you too

I breathe a sigh of relief when I put my phone back under my pillow. She'll likely stay at Martha's until all the roads clear, so we're safe for a little while.

I wiggle trying to get comfortable, when really my brain is running a mile a minute due to the sole fact that there's only a hoodie separating Midnight's hand from my stomach.

"Stop moving," he mumbles against the back of my neck.

"Sorry." I bite my bottom lip. "It's just that I'm used to waking up early." I have this annoying alarm clock in my head that says *four a.m. is where it's at.* Usually, I play games on my phone, scroll through TikTok, then pass out an hour before my alarm goes off at seven. It's a vicious cycle I can't break.

I tap my fingers against the mattress, then click my tongue against the roof of my mouth.

"Shh," he tells me.

"I can't *shhh*," I say, grinning. "I'm in bed with a boy in my room, and it's weird, okay?"

He stiffens, yanking his arm away like he just now realizes what he's doing. "Sorry."

"It's fine." But the weird tension that follows says otherwise.

I move my feet, trying to warm them, only to accidently brush them against the top of his.

"What the hell?" He rolls off the bed, landing with a thud on the floor.

I slap a hand over my mouth to hide a laugh, then crawl to the edge of the bed so I can look down at him. "My bad."

He groans and throws an arm over his eyes.

"It's freezing in here," I tell him. "The window was left open all night."

His eyes fly open, locking with mine. "What?"

"I said..." I roll over and out of bed, a blanket wrapped around my shoulders. "The window was left open all night."

When I look outside, all I see is snow. It's piled high on the roof, lighting the super dark morning. The shadows of the trees move in the distance, but I have a feeling each one is covered in layers of ice.

The wood of the window squeaks when I close it, and snow falls onto my already icy toes.

Wonderful.

I turn and rush back to my bed, sliding in, and burying myself under the covers again to where only my eyes and the top of my head are visible.

"I closed it last night." Midnight's on his knees, staring at me from the floor.

"It's fine. Normally I do sleep with it open because it gets hot up here. But since the power went out and there is literally no heat on, it's freezing." I tuck both feet within the confines of my sheets, tangling them between that and the comforter.

"The power went out?" Midnight stands, as shirtless as the night before.

I swallow, trying not to ogle him. "All the ice, I'm guessing."

My mouth dries as I look at him. Even through the dark he's a vision. One that has my entire body tightening. Low-slung sweats, hip bones sticking out from over the top, and a flat stomach that is undeniably attractive. I blink, lifting my eyes to trace them over the rest of him.

Midnight is incredibly beautiful.

Oblivious to my lingering stare, he walks to the window. My gaze latches onto to his back, and that same lump from the night before shows up in my throat again.

It's amazing how I can go from lusting after his body to feeling like absolute trash fire over the fact that he's so broken within seconds.

"When did it go out?" he asks, reopening the window, then sticking his head out of it.

I prop myself up on my elbows and watch him. "Um, not sure. My mom texted me a little bit ago and said the power's out at the bar too, so she's staying with her friend. Why?"

Slowly, he pulls his head back into the room, standing at his full height when he turns to face me. There's a line between his deep-set blue eyes that I have a desperate urge to smooth out with my thumb.

"I see footprints out there," he says, his voice rising.

"It's probably the neighborhood raccoon," I say. "They're always up there, getting stuck inside our roof vents."

"These are people prints, Bex."

I jump out of bed and move in next to him, confused. "Where?"

He points to the edge and I look, noticing the fresh trail. Smaller footprints. Kid size, maybe? But that can't be right.

"That's weird." I frown.

"We need to go." He shuts the window, locks it, then closes the curtains.

"Um, why?"

"Because someone was out there watching us."

"Seriously. It's probably the landlord's prints that got partially covered or something. I'm guessing he was either trying to get the raccoons out or spraying off his satellite at some point before the power went out." Though you'd think I would've heard him.

"No." Midnight shakes his head. "No, it's not. It's him."

I jerk my head back, brows furrowed. "Him who?"

As fast as humanly possible, he rushes to my closet and grabs my bookbag. Books are strewn across the room, followed by pencils, folders...everything in my bag.

"Midnight, stop," I say.

"No, we have to... We need..."

I jump in front of him and grab his forearms, holding him in place. "Stop."

Slowly, he lifts his eyes, and the terror in them has me faltering. Someone's got to be the tough guy here though, and it won't be him.

I lift my chin. "Turn off whatever is in your mind right now. I'm safe. You're safe. We both are."

"I can't." He holds his breath, squeezes his eyes shut. "Bex, I just..."

"We're here in my room. We're not *there*, okay?"

He winces, obviously realizing what I mean by *there*. That place, the people, everything he went through. He's still got so much to tell me, but from his outburst on Monday, now this, I'm getting the gist of how terrible it was.

"Do you want to talk about it some more?" I hold my breath, wait for him to answer.

He tries to pull back to wipe his teary face, but I shake my head. "Let me, okay?"

He nods, not even knowing what I'm about to do. It's the biggest gift he can give me—his trust. And I won't screw it up.

I release his arms, slowly move my hands up his shoulders, his neck, then finally to his cheeks. With soft strokes, I brush away the tears with my thumbs. His face is warm and soft, flawless like his chest, with hidden marks that have made him into an entirely different person. I wish could take his pain away, but his demons aren't mine and battling them will be the only way for him to get control of his life.

When I'm finished, I meet his gaze head on once more, finding something new written on his face. Red cheeks and parted lips, a hint of softness in his eyes that makes my belly flutter. It's vulnerability, an opening for me to get questions answered once and for all. I shouldn't take advantage of it, but if he wants to heal, he needs to let go of his secrets to someone.

"Do you want to tell me the real reason you don't like the cold? Why you pull girls under tables? Why you think someone was looking through my window?"

Midnight doesn't move. Doesn't nod. Doesn't speak. But the light in his eyes darkens as he finally says, "Okay. I'll tell you."

CHAPTER 19: MIDNIGHT
FEBRUARY 2021

NOAH HADN'T BEEN AROUND to lead me to the afternoon Gentlemen Services like normal for almost two weeks. In fact, I hadn't seen him for a good seven or eight days. That sucked because he was the one person who'd talk to me. And in order to get Eve and me out of there, I had to know a few things about our location. Where we were in relation to Eve's house, especially.

Simon had taken over for him for some reason. When I'd asked about Noah, he'd barked at me, said if I knew what was good for me, I'd shut up. Whatever the hell that meant. Otherwise, Simon had been ignoring me too.

Emmanuel showed up to lead the Gentlemen Services still in the afternoon, but even he'd been tamer. His greetings were minimal, and when I didn't do something fast enough, he ignored me instead of beating me.

Hell, everyone ignored me, really.

Except for Eve, who'd been coming on stronger than ever over the last week.

Every night she tried to kiss me and touch me. And every night I continued to reject her. I tried to tell her that my rejections were for her own good, but she kept saying we had to or else we'd get punished. Still, I kept refusing, confident we could get out before it came down to that.

Usually, Eve let it go. But last night, after I'd fallen asleep, she'd taken things a step further and gotten naked in bed. I'd woken up to the feel of her lips on my throat and body on top of me. It freaked me out a little, though I'm not sure why. She was pretty and nice and I should've been okay with it, but...I wasn't. When I told her I couldn't do what she wanted, she'd started crying again.

You don't love me, she'd said. *You never will.*

I did love her, yeah. But not in the way she loved me —though I didn't tell her that.

She'd fallen asleep in my arms right after, at least her soft prayers against my chest like a soothing lullaby, though I had no idea what they'd meant.

Ángele Dei,

Qui custos es mei,

Me, tibi commíssum pietáte supérna,

Illúmine, custódi

Rege et gubérna

Amen

It was on the fourth day of the second week without Noah around when I realized something wasn't right. I was to line up by the door that led to the courtyard at ten p.m. Emmanuel had called an emergency Gentlemen Service through the intercom. Nine other men and I were told to meet there.

"What's this all about?" Eve sat on the bed beside me while I put on my boots.

"No idea."

"Oh, well, maybe you shouldn't go."

"Yeah, and get another beating?" I scoffed. "Don't think so."

She sighed. "If you're going outside, don't you think you should take a coat?"

I shook my head and finished tying my other shoe. "We're not allowed to bring anything to Service but our bibles."

"But it sounds like you'll be outside if you're meeting at the courtyard doors, right?"

I shrugged and put both feet on the floor before grabbing her hand and squeezing it in reassurance. "I'm sure it'll be fine."

And if it isn't?

The thought ran through my head like a bulldozer. Every time Eve and I separated for Services, or any reason really, my body turned into this live wire that didn't shut down until we were together again. It was stupid to feel this way, like I was constantly worried something would happen to her or myself. But that's what happened when everything good in your life got taken away.

I kissed her on the cheek and said goodbye, telling her not to wait up. When I got to the hall, though, she rushed after me, her bottom lip tugged between her teeth.

"What is it?" I asked.

She shook her head and jumped forward, wrapping both arms around my waist. She held me, shaking and crying, to the point where I lost my smile and realized that something was wrong.

"Hey," I pulled back to look down at her. "What's wrong?"

Instead of telling me, she threaded fingers through

my hair and kissed me hard, losing herself, it felt like. I let her, not reciprocating, though that didn't stop her.

When she pulled away, all glassy eyed and smiling, she said, "Tonight. Let's leave. You and me."

"Really?" I widened my eyes, not sure what had changed her mind, but not wanting to question it either.

"Yes. We'll sneak out at dawn. That's when almost everyone is asleep."

"Okay. You're sure?"

She kissed my cheek. "Never been surer in my life."

We separated, the two of us watching one another until I was forced to turn around to see where I was going.

My grin stayed on my face the entire walk to the courtyard doors. So much so that I didn't realize I'd forgotten my bible till I saw the others with theirs.

Shit.

A strange guy at the head of the line stood by the door instead of Simon. I didn't know him. He had thin hair and a gray beard to match. He wore a black robe and held a bible in his hands too.

"Who's that?" I asked a dude in front of me.

"No idea," he whispered back.

I blinked, studying the stranger's profile, uneasiness building in my stomach.

"Follow me, young Shepherds," the new guy said, his bible pressed to his chest as he pushed through the door.

We followed him outside, walked through the dark courtyard, then headed between the small homes separated from the two main buildings. The ones I'd only ever seen through the gates. Each one was small, a cookie-cutter version of the other. But not all were lit up with life.

Emmanuel had told us in the beginning of our relationship that once Eve and I proved worthy of being stable life partners, the two of us could live in one of the empty homes. It might have been easier to escape if we did, but I wasn't willing to wait that long.

The temperatures were below zero outside, and the wind smacked us all in the faces like creatures looking for blood. I shivered, trying to read the faces on some of the other guys with me, but it was too dark to see much of anything.

"This way," the bearded stranger said, pulling the hood of his coat over his head.

The ground was icy and snow-filled, and my shoes sunk in deeply, making it hard to walk. I'd heard that tonight was supposed to be the coldest weather of the year so far, which was why it didn't make sense that we were gonna be outside for whatever this was about to be.

I shivered again, wrapping my arms around my hardening gut.

"Shouldn't we get our coats?" someone asked.

The guy ignored him and moved quicker, leading us to the very back of the land, to the farthest building—one I'd never seen before. I blinked and took it all in. It was pressed up next to the fence line, reminding me of an outhouse, only big enough that a group of ten or less people—the number with me—could easily fit inside.

"Brother Zacharia." Another guy I'd never seen before moved to the front of the line and grabbed the Simon-and-Noah replacement's shoulder. At least someone knew him. "Are we having Service in here?" the guy asked. "It's freezing cold."

The Zacharia old man lifted his chin and looked over the guy's head. Instead of answering, he opened the door and waved us all in like we were literal sheep he was guiding. The nine others with me followed orders, leaving me by the door, alone.

I stepped up to the threshold and looked inside, my neck and shoulders tensing as I studied the room's layout. It was a ten-by-thirteen room made up with red painted walls and one lone light that hung from the center of the ceiling. It swayed back and forth from the wind whipping through the door, a creak filling the air from the metal it hung off.

The floor was made up of uneven bricks. The kind you could trip over easily if you didn't watch where you were going. There were no chairs inside to sit on, no soft rugs or anything to rest our knees on while we prayed. Not even a space heater or fireplace. It also smelled like mildew.

"Enter, Brother Midnight," Zacharia said, grabbing my upper arm.

I stared down at his hand with narrowed eyes. "I forgot my bible, Brother Zacharia. May I run back in and grab it?"

Instead of answering, he shoved me inside, catching me off guard.

I fell to my knees, wincing when the brick dug into my pants. I glanced back over my shoulder, ready to pounce, but the door was already shut and Zacharia was gone.

Pushing hair from my face, I got to my feet and looked around again. Every time the wind started to blow outside, it snuck through small cracks at the base of the walls making us all shiver.

The ends of my pants were wet and already freezing to my ankles. I looked down, peeling them off the best I could. I'd been out here five minute and things had already started to go bad. I pulled my hands inside my shirt sleeves to try to warm them up, unable to ignore the thud of my heart in my ears. Something *really* wasn't right.

I looked around, then up. At the top of two of the walls four walls, a prayer was butted up against the ceiling and written in Latin. It didn't look familiar.

Domine Iesu, dimitte nobis debita nostra, salva nos ab igne inferiori, perduc in caelum omnes animas, praesertim eas, quae misericordiae tuae maxime indigent.

The rest of the guys huddled together, probably trying to get warm. None of them seemed *too* weirded out by what was happening, until one of the oldest men there began translating the prayer into English.

"O my Jesus, forgive us our sins, save us from the fires of Hell, lead all souls to heaven, especially those in most need of Thy mercy."

"What does that mean?" someone asked.

The translator looked his way, then around at everyone else, his eyes bulged wide but his mouth staying closed.

"Answer him," someone shouted.

"I..." The guy shook his head and stepped back.

I shivered again, this time not from the cold.

From what I could tell, there were no windows, one door, but there were large cracks in the bases of the walls. Way too small to get out of, but just wide enough that the cold air could freeze us in minutes if we were out there too long.

This was nothing. It had to be. Just some weird Emmanuel shit. He did stuff like this all the time, like once when we'd had to go onto the roof and stand there for hours because *God* was supposed to be sending messages through us all. Obviously, I'd gotten nothing from the Big Guy, other than windburn on my face and a sprained ankle from climbing the ladder too quickly.

There was no reason to get freaked out.

At least not yet.

"Bonum diem pastores." *Good day, Shepherds.* The door we'd entered reopened. I turned around and saw Emmanuel walk inside, a wide smile on his face. Unlike his normal white robe, today he was wearing a black one like the Zacharia had been wearing.

Emmanuel scanned the room like we were nothing but rats at his feet—a waste of his time on a Saturday night.

"Oremus," he started, bowing his head.

When I got onto the floor, the prayers started, along with some loud music outside the door. I frowned, turning my head to the side like I could see it. Some of the other guys did the same, even throwing looks at each other, while the rest seemed to stiffen or ignore it.

"What is that?" I heard someone whisper.

"It sounds like guitars," another guy answered.

Emmanuel's prayers grew louder, like the music was nothing but background noise. Like he'd been *expecting* it. Soon, everything was so jumbled together and chaotic that nobody was listening to the prayers anymore. And not once did Emmanuel tell anyone to resume their positions.

Slowly, I lifted my head and rose up onto my knees, watching as Emmanuel stepped toward the exit. My body twitched; the need to run and beat him to the door was strong. I had to keep him from leaving because I had a feeling he wouldn't take us with him.

"Prophet," I yelled when I got to my feet.

He turned and looked my way, as if just noticing I was in there. But instead of his normal scowl, he smiled and yelled over the music, "Death rather than dishonor, my son."

Seconds later, the door opened, and he stepped out before I could make my way to him. Still, I ran over, yanked and twisted the handle.

"Let us out!" I pounded on the metal with a fist, then kicked it with the end of my shoe. It didn't budge, not even when I rammed my shoulder against it.

"Brother Midnight." A guy I didn't recognize ran over to me. "What's this all about?"

"You think I know?" I stepped back, hands running through my hair, gaze flopping from the door to him to the rest of the guys in the room now staring at me. "What?" I shouted at them all. "Stop looking at me like I'm your savior."

Several bowed their heads, others blinked like they couldn't believe I was yelling. I knew one thing for sure. They'd trapped us in here for a reason. And I was pretty sure we wouldn't be alive when it was all said and done.

CHAPTER 20: BEX

MIDNIGHT SHAKES SO BADLY I can't tell if he's cold or terrified of his own memory. I want to tell him he can stop talking about it, that I'm pretty sure I know what comes next in his story. But if I do, I don't know if that'll help him or hurt him more. It's obvious he needs to talk to someone about this though. Because from what I can tell I'm the first person outside of his cult life that he's opened up to. That can't be healthy.

"What happened..." I swallow, brave enough to reach for his hand, "after you were all locked in that building?"

He blows out a slow breath and closes his eyes, surprising me when he interlaces our fingers. It's for support—completely platonic, that's all. Because I won't let my thoughts take me down a path that he likely has no interest in traveling with me. I'm his friend. His companion. His vault. That's it.

"It's a blur," he says. "I can't remember much."

I pull a knee up on the bed, facing him, and keeping his hand in mine. "It's not going to get easier if all you do is keep it in."

He glares at me.

"What?" I shrug. "I used to be the same way when it came to talking about my dad. All that did was get me transported to this lovely town."

"I don't..." He shakes his head and stares at the bed.

"Midnight." I lift my free hand and press it to his cheek, urging him to look at me. He does, but I can see how hard this is for him—the twitch in his left eye, the hardening of his jaw beneath my palm. It's obvious he's not the type of person who wants to be pushed. But if I don't, then I can't help him. "You want to talk about this, I know you do. But if it hurts too much to spill it all at once, then we can take it one day at a time." I smile at him. "I'm not going anywhere."

He turns his head away and pulls his hand out of mine. I try not to take it personally, but something in my stomach tightens regardless. He's such a complicated person. If only he'd unload some of those *complications* onto me. I can take it. My shell is already broken, so there's nothing more he can crack.

"It's okay," he says. "I mean, I'm okay."

"I know you are."

This has him looking at me again, narrowed eyes searching my face. "How?"

"How do I know that you're okay?"

He nods.

"Because you're alive."

"Sometimes I think death would've been better." He shrugs.

I bump his thigh with my knee. "If that was the case, then you wouldn't be able to talk to amazingly awesome people like me."

He grins the tiniest bit at my lame joke, which reveals the smallest dimple in his right cheek. My heart does this fluttering thing at the sight of it, and I can't stop my grin from widening.

Like he senses I'm a giant mess for him, he turns toward me fully, bringing his knee up on to the bed, matching my position.

Dreamy blue eyes search my face as he says, "You're really pushy."

"I know," I say. "I've been told that a time or two."

Our eyes hold for five long seconds. He blinks. I blink, and it's like something has rooted itself between us. Two broken souls, brought together by tragic pasts. Two lives that can be whole again, with the right support. The right friend.

But what happens when that right friend also becomes someone who wants to kiss you? Because right then and there, so close, so wrapped up in the way he's staring at me, that's all I can think about. But like always when it comes to Midnight and me, the timing doesn't match up. He's got demons. And I'm here to help him slay them once and for all.

CHAPTER 21: MIDNIGHT
FEBRUARY 2021

THE LIGHTS FLICKERED on and off. I looked up, blinking when they went out permanently.

"What's happening?" another guy asked me, his hand shooting out to grab my upper arm.

"I told you." I jerked away. "I don't know."

Everyone talked over each other then, moving away from me, the words *do something, Midnight* filling the air. I pushed away everyone who got close to me, running my hand along the walls and looking for a way out. There had to be some secret passageway or a thin piece of the wall that we could break down. I kicked, punched even, but with every step I took, every inch of the wall I ran my hand over, my hope died.

"Goddamn it," I yelled, finishing where I'd started. Hands in my hair, I leaned back against a wall, crouching until I landed on my ass. I didn't want to freeze to death. Hell, I didn't want to die at all anymore. Not if meant leaving Eve behind.

Don't you think you should take a coat?
Don't you think you should take a coat?

Don't you think you should take a coat?

"Yes," I screamed out loud like she could hear me. Like she was right there. "Damn it, yes."

The room grew silent after that. Like my loud voice would bring on more trouble. But these guys were idiots if they thought I was the whole reason we were in there.

Ten minutes passed.

Twenty.

Thirty.

An hour.

"Why is it so hot?" someone mumbled. "Turn off the heater. I'm too hot."

I pressed my right cheek against the freezing wall and shut my eyes.

"Shut up, man," someone else said. "You're gonna get us all killed."

"I'm already dying. It's so hot! How are you not hot?"

I bit the inside of my cheek, drawing blood. The sound of my chattering teeth made my head hurt. The shouting men made it hurt even more.

Another twenty minutes went by. Someone started to cry then.

A pounding echoed through the room.

"Stop knocking," a garbled voice said.

The world started to spin. It was hard to keep my head up because of it, so I laid down flat on the bricks. The guy was right. It was hot in here. Like someone had turned on the summer heat.

The smell of piss filled the air when I inhaled, and I gagged but nothing came out. I'd eaten dinner, so that didn't make sense.

Look, it's your favorite tonight, Eve had said, pointing to the mac and cheese.

But it wasn't my favorite. I hated macaroni because

that was all I'd eaten for years whenever Mom had forgotten to cook for me. Eve had said it reminded her of home, but that made no sense because she hated home and...

I puked then. All the macaroni and cheese. I hated it so much.

Someone else did too. At least it sounded that way. My ears were so fuzzy I couldn't make out sounds well. Until the shouting started again.

"Brother Jonathon? John? John, wake up, man. Please, wake up."

Nobody said anything about the shouting this time.

Behind my eyelids, everything spun, and in the darkness there was one light. Mom stood there, smiling at me. Waving me over. Next to her was Eve, who was smiling too. But next to Eve was Emmanuel. He wasn't smiling. He was scowling and shaking his head, the same words coming out of his mouth, over and over and over again.

Fiat voluntas Dei. Fiat voluntas Dei. Fiat voluntas Dei.

I sucked in a breath but couldn't feel it move through my lungs anymore.

Instead, I choked. I coughed. I puked again.

"He's not moving!" that same voice rang out. "H-he's not breathing. John, John!"

"Mom?" someone else cried.

"I-I d-don't..." someone started but couldn't finish.

I gritted my teeth to keep them from chattering when I finished and laid on my back, frozen fingers gripping the inside of my shirt. For the first time in all of my time being at Children of His Mercy, I did say a prayer. I said it in my head, until the voices faded away completely. Until the only thing I could hear was the sound of my dying heart.

Eternal rest grant unto them, O Lord, and let perpetual light shine upon them.

May the souls of all the faithful departed, through the mercy of God, rest in peace.

CHAPTER 22: BEX
FEBRUARY 2022

I DON'T CRY. Ever. But Midnight's story has me blubbering into his shoulder with full-on snot and tears. He doesn't stop to try to stop and comfort me, which I don't expect him to. Instead, he stares at my wall, lost in his head or memories—wherever place this is all coming from.

Hugger or not, I wonder if he'd let me wrap my arms around him. I'm willing to take the chance, of course, if only because I'm selfish and need to make myself feel better.

No second thoughts, I spread my legs on the bed, then yank him close, between my thighs until he's snuggled against my chest. I stroke his hair, no time to think about how soft it feels.

"Midnight." I close my eyes and lay my head on top of his. "This shouldn't have happened to you."

He curls his knees to his chest, holding them as he softly cries.

Needing to comfort him more, I press my lips to the top of his head, reminded of that day not long ago under the lab table when our positions had been in reversed. When I'd been between his legs, in his arms. If I would've known we'd be where we are today, then I probably wouldn't have run. If anything, I would've stayed there with him until he felt better. Just like I'd done last night. And just like I'd do today...and however many more days he allows me to be close to him.

Midnight shakes his head, surprising me again as he wraps both arms around my thighs. I'm like his human body pillow, but nothing about the feeling, our position feels wrong.

"It was so cold, Bex," he says with a strained sob. "And all I could smell was piss and...and death."

I bend down and bury my nose into his hair, tightening my arms around his shoulder.

"Later, when I woke up," he continues. "I-I was in another room. Eve wasn't there. But Noah was. Another guy too—Simon was his name."

I frown, trying not to get hung up on the girl's name.

"Noah had to..." he shudders, "cut off one of my toes."

I swallow another lump in my throat, choking back more tears.

"I-I don't remember much, but the pain..."

"Why the *hell* didn't they get a doctor for you? O-or call an ambulance, for that matter?"

"Because I wasn't supposed to be alive. Emmanuel was trying to kill me and the other men I was with."

"Who's Emmanuel?"

"My prophet," he whispers, "and my father."

"Holy shit," I whisper, throat tightening.

When I gather my wits and know for a fact I'm not gonna cry anymore, I say, "Tell me more."

"Like what?" he whispers.

"Whatever you feel comfortable sharing."

Deep down, I want to ask who Eve is, but I also don't want to seem like a jealous girlfriend. So for now, I'll settle for whatever he's willing to share.

"Noah's the one who found me." He shivers a little. "I was the only one alive when he got there."

The thought of him freezing to death, of staying in some sort of building with nine dead bodies surrounding him while he was the last to die, of him not being here at all...?

It undoes me.

I push him up by the shoulders, voice cracking with tears. "Sit up."

He lifts his head and looks back at me through empty eyes. "I'm sorry," he manages. "You think I'm a freak. This is why I didn't wanna tell—"

"Stop," I say, forcing him upright. "Don't you dare."

I don't want to snap, and I don't want him to be my target because of my ugly emotions. But if he doesn't do what I ask, then I won't be able to do what I'm about to do, and I *need* to do it before I chicken out.

Slowly, Midnight sits up, dark brows pushed together.

"Listen to me," I say. In a move I never thought I'd make, I crawl onto his lap and straddle him, draping my legs around both sides of his waist. He stiffens but doesn't push me off.

I cup his face with both hands this time. "You are the most amazing person I've ever met and not at all a freak." I press my forehead to his, brushing long strands of dark hair behind his ears. "So far from a freak it's not even funny."

When I finish, he relaxes against me, not hesitating to wrap both arms around my waist in return. I do the same, and the hug is so tight and so long that it feels as if he's trying to crawl inside of me. My ribs ache, lungs practically puncturing from pressure. But the pain feels so good.

"I'm so sorry that happened to you." I bury my face against his neck, inhaling the soapy scent of his skin. "It wasn't right." It was cruel, actually, though my saying so won't make a difference either way.

"S'okay," he manages. "I'm okay."

"Are you though?" I pull back just enough to look into his eyes, settling my hands against the side of his neck. He doesn't answer my question, and I'm worried I pushed him too far. But I need to know him in order to help him and his heart heal, so the tough questions have to come if he's looking to get past his pain.

If he even *wants* to get past it.

"I don't know," he finally says. "I...I don't think I am."

I nod. "There's no rush when it comes to being okay. Sometimes you never will be."

"Yeah?"

"Absolutely. But talking about it helps, believe it or not."

By admitting to me what happened in his past, he's already taken the first step toward healing.

A few more minutes pass and the knot dislodges inside my throat. I can breathe a little easier—at least through my mouth. My nose, on the other hand, feels like it's been stuffed with cotton.

Quickly, as if just realizing what a mess I am, I wiggle a little, reaching up to wipe at my wet cheeks. God, I'd do anything for a tissue right now.

"Ugh," I tell him. "Nobody's seen me ugly cry before."

Before I can wipe the last of my tears, he pulls my hand back and starts to do it for me, thumb stroking across my cheek.

"I don't like it when you cry for me," he says.

"If I don't cry for you, then who will?"

"I don't need your tears." He blinks so slowly it feels as though everything is in slow motion. "I need your smile. It reminds me that life isn't bad anymore." He swallows hard, and I can just barely see his throat bob as he finishes with, "When I'm with you, Bex, I feel safe."

My stomach flips even more.

Safe. He feels *safe*. With *me*.

We move to sit at the head of my bed, leaning back against the wall. I turn to look at him, finding his face within inches of mine.

"Bex?"

"Yeah?"

"I...didn't expect you."

I pinch my lips together to hide my grin. "I'm pretty unexpectable." I curl my nose. "Wait. Is that even a word? Unexpectable?"

Midnight shrugs, and for a small moment, his lips kick up on both sides. It's a powerful view, magnificent really. Like he's got this light bursting from his entire face from that smile alone. Of course it doesn't last long —happiness never does when it comes to Midnight, it seems. It's almost as if he's scared to let any goodness inside.

"It's okay to be happy." I brush a thumb across his jaw, surprised by how easy it is to touch him.

"Not for me it isn't."

"Why? Because you've been through years' worth of hell and trauma, therefore you think that's the only thing you deserve?"

He stares back at me but doesn't answer.

I roll my eyes. "That's a crap attitude, you know."

He blinks.

"What?" I huff. "All I'm saying is that whatever you think you deserve, it's likely far from what you *actually* deserve."

He lowers his chin to his chest and says, "I should have left that place sooner."

I press my free hand to the other side of his face, forcing him to look me in the eyes again. "Don't blame yourself. You did nothing to deserve that."

Midnight shuts his eyes and shrugs. "I guess."

"No 'I guess'." I lay my head on his shoulder. "That's an *oh, Bex, you're so smart and right about everything*."

He laughs softly, the sound warming me as much as his body. Right then, I make it my duty to be the one to make him laugh from here on out. The one who also gets to hold his hand and be the person who he can cry against when the memories get to be too much.

"Hey, Midnight?" I whisper against his bare neck.

"Hm?" he murmurs back, sounding as tired as I feel.

I swallow hard, not prepared for the answer I'm about to get with my question. Knowing, at the same time, I have to ask it in order to see if he's ready to move forward.

"Who is Eve? You said her name."

He freezes in place. It's almost like he's stopped breathing too. But those fingers I can't stop staring at fold together as he cracks each knuckle. At first, it feels like he's not going to answer me, but then he clears his throat and starts in, his voice cracking as though there are a thousand knives being dragged up and down his throat.

"Eve is... I mean, she was..." He pauses, this time twisting his hands together.

Maybe I should've asked the easier question first: who is Noah? And Simon too. But my curiosity is in full force—the journalist in me taking control. Dad said once I was bound to follow in his footsteps for as curious as I was, but I've only ever seen myself as a behind-the-scenes person, not the one who ask the hard questions. Until now.

A full minute passes before he speaks. Empty air like this makes me uncomfortable, so I decide to let it go. "Never mind. You don't have to tell—"

"I want to tell you," he jumps in. "I just don't know what you'll think when I do."

"I don't judge, remember?" I sit up and turn to face, pretzel-ing my legs. "Whatever you're comfortable telling me, I swear I won't bat an eye."

Midnight turns to face me, mirroring my position. Our knees touch, but neither of us pull back. Yet the second the words are out, all of my preconceived notions about not being jealous go right out the window because...holy shit.

"Eve, she was my life partner."

I jerk my head back. "Your what?"

"In generalized terms, she was my wife."

CHAPTER 23: MIDNIGHT

FEBRUARY 2021

DARKNESS.

Men yelling.

The pain.

A pain so intense in my foot I couldn't breathe for reasons aside from the squeezing of my lungs from no air. A ripping I could feel inside my bones.

Let me die, I remembered thinking. Anything so I hadn't had to feel the burn. Then darkness had hit again, until now.

The voices around me were muffled. My skin burned, yet I was numb at the same time, like when your legs fell asleep, then started to wake up. The pain in my foot had dulled to a low ache, thankfully. I was also alive, though I shouldn't have been.

I was alive and no longer cold. If anything, I was hot.

"He'll make it," a deep voice said. I recognized it without even opening my eyes. "I have training in this, remember?"

Simon.

"But he should be awake by now. Why isn't he? We should've called the doctor." Noah.

"No way in hell," Simon growled.

"But you told me—"

"Shh," Simon hissed. "If anyone finds out I brought him here, it'll be the end for us all."

Feet scuffled across the floor a few minutes later, pacing back and forth. Only then did I open my eyes and find Simon glaring down at me.

"You're lucky, kid," was the first thing he said to me.

Noah took a seat in the chair next to the bed I was lying in. "Brother Simon found out what had happened. If he hadn't saved you, you'd be dead."

I blinked a few times and swallowed hard, trying not to let any emotions show when I looked up at Simon again. "Why would you save me?"

His jaw clenched. "Because believe it or not, I'm on your side."

I opened my mouth, then shut it, trying to take in what he'd said. When the words got stuck in my throat, I looked around, desperate to figure out where the hell we were.

The square room we were in was small. It had no windows, and one lone door. A dresser sat in the corner, and on top of it were several candles to light the room along with a picture that had two people in it.

Then there was the chair Noah was sitting in, and the small bed I was in too. My feet hung over the end, and I looked down, wiggling my toes, then spotting a bandage on top with blood soaking through.

"W-what happened?" I choked out, remembering the pain, the throbbing, the cold.

"Brother Simon had to cut it off. I'm so sorry." Noah

moved forward in his seat and set his elbows on his knees. "You had such extreme frostbite that—"

"I-I get it." I shut my eyes.

There'd be time to worry about that later. For now, I needed other answers. "Where have you been?" I asked. "A-and how did Simon know where to find you?"

"I've been here." Noah stretched out his arms and leaned back in his chair.

"Where's here?" I ask.

"A separate building about three miles from the main compound. Abandoned. Nobody knows it's here but Simon and I." He looked at Simon, who nodded. "Brother Emmanuel thinks I'm on a recruitment trip. To find other like-minded individuals to join Children of His Mercy. It's why he did what he did...to you."

"Why would he care what you thought?" I curl my upper lip. "You're just like him?"

He set his elbows on his knees and studied me for a minute, his jaw clenching as he spoke. "Believe it or not, Midnight. My heart isn't filled with the hatred that Brother Emmanuel's is."

I shook my head, not caring about anything but Eve right then. "Where's Eve?" I looked at Simon. "Did you get her out too?"

Noah stood and stepped between us, clearing his throat. "You should sleep. There will be time for this all later."

Leaning over, he put a pillow behind my neck and helped me sit up. It hurt—everything in my body did— maybe even more than my toe. But I needed to know. She was my only priority.

"Tell me. Now," I whispered. "Please. Where is Eve?"

Noah bowed his head, letting it hang there. "She's safe."

When I looked to Simon for confirmation, he turned and left the room, slamming the door behind him. I stared at the door, a pit in my stomach.

"I've been Emmanuel's faithful servant since the age of twenty-two," Noah said, sitting on the side of the bed. "He's three years older than me. And he is also my brother."

"Cut the religious *brother* crap," I growled. "How do you *really* know him?"

"He is my *brother*," Noah nearly yelled. "As in we shared the same mother and father."

I blinked. Shit. He wasn't lying.

"Our parents ran Children of His Mercy for many years, but both were murdered on a mission trip."

"So, this was a hand-me-down-cult, then." I nearly laughed.

His parents were dead. *My* grandparents. I probably should've been nicer, but anyone who shared the same blood as Emmanuel made me feel nothing but bitterness.

"This isn't a cult," Noah said, his voice angrier than it'd been.

"Bullshit."

"It's not." He hit his thigh with a closed fist.

"Then what is it, huh?"

"This is a home for those who need something to believe in," he said. "A place for those to go who admire traditionalism and not the bizarreness of the real world."

"Exactly," I curled my upper lip. "A *cult*."

He narrowed his eyes but didn't argue this time. For being Emmanuel's brother, he sure as hell didn't share the same temperament.

"You can't tell me that you're okay with everything that happens here," I said.

He looked away. "I believe in the teachings at Children of His Mercy."

"You believe in torture and murder, then."

"No. I don't." His squared his shoulders. "But those men with you tonight were not good. They didn't belong here."

"So, you *knew* this was going to happen, then?"

He rubbed his temples. "Yes, I knew of the Reckoning Night and the Reckoning Room."

"You son of a bitch." I gritted my teeth.

"You have to believe me when I say that I did not know *you* would be there." He looked me in the eyes. "You didn't deserve it, Midnight. Not like they did."

"Then why was I there?"

"That reason has yet to be seen." He rolled his shoulders. "Brother Simon has been digging. He's close to finding out the truth."

"Simon, as in the dude who's hated me from the second we met?" I nearly laughed again. "Why the hell should I trust him? Or even you, for that matter?"

"Because he's the one who got you out of there."

"Why, huh? Why is my life worth being saved?"

Noah looked away. "I can't tell you yet."

"Of course you can't." I grabbed my hair and tugged at the ends. I wouldn't cry, damn it. I couldn't. Now more than ever, I had to be strong to get Eve out. Maybe if I played my cards right, Noah could help me without actually knowing what my plan was.

"What did they do?" I swallowed. "Those men, I mean. What did they do to deserve..." I couldn't even finish.

"The unspeakable," he whispered. "They hurt their life partners. Their precious lambs."

"I would never hurt Eve," I said with so much surety, I felt it in my bones.

"I know this." Noah nodded. "I've witnessed you with Eve. You wouldn't hurt her. That's why I'm so confused."

"I'm not. Emmanuel put me in there because he hates me."

Noah opened his mouth to say something, but a knock on the door interrupted him. He jumped to his feet, fidgeting with his hands as he called out, "Who's there?"

"It's me," Simon called from the other side.

Noah's shoulders slumped. "Come in."

Simon walked to the end of the bed and set a small bag at my feet. "Food for the kid."

"Did you poison it?" I asked.

"Should've." Simon winked, then looked at Noah. "You tell him yet?"

He cleared his throat and pulled at the neck of his shirt. "Not yet."

"Tell me what?" I asked.

Noah reached over and grabbed a bottle from inside the lone dresser. "Take these." He handed them to me. "You're going to be in pain soon again."

"No." I shoved his hand away and the pills went flying. "Tell me what the hell he's talking about."

"Ya might as well get it over with." Simon shrugged, wearing that ugly smirk I always wanted to cut off. "Kid's gonna find out soon enough."

It was the first time I'd ever agreed with the guy.

Noah looked between us with a scowl, then bent down to grab the scattered pills. When he stood, he motioned for me to put my hand out.

"You gonna tell me what's up?" I lifted an eyebrow.

"You take the pills and I will."

I pursed my lips but did what he asked, swallowing them dry. When I was finished, I folded my arms across my gut, the searing pain returning in my foot already. I hated how he was right.

"Tell me," I said.

Noah sat on the foot of my bed, staring at the pill container as he spoke. "Seventeen years ago, I had a life partner. She was the love of my life." He sighed and stared at his hands. "And her name was April."

I jerked my head back. "April?"

"Yes, Midnight." He nods. "April, as in your mother."

CHAPTER 24: BEX
FEBRUARY 2022

"THEY MET AT MIDNIGHT ON A TUESDAY," Midnight continues, his face blank, even though his throat cracks with emotion not written on his face. He must have gotten super good at hiding his feelings throughout the years. That breaks my heart as much as much as hearing his truth did.

"Your mom and this Noah guy?" I ask.

He nods.

I take a second to try to understand things. That place and their rules, forcing young girls to marry and get pregnant... It's disgusting, and I don't understand how they got by without getting caught.

Then I start thinking about Eve, my heart thudding harder when I do. I wonder if she's pretty, what she sounds like, where she is now. Midnight didn't say much about her, other than explaining how they'd been paired up and expected to have kids. But there's no way I can ignore the tension that was in his shoulders when he first mentioned her. Maybe it hurts for him to talk about because he's secretly still in love with her.

The possibility of that sends a pang of jealousy throughout my stomach. I shouldn't feel this way. It's wrong. I didn't even know the girl.

"I don't know the whole story," he eventually continues. "At least not much more than what Noah told me."

"And what was it that he told you?" I hold my breath.

"That my mom had really bad parents. And Noah was a recruiter of sorts. Went around spreading the word to others throughout the country about Emmanuel's teachings. He found my mother in a homeless shelter in southern Missouri, told her he had a place that'd take her in, provide food, shelter, and stability. Apparently she had to get a new name, Cora, or something like that, so her parents didn't hunt her down. I dunno."

"So this place was Children of His Mercy?" I ask.

He nods.

"And is Noah your real father?"

"No." He rubbed a hand across his mouth. "Apparently when my mom got there, Emmanuel developed this..." he scrunches up his face, "*obsession* with her. But since he didn't allow himself to take life partners, he said the next best person to do it would be his brother. But when Noah refused to have sex with her, Emmanuel took over, and...here I am."

I scowl, a million emotions running through me. Angry, sad, disgusted...all the things, really. Empathy is a chaotic bitch, and I wish for just once I could put on a blank face and pretend that his pain isn't mine.

Thankfully, Midnight is too busy talking with his head down to notice how his words affect me. But the truth is my chest is so tight I can hardly breathe. My nails are digging marks into my palms too. This wonderful, kind, loving boy was brought into this world through the most horrible circumstances, and I want to scream in outrage for him.

But I don't.

I *can't* is more like it.

If I do, I'm pretty sure I'll start to cry again. Then the anger I feel will boil over into something I'll regret.

"Why wouldn't Emmanuel take a life partner?" I ask.

"Something about his position as Prophet and not allowing himself to be intimate with a woman."

I look at him again, take in his profile, the bob of his Adam's apple as he swallows.

He turns to me and meets my stare, chewing on the corner of his mouth. "What are you thinking right now?"

I purse my lips, then ask the most obscure question. "Is that why your name is Midnight? Because Noah found your mom at midnight?"

"I don't know." His eyebrows furrow. "I've never asked. But I can."

"Who will you ask?"

He shifts closer. "Remember the other day in the nurse's office?"

"How could I forget?" I grin, trying to ease the tension.

His rubs a hand down his face, probably trying to hide a blush I can't even see. "I mentioned having a guardian."

"You did, yes." I hold my breath, waiting.

This is it. I'm finally going to learn something about him that's current. I don't know whether to cry tears of joy or screech. Either wouldn't bode well with a guy who's currently baring his soul to me, so I tame down my excitement until it's an internal blip on the Bex-dar.

"It's Simon."

"The guy who you said was always a dick to you?" I gasp.

He smirks a little. "I don't actually stay with him. I stay with his friend."

"Oh, gotcha."

"And technically I don't need a guardian since I'm eighteen, but he takes care of things I can't get for myself yet, ya know?"

"Understandable," I say. If I was left alone at eighteen, I'm pretty sure I'd be a hot mess. I need my mom still—despite how annoying she can be.

"What about Noah?" I ask.

He shrugs. "He's...not around."

"Not around? As in dead or disappeared?"

Midnight opens his mouth to answer, set of footsteps clunk outside my door, followed by a familiar voice.

"Bex, I'm home."

My mouth makes an O. I shoot a wide-eyed look to Midnight, then the window, and finally my closet. "You have to hide," I tell him. "My mom's home."

He narrows his eyes. "Hide?"

"Yes, if she knows you're in here, she'll kill me." I jump up off the bed, grab his hand, and yank him toward my closet. "I'm sorry," I say as I turn the knob. "It's gonna be tight."

His face pales as he looks between me and the tiny space that's honestly more of a cubby than a closet. I feel like crap for forcing him in there, especially after what he just told me he'd been through, but I don't know what else to do.

"Please, Midnight," I beg, bouncing on the tips of my toes. "I'll do anything."

Mom's footsteps hit the hallway floor. "You awake?" she calls out. "I figured you would be since it's a snow day and all." She laughs. "You're usually up with the sled by now."

Slower than I want him to, Midnight slides in, crouching down beneath the lowest shelf. He's like a dang turtle in a snail race, though I can't expect a rabbit when he's likely freaking out inside.

"Hey," I whisper once he's settled. "I'm gonna make this up to you. I swear it."

He blinks up at me, expressionless. God, what I wouldn't give to have a bedframe on my floor so he could've at least hid under there.

"Okay?" I whisper, needing a yes. Otherwise I won't be able to shut the door.

Finally, he nods, closing his eyes seconds later.

The last thing I see before shutting him in is the top of his head, hands buried deep in his hair. A tear falls from my eye when I turn to lean against the wall. I'm seriously going to go to hell for this.

My room door opens then, shakes. "Hey, is the door locked?" Mom asks. "Bex, answer me."

I rush across the room and whip the chair out of the way. It crashes to the floor, knocks over a pile of clothes, then hits the wall with a thump.

Seconds later, Mom throws the door open. "Bex, what in the world?"

"Hey, sorry." I clear my throat, fold my arms, unfold them, and mostly struggle with staying cool. "I thought I heard someone in the house last night, which is why I, um, put a chair under the door handle."

She stares at the chair lying sideways on the floor. "You all right? Did you call anyone? Why didn't you tell me this morning when I texted?"

"It was just the wind, and I fell back asleep. I just

forgot to move the chair." I wave a hand away. "So, what's up?"

She folds her arm, looks over my shoulder at the bed. I don't know if she suspects anything. If she does, she keeps quiet about it—thank God. "You headed out?" she asks.

"Uh-huh." I clear my throat. "Just looking for my snow boots."

On a normal snow day, when we lived in Chicago, Dad would usually take the day off work and the two of us would drive to a local suburb, find a random rich-people neighborhood with hills, and sled until our legs felt like jelly and we couldn't feel our noses. Hot chocolate would follow, with extra whipped cream too.

I make a note to myself that I have to take Midnight sledding. Let him have that experience that always made me so happy. Granted he hates the cold for very good reasons, but therapy in the form of facing your fears can be helpful. Not that I'm a doctor.

"They're in the hall closet by the front door." She tips her head to one side. "You sure you're okay?"

I force a tired smile. "Yep. Just looking to get to the hills early so I don't have to fight with the kids for space."

"You're sure?"

"Absolutely." I nod.

"You're lucky we've got insurance." Mom shakes her head. "You and Dad always scared the crap outta me when you'd go sledding all day."

I bite my bottom lip, watching as my mom lowers her chin to her chest. "Why didn't you ever go with?" I ask.

She shrugs. "That was you and your dad's thing."

"But we wanted you there too."

She looks up and smiled at me. "Sugar, you and dad

would've had the worst time. You know I don't like that kinda stuff."

It's true. She doesn't. But I never understood why she couldn't just come and watch. I didn't ask, though, because what was the point. Things happen for a reason, and those days with my dad, just him and me, are some of the best memories I have.

"How was work?" I ask, yanking out a pair of long johns from my dresser, followed by wooly socks.

"Slow." She shrugs and looks at her hands, picking a hangnail.

I lift a brow. She's got secrets—hangnail picking is her tell. I wonder if it's about her new mystery man. The one she'd been texting. I'd ask her what's up, but I need her gone more than anything right now.

"I'm gonna change now." I force a smile and shake the pants in front of me.

She smiles too, but there's something sad about it. I should feel guilty for pushing her away when she just got home. But Midnight doesn't deserve to be locked up in my closet either.

"Right. Okay. I'm going to head to bed. Be sure to text me later," she finally says.

"Will do." I turn back to the door and hold my breath.

"Can we do dinner tonight?" she asks from behind.

"Sure," I smile over my shoulder at her. "I'd love that."

She opens her mouth like she wants to say something else but nods and heads to the hall. The door closes with a barely audible click behind her, but my ears feel like they're rushing with blood. When the sound of her bedroom door shuts down the hall, I rush to the closet, open the door, and find Midnight in the exact position I left him in.

"Shit," I mutter, dropping to my knees in front of him.

The view of his face between his knees, his body rocking slightly, makes my insides cold. "Midnight, hey. I'm so sorry. I'm here."

I brush a few fingers through his tangled black hair, and he immediately goes still.

"I'm so sorry," I whisper again.

Slowly, he lifts his head, eyes meeting mine in the early morning light. The look on his face is a mixture of terrified and exhausted, those normal dark shadows beneath his eyes more prominent than usual. My heart breaks into pieces at the sight.

"S'okay," he whispers, reaching for my hand. "Need a little help though."

"Of course." I take it, his smooth palm sliding across mine. Swallowing down my tears, I help him to his feet, graze the back of his hand with my thumb as I do.

"Do these hurt?" I ask, looking down at his scars. His hands are still in mine, and I lift them higher to look closer.

"Not anymore."

"Hmm." Using the fingers of my other hand, I trace the raised and welted paths.

Anger pricks at my throat, but I don't say anything because words won't ease the heartache. Instead, I lift his hand and press my lips to the skin, lingering like I can pull the pain from his body through one kiss, then push it away for good.

His breathing gets heavier the longer I linger, and his hand starts to shake too. But instead of telling me to stop, he moves closer, his bare chest and warm thighs now pressed against mine.

"You scare me," he says.

I look into his eyes—eyes that make my knees weak. I lower his hands but don't let go. "How do you mean?"

"I mean…" He studies to our hands. "I'm scared of you. Of what might happen if you…"

"If I what?"

Slowly, like he's afraid of breaking the invisible, thin glass that he's put between us, he moves even closer, setting his forehead against my shoulder. "I'm scared of what might happen if you leave."

I shiver a little, but the last of the walls surrounding my heart fall away.

"Midnight," I say, lifting my free hand to brush through the back of his hair. "I'm not going anywhere."

"You say that, but sometimes things happen." He wraps his arms round my waist, squeezing me tight. "My mom left me. Eve, she…"

"She what?"

He shakes his head, and I know already that he's not going to tell me.

I should be upset, but for once, I'm not. Midnight's been open with me all morning. A few secrets kept for later are not deal breakers.

"Look," I say, leaning back to see his face again. "I'm not them. I won't be them. I'm here and you're here and…"

He blinks. "And what?"

"We can just be us, okay?" I smile sadly, wishing I could give him the world. Make everything from his past disappear. But I know for a fact that history builds people, and without that history, we wouldn't be here with each other.

"Okay." He nods. "But can you do one thing for me?"

"Anything."

"Can you distract me for a while?"

I grin, trying to play it cool, though deep down I do want to distract him, but in all the ways I know I shouldn't. Like, with lips and hands and—

"No," I mumble under my breath, gaze locking onto his chest.

"Oh." Midnight takes a step back. "Sorry. I shouldn't have asked."

"Wait." I lift my hands and press them out in front of me, widening my eyes. "I was just in my head about something. That wasn't a no to you."

"You sure?" He chews on the inside of his cheek—it's his nervous tick, I've come to discover.

"Absolutely sure. Plus I can *help* you with something at the same time, if you'll let me."

He squints. "Help me with what?"

"I don't want to tell you until we get there."

Midnight doesn't answer right away. But he studies me with this intensity that makes my skin itch. Still, I don't back down. We've come too far for me to get nervous about something so simple—even if it may terrify him. It's probably the worst idea ever. But some-times the worst things can be exactly what mends the soul.

"You can tell me no if you want," I say.

He sighs so deeply I can feel my heart jump. But it's his affirmation that gives me life. "It's fine. I trust you."

CHAPTER 25: MIDNIGHT
FEBRUARY 2021

IT TOOK me five minutes to process what Noah had said.

He'd been in love with my mother. And his own brother had stolen her from him. I knew Emmanuel was sick, but this was beyond another level.

The drugs he'd given me had knocked my ass out. It was easier to just sleep than try to ask questions anyway. But when I woke up a good twenty-four hours later, in more pain than I'd been before, all I wanted was to find Eve, then get the hell out of this place once and for all. Away from Emmanuel, Simon, *and* Noah.

"You're not ready."

Noah grabbed my arm when I reached the bedroom door. He'd been in the bathroom, and it was dark in there, so I'd tried to sneak out. But walking was almost impossible.

"Let me go." I tried to rip my arm away, but he tightened his grip.

"You're not strong enough. And if you go out there

and Emmanuel realizes you're still alive, it won't end well for you."

"He probably already knows I'm alive anyway, so what's the point in hiding?" It wasn't like the son of a bitch would leave nine lifeless bodies in plain sight forever. If anything, he'd probably want to see the dead with his own eyes, especially me. The guy was an ass, but he wasn't dumb.

"He's unaware of your escape, Midnight." He sighed. "The Reckoning Room was burned just thirty minutes after we got you out."

"Burned?" My stomach rolled.

Noah nodded and let go of my arm. "The thing is nobody knows that you were in there at all. Only Zacharia and Emmanuel."

"Was that the old man?"

He nodded. "Zacharia was a former Shepherd who was forced off years ago by our parents," Noah said. "He'd been a close friend once to our father until he inappropriately punished our mother during Service." He rubbed a hand over his mouth. "He and Emmanuel share the same beliefs when it comes to punishment, which is why he's been invited back to lead the Young Men Services."

"Well, that *Zacharia* dick isn't gonna make this place any better," I sneered, setting both legs on the bed.

"I'm aware," was all he said.

I thought about things a little more, coming up with one conclusion to my issues. "Nobody's gonna care if I'm alive or dead, other than Emmanuel. So why can't you just help me and Eve escape?"

Noah put a pillow beneath my bad foot, propping it up. I cringed through the pain but let him do it anyway. "Your sole purpose at Children of His Mercy is to procreate with a lamb. You're right in the sense that nobody will miss you. But they *would* miss Eve."

"Get someone else, then. Get another woman or girl to take her place."

"Sacrifice her life for someone else's?"

I winced, realizing how bad that sounded. But I was desperate.

"The female population is precious to us here. As Christ himself was birthed from Mary, we believe that every woman be treated as though she is carrying the next sacred child who will save us all from evil. And since you are Emmanuel's son and have fallen in love with her, he believes that she is to birth him a second child."

"I'm not in love with her," I growled. But it doesn't matter. You can't let that happen."

He tilted his head to one side and stared at me, blinking. "I want to make you happy, Midnight. I want to do it for your mother. But my faith is still strong, and some of my beliefs match with Emmanuel's."

"You're an idiot."

He shrugged. "Maybe. But I do know that if we continue down the path of non-traditionalism in this world, our population will decrease and soon there will be fewer children left in the world to spread His word."

"Kids will be born, you know. That ain't gonna stop."

He ran a hand down the front of his face. "You're missing the point, Midnight. Christ is losing his followers on a daily basis and—"

"Save it. You don't gotta preach to me, dude. I'm not gonna be converted, and I'm *not* going to build some *Godly* empire here either. I'm out as soon as I can get to Eve."

Noah leaned back in his chair. "I don't expect you to

stay. This isn't your life. But that doesn't mean others won't want to be here, including Eve."

"You're just as bad as he is, you know that?" Only difference was Emmanuel like to use force to make others believe, while Noah used his words.

He held his hands up and stood. "I believe in one thing, but you are free to believe what you want as well."

I nodded, not knowing what else to say on the subject. We had other issues to deal with anyway. Like getting me out of here—getting me to Eve, most of all.

He patted my knee, then walked to the door like he was about to leave.

"What about Eve?" I asked his back, sitting up straighter. "Where is she? And can you bring her here so I can make sure she's okay?"

"Eve is fine." Noah said, staring at the wall. "Simon is watching over her. He's been assigned as her guardian until she's paired up with a new life partner."

"What the hell? Someone *new*?"

"I know you're upset." He turned around and folded his hands across his waist. "But trust me when I say it's for the best. Eve is truly happy here. You taking her away would only hurt her."

"No," I growled. "She *wants* to go with me. She told me."

"Hmm." He nodded. "Just rest. Tomorrow I will get you up and moving around properly. Simon will be by to help."

I balled my hands into fists, exhausted but more than ready to fight if I had to. I hated him. I hated this place. I hated what his plans were, most of all. But he was right on one thing. I couldn't get out of this room without falling on my ass, so there was no way in hell I'd get Eve out. Not when I couldn't even help myself.

TWO WEEKS HAD PASSED since everything happened, and I was getting stronger every day. Noah was always there watching over me. Simon on occasion too. The two of them took turns getting me on my feet and moving around, but the world outside this building stayed quiet, and I didn't even have a window to tell when it was night and day.

Simon talked more than Noah did, surprisingly. He mentioned once when he was walking down the hall with me that this building had been the original home for Children of His Mercy years ago. But when Emmanuel had bought the many acres surrounding it, he'd created a new commune, along with the thirty houses surrounding the building for the life partners and their families to live in.

Why don't you have a life partner? I'd asked one day.

His answer surprised me. *I don't believe in them.*

I wasn't sure where Simon was from, how long he'd been here or been a part of this community. But from the sleeves of tats on his arms I sometimes saw, I knew this place hadn't been his first home.

After walking all day, I was usually weak and tired, to the point where I couldn't even think about leaving. It got to a point where nothing mattered to me but sleep, though even that wasn't easy to come by.

No matter how tired I was, my body was restless, like something big was coming and I had to be ready. I wanted out of there but had no idea where *there* even was in relation to the commune.

It was a Friday when I was ready to just say *fuck it all*, push through my weakness, and do whatever I could to leave. Fate, though, had other plans when the unmistakable sound of running feet filled the hall outside my door.

I propped myself up on my elbows and turned to look at the door just as the knob twisted. I should've been scared. It could've been anyone. But when Noah rushed inside, I knew right away something was wrong.

"It's time." He ran over and grabbed me under the arms like I weighed nothing.

"What're you talking about?"

"To leave. The timing is right for you to leave here." He set me on my feet like I was Jell-O, then ran across the room and grabbed the picture frame, tucking it inside the waist of his pants and under his shirt.

"What are you talking about?"

"There's no time for details. We need to get you as far from here as we can. Tonight, while we still can."

When I managed to step in front of him, I gripped the front of his shirt and shook it. "I'm not leaving without Eve."

He covered his mouth and looked away, his left eye twitching. An unsettling knot filled my chest then. I let him go, stretched my fingers in and out against my palm. It felt like someone had put a hundred bricks inside my body, demanding me to walk through the pain.

"Where is she? Where is Eve?"

"There's no time."

"What? I don't get it. You've been calm for two weeks about this, and now—"

"Tonight is another ceremony," he blurted. "There is a pairing going on. Everyone will be there, so it's your only chance to leave unnoticed."

My body grew cold. "Whose pairing?"

He didn't answer, just grabbed my elbow and rushed me to the door.

"Answer me, damn it." I slammed it shut and got in his face, breathing hard.

Noah lifted his chin and looked me in the eye, his words a punch to the throat.

"Eve will be Emmanuel's lamb now."

CHAPTER 26: BEX
FEBRUARY 2022

WHEN I PULL into the park parking a half hour later, the first thing I do is look at Midnight in the passenger seat. He stares at the hill, blinking a few times like he's not sure where he is or how he got there.

I reach over and touch his wrist. "Hey, if you don't want to get out and do this, that's fine."

He stays silent. Doesn't even nod.

I knew this probably wasn't a good idea the second I'd thrown my mittens and a pair of my dad's long underwear at him. The horror on his face nearly undid me.

It'll be fun. Just me, you, and about fifteen other little kids. Trust me.

His answering stare was worse than the one I'm looking at now.

In a way, it's kinda inconsiderate what I'm making him do, especially after what he just told me. But it's not my intention to make him uncomfortable or upset. Normally, I'm a logical-thinking person, but sometimes I forget that other people aren't necessarily into pushing past their demons like I am.

His nostrils flare when he finally looks at me. "I-I can't do it. I'm sorry, Bex."

"Totally cool," I say, feigning nonchalance so I don't upset him. "We don't need to. It was kind of dumb of me anyway, what with your fear of the cold and all."

With Midnight, I feel like I'm two levels below him in maturity. Normally stuff like that wouldn't bother me, but it kind of does in this case. I want to be worthy of him. Mature, but still me at the same time.

I bite my bottom lip and look out the front window. "You're gonna think I'm dumb for this, but I'm still gonna go. Just once though." I reach over and touch the back of his hand. "I'll be quick, promise. It's just that this is a tradition I do after a big snowfall." I shrug. "For my dad and stuff."

Now that I say it out loud, it sounds pathetic. But I can't expect him to understand when he's been through what he has. Comparing tragedies is like comparing onions to Brussels sprouts—they're both nasty, but in their own way.

"Okay," he says, staring down at his palms.

A few families are already here. Midnight looks up and watches them, chewing on the corner of his mouth. I want to ask what he's thinking, but I know better now. I've come to learn that Midnight shares things at his own pace.

I slide out of the car, giving him a quick wave as I do. After I grab my sled from the trunk then move to stand in front of the car, I can practically feel the burn of his gaze on my back. It sends a shiver up my spine, forcing me to zip my coat all the way to my chin, then pull the hood over my head tighter than normal.

A few minutes later, when I reach the top of the hill and battle off a couple of rug rats rushing to get in front of me, I hear a set of heavy footsteps crunching in the snow from behind. I know it's Midnight before I bother to look—his energy is hot and makes me glow like a radioactive incinerator.

"Did you change your mind?" I ask, staring down at my yellow plastic sled.

"N-no." His teeth chatter, echoing through the air. "Y-yes."

I swivel around to face him, blinking a few times before eying him from head to toe. He's dressed in everything I gave him, down to the old pair of work boots I'd found in my mom's closet that I'm pretty sure belonged to one of her old biker friends. I stare at them a while, wondering if it's hard for him to walk with a missing toe. I've never noticed him limping before, but I'll keep an eye out now.

I slowly lift my gaze to meet his. "Yes, as in you'll sled with me?"

He shakes his head no, but his words don't match. "Yes."

"Okay," is all I say—mostly because I'm not sure if he's doing this to make me happy or for his own self. Either way, I pretend it's cool, then start to drag the sled behind me. Seconds later, he follows.

We get to the hill I'd been eying. "You don't have to do this," I tell him again.

His mouth twists. "I do."

I turn and grip the end of his shirt, then give it a small tug. "No. You don't."

"But—"

"Stop." I spread my hand over his chest. "This was stupid of me to bring you here. I get that now. What you went through?" I wince. "God, Midnight. All I wanna do is make it better for you. But sometimes my ways of helping are not necessarily good for others. I just need you to tell me what makes you comfortable, okay?"

Slowly, he slides his thumb and forefinger beneath my chin, urging my head up and forcing my gaze to meet his. His cheeks are flushed, and his eyes are as blue as the winter sky.

"You've already made it better," he whispers.

"How so?" I whisper back, struggling to ignore the butterflies in my belly.

He searches my face. "You've made it better by being you." Then without warning, he leans in and presses his lips to mine.

Oh.

Oh god.

I stiffen, eyes going wide for a hot second before I slam them shut and just...let it go. I'm not scared. I'm not angry either. If this was any other guy, I'd be mortified over the fact that he was stealing my first kiss without consent. But with Midnight, I'll happily lose every number one with him and then some—feminism be damned.

A low groan builds in his throat, and his left hand tightens in the back of my hair. He lowers his right hand, settling it against my hip where he squeezes just enough that I can feel it through the thick fabric of my coat. It doesn't hurt, but it makes me want to do the same to him. Midnight weakens my knees and makes me needy between my legs.

Not once do his lips move against mine is the thing. He doesn't urge for me to open up or even try to slide his tongue inside. He just stands there, pressed hard against me, likely waiting for me to do something. Say something. His entire body shakes, chest rising and falling like he's terrified I'll run. Or maybe he's as terrified this might all disappear like I am.

At the thought of it ending, I move until his chest is against my chest and our bodies are nearly one, even with the layers of clothes we wear. The wind picks up around us, carrying with it the giggles of kids. I smile a little against his mouth and he does the same, neither of us seeming to care that we've got an audience.

"Midnight," I whisper, pulling back just enough to look him in the eyes. Eyes that are as wide as saucers—blue and sharp and eager. Boyish, even. My heart skips a thousand beats, and I nearly forget what I'm going to say because right then, it feels like he's a different person. Someone made for only me.

"Let's go," he whispers, taking my hand.

"As in leave?" I say, chasing him with my lips—breathless and fiery, like his kiss alone stole the air from my lungs. He's burning me from the inside out.

More, more, more, my body says.

Midnight is clueless.

"No, not leave." Reaching down with his free hand, he grabs the rope attached to the sled, pulling it behind him as we walk.

I blink a few times, trying to come out of my state of delirium. It feels very much like I'm making this up in my head. "You don't have to do this. I told you."

He looks over his shoulder and smiles. And not just a half smile either. It's real and beaming and bright, explosive like a blast of sun has chipped away from the sky and landed right on his lips.

"S'okay," he says. "I'm ready."

We don't wind up where I was intending—the longest and steepest portion of the hill. Yet it doesn't bother me either because where he takes me is even better. This hill is much smaller. More importantly, it's private. At this point, I don't need a bigger rush than his kiss. That alone was exhilarating enough. Anything more will have me passing out.

"Here okay?" he asks, his voice low, a little bashful even. He's nervous, probably because he thinks I'll make fun of him for picking the shortest hill in the park.

No way, Mr. Midnight. No freaking way.

"This is perfect." I take the sled rope from his hands and set it down, stepping on it once to make sure it won't go anywhere until we're ready. "I'll sit in the front. You can sit behind me."

I look up, finding his eyes on the sled, narrowed a little.

"What?"

"It's not very big. How will we both fit?"

"We will." I wink.

He looks at me, stoic-faced, and nods, taking his position in the back like this is something he's done his entire life. Maybe before he went to that *place*, when he was still with his mom, he'd done stuff like this. Normal things.

I watch him get comfortable, biting my lip when I realize his legs are longer than the sled. His feet hang over the front end by at least four inches, but he's thin, so the space between his legs is decently wide. Problem is my *ass* may be decently wider.

Good thing I like a challenge.

"Okay," I whisper, more to myself, before squatting then sliding into the tight space between his thighs. "You ready?"

Not answering with words, he wraps both arms around my waist and pulls me back, firm against his chest. I grin, trying not to laugh at how weird we probably look. The sled is meant for an older kid—or someone short like me. Not a six-foot-two teenage boy and his lap mate.

"This okay?" He sets his chin on my shoulder, warm breath sliding across my ear and exposed neck.

I bite my lip and nod, interlocking our legs so we're both on the plastic more.

After I slide my butt back and center myself between his thighs fully, a shudder runs through him.

"Yep." I smile. "This okay for you?"

I look at him from over my shoulder when he doesn't respond right away. His eyes are an impossible shade of navy blue right now. I swear they change colors like a chameleon with every blink. The urge to push our kiss from earlier into the *further* category has me lifting my chin, parting my lips, and whispering his name...

"Midnight?"

He stares at me, wearing a ghost of a smile that says he knows exactly what I'm thinking. But seconds before I can close the distance between us, he shoves at the ground with both hands and off we go down the hill.

I gasp when the icy air hits my cheek, but I can't look away from his face. It changes within seconds. His eyes are wide with what looks like delight, and that smile grows larger than I've ever seen before. My heart thumps faster than the adrenaline I normally get from sledding, and before I can stop myself, I lean up and kiss his neck, burying my face between his throat and his shoulder.

His arms tighten around me, interlocking at my waist, and I smile, knowing I'm safe there, that even if we did fall off, it wouldn't hurt as much because I'm cushioned in his arms.

Eventually we stop—too soon for my liking. But

when I look around and realize we're alone in this small little ravine, the adrenaline rush of the ride is the last thing I want.

"That was…" He breathes the words out, laughing just the smallest bit.

"Amazing." Though it's him I'm talking about, not the sled ride.

He laughs again, oblivious to my meaning. He may have kissed me, but he doesn't know the extent of my feelings for him. How I'm bursting with this energy that has me wanting to scream into the world, *Midnight Turner is my sun.*

Snow has seeped into the sled, coating my jeans, and soaking through my long johns. I see the wetness through his pants too, but he doesn't complain. Doesn't freak out or begin to shake. Away from the big hill, the kids, in the quiet murmurs of the wind and the crackling trees, I realize that there's no better time to make my move.

With a speed I didn't know I was capable of, I turn and face him, propping myself on my knees between his calves. He looks at me, his brows dipped together, but I don't give him a chance to ask what's up. Instead, I slide onto his lap, wrapping my legs around his waist, until we're pressed so close I can't think straight.

"Bex," he whispers my name with the kind of reverence a girl can only dream of…then takes it a step further, sliding both hands to my hips.

I'd stay like this forever if he let me.

"You okay?" he asks.

It's a switch in the normal between us. During our time spent together, it's always been me checking on him. And though I don't mind, I find myself grasping for this unfamiliar rush of devotion. It's the kind that sinks heavy inside your chest and roots itself within you. The kind I haven't felt since my dad.

"I'm good." I lift my hand and brush some damp, snowy hair away from his cheek. "But I want to kiss you again, if you'll let me."

His lips part. He looks me in the eye, shock capturing his stare. He doesn't say yes. He doesn't say no either. Instead, he pulls me close, closes his eyes, and lets me lead this time.

CHAPTER 27: MIDNIGHT
MARCH 2021

"NO." I gritted my teeth.

No way was I leaving this place without Eve.

And no way would Eve ever be Emmanuel's life partner.

I'd die before I let either of those things happen.

"We have to go," Noah mumbled. "I know this is upsetting, but—"

"You have no damn idea how *upsetting* this is to me." I poked him in the chest. "You lied. You said she was safe, but she's not."

Without warning, he scooped me up and over his shoulders, letting my head hang down his back.

"Put me down, asshole." I beat a fist against his back.

"We don't have time for you to get your sea legs back."

"I already got them. Now put me. The hell. Down."

Instead of listening, Noah's hand tightened around my thighs. He didn't respond to my fists against his spine or my screams in his ear. He just continued down the short halls I'd barely begun to get familiar with, shoes thudding and squeaking against the linoleum as fast as my heartbeat.

The second we stepped outside the cold hit me hard, and a blast of wind smacked me from behind. I stiffened, almost forgetting for one second that I'd nearly been frozen alive.

I started to shake so badly my teeth chattered together. The tips of my fingers burned, and I fisted them into balls, not caring if my nails broke skin if it meant finding some sort of heat.

I couldn't be out there.

I had to get to Eve.

I needed to...

"Calm down." When the doors shut behind us, Noah set me on my feet. He leaned me back against the brick building, wrapped a coat around my shoulders, then zipped it up. Somehow, he even got my arms through the sleeves.

"You're safe, Midnight."

I shook my head, opened my mouth, then squeezed my eyes shut.

But the memories were there, creeping inside my head like weeds that never died. The cries, the room, the smell...

"We won't be out here long," Noah said.

I opened my eyes then, clenched my teeth when I glared at him. "This is your fault."

Noah flinched a little but otherwise ignored me. He looked around the building's edge. "There's a car coming to take you away from here." He pointed to a snowmobile just a few feet behind him on the side of a hill. "We'll have to ride that first to get you up the hill since there's no way you'll be able to walk."

I looked around and finally took everything in. We

were deep in the woods somewhere, down in a ravine. The building we'd been staying in was old with a cracked foundation, broken windows making up most of the walls. Trees surrounded us on every side but for the small path the snowmobile was on.

"W-where is she?" I asked, finally coming to.

"Who?"

"Eve," I yelled. "Where is she? Is she on the commune?"

He pinched his lips together.

"Answer me!" I yelled.

"Emmanuel will have you killed on sight if you try anything. He's told everyone that you hurt her and deserved to die in the fire. That he's doing the girl a favor by taking her as his lamb. Imagine if your brothers—"

"They're not my *brothers*." I jammed a finger against his chest. "And I sure as hell didn't hurt her."

He stared at me, blinking. "I know."

"Then why are you not doing something about it?" I threw both hands up.

"It's not that easy." He covered his face with both hands.

"Why not? You have Simon, right? And if you're allowed to leave, then go to the police. O-or go get a gun, even."

"I will take care of things on my own."

"Liar." I shoved him against the wall. "All you you've done is lie to me since I've gotten here. About who you are and what I was going to go through. You don't care about me, and you sure as hell don't care about Eve."

"I'm trying to get you out of here, don't you get it?"

"Then why did you leave Eve behind?" I got in his face, months' worth of rage and hate exploding.

"Because *she* is not mine to worry about. *You* are."

"The hell are you talking about?"

"Your mother..." He looked down at the ground.

"My mother *what*?"

"She found me one month after you came to Children of His Mercy. I was out on another recruitment trip. She asked me to take care of you. Keep you safe. Then when the time was right, to bring you to her."

"Where is she?"

"She's waiting for you in a town about six hours away. You just need to go with Brother Simon. He'll take you there."

My stomach hardened. I shook my head, staring at him. "You think I care about my mother right now?" I lied. The truth was, I did care. Too much. I was ready to goddamn cry at the thought of her being alive, of being able to see her again. Mom had gotten away after all. She was *waiting* for me and had been trying to get me out of here. I wasn't the forgotten son lost. Still, as much as I wanted to go to her, I knew I couldn't. Not without Eve.

"We have a safe place for you two to go, Midnight, until things calmed down. A real home up in Illinois."

I stepped away, needing some distance to think. A real home. With Mom. No more running, no more worries. No more Children of His Mercy. And most of all: No. More. Emmanuel.

But as much as I wanted that, I knew it wasn't an option. Not without Eve.

I looked at the snowmobile, the hill we'd go up.

"I know what you're thinking." Noah sighed, like he was bored. "But what will you do when you see Emmanuel, huh? Kill him with fists?" He laughed bitterly. "You're seventeen years old, Midnight. Injured and weak... You have nothing to protect yourself with and have likely never even ridden on a snowmobile by yourself."

That's where he was wrong. I might've had a crap life growing up, yeah, but there'd been a few moments of normalcy I'd experienced. Like the time one of Mom's exes had taken me and her to ride snowmobiles one Saturday. We'd left the next weekend, leaving all our crap behind to move to Texas—one of the twenty places we'd lived since I was five. But that ride wasn't something I'd ever forgotten.

"Besides that, the commune is three miles from here," he continued. "You wouldn't make it in the cold."

I would on that snowmobile. Just had to figure out how to get to it without him stopping me. Create a distraction? Shoving him off at the last minute? I'd need to do both to make this happen, even if it killed me.

"H-how did my mom get out of here?" I stared at him.

"It's complicated," Noah said.

"Was it you?" I asked. "Did *you* help her?"

He looked me in the eye and nodded once.

I unclenched my jaw a little. It was hard to hate the guy when he'd at least gotten my mom out. Granted, that was *all* he'd done for her back then. I shook my head. It wasn't time to get bitter.

"You should've done more for Eve. Like you did her," I told him.

"She has never been my priority."

"Yeah. And I'm not your *priority* either."

Noah opened his mouth but closed it when something beeped from inside his pocket. I watched him pull out a cell phone and run a thumb across the screen.

"Since when did you have a phone?" I asked.

He ignored me. "He's here. It's time."

"Who's here?"

"Brother Simon." He bent down and grabbed a backpack I hadn't noticed before. Quickly, he unzipped it and pulled out some paperwork. "Here. It's all the information about your new life. Where you're going. Who you're staying with as well."

I didn't reach for it. I didn't even look at him because there was no point. What I needed to do was get to Eve and get her as far from this place as possible. And only then would I think about the future.

He stuffed a file folder inside my zippered coat, then threw the backpack onto his shoulders again. "You're finally going to get the life you deserve."

But it wouldn't be a life without her. Which was why I needed to play Noah's game, pretend that he was winning this, when he'd lost the second he showed me that snowmobile.

"Promise me you'll try to get her out," I said, throat burning despite knowing what I was about to do.

"I'll try." He looked away, clearly lying. I wanted to call him out on it, but it was pointless to waste the energy.

His phone beeped again. "Damn it."

I frowned. "Simon?"

"Yes—he's impatient." Noah grabbed my arm and slowly led me away from the building toward the snowmobile. "You're good to walk this short distance, right?"

I nodded, struggling to figure out why Simon was the one who was taking me but knowing there wasn't time to question something that wasn't gonna happen.

We headed through the snow drifts, slower than Noah probably wanted. I could see him from the corner of my eye, trying to text with one hand. He was a fast typer. Too fast for a guy who'd been living the cult life for as many years as he had.

He flicked the screen off and slid it into the side of his backpack. "All right. I'm going to get on first. You, then, climb on behind me and wrap both arms around my waist."

I hesitated, staring back through the woods. If I managed to pull this off, it'd be a miracle. Still, I had to try.

Noah started the engine, then signaled for me to get on. Slowly, I lifted my bad leg and sat behind him, testing out how much room I had. It was a tight squeeze, but at least I had the upper-arm strength to try to pull this off.

"You ready?" he yelled over the engine.

"Yeah."

Seconds later, he took off through the woods, in the opposite of the way of the commune, I assumed. The back of the snowmobile slid right then left the whole time. Noah cursed when we got stuck on something a few minutes later. Another thing I'd never heard was a cussword falling out of his mouth. Twice in five minutes.

"We're stuck," he yelled over the engine. "I'm going to have to get out and push."

"Okay." I nodded. This was my chance.

"I'm going to need you to give it just a little gas, but not so much that you're pushing me backward, all right?"

I nodded again, my heart racing even faster.

He slid off and got behind me, yelling over the motor, "On three?"

"Yeah," I managed, gaze shooting up the hill, only to notice a set of headlights.

"One, two—"

We were out on *two*, but instead of stopping like he'd said, I veered the snowmobile to the left and took off in the opposite direction, grinning for the first time in a week. From the corner of my eye, I saw him run after me, his hands up and yelling my name.

What I didn't do, though, was stop.

CHAPTER 28: BEX

FEBRUARY 2022

MIDNIGHT TURNER KISSES LIKE A DREAM—
THE kind I never want to wake up from. The kind that
has my entire body careening off a ledge the second he
lies back on the sled and pulls me on top of him.

"Tell me this is okay," I whisper, looking into his eyes.

The pools of blue drown me to the point where I
don't even care that I can't breathe. Dying under the
hypnotic spell of this boy would be worth it.

He smiles. It's soft and sweet—not hard or nervous
like the other times he's done so—and I melt against him
even more, forehead pressed to his.

"More than okay," he finally whispers.

Without another word, Midnight slides his cool
hands beneath my coat, taking care to keep them over
my thermal. I hiss, arching my back on a gasp despite the
barrier between his palms and my skin. His hands are
ice, yet it feels as though I'm burning up inside when he
touches me. Tossed over a ledge into a free fall, like my
mind is left behind and my body's ten seconds ahead
of it.

A moment later, he squeezes me even closer, slanting his mouth over mine. This time our kiss is faster, all heated breaths and freezing hands that graze and grip and tighten around each other's clothes like we're seconds from tearing them off, right here in the middle of a public park.

Spreading my legs, I drag my hips across his, not wholly understanding what this feeling is inside me— knowing, at the same time, I'll never be able to quit it. My stomach is hard, but my insides are soft, and I'm his to mold like his own brand of putty.

He parts his lips, and I don't hesitate to slide my tongue inside. But he stiffens when I do, fists tightening around my clothes at the same time.

"Shit," I whisper, lifting my head. "I'm sorry. I shouldn't have..." Wincing, I try to pull away so I can make sure he's okay, but Midnight shakes his head and pulls my mouth back to his, reciprocating with gentle, tentative swipes of his tongue against mine.

I shudder. It's like he's memorizing every second of this kiss. Like it's his first time making out too and he's not sure what to do but knows he wants to keep doing it.

Over time, our kiss slows, a lingering experience of taste and touch. We explore each other's mouths and bodies. Hands slide up the front of my shirt, and his fingers spread across my bare stomach this time. I gasp, press my forehead against his neck. I need air to get me through whatever he's about to do to me.

Fingers slide up higher, hitting just beneath my bra. I wanna kiss him forever, and then some. I want to be touched and I want to touch him. For a fact, I know I'd be willing to die today if this was my visit to hell.

He drags his hands out from beneath my coat, never touching where I want him to. I bite my lip to hold back a frustrated moan. Maybe he's scared. Or it could be that he's not a sudden voyeur like I'm turning into. Instead, he moves those palms up my back, then fist his fingers through my hair, forcing me to lift my head and kiss him again.

A low groan sounds from his throat, and I know it's because my hips won't stop moving against his—wild and without abandon, like my body is seconds from exploding into fireworks.

We should probably stop. Seriously. We're in the middle of a park on a snow-covered hill. This kiss is close to obscene, and kids could come running through here at any time. Still, dragging myself away feels like torture, and I'm not a masochist by any means, so I keep going and going until I'm out of breath. Until he's cupping my cheeks with both hands and smiling up at me with eyes so sparkling that they burn hotter than the sun against my skin on a midsummer day.

The echo of giggles from somewhere up above has me biting my lip. He does the same, a playful look I've not seen before in his eyes.

"Nosy brats," I mumble.

He says nothing, just stares at me, losing his smile.

"What?" My grin turns into a frown.

"You're so..."

"Soooo?"

"*Decorsis,*" he whispers.

Shutting my eyes, I press my forehead to his again, remembering what that word means. An unfamiliar ache forms in my chest. It's painful. More of a pressure, squeezing kind of pain, though, than I want-it-gone-now pain. To ease the ache, I decide it's probably best if I get off his lap—give us space so I'm not tempted to give him my V-card right here, right now. But it's difficult to do, maybe even more emotionally than in the physical sense.

Being so close to him makes my wobbly world right again.

He watches me as I get situated on the snow-covered dirt, eyes practically burning a hole into the side of my head. "I'm sorry," he says.

"For what?"

Like me, he sits up, and I'm pretty sure he has to adjust himself because when I glance at his face, his cheeks are kissed by the color pink. "If I made you uncomfortable."

"No," I say. "You're amazing, Midnight. And I didn't wanna stop, but..." I tip my chin toward the top of the hill where a small group of three kids and a dad have gathered. They're watching us, the dad with a scowl.

He looks where I'm looking. "Oh."

"'Oh' is right." I laugh.

Regardless of our audience, neither of us make a move to get up and leave. Instead, I pull both knees to my chest and scoot until our shoulders are pressed together. I set my chin onto of my knees, internally sighing like a lovesick puppy. I'm not sure what this means or what's next, but I feel awake for the first time in a long while. Like my mind is on fire with thoughts and my body is alive with desire. I'm wild with sparks that can't possibly last forever because nothing this good is meant to last. I don't want to think like that right now though. The here and now is more important than tomorrow—though I have zero idea what that'll bring us.

I think I'd like this day to last forever, thank-you-very-much.

We both stare straight ahead, not at anything in

particular. It's Midnight who notices what I see right away, his voice almost childlike in wonder.

"It's a deer." He points to the edge of the woods on top of the other side of the hill.

"It is." I swallow hard, then grab his fingers, not thinking much when I interlock them with mine. "It's beautiful."

"Hmm," he says, nodding in agreement.

He stares down at our joined hands, a smile on his lips. It's charming and endearing, sending my heart racing like bulls running to red. It's the perfect kind of smile because I know he's relaxed—dare I say happy, even.

"They don't scare as easily as you think," he continues. "Sometimes they're even drawn to humans."

"Like the whole deer-in-headlights thing, right?"

He nods, trading his smile for an instant frown.

"Hey." I reach up with my free hand to tap his chin. I need his eyes on me, and he doesn't disappoint. "Where'd you go just now?"

He doesn't hesitate, words coming freer the more time we spend together. At least it feels that way. "Where I always go."

I nod, understanding. I hate that I know the place he's talking about.

"Things trigger you," I say more than ask. I already know the answer.

His jaw tightens, but he doesn't speak. He doesn't nod this time either.

"When I lost my dad, I had nightmares every night for a straight year." I blow out a slow breath, and Midnight squeezes my hands. "What I'm saying is it's okay to think about your triggers. Even talk to someone about them." I shrug. "I did. Still do actually, especially a few months leading up to the anniversary of his death."

"I've seen a counselor before if that's what you mean. My guardian insisted that when I moved here I saw someone to help me reacclimate."

"Did it help?"

"For a while."

"But not anymore?"

He shrugs.

The wind picks up and ice shards start to break off the trees. He looks up first, eyes me, then gets to his feet. "We should get going."

My stomach sinks. "Oh. Yeah…sure."

I want to tell him that home is the last place I want to be—that getting to know him is the only thing giving me life at the moment. But I realize how creepy that sounds in my head, so I keep it there.

By the time we leave the parking lot, we're back to that awkward pre-kiss, pre-spent-the-night-together state. It's unnerving, and I don't like this roller coaster. That's probably why I say what I do next.

"Hot chocolate." I feel his stare on my cheek as I drive away from the park.

"What?"

"It's the second part of my annual snow tradition. Dad and I would always stop by a coffee shop and have hot chocolate when we finished sledding." I bite my lip and quickly glance at him when we reach a stoplight. He's still looking at me, but his expression is softer, as are those ocean-blue eyes.

"You want to do that with me?" he asks.

"Of course I do." It's sad how clueless he is, how sheltered he seems too. "I wouldn't have asked you if I didn't."

"But the power," he says. "Isn't it out everywhere?"

"Well, yeah, unless you have a gas stove."

"Oh."

I laugh. "Come on, dork. It's time I make your taste buds cry with joy."

CHAPTER 29: MIDNIGHT
MARCH 2021

THE WIND WAS BRUTAL. The faster I drove, the harder tiny pieces of ice kept slapping my face. It was almost impossible to steer the snowmobile when it was blowing like that. But I managed, holding on as tight as I could.

I'd long gotten away from Noah, but that didn't mean I was safe. Deep in the dark woods at night like this anyone of Emmanuel's dudes could be out there hiding. And just like Noah had said, I had nothing to protect myself with.

The commune was west, I hoped, so I headed that way. Stuff like basic directions didn't come easy to me, though, and my dizziness was getting worse by the second, making it hard to see what was left and right.

Ten minutes later, the snowmobile started puttering. I was half up a hill to where I thought would be the last stop when it shut down completely.

"Damn it." I slammed a fist against the handlebar, breath fogging up the air.

A rustle sounded, followed by a few scattered footsteps. I looked up and to my left, eyes widening some when I realized what I was seeing. There was a deer standing there, unmoving and staring right at me.

I pulled my bad foot around to the side of the snow-mobile, along with my good one, and held my breath, watching it under the moonlight.

One time my mom had run over a deer when we'd been rushing to get to the next town—away from the threats I'd always assumed had been in her head. The stupid thing had just stood in the middle of the road, watching, and instead of slowing down, Mom had sped up.

I'd asked her why she'd hit it. And her response had been typical weird-mom stuff.

If a deer stares you down, Midnight, it means they can read your emotions. And I refuse to let that happen anymore.

Thinking back on it, I wondered if that deer had been a metaphor for Emmanuel. Her need to kill him—and make sure her thoughts stayed her own. It made sense. Emmanuel was a brainwashing king. I hadn't gotten that then, but I sure as hell did now.

Seconds later, the deer took off, leaving me alone in the quiet.

I listened for voices or the sound of human footsteps after that. But no matter how wide I stretched my hear-ing, the only thing I heard was an owl and the crackle of the ice on the branches as they moved with the wind.

Knowing I didn't have much time, I walked up the hill, knee-deep in the snow. I'd barely been out of bed for more than an hour these past two weeks, and I was feeling it with every step. Sweat beaded my temples, even though it was freezing out, making my hair wet for reasons besides ice.

Once I reached the top, I spotted the commune chain-link surrounding the land about ten feet tall. Nobody was outside as far as I could tell. But a large light was on. It flickered on and off like a cop car, spinning in circles. Green and yellow, green and yellow, over and over and over. I'd never seen it before.

I moved along the edge of the fence toward the front gate, through the snow, limping, stopping to catch my breath, then limping again until I could feel the blood pool between my toes.

Five minutes later, I reached the entrance, dizzier than I'd been before.

That was when the front door of the main building opened.

I blinked a few times, thinking I was seeing things. A dude dressed in an outfit like mine exited...and his shoes and pants were on fire.

"Shit." I shook the gate to get his attention, then yelled, "Take your clothes off!"

He lifted his head and howled louder at the sight of me, panicking and running my way. All that did was send the fire up his body quicker, until it hit the bottom of his shirt.

"Stop running!" I yelled.

Seconds later, a gunshot sounded.

The dude fell on his face, hands out at his side. His body continued to burn, but from the silence that followed, I knew he was dead before he'd hit the ground.

"No," I groaned. "No, no, no." I looked around at several of the houses on the commune, then the main building, trying to see where the shooter had come from. But it was too dark to see.

I backed away, bent over, and puked my guts out.

Before I could lift my arm and drag it across my

mouth, I was jerked back from the fence, arms around my waist.

"Stay back," Simon's growly voice filled my ear.

I fought against him, elbows shooting against his ribs as I twisted my body. When I got too weak to move and realized he was too strong for me, I gave up and bowed my head, chest still heaving.

"You done yet?" he asked.

I shook my head. "I-I need to find Eve."

"She's with Emmanuel. It's too late."

"That's why I need to find her." I spun around, getting in Simon's face...only to realize a minute later what I was looking at. "What the..."

Glasses sat on his nose, thick and brown. He pushed them up, eyebrows lifted as he stared back at me. "What?"

"Who the hell are you?" I asked, looking him over. He wore jeans, a white shirt, and a puffy winter coat. Plain street clothes. His once long and greasy black hair was cut and styled on top of his head. He looked like a normal dude off the streets.

"The car is just up the road," he said, not bothering to explain himself. "We gotta get you there before the authorities show."

"The authorities?"

He glanced at his watch—tapped it. Where the hell had he gotten that thing? First Noah with his phone, now this dude with an Apple watch.

I shook my head and looked at the commune from over my shoulder. Everything started spinning faster when I did.

"Fire trucks, squad cars, negotiators," Simon muttered.

I narrowed my eyes, blinked to try and steady myself with a hand on the fence. "I'm not *leaving* without *Eve*."

He glanced toward the road that led to the interstate. He looked different like this, yeah, but even his attitude had changed too. Gone was the grumpy asshole who looked like he wanted to murder me. In his place was a dude who not only looked like a dad but also acted like a guy who was there to help me, not hurt me. The Simon I'd once known and hated had become nothing more than a figment of my imagination.

Sirens filled the air then.

"Shit," Simon yelled. "Shit, shit, shit!" He made like he was gonna storm the road but seemed to think twice about it, grabbed my arm and pulled me with him. "Stay close. We don't have time to get you there, which means we're going with Plan B."

"Why are they here?" I asked, knowing damn well the only plan would be one I'd come up with on my own.

Ignoring me, Simon let my arm go to raise his hands over his head to wave. The police up front cut their siren, but there were more in the distance growing louder the closer they got.

"Radio them," he yelled at the officer who'd jumped out of his door. "Tell 'em to cut the noise. What were you all thinking? He's going to know now, damn it. There's no way we can get those guys out now."

My stomach twisted. *Get those guys out...*

Black cars with tinted windows drove up next, followed by a couple of ambulances and a fire truck. I watched, finally understanding what was happening when they all pulled up to the gate's entrance. This was a raid.

I yanked Simon around to face me, face growing colder, but not from the air. "Who the hell are you?"

He hesitated, then said the last thing I'd ever expected to her. "I'm FBI, Midnight. And now your ticket out of here." He rushed toward a car with tinted windows, leaving me behind. But before I could even try to understand what the hell he'd just said, an explosion burst from the commune building.

I yelped, turned around, and sucked in a breath when I saw what was happening. Glass shattered, falling to the ground from the top floor of the building. Orange flames danced from windows and the roof. Smoke alarms rang out from the inside, and I covered my ears even though it wasn't loud. The Children of His Mercy's building wasn't small, but the flames were taking it over like wood soaked in gas. And inside, there were people.

"Eve," I whispered.

Panic grabbed me by the throat and squeezed when I looked left and right for a way inside. The gates were padlocked, and unless someone was going to run it down with their car, I knew getting inside that way wasn't happening.

Simon pointed from one end of the building to the other, hollering at everyone he came in contact with. The fire trucks were the closest, and two guys jumped out. One ran to the back of the truck to get a ladder, the other snatched an ax and went to town on the gate.

Hoses were dragged out by another fire truck, and soon the long ladder was lifted high and over the fence. But before Simon or I could warn them that someone inside had a weapon, another shot rang out, this time taking down the firefighter who was axing away at the padlocks.

I winced when his head cracked against the side of the truck beside him, the sound like a drum in the night.

Someone yelled. Someone else cried out. People rushed the guy, ignoring everyone and everything.

Gunfire filled the air, this time from outside the gate. A lone cop took to shooting, only for another shot to take him down next.

Shouting filled the air, followed by a few more gunshots. Someone yelled, "Don't shoot, don't shoot!" But I couldn't tell where it was coming from.

Simon was nowhere to be seen.

Using his absence to my advantage, I snuck right, rounded an ambulance, and headed straight toward the corner of the fence. Nobody saw me, the shadows kept me hidden. I started toward the back of the commune through the wooded surroundings, keeping low. I needed to get to the courtyard. The entrance back there led to the main stairs where Services were held. And I knew without a doubt that was where everyone was—including Eve.

My foot throbbed with every step; a burning pressure that made me feel like it was asleep. But I ignored it the best I could and kept moving, hanging out in the shadows like that deer I'd seen.

The hole in the fence was easy to locate. Eve had once pointed it out when we'd gotten to walk the perimeter together this summer. It felt like a sign, knowing she'd found it back then. If she hadn't, I wasn't sure how I would've gotten in.

I dropped onto my stomach and dug out the snow. My fingers grew numb right away, but adrenaline fueled me on enough that I got it mostly cleared out. I slid through, army crawling with my elbows. The gate wires caught the back of my coat, digging in just deep enough that it scraped some of the scars on my back. I winced but kept going, only one thing running through my mind: *Find Eve.*

I kicked the snow back how I'd found it so nobody would notice I'd snuck through, then hurried toward the first house that sat empty on the property. Footsteps crunched through branches and snow from the other side of the fence a minute later, so I hid in the shadowed roof overhang, my back pressed against the siding.

Thank God it was dark.

Thank God all the houses seemed empty too.

"I know you're in there, kid," Simon hissed. "You go where I think you're going, then it's not gonna end well for you."

I gritted my teeth and leaned my head back against the house, breathing through my nose. Letting him know I was there would be the worst mistake I could make. Especially when I still didn't trust him fully.

The crackle of a walkie-talkie filled the air. "Lost him," Simon said.

Another crackle, followed another beep. "Where is he?" Noah.

"Think he got through the gate, but I can't see. The lights are off back there."

"Power's been cut," Noah said. "There's a hole back there in the fence. Find it and go in."

Simon's voice grew distant.

I've got the...

Doesn't want to be...

No time to...

I missed the rest of their conversation, not caring either way. I didn't need anybody to save me. *Eve* did. Luckily, I knew this building well, so I could do it myself. I'd been mapping it out in my head all year.

Another explosion sounded from up front, but I

ignored it and moved closer to the building. My limp was getting worse, and my bad foot was now numb like my hands. That probably wasn't good, but I didn't have time to stop and care.

It was quiet back there—no fires, no sign of life, like a whole other world compared to the front. So when I tugged the back door and it thumped against the lock, it felt like I was waking an army.

"Damn it."

I looked at different windows, walking along the edge until eventually I crouched in front of a lower one. I banged on it with my elbow, but nothing broke. Standing, I used my good foot and kicked, losing my balance and falling against the building in the process. Determined as ever, I stood upright again, running both hands through my hair as I tried to figure out what to do.

I looked around, focused eventually on the fountain that never ran. The stone eyes of Emmanuel seemed to glare at me through the dark. If I could, I'd tear the thing in half, use it to knock the door down. But it was too heavy. And I was running out of time.

Reaching forward, I ran my hand along the edge of the building beneath the snow. Something round and hard filled my palm, and I picked it up, struggling to wrap my hands around it. A rock, large enough to do some damage.

I turned it over in my palm, not thinking twice when I smashed it against the window—one, two, three, four times... Pieces eventually broke, falling in and out of the building. A few small shards jammed into my knuckles, reminding me of the night Mom had jumped from my window and I'd been left behind in my room.

Ignoring the pain and memories, I yanked the glass back from the frame, piece by piece, until there was nothing left. Then I sank down onto my knees, ready to crawl in.

"Don't think so," a voice behind me said. Arms wrapped around my waist and yanked me back. I groaned when I realized who it was. Freaking Noah.

This shit was getting old.

"Let me go," I hissed.

"It's too late." Noah pulled me back and set me onto to my feet.

"It's not. Get your hands off me." I struggled against him like I'd done Simon, somehow escaping.

He followed me. "Midnight, stay b—"

Fire burst through the window I'd just broken. I fell onto my ass, then scrambled away on my hands. Smoke filled my lungs and I coughed so hard I saw stars. Noah was there with me, standing but bent over at the waist, coughing too.

"No, no, no." I covered my face and shook my head.

"I'm sorry." Noah kneeled down beside me and set a hand on my shoulder. "I'm so, so sorry."

"Shut up. This is all your fault," I yelled.

He took his hand off my shoulder and scrubbed at his forehead. "Maybe it is, maybe it isn't," he said. "But this conversation is going to have to wait."

"You say that like I'm actually gonna leave." I threw a hand in the air.

"You are—either in a body bag or in Simon's car. Those are your choices."

I flipped him off and turned to face the building, just in time for the wind to pick up speed. Like it was taunting me, the flames pushed up the walls and captured the vines attached to the building. Another window blew out beside the one I'd busted, and before I could blink the fire grabbed hold of one of the decks on the third floor.

Ignoring Noah, I limped-ran to the door again. Just the thought of Eve inside, possibly burning alive, had me losing my shit.

Noah dragged me back by the elbow when I tried tugging the door again.

"Stop. I have to get in there and—"

"Midnight?" The building's door creaked open. I held my breath and blinked when I realized who was standing just ten feet in front of me.

Like an angel of the night, Eve stood at the door. Alive, alone, and staring at me like I was her entire world.

"Eve," I whispered.

My heart dropped into my stomach when I took her in completely. She wore the same dress as the night we'd been paired, only this time her braids were in a crown on top of her head. She was filthy though. Her face smoky and gray, her eyes wide with panic and tears.

She was terrified. And her eyes said what her mouth didn't: *Help me.*

I went to rush her, but Noah wrapped an arm around my ribs before I could even move. "No, Midnight. It's a trick."

Seconds later another voice sounded from behind her. I lifted my gaze and sucked in a sharp breath when I saw Emmanuel.

"Son," was all he said as he stood beside her.

I sneered at him, head to toe, blinking and blinking and blinking again. He was dressed in a white smock. It was like Eve's dress, only he wore a bright red sash around the middle that tied on one side. His face was also covered in ash, but his teeth were blinding white when he smiled at me.

"I would say I'm happy to see you, but that would be a lie." He put an arm around Eve's waist like she was some sort of prize, yanking her against him.

She winced, pressing a hand to her mouth to hide a cry.

I bit my tongue, tasting blood.

He'd hurt her. I'd kill him twice now.

"Get your hands off of her," I yelled.

"Stop," Noah whispered in my ear. "Threats won't save her."

"My instincts were right after all." Emmanuel rubbed a hand over his mouth, eyes on Noah as he finished. "Pity. Those boys were excellent flock members. True future leaders of our community."

I stiffened. "W-what are you talking about?"

"Let's go," Noah hissed.

"*You* were supposed to bring me a successor, Midnight," Emmanuel said. "The prophet's son and the girl he fell in love with would birth a child. The next savior." He frowned, gaze on Noah. "It was just what we envisioned, remember? You, me, Brother Simon, the night we sat praying for a sign after Cora left."

Go forth and create my miracle.

I sucked in a breath and looked at Eve, who's eyes were on mine. She'd known this would happen. It was why she'd pushed so hard to get me to have sex with her. All our months together she'd been trying to make it happen. Not only to save herself but me too. Yet I'd been so confident that I could get us out of that place I'd wound up failing us both.

I was damn fool.

"Tell him Brother Noah," Emmanuel jumped in. "If

you value his life over this community so much, then why have you waited until now to say anything?"

"Not here," Noah said.

"Tell me what?" I spit out.

Noah slammed his lips together, the refusal written in his eyes when he looked at me.

Emmanuel, once again, didn't mind telling the story it seemed. "Since you weren't able to give me what I needed, Midnight, we had to go with God's plan instead. Just like I had to do with your mother. Unlike Cora, though, Eve here was a lot more amenable when it came down to her agreeing to have a son with me."

My chest burned hot.

I looked at Eve, who started to quietly cry.

"No. Don't you touch her, damn it. Don't you dare." I gritted my teeth and took a step forward, ignoring the dig of Noah's nails into my skin as I glared at Emmanuel.

"*Qui cum Patre et Filio simul adoratur et conglorificatur: qui locutus est per prophetas,*" he said. "Who, with the Father and the Son, is adored and glorified: who has spoken through the Prophets." Emmanuel smiled. "In case you didn't know what that meant, of course."

"Emmanuel, please," she cried out.

"*Taceo,*" *Quiet,* Emmanuel growled, putting a hand on the back of Eve's neck. He shoved her down and onto her knees seconds later.

"Eve," I cried out, falling to my knees too.

She lifted her head, stared at me with eyes so wide I could feel her pain right in my gut.

I'm sorry, she mouthed back.

I reared back. "No."

"You see," Emmanuel said, reaching down to pet the top of her blonde hair. "We needed you to give her a child, Midnight. It was the only way to go about getting the bloodlines right for a new Prophet." He sighed. "But when I realized you wanted nothing to do with my plan and our glorious community, I understood that I needed a new path. So I prayed. And I prayed for a week, my son, asking the Lord what to do."

All the blood drained from my face. I shook my head, eyes locked with Eve's once more.

I love you, she mouthed.

"Eve, no," I called out. "Don't say goodbye, damn it."

She bowed her head, keeping it there, her shoulders shaking even harder than before.

"Let's go." Noah grabbed me beneath the arms and pulled me to my feet. "Hearing the rest will only hurt you more."

"Ah, but he should know the rest, don't you think, brother?" Emmanuel asked.

"I think this is not what our parents intended, *brother.*"

Ignoring Noah, Emmanuel kept going. "You see, Midnight, the Lord came to me in a dream, saying in order to full fill my legacy someday, I would need to sacrifice your life so I could create a new one with Eve. A Prophet who would appreciate what I'm leaving for him."

"Fuck you," I spat.

He laughed. "Don't get me wrong. It wasn't easy. I mean, you are my first and only son as of right now." He shook his head. "But imagine my surprise when I found out you were alive. I knew it was His will that our Savior didn't, in fact, want you dead. That instead, I'd have to sacrifice your brothers for your sins and lies, then create a new Prophet of my own with the woman you deeply loved."

The guys in the basement that Simon had mentioned earlier.

The ones I barely even knew had all been killed because of me.

I squeezed my eyes shut, balled my hands into fists too.

"W-where're the others?" I asked. "The people not inside, the kids, the families..."

"Away from here." Emmanuel folded his hands at the waist. "At least...the women, the elder Shepherds, and all life partners. Brother Zacharia is taking very good care of them until I can find us a new home. One not tainted by you and your lies."

I grabbed onto Noah's arm, needing it to hold myself up.

"If it makes you feel any better, son, most of the younger Shepherds were honored to make the sacrifice." Emmanuel winced, finishing with, "Obviously there was at least one that didn't agree with the outcome, unfortunately."

The guy out front on fire. I curled my lip, stood, and lunged. "You son of a—"

"Stop." Noah jumped in front of me, grabbed my shoulders and shook.

"You told me he thought I was dead," I yelled at him. "You told me the building with the bodies were burned. How did he find out?"

Noah bowed his head. "I had to lie to keep you safe, Midnight."

I shoved him in the chest, then took several steps back, hands in my hair gripping the ends.

"It's time now, Eve," Emmanuel said, smiling down at her.

"Leave her," I called out. "Take me. *Kill* me. Just...let her go. Please."

She got to her feet and took a step toward me. "I-I'll be okay, Midnight. Promise."

"Eve, no," I cried out.

She mouthed *I love you* one more time, then turned to Emmanuel and said, "Let's go."

Instead of letting her walk, Emmanuel grinned and scooped her up into his arms, cradling her against his chest as he turned to face me.

"Until next time, Midnight." He nodded my way, then walked toward the gate a few yards ahead.

"Do something," I yelled at Noah, who'd since grabbed the front of my shirt to hold me back.

"I-I can't," he said, looking me in the eyes now. "I'm sorry, Midnight."

"Why not?"

"Because I love your mother," he said. "So you're my priority, not Eve."

"Screw my mom," I hissed, then screamed, "Eve, I'm coming. I swear I'll get you." I broke free from Noah's hold and took off. Not even seconds later though, he tackled me from behind. I fell face first onto the snow, tasting blood.

"Stop," he said, pinning me down. "It's too late, Midnight. I'm sorry."

"No. It's not." With all I had left in me, I moved out from underneath Noah, kicking him with my good foot in his balls. He groaned and rolled off of me.

I got back on my feet, dizzy, eyes blurring to black. Still, I made it to the gate Eve and Emmanuel had left through, stopping when a flood of flashing lights filled the air as cops pulled in front of me.

Doors slammed as they exited their cars, loud voices

filling the air. A fire truck pulled in as well, parked close to the edge of the building. A horn honked. Then another. There was too much going on.

Blinking to clear my vision, I looked ahead spotting a car beyond the rest, its brake lights flickering on, but no sign of Eve or Emmanuel.

They were in there though. Had to be.

"They're in that car," I yelled out to anyone who'd listen. "They're getting away. Stop them."

Seconds later, Simon was in front of me. "Don't move, kid. You're hurt."

Fat tears rolled down my face when I looked up at him. "Emmanuel and Eve are in that car!"

Before I could take a breath, gunshots rang out, pinging through the air then hitting metal. Simon looked to where I was pointing, eyes going wide.

"Shit." He then yanked out his phone and yelled through the speaker at someone, "Stop firing. The girl's inside." But by the time they did, it was too late because another shot rang out, hitting one of the tires. The car swerved then flipped down a hill, once, twice, three times, before it disappeared into a ravine.

CHAPTER 30: BEX

FEBRUARY 2022

"DO YOU NOT LIKE IT?" I sit down across from Midnight at my kitchen table, second cup of hot chocolate in hand.

He's barely touched his first, having only taken a few drinks. Instead, he stares at the foamy whipped cream, brows furrowing like it's an abomination, not the most delicious drink on the planet.

"Okay, then." I sit back in my chair and kick my feet out in front of me.

A minute later, the telltale sound of a slurp sounds. I bite my bottom lip, not needing to look at him to see the satisfaction on his face when he swallows. I feel it in his energy and hear it when he takes his third, then fourth slurp.

We sit like that for a while, drinking and slurping, until his empty cup hits the table with a soft clunk. Mine's still half-full, but only because I love the warmth between my fingers on a second cup more than the taste.

I want to ask him if he needs to go or if there's someone he should call. But I don't want to scare him away. He's still a bit of a flight risk when it comes to this thing between us, and I'm paranoid I'm going to do or say something that will send him away. In normal circumstances with normal dudes, I'm pretty sure that'd be a red flag. But people don't go through what he did and not have some major issues when it's done.

"So..." I chew the inside of my cheek, finally looking his way. "Do you want to maybe watch a movie or something?"

Midnight's phone buzzes before he can answer me. He slips it from his pocket, frowning at the screen.

"Everything okay?" I ask.

"Yeah, I just..." He clears his throat, then sends off a flurry of texts before pocketing it again. "I should go."

My stomach sinks. It's dumb to feel this desperate need to cling to his legs like a toddler. That's not who I am. And it's not going to be the person I become. But still. I want to be with him more than I need air right now, and that terrifies me. I've gotten way too attached to this guy.

"Sure, yeah." I force a smile and get to my feet. "Let me grab my keys and I can drive you."

He rubs the back of his neck, cringing when he stands. "It's okay. I'll take the bus."

My shoulders slump. "Oh. Okay."

Slowly, he comes around the table until he's in front of me, sock-covered toes touching mine. His pillow-soft lips part just slightly, and his eyes are warm too. He looks happy for once. And if that's because of me, then color me confused because I have zero idea where we stand.

"Thank you," he says.

I grin. "For what?"

"Today. Last night."

"I didn't do anything."

"You did *everything*, Bex."

"Nuh-uh." I roll my eyes, pushing the heart flutters away with my words. "If anything, I was selfish, pushing you like I did today."

"Did I say you were?" He frowned, looking generally confused.

"No. You said nothing like that actually."

The thing about Midnight is he takes everything literally, while I'm the biggest smartass ever. We make an interesting pair.

He blows out a slow breath. "Okay."

My belly somersaults. I open my mouth to say sorry and ask if he's okay, but he speaks first, lifting his hand to touch the side of my neck.

I shiver when the tips of his fingers graze skin, instantly imagining them on other parts of my body. My palms sweat at the thought, and holy crap…I am in deep, deep trouble.

"Walk me to the door?" he asks, so obviously clueless.

I nod. "Sure."

He hesitates—I feel it in the weight of his stare, his unmoving feet. But I can't look at him. Not when I'm terrified of seeing rejection on his face. We shared two amazing kisses, yeah, but that could've just been a lost-in-the-moment thing for him. There's so much he hasn't told me about his past, his life with his…his whatever that Eve girl was. So it's possible I'm a rebound for him, which isn't something I ever wanted to label myself as. But at the same time, I don't want to *not* be with him in some way either.

Without looking into his eyes, I walk around him and head to the front door, heart in my throat. When

Midnight and I reach it, I clear my throat, turn, and finally look up at him.

"Did I do something wrong?" he asks.

I squint at him. "No, why?"

"You seem upset." His brows furrow. "I'm sorry I can't stay. My guardian is coming by in a half hour, and I forgot about it. He's the one who just texted me."

It's on the tip of my tongue to ask where he's staying, and if I could come meet the people he's staying with—his guardian too. But that'd be a little obsessive and I'm not about to be *that* girl. Still, it sucks because I feel like I know so much about him but so little at the same time. That's why doubts ring like bells in my head, telling me this is a bad idea—that *he's* a bad idea. Even though my heart says otherwise.

Without warning, Midnight closes the distance between us, moving even closer to me than he'd been in the kitchen. And just like that, all my silly doubts slide away when I look up just in time to see his Adam's apple bob with a swallow. He's nervous. And when Midnight is nervous, it's usually because he's about to tell me something.

"Bex?"

I lick my lips and can't help but stare at his. "Yeah?"

"Can I..."

"Can you what?" I hold my breath and look into his eyes. Those eyes, so blue, damn it... They're making me weak in the knees and the heart.

"Can I come over tonight after my guardian leaves and stay the night again?" He releases a slow breath. "You...you make me feel safe."

I nod without hesitancy, knowing my throat's too dry to speak the words.

"One more thing," he whispers.

"What's that?"

Midnight searches my face like it holds the answers to long-lost secrets. *Reverent* would be the perfect way to describe it—I'm a treasure he's only now discovering. Or maybe that's just me, doing the same with him.

"I want to kiss you again," he whispers. "But I don't know if you want to kiss me."

I smile and bite my bottom lip. "I wouldn't be opposed."

For once he must pick up on my sarcasm because one side of his mouth tips up. "Is that a yes, then?"

Without words, I slide my hand into the back of his hair, pulling him down until our noses touch. His breath catches against mine and he shudders. *Success.*

"That's a hell yes." Then I press my lips to his.

CHAPTER 31: MIDNIGHT
MAY 2021

THREE MONTHS. That was how long it'd been since everything in my life had fallen apart. Since I'd last seen the blonde, braided crown of the girl I hadn't been able to save. She'd exited my life the way she'd entered, like a firestorm. And I'd never get over losing her.

"You're gonna like it here," Simon said for the fourteenth time from the driver's seat of his car. "They're good people."

I pinched my lips together and stared out the window, not sure who he was trying to convince more. Me or himself. Either way, I was still pissed that this was how it was gonna go down, especially since he'd been my guardian since the night we left Children of His Mercy.

It was no surprise my mom had vanished into thin air, leaving me with no place to stay. Normally, I would've been worried about her, but with Emmanuel being dead, I figured she was just done being a mom, or something. I tried not to take it personally, but it was harder than I thought it'd be, knowing I wasn't wanted by my own blood.

So, for twelve weeks Simon and I had lived in his tiny apartment above a bar in northern Missouri. He hadn't been home a lot. Something about him having work to do and things to take care of. I hadn't minded because I liked the quiet. It'd worked out well.

At least I'd thought it had until six in the morning today.

He'd come into my room and told me to pack up what little stuff I had. Said he'd found a place for me to stay and repeated over and over that they were good people—just like he'd said a minute ago. Even if they weren't good, I didn't care. I'd been through the worst kind of hell imaginable, so nothing fazed me.

"You hungry?"

I blinked. "I'm good."

Simon grunted. He did that a lot. "Won't be long now until we get there anyway."

I leaned my head back against the seat. "Will you tell me who I'm staying with?"

He tapped his thumbs against the steering wheel. I half expected a no. He'd been so vague about everything since that day, and other than telling me he worked for the FBI, I knew little about him.

When he did finally tell me, I wished he wouldn't have.

"You're staying with Eve's family."

I shot up in my seat and faced him. "No. I'm not staying—"

"You don't have anywhere else to go."

"Why can't I just stay with you?" I asked.

He rubbed a hand over his mouth. "You don't want me, kid, I told you that. I'm a loose cannon, never home, always got shit to do and can't be there when you need me."

"That's the best part. I don't need anyone to take care of me." Which was why it made sense for me to stay with him.

"Of course ya do. You're still a kid."

"No. I'll be eighteen in December."

"Exactly. Still a kid."

"This is bullshit." I crossed my arms.

"Yeah, well, life is bullshit, and the papers have already been signed."

"Asshole."

"I know I am."

My stomach twisted so tightly into knots it hurt to breathe. I thought there'd be no hell worse than Children of His Mercy, but I'd been wrong. Because now he was saying I had to live under the same roof as the family of the girl I'd let die. A girl who'd died *for* me.

"I'm still your legal guardian and will be until your birthday. But I've got stuff I gotta take care of right now, which is why I can't be the guy you need."

"What are you doing, huh? You owe me that much of an explanation."

He sighed. "Don't be dramatic, kid. I—"

"Tell. Me." I reached over and grabbed his arm, squeezing so tight I probably could've broken his bone. He barely flinched. The guy was some sort of superhero strong, and my squeeze probably felt like a love pat.

Simon flexed his hands over the wheel, his knuckles turning white. "I'm going to look for your mom."

"My mom," I deadpanned.

He nodded. "Yeah."

I narrowed my eyes and looked out the front window, letting go of his arm. That...wasn't what I'd been expecting to hear.

"What's the point?"

He cleared his throat. "I owe it to you. For everything that happened. For losing Eve…"

"I don't want anything from you." I scoffed.

"Well, that's too damn bad."

We drove in the silence down a long highway for another hour until we hit a side road, followed by a long driveway that led up a house that was big and rich and nothing like Eve.

Simon looked at me when we parked. "Midnight, I—"

"Don't," I said, staring at the front door of the house. *Eve's* house.

A second later, the driver's side door opened. I looked out the window, not at Simon when he came to my side but the people who stood in the opened doorway of the house, watching us.

A guy was in front. Tall and skinny, dark hair. A pretty, older blonde lady was beside him. And to her right was…

My eyes bugged out and my palms started to sweat. I rubbed them up and down my pants, shaking my head over and over. "I can't. Simon, that's—"

"Eve's twin. Her name is Jo, Midnight. Jo Donahue."

CHAPTER 32: BEX
FEBRUARY 2022

THE POWER CAME on about an hour ago, so in a move that's unlike her, Mom's cooking supper.

"Grab the plates." She points at the cupboard.

I take two out and set them on the counter.

"Um, grab three, would you? I invited someone to dinner."

I cross my arms. "Who?"

"A friend." She shrugs. "The one I mentioned."

I lift my brows. "And you didn't tell me, why?"

She licks tomato sauce off her finger. "I did the other night when you went to the pond?"

I frown, not mad. Just not ready.

"He's nice," Mom says. "I think you'll like him."

I blow out a breath and nod. I'd rather it just be the two of us tonight, but at the same time I'm curious as to who this mystery friend is and why Mom's so dressed up to see him. She's wearing makeup that's ten times tamer than usual. Lip gloss and mascara, no heavily lidded eyes like she's going to work. Her outfit's different too. More Midwest Mom than I've ever seen it before. A pink-and-brown striped sweater dress with cream tights and bare feet. No leather. No red. No...*Mom*.

Whatever. I've got too many other things on my mind to figure out what brought on this change. Like life and one certain boy who has flipped my entire world upside down...

"You're thinking about him, aren't you," Mom says, leaning her hip against the counter.

I turn and grab an apple off the counter, taking a bite to try to chill out. She doesn't know about *Midnight*. There's no way. Yet the gleam in her eyes says she does know *something*.

"I'm not thinking about anyone," I say.

"Please." She laughs and turns back to the stove. "I know all about your all-night rendezvous, sugar. Don't think I had those security cameras out front for no reason."

I choke on a bite of my apple, spitting it into a napkin a minute later.

Mom shakes her head and laughs. "I saw that boy jumping off the roof this morning." She *tsked*. "All long legs, wearing your dad's sweats too."

I drop the apple onto the floor. "Shit. I'm sorry. I'll get them back. I swear it."

She snort-laughs, which is pretty much the opposite of how I thought she'd react.

"Please. You ain't sorry."

"I am. Swear it." Okay, so that was a little off the truth path, but still.

"Look," she says, setting aside the mixture for lasagna. "I could tell something was changing with you, baby. Your whole vibe's been off, in a good way, these last few weeks." She shrugs. "But having a boyfriend is the least of my worries about you."

Out of everything she just said, there's only one word that trips me up—and it's not *boyfriend*. "Did you just say my *vibe*?"

"Yep." She walks to the freezer and pulls out some garlic rolls, placing them on a cookie sheet.

After I bend over and grab my apple, I prop myself up on top of the counter like I used to do whenever she and Dad would cook dinner together.

She's right though. My *vibe* has been off, but in a good way. And it is because of Midnight. In a way, he's changed me. Made me bolder, but also given me something to distract myself with. Something to make me feel like an actual senior in high school, not just a grieving teenager.

She grabs her mixture and adds more seasoning. "Tell me about him."

I bite my bottom lip, hesitating. Mom and I don't talk boys and dating. We barely talk about anything other than superficial stuff actually. We're close, but not in a friend way—which is fine and all. But with my dad, we told each other every single detail of our lives—well, to an extent. Needless to say, I've missed the hell out of it.

"Well…" I draw out the word, wondering where to start. It's not like I can mention his former cult status and the hell he's been through. But I've got to begin somewhere. "His name's Midnight. He's, um, in my Chemistry class. We're friends."

"Sure." Mom clicks her tongue against the roof of her mouth. "Someone who's *just friends* with a boy doesn't turn hot pink from the sheer mention of him."

"It's hot in here," I say, shaking out the front of my sweatshirt.

Mom throws her head back and laughs.

"What?" I huff. "We are friends. That's it." *Friends*

who've kissed. Not that she needs to know *all* the details in my life.

"Oh boy," Mom whispers, losing her teasing tone.

I jerk my head up, eyes narrowing. "What?"

"It's happened." She stops mixing.

"What's *happened*?"

"Damn it, John." She rubs a shaky hand down her face.

I jerk my head back. "What does Dad have to do with this?"

"This was supposed to be *his* thing, not mine." She looks me dead-on, and I notice right away that her eyes are all watery. "The whole love thing is, well..." She presses her lips into a flat line, looking like she's trying to gather her words or maybe just trying not to cry.

I reach my hand out to touch hers, stopping halfway when she blurts out, "Do you need to be put on the pill?"

"What? No. Jesus, Mom."

"I have condoms upstairs until then. But I'll call my doc. Or Planned Parenthood, even. See if they can get you in sooner."

"Mom," I hiss, my whole face burning. "I don't need birth control. Seriously."

"You say that now, but it's my job to prepare for this part." She looks at the floor, *her* cheeks bright red this time. "Dad was supposed to be in charge of everything else you're going through right now. The emotional stuff. The sex was mine."

"For one, I'm not *having* sex. And another, what *exactly* am I going through?"

Her watery eyes meet mine. "You're falling in love, Bex."

"I... No." I curl my nose. "That's... *No.* I'm...no."

Oh, crap.

I can't defend myself. Or tell her no either because I think, deep down, she might be right. But it's way too soon for declarations. We've only kissed. Only started talking, like, real-ass sentences outside of the classroom a month ago.

But there's no denying the belly flutters I get whenever I think about him. The ache in my chest that's never been there before when I see him either.

"Oh God," I groan and cover my face.

"Uh-huh. See? Told you," Mom says.

Shit. If that's what it feels like to fall in love with someone, then maybe I am.

That's probably not a good thing.

"Look." Mom sets both hands on my shoulders and looks me in the eyes. "I've never been too good at my own relationships. But if you think you're feeling something like that, then I'm happy for you."

"But you and dad were good at relationships." I'd never seen two people more in love in my life actually.

She laughs. "Dad and I had our problems like everyone else."

I keep silent, struggling to believe that she and Dad could be anything other than happy. Whenever I saw them together, they were always cuddled up or kissing. Staring at each other, holding hands...normal couple-ish stuff. It was gross at the time, but now that I think about it more I realize just how damn awesome it was growing up and watching them get to be so in love. It's like they found the once-in-a-lifetime storybook, fairytale stuff that not everybody gets.

"Look, sugar. I'm not trying to rain on your happiness." She reaches over, tugging on the tie of my hoodie. "But if you're already in deep, all I'm saying is it's gonna come with some roadblocks. And as your mom, I just want to warn you. Good things take time. Hard things are the ones that make things worth it." She winks at me.

"But what if I'm not in deep? What if I'm only putting a toe in the water to test it out?"

She shakes her head. "If there's one thing I know in life, it's that falling in love with someone ain't your fault, even if you try to avoid it."

Before I can get to open my mouth to ask what she means, there's a knock on the door. Mom's face pales a little, and her gaze darts toward the hallway.

I roll my eyes. "You want me to get it?"

"Would you mind?" She presses her hands together like she's praying.

I do mind, but this talk of ours is too fluffy and serious for my taste, which is why I don't hesitate. "Sure thing."

Slowly, I unlock the deadbolt, then slide the other lock off before pulling the door open. I'm met with a wide, male chest in a black sweater. I look down, noticing checkered Vans and jeans. *Weird.* When I meet him head on, the first thing I notice is his smile. It's toothy and big. He's handsome for an old guy, with super dark brown hair that curls at the temples.

"Hi," he says, waving with one hand while he clings to flowers with the other. "You must be Bex."

I clear my throat and take a step back, realizing I've been staring for way too long. "That'd be me."

"It's good to meet you." He reaches out and shakes my hand.

"You too." I think.

I shut the door behind him and offer to take his gloves—his mittens actually. Black, like his sweater. And

I'm pretty sure they're both that rich-ass material—cashmere, I think it's called.

He hands them over, eying the room. Without asking, he sits on the end of the couch—minus two points for sitting on the arm. Dad used to freak when I did that as a kid. Mom would come into the room, though, and do the same five seconds later but on purpose. I'd "snitch" as she liked to call it. Then Dad would tackle her, and they'd have a wrestling match on the floor while I bounced up and down on the couch cushions, cheering and grinning so big it hurt.

I blink the memory away, go back to studying the stranger. He smiles at me again. It's an easy smile, casual like we've known each other way longer than two minutes.

"Did you have fun today?" he asks.

I tip my head to one side. "Umm..."

He stares at me for a few more uncomfortable seconds, then clears his throat. "Your mom told me you went sledding."

"Oh, right. Yeah. I did."

Mom walks into the room then, wearing this huge smile I haven't seen in, well, months. "Hey, you. I'm glad you made it."

"Good to see you too, Sara. Looking beautiful as always."

My stomach churns at the view of him scanning her body, the way he grabs her elbows and pulls her in to kiss her cheek too.

She blushes and looks at me when she backs up, running her palms down the front of her dress. She's preening, and it's more disgusting than him kissing her cheek.

I step back and let them have their moment, eying the

door to my room down the hall at the same time. Whether I want to believe it or not, I know for sure this isn't just some old friend of my mom's. This is someone who's trying super hard to get with her.

"Soooo," I say, clearing my throat.

Mom looks at me, her eyes widening like she forgot I was in the room. Her blush runs right past the point of tomato into full-on July Sunburn.

"What's up, sugar?" She takes the guy's arm and pulls him around to face me. This time, I don't bother looking at him.

I jab my thumb back toward the hall. "If you don't mind, I think I'm gonna just eat dinner in my room tonight. I've got some homework to catch up on."

"What?" Mom looks at me with sad puppy-dog eyes. "I was hoping—"

"It's okay," the guy tells her, patting her hand. "Bex and I can get to know each other another time, right?"

For a second I stare at the guy, finding a momentary and mutual agreement in his eyes. He wants to be alone with my mom. And I want to be away from them both. Homework sucks, but it sounds more appealing than sitting through a dinner with these two. Besides that, I need to shower, get ready for tonight. For Midnight.

"Dessert later, then? I made a cake." Mom holds her breath, waiting for my answer.

"Sure." I force a smile.

Her shoulders slump in obvious relief before she turns and steers the guy toward the kitchen. The pair walk with their heads touching and their shoulders brushing together too.

I realize then that I didn't even get the guy's name.

"Hey, dude?" I call after him.

He stops, turns and looks my way. "Yeah?"

I poke my tongue against the side of my mouth, wondering if he's trustworthy or not. "What's your name by the way?"

Mom opens her mouth, but the guy beats her to it, his lip curling in a crooked smile as he says, "You can call me Sam."

CHAPTER 33: MIDNIGHT

JULY 2021

THERE WAS a knock on the door of the room I stayed in at the Donahue house. I didn't get up to answer, just kept throwing the hacky sack I'd found under the bed at the ceiling, then catching it when it fell. I'd been doing it for a half hour, mostly so I didn't have to face the person on the other side of the door.

"I know you're in there," Jo hollered at me. "There's no point in hiding."

I groaned and sat up, kicked my feet over the bed, pissed that I had to be such a damn pushover. But every time I looked at her, even three months after coming here to live in this house, it felt like someone had shoved a knife into my chest and twisted it until I lost the ability to breathe. She had the same eyes, the same hair, if not a little lighter, the same soft-looking skin too. But instead of being the kind, inno-cent, and generous person Eve had been, Jo was a snappy know-it-all brat who always got what she wanted.

"It's open," I said, staring at the wall.

Jo rushed in and sat down beside me on the bed. "You're coming tonight."

I stared down at my hands, flexed them on my lap, and shrugged.

"Ugh, don't be like that. It'll be fun." She wrapped her hand around my upper arm and laid her head on my shoulder.

My stomach twisted in that way it always did whenever she touched me.

"I'm tired," I said. "Think I wanna go to bed early."

"What are you, eighty?" She laughed and shoved me away.

I flinched but said nothing. Parties weren't for me. Hell, nothing about this town or Eve's family was. Every other night I texted Simon, begging to come back and stay with him. But his answer was always the same.

Can't happen—sorry, kid.

"Miiiiid-night," Jo sang. "You start school next month. Don't you wanna make friends and shit? Eve would want you—"

"Shut up." I gritted my teeth. "Stop using her against me."

She scoffed and let go of my wrist. "She's dead, you know."

I squeezed my eyes shut. "Shut. Up."

"And she's never. Coming. Back." Her voice was calm and even. Empty in a way that sent shivers up my spine.

"Please, Jo," I pleaded.

She knew how to play the Eve card and use it against me a lot—pretty much since I'd showed up here. She'd decided I was gonna be this toy of hers for some reason. Too bad for her, I knew her truth—the real truth she hid away from everyone.

These walls were thin, and every single night I heard

her crying. For her sister, and sometimes even her brother too. Jo was masking her pain until she was all alone because she likely didn't want to seem weak.

Which was exactly why it was so damn hard to say no to her.

"Jesus, you need to lighten up." She stood and moved in front of me, her hands on her hips. "I'm living for her. You're not."

I covered my face.

"You gonna cry about it again?" She laughed. "Because we both knows tears won't bring her back when *you* yourself couldn't."

"Enough!" I jumped to my feet, towering over her, my breath coming out so quick I got dizzy.

Instead of cowering like I'd hoped she would, Jo shoved my chest and laughed. "You're strung too tight. I was kidding." She reached a hand up and pressed her palm against my chest. "Which is exactly *why* you will be coming tonight."

Heart in my throat, I stepped back, needing distance, a way to relieve this pain in my head. The sudden urge to ram my face against a wall just so I didn't have to see her smirking face was real and scary.

Maybe Simon was right.

Maybe I needed to double down on therapy. Get something to help me sleep at night too.

For months, I'd been trying to give Jo the benefit of the doubt. It wasn't her fault she was the way she was. Spoiled and pushy, always getting her way, always reckless. She had crappy parents who had no idea how truly messed up their daughter was.

The one time I did try to say something, Mr. and Mrs. Donahue had told me I hadn't known what I was talking about. That Jo was just overdramatic. That she was thriving in school and her social life. Not once did they mention anything about healing or grieving from losing not one but two siblings in the span of a year.

The two of them were just as bad. In fact, the only time they'd ever asked about Eve had been on the second night I'd been there, and it had only been one question at that.

Did you see her die?

Neither of them had even cried. It was like they had no emotions left in their bodies. At least not when they were around each other. But at least I understood the dynamics of this family. Why Eve didn't want to come back. Her mom drank too much, and her dad was never home. Then when he was home, he treated me like a replacement son, taking me places and allowing me to use his things. Buying me stuff I never used, like gaming and VR crap. One time he'd taken me camping, just us two. But he drank a lot too and kept insisting I was his dead son.

I was also pretty sure he was cheating on Mrs. Donahue. And that she was doing the same. Not that it was my business. Nor was I gonna make it my business. Once I turned eighteen, I'd do what I want. Leave—never look back most of all.

"Just go, all right?" I whispered again, bowing my head, way too tired to argue.

"Whatever," she snapped at me. "Just be downstairs and ready to go by eleven."

The door slammed in her wake. She was pissed, not for the first time since I'd learned to stand up to her. But instead of running after her and apologizing like I always did, I laid back down on the bed and started throwing the hacky sack once more, struggling to imagine a world

where Eve had lived here with these people who were
nothing like her.

———

LIKE THE LAST time I'd been to the Donahue party
farm, Jo left me five minutes after we showed. I didn't
mind it because it meant I could sneak away and go
down to the pond for some quiet. But it was storming
out tonight, so I was stuck. Which only made my bad
mood worsen.

I sat at one of the tables farthest from the makeshift
dance floor and looked around. This place was the
Donahue moneymaker, yet it felt cold and dark and
nothing like I'd expected when they'd told me they ran
weddings and receptions out of there.

"Hey, Cult Boy." The chair beside me screeched
across the barn floor. I turned and took in the familiar
face. Pink hair, dark eyeliner, black lipstick. Gia was her
name. She was friends with Jo.

I leaned back in the seat, ignoring her. When I didn't
talk, people left me alone. But not Jo's friends. Especially
this one.

"So it's gonna be like that tonight, hmm?"

I gritted my teeth.

"Car, c'mere." She yelled over the music. "Say hi to
Cult Boy."

I fucking hated that name. But I also didn't stop her
from using it either. People knowing I'd lived at Children
of His Mercy meant they tended to stay away from me,
like I was a leper. At least the guys, that is. But the attention from girls was nonstop, and I hated every second of
it. It was like they all thought I was something to toy
with, or maybe even claim. But none of them knew the

truth. That my heart stopped working when I lost Eve. That if I couldn't save her, I wasn't worthy of being happy again.

The other friend, Carson, zigzagged through the crowd. She nodded my way, but she rarely spoke to me. I respected her more because of that. She wasn't one of *them*. Like the four girls who'd been sitting at the table next to mine all night, staring, giggling, waving, and winking at me.

"So who do you think it's gonna be tonight?" Gia lifted a bottle with something pink inside and took a drink, staring at Carson when she sat down.

"Bryan or Xavier. One of those two, I'm betting." Carson shrugged, looking bored and uninterested. "But I see some new faces here tonight. Guessing the same ones are getting boring to her."

"Probably." Gia shrugged. "I saw some college dudes here tonight. Pretty sure she invited them. They all looked like they had money shoved up their asses, which means they'll inevitably be dicks."

Carson sighed. "Why does she do this to herself?"

"No clue. But it's not healthy." Gia rubbed a finger across her mouth, staring across the room at Jo like she was thinking. "I've tried to talk to her about it, but she just flips out on me when I do and tells me to mind my own business."

They both turned to look at me. "What about you?" Carson asked. "Does she...mention anything?"

They knew enough about where I'd come from and how I'd been with Eve. But not everything. Jo only knew what she wanted to know too, despite the mountains of paperwork that sat on her dad's desk about me, her sister, and Children of His Mercy.

"No," I said. "Not really."

It was the truth, mostly. The Jo I knew, the one who found a new guy to go off with during these parties, wasn't the one I knew at home. Yeah, she pushed for me to be one of the dudes to fall at her feet, but I did so for another reason: Eve.

The rest of their conversation went over my head, the two talking about the people there and the start of school coming up. All the crap I tried to avoid thinking about. The whole time, though, I felt someone's gaze on me from the table with the four girls, only for one of them to finally get up and sit beside me.

"Hey. You're Midnight, right?" she asked.

I didn't say anything, just kept looking forward.

"I'm Sadie."

Still nothing.

"Um, you live with Jo's family, right?"

"Eve's," I say. "I live with Eve's family."

"Oh, right. I, um, didn't talk to Eve a lot in school. I feel bad, though, for what happened."

"*Discendo*," I said. *Leave.*

"That's really pretty. What does it mean?"

I didn't tell her.

Her friends giggled. Obviously, they thought I was sweet-talking.

The girl said something else to me, touched my arm without permission too. Everyone looked at me like a shiny toy, when I was like an evil doll, ready to come alive and haunt them for eternity. I was seconds away from telling her to get the hell away from me when a loud screech filled the room.

I stiffened and eyed the crowd, though nobody else seemed to hear the noise. The music was loud, and everyone was dancing, but then I heard it again, louder this time.

"Did you hear what I said?" The girl touched the back of my hand this time, and I looked down, eying her finger as it traced the scars.

I yanked it away. "Don't touch me. Ever. Fucking. Again."

Her eyes widened, and I jumped out of my chair, searching the crowd again, hearing the screech turn into a squeal.

"Where is she?" I asked Gia and Carson.

"Who?" one of them said.

"Eve. Where's Eve?"

Neither answered but instead stared up at me like I'd grown a second head. Their quiet pissed me the hell off because they had to know where she was.

Not waiting any longer, I pushed through the crowd, stopping when I saw them go inside one of the bathrooms. She was hanging over his shoulder, his hand was on the back of her thighs.

Prophet, please let me go.

Eve. Eve. Eve. Eve.

I growled and continued chanting her name in my head, feeling like a monster who was ready to rip arms off bodies, heads off necks.

My throat burned as I rushed after them, flashes of Eve sitting in the courtyard, our hands bound together in our room, the blood on our palms.

No. Stop it. No. I shook my head and ran a little faster.

"Damn, bro. Watch where you're going," someone called out to me when I slammed into them.

A flash of black hair with gray streaks. A white robe. Tall. Broad shoulders.

I shook my head and yelled, "No!"

When I got to the bathroom, I pushed on the door, but it was locked.

"Open up!" I cried out. Pounding and calling her name, "Eve, Eve, it's me! I'm here. I'm not gonna let him hurt you."

Seconds later, the door swung open, and I didn't stop to think, just grabbed the dude by the front of his shirt and shoved him against the wall. I nailed him in the nose, feeling bones break—his or mine. He went down right away, hands covering his face and blood streaming through fingers. That didn't stop me though.

"What the hell, Midnight?" a voice cried out from behind me. "Stop it!"

Ignoring the voice, I straddled the guy's stomach and hit the side of his temples with my fists. More blood filled my vision. Over and over and over I punched him, death on my mind, Eve crying my name…

Midnight, help. Midnight, I love you.

The fire. It was so hot. My feet were numb, I think, but I didn't stop swinging.

"Someone help! He's going to kill him."

Footsteps sounded, hands grabbed my shirt and yanked me back. My ass hit the floor, my head next when it collided with the underside of the sink. Even still, I kept swinging and kicking and crying and crying and crying…

"Let me go," I yelled. "Let me end him. Let me kill him now."

Someone jumped on top of me, their arm pressing against my throat. I coughed. I choked. I blinked. *Simon.*

"Stop fighting, and I'll let you go," the voice above me said, blurring in and out of focus.

Not Simon. But he had to be bad if he was there with Emmanuel.

"This guy is psycho," someone said.

"I called nine-one-one," someone else cried out.

In the distance, I heard sobbing.

"Eve," I cried out. "Save Eve."

But nobody saved her.

She was dead.

And I deserved to die too.

CHAPTER 34: BEX

FEBRUARY 2022

IT'S past two in the morning when the scuffle of shoes on shingles wakes me. I smile, knowing right away who's outside my window.

Then jerk upright with a gasp when I realize—for a second time—who it is.

Midnight.

He's here.

I swing my legs over the side of the bed in time to see him slide a leg inside. As always, he's quiet, but it doesn't bother me anymore now that I know it doesn't have anything to do with me. It's a Midnight-ism I'm starting to adore.

"Hey, you," I whisper, my throat scratchy from sleep.

He lifts his head once he's fully inside, immediately zeroing in on me from across the room. I swallow at the view—the intensity of his stare in the near dark is almost too much, but in a good way.

Goose bumps cover my skin, and I rub my hands over my naked arms. "You okay?"

Midnight closes and locks the window, then steps

toward me, stopping when he's between my parted thighs. Bending over, he takes my face between his palms and the smallest, sweetest smile lights up his face.

"Yeah," he murmurs. "I'm good."

My stomach flutters with the touch, the smile, his words. They bombard me to the point where I'm overwhelmed and ready to tackle him. And that's all before he decides to kiss me.

Mom was right. I am falling in love with him.

Or maybe I already have.

Flutters travel to my chest when our lips touch, only to burst free when he slides one hand to my neck. His palm is damp and cold, yet there's this fire inside of him whenever he kisses me that makes it feel like we're a candle ready to ignite into a bonfire.

I shudder at the thought, wanting the explosion, clinging to his forearms as our kiss deepens. Midnight kisses me like he's terrified he'll break me into pieces. It's the best kind of torture there is. But after our day and knowing what he tastes and feels like, it's not enough for my greedy self. I *need* him to give me everything he has, if only to make sure I'm not living in a fantasy world.

"Midnight," I gasp against his mouth, his hot breaths mirroring mine, our foreheads touching. "Don't hold back, okay?"

He leans back just a little and blinks down at me as if he's not sure what I mean.

My face heats, and I bite my bottom lip. "I want you to...you know, *touch* me."

His eyes widen, and an immediate groan fills his throat. But instead of backing away, he wraps his arm around my waist and yanks me close. Once we're pressed together everywhere we can be, he turns his head one way, I the other, and just like that, all of my two-in-the-morning wishes come true as I fall back onto the bed, and he lowers his body on top of me.

His hips straddle mine, and we mold together like two halves of a whole. Two various sculptures forming into one perfect image in my head. He's warm where I am, heavy where I want him to be, and when his hips move just the slight bit, I can't help but grip his hair and moan.

He mirrors the noise, but it's more like a growl—something feral and wild. Our breathing grows heavier between our kisses, and the bed seems to rock just the slightest whenever he moves against me. I should be worried about my mom being in the room across the hall, but I can't think about anything other than feeling good and feeling *him*.

Fingers slide around to the back of my head, and he pulls my chin up as he arches my neck.

"In perpetuum et unum diem," he whispers against my throat, lowering lips to my pulse until he's nipping and biting and sucking.

Those words, whatever they mean, wrap around me like a warm blanket that promises safety and heat and forever. I want to hear them again and again, despite the fact that I have no idea what they mean.

I wrap my legs around his waist and hips instead, eyes widening when he starts to move against me again even faster. Another one of his groans fill the room as he does, and the vibration has me wild with feelings that build and push until they're carving a space inside my stomach and crawling lower and lower...

With every passing second, our kisses grow more desperate, the kind of kiss that consumes my entire soul. And when the hand behind my back moves to grip my hip, I shiver, wishing for things that don't make sense. Like nakedness and sex and limits I've never thought about crossing.

Until now.

I squeeze my legs even tighter around him, wondering if he feels it too.

"Bex," he whispers, lifting his head up. When our eyes lock, I get my answer.

Tears fill my eyes—stupid tears I shouldn't be shedding but am. But instead of acknowledging them with a wipe, I press a soft kiss to his chin, letting my lips slide across *his* neck this time. It's smooth, so much so that I rub my nose against it like a cat.

"More," I say with a shiver.

Midnight shivers too but must understand what I need because soon the tips of his fingers do a slow dance across my stomach, almost tiptoeing up to my chest. He doesn't touch me though, just traces the outline of my breasts, his knuckles grazing the underside.

My eyelids droop down to the point where I have to shut them again. I'm dizzy with need, too flustered to say words, and decide right then to communicate with my hands like he's doing with his.

Slowly, I slide my palms under the back of his shirt, go to lift them, and…

He stiffens, his entire body like a sudden cube of ice.

"Crap," I say, realizing what I'm doing. Except when I try to yank my hands out, he shakes his head, his narrowing eyes locking with mine.

"No." His Adam's apple bobs with a swallow. "Please…don't stop."

My throat tightens a little and I blink to clear my vision. It's painful to watch him, knowing I'm the cause of his sudden fear. "I shouldn't have touched you there without permission," I whisper. "I'm so sorry."

"It's okay," he says with a sigh. "I like it when you touch me."

"Are you sure?" Because those scars are a part of him, not me, and I don't want to intrude. I don't say that though. Instead, I'm hoping he gets it, that I'm scared of crossing that line.

He nods once, his lips kicking up on one side. "Yeah. I'm sure."

Swallowing hard, I go back to where I was, slower this time as I let my hands graze his bare skin. This has to be a big deal for him. Being vulnerable and letting me explore his scars—physical links to a past that never should have existed at all.

Midnight shudders, lowers his lips to my neck again, where he kisses and nips like before. Only this time, the feel of his fingers shaking against me has my heart racing even faster.

"Tell me to stop if you want," I say.

He says nothing, just keeps kissing my skin.

With light fingertips, I start at the base of his spine, slowly moving upward. The scars are rigid, getting deeper the higher my hands go. With each one I touch my nose and eyes burn with a sudden urge to cry for his past pain. I wonder, not for the first time, how he could've survived something like this.

Tears escape before I can stop them. Midnight stiffens, probably because he can feel the wetness. Seconds later he rolls off of me, turning sideways. I do the same, smiling at him, despite the wobble of my bottom lip.

"I'm sorry," I say again. Not just for crying but sorry for what he went through. For making him uncomfortable. For not being able to turn back time and save him, most of all.

Midnight reaches out and wipes my tear streaks away with his thumb. "Don't say sorry. I like it when you touch me," he whispers, pressing his forehead to mine. "You make me feel alive again. I'm just not used to it."

"I make you feel that way? Really?" I bite my bottom lip.

He nods, his ocean eyes sparkling beneath my LED lights.

We study each other for a minute, our breathing slower now, nearly in sync. Surprisingly, he's the first to break the quiet. "I don't know what this is, Bex," he whispers.

"What do you mean?"

"This." He waves a hand between us. "Us. I don't…"

He thinks there's an us.

An *us* he's not sure of, but an *us* all the same.

"I don't know either." I swallow hard. "But I do know it doesn't *have* to be anything labeled if you don't want it to be."

He scoots even closer, setting his hand on my hip again. "I want it to be something is the thing."

I hesitate. Not because I don't agree but because I wonder if what he's feeling is true. The thought of being the rebound girl does nothing for my ego, but this isn't about me. I'm worried this is too fast for him. That maybe he's just clinging to me to try to fill a gap in his heart that Eve put there. I don't want to be a filler for him, despite my own feelings.

"What do you want it to be?" I ask.

"More." He blinks, his smile widening. "Everything."

I say nothing and stare at his mouth. His eyes are

excited and happy, which I love. But I'm terrified of the sudden change too.

"What?" he asks, tipping my chin up. His smile slides away, and I hate that I can't be happy. "Do you not want—"

"Stop." I grab his wrist when he goes to pull his hand off my hip. "I really like you, Midnight. Like, I don't think I've ever felt this way about anyone. Or even *wanted* to feel this way about anyone until you showed up." I release a slow breath, trying to keep my heart from racing. "I'm just worried things are moving too fast."

The messy side of my brain that wants to make this real is all about ignoring the reality of the situation. But the side of my brain that speaks the truth is winning. It sucks to have morals, honestly. Especially when being non-morally correct has become the highlight of my life recently. Dad would be proud though, and I've always followed his lead. But Mom, on the other hand, would be telling me the heart wants what it wants and to go for it.

Midnight shakes his head, frown lines crawling across his forehead. "When I'm with you, I feel okay again. I can forget about the things that happened to me for a little while."

"So I'm a distraction."

"No! God, no." He lifts his hand from my hip and cups my cheek. "Breathing isn't a chore when we're together, that's what I mean. And life feels real and good. I have actual choices with you that won't lead to destruction."

I bite my lip, not wanting to sound like a jealous girlfriend, but the question has to be asked. "Isn't that how it was with Eve?"

He blinks, then jerks his head back like I've slapped him. "No. It's the exact opposite actually. With Eve, all I could think about was saving her and getting her out of there. And there were only two choices: I lived or I died."

I swallow a hard lump in my throat. "You love her a lot, don't you?"

He pulls his hand off my face, brows furrowing. "I *loved* her," he says.

"Loved?" As in...

Oh god. Eve is dead.

It's no wonder he's so broken.

"Yeah." He looks at me, nods, but doesn't say the words. I don't expect him to.

"I'm so sorry," I say.

"Me too."

He rolls over onto his back, still sharing my pillow, though it feels like he's a million miles away. I don't roll away though. Instead, I watch him, study his profile. Breathe him in.

He sighs deeply. "Part of the deal at Children of His Mercy was the fact that I was supposed to get her pregnant."

My eyes widen a little and my lips make an O.

"Eve knew all along what would happen if we didn't do it." He blows out a long breath. "But I kept putting it off. I told myself we were too young and that it wasn't the time. But the truth was I didn't want to because I wasn't *in* love with her. And I also didn't want to live a life there."

I touch his cheek and urge him to look at me again. "God, Midnight, you were, what, fifteen, sixteen? Of course you weren't ready for that kind of commitment."

"Yeah." He clears his throat. "But I could have saved her life if I did."

"And lost your life anyway." I wrap my arm around his waist and pull him close, settling my head beneath his chin while burying my face against his chest, so thankful that he didn't make that decision. But feeling terrible for thinking so at the same time because Eve might still be alive.

"*Vita ad vitam,*" he whispers.

I don't ask him what it means, but I do hold on to him a little longer. Maybe getting him to admit things out loud is a good place to start when it comes to healing. Because without having this conversation, I don't think we can move on, despite my body cursing me for the rational decision.

"The guilt won't go away," he tells me.

"It won't," I whisper, remembering my own guilt. How I'd barely said goodbye to my dad the night he died.

Midnight wraps his arm around my waist like I am him, squeezing me so tight it feels like we're connected all over. Superglued together with the kind of emotions that I didn't know I could feel. I'm content. Happy. Sleepy, but calm. And even though I know the two of us have a ways to go until we can find out what lies ahead of us, I will do everything I can to enjoy the moments like these.

"Can we sleep now?" he finally asks.

I squeeze the front of his hoodie and urged him onto his back, laying my head on his chest again. "Yeah. We can do that."

CHAPTER 35: MIDNIGHT
AUGUST 2021

THE HALLWAYS WERE CROWDED and overwhelming. Everyone talked too loud and stared at me when I walked by, like they knew who I was—most probably did after what had happened last month. What I'd done to that kid. I might have been new to this school, but I wasn't new to the town.

I took my phone out of my pocket and texted Simon when I got to the third floor.

Me: I don't like it here

Simon: Too bad.

Me: It's smells like sweat and perfume

Simon typed for a second. I waited, watched when the dotted lines popped up and then, eventually, just stopped.

"Asshole." I tucked my phone into the back pocket of my shorts.

I'd barely made it ten feet down the hall before the urge to puke took over. Nerves, the smells, the crowded spaces...

I rushed into the first bathroom I could find and

hurled in a toilet without closing the door behind me. Someone started laughing—dickhead. Someone accused me of being hungover—double dickhead. I hated this place already.

When I finished, I wiped my face with a paper towel at the sink and stared back at myself in the mirror. My skin was paler than ever. And my eyes were practically sunken into their sockets. I shook my head, gathered some water in my hands, and took a drink, swishing it then spitting it out into the sink a second later.

A bell rang when I made it back into the hall—feeling no better. Instead of nerves, dread pummeled my chest this time.

What if I couldn't do this?

Simon told me this was a place where I could start over, not think about the shit I'd gone through. But the more I looked around, the more my head spun, and I realized just how wrong he'd been.

Eve. Do this for Eve.

I started down the hall, my chin a little higher, only to spot Jo on the right. She was leaned back against her locker, arms folded, her blonde hair piled on top of her head in a bun. Her friends were close, rounding out their three-person circle. All of them were laughing—Jo too, until her eyes locked with mine over Carson's shoulder. Her entire body grew rigid, but that wouldn't stop me from doing what I had to do.

My hands shook as I made my way over to her. I skidded to a stop a few feet behind Carson. "Hey," I said. "Can we talk?"

"Go screw yourself." She tucked her arms through Gia's and Carson's and took off in the opposite direction.

My shoulders slumped, and I bowed my head in defeat.

Lunch. I'd try to do it again at lunch. Then if it didn't happen today, I'd try again tomorrow, and the day after that, until she realized how sorry I was. That what I'd done to her boyfriend hadn't been on purpose. Not that it would make a difference.

Chemistry, room three hundred. That's where I headed. But as I made my way to the last door on the right, I couldn't remember what I was even supposed to bring to class. Hell, I could barely remember my own name some days and had to say it over and over in my head, remind myself that this was where I was supposed to be, even if I didn't wanna be there. I hadn't been inside a real school in a long ass time and it was even worse than I'd remembered.

When I stepped through the door, I barely registered what the teacher said, other than *find a seat*. I grabbed the one closest to the hall, not caring who I sat beside. I wasn't at this school to make friends. I wasn't there to...

God, I didn't even know *what* I was there for.

Normalcy wasn't right, and it sure as hell wasn't *fairness* either. Simon's idea of starting out my junior year when I was almost eighteen sucked. Not only because I was nearly an adult, but because it was embarrassing. Even if I did manage to make it through this year and next, what kind of life would a loser like me ever have when he'd failed everyone he'd ever loved?

"Each of you should have a syllabus sitting on the table in front of you. It's only a few pages long, but it explains what's expected of you this year as far as workload, homework..."

The teacher went on and on. I tuned him out, doodling on his stupid syllabus with the only pencil I'd brought. A snapped-in-half generic number two. That was also the only reason I noticed the set of hands on the table next to mine. Her fancy pencil was a hell of a lot better, not to mention glittery and black.

Short, thin fingers; nails painted a pale pink; freckles on the back of her hand. She was short—even sitting down I could tell. I bit the inside of my cheek, debating on whether or not I wanted to match the hand with a face.

In the end, I did, but slyly to the point where she'd hopefully not notice.

Long brown hair, a few freckles on her cheeks. Wide eyes, though I didn't know what color they were. If I had to guess, they were probably brown, like her hair.

As if she could feel me staring, she glanced at me from the corner of her eye and pinched her lips together. Our stares locked, mine longer than hers, before she cleared her throat and went back to doing whatever she was doing.

It annoyed me how she'd looked away first. It was also refreshing too. I didn't want to be noticed. I wanted to just...be.

For fifteen minutes, I sat there staring at the papers, the words blurring in and out of focus as badly as the teacher's voice. Even when the teacher announced that our seatmate would be our lab partner, I said nothing. Didn't react either. I heard the girl groan though. I didn't blame her. I was dead weight.

"We have to read this article," she said to me, tapping something on the screen of her Chromebook. "Then we have to answer question one through ten, which is freaking stupid because this is the first day."

I looked around, noting everyone else had their computer out too.

That was what I'd forgotten.

"Hey," she said again. "Did you hear what I said?"

Answering felt pointless, so I didn't. Instead, I turned my chair and stared at her computer, pretending to read it on her screen.

"Do you not have a Chromebook, or...?"

I said nothing again.

"Okay, then." She huffed out an insult out under her breath.

Dick-for-brains was what it was.

"I'm down with silent reading," she said a few seconds later. "And sharing apparently too. When we're finished, I'll answer the top five questions and you can do the bottom."

She handed me a worksheet.

I stared at it, then looked at my pencil. If Emmanuel were here, he'd probably take her pretty pencil and stab me in the back of the neck with it. Then he'd laugh.

"Look," the girl said, interrupting my deranged fantasy. "I don't want to be your partner any more than you wanna be mine. But I *have* to pass this class, get me?" She dropped her voice to a whisper. "I am the *only* senior in here. It's embarrassing."

I wanted to tell her that there were a lot worse things in life than being a senior in a junior class. I even thought about telling her that I was being held back a year too. But that'd lead to questions I wasn't in the mood to answer—ever if I had my way.

Feeling her annoyed gaze on my face, I finally looked at her full-on, swallowing a little harder than normal when I did. She was...pretty. Different pretty than Eve. Harder and angrier, but also had this take-no-shit kind of look about her too. Her hair was mostly straight but for a few pieces underneath that almost looked like she'd forgotten to brush.

She said something else, then smashed her lips together.

"You gonna answer me today, or...?"

"Yeah," I cleared my throat. "Okay."

Satisfied, it seemed, she turned and started reading the article again, staying quiet as she did. Meanwhile, I spent the next twenty minutes studying the waves under her hair and the tiny freckles sitting just underneath her right eye.

———

I WASN'T PLANNING on eating today. But I *was* hoping to catch Jo, which was why I went to the lunchroom. I narrowed my eyes when I stepped through the doorways. It was a zoo in there, and damn if my gut didn't churn the second the doors swung shut behind me. Instead of sweat and perfume I smelled fried foods. Old fries, greasy hamburgers, stuff I wasn't used to eating.

My stomach churned. I had to hurry and find her. Get out of there and maybe spend a few minutes of quiet in the hall to text Simon and beg him to call me out. Not that he would.

The tables were round and easy to maneuver between. But every time I saw a blonde head of hair it made me think of Eve and that day in the courtyard when I'd first seen her braids. I shivered, not watching where I was going because in the next second I rammed my hip against an empty table next to Jo's. Only she wasn't alone. And she wasn't with Carson and Gia either. Chem Girl was there, head in a book, and one hundred percent ignorant of the girl who'd just sat down beside her.

Jo, who took matters into her own hands, swiped the book right out of Chem Girl's hands. I stiffened, protective for some reason. Until I saw the look the girl gave Jo. It was cruel and condescending, like she knew how to fight with fists and would knock Jo out in a second if given the chance.

Before I could walk over to Jo and start talking, she stood and tucked her arm through Chem Girl's, yanking her onto her feet. Jo then grabbed the girl's tray and set the book she'd swiped on top of it, saying something I couldn't hear. Chem Girl frowned but followed Jo who led her across the room, talking the entire time with wild, animated hands.

I scooted back and hid behind a cardboard cutout, watching as Jo pointed to a seat at the new table. Carson and Gia were there, smiling.

"She conned you over here, huh." Carson laughed.

Chem Girl smirked and shook her head. "No. I was good where I was. She just insisted I would be better here."

"Which you will be." Jo tugged Chem Girl down onto a chair besides her. "Ladies," she said looking between Gia and Carson. "This girl right here is going to be the fourth corner of our square."

"That's corny." Gia curled her nose. "But still, glad to have you."

Chem Girl cringed and said, "Thanks." After that, she yanked her tray closer, grabbed her book, and tucked it onto her lap.

"You're in my English class," Carson said to her.

"Yep." Chem Girl nodded and took a bite of her burger, spitting it out into her napkin.

The three of them laughed. Jo was the first to say something. "You don't wanna eat the main lunch line.

Stick with us, and we'll do the salad-and-wraps line from now on. It's pricier but worth it."

"But—"

"Trust her," Gia said. "That crap isn't worth it."

I chewed on the inside of my cheek, listening as they spoke, while staying focused on Chem Girl and the way her cheeks had turned bright red. After that, their voices grew softer and I couldn't hear much of what they said, other than an occasional laugh. What I did notice, though, was that Chem Girl was hardly paying attention. Instead, she read the book on her lap.

"So, tell them what your name is," Jo said just loud enough that my interest piqued. She set her elbows on the table and her chin on her hands. "It's the freaking coolest name ever. Like, I'm jealous. So much better than Josephine."

Chem Girl jerked her head up, blinking a few times. "Um, what? Sorry. I didn't hear what you said."

"Your name." Jo rolled her eyes. "Tell them what it is."

"Oh, right…" She looked between the three of them, and I found myself holding my breath. I didn't know her name. I didn't *want* to know her name. But I needed to, if only so I'd stop calling her *Chem Girl* in my head.

"My name's Bex."

"Bex?" Gia's eyes widened. "That is a cool name."

"Thanks. It was my Dad's favorite author's name. Bex Capone."

"Like, Al Capone?" Gia asked.

"No." Bex bit her bottom lip and looked at her lap. "There's, uh, no relation."

I swallowed, silently saying her name in my head.

Bex.

Bex.

Bex.

I hated that the name had three letters.

I hated that I liked the name too.

And most of all, I hated that the girl named *Bex* was the first girl who'd made me open my eyes a little wider since losing Eve.

CHAPTER 36: MIDNIGHT

NOVEMBER 2021

IT WAS THANKSGIVING, but I didn't celebrate—at least not with the Donahues. They were at some country club, having brunch with a bunch of rich people. They'd asked me to come, but I'd said no because Simon was coming into town to take me out to lunch—though he was late as hell by the time he pulled into the driveway.

"Sorry, kid. Traffic was bad," he said when I hopped into his truck. It was new. Big too. FBI agents who did undercover work must've made good money.

"It's fine." I looked around, taking the interior in. The first thing I noticed was a picture on the rearview mirror. I pointed at it, the woman with dark hair. "Who's that?"

He yanked it down and put it in the front of his button-up shirt pocket. "Nobody."

I grinned. "You got a girlfriend?"

"None of your business."

I shook my head and leaned back against the seat, watching the rain outside the window. It wasn't cold yet, but it wasn't warm either. The heaven before hell in the weather sense, guess you could say. The first snowfall,

I'd be faking illness, if only so I didn't have to feel it or see it.

"So, talk to me, kid. How are things?"

I shrugged. "Fine."

"Fine? That's it?"

I *could* tell him things if I wanted. About how Jo's boyfriend was off at college now. How he'd broken things off with Jo by sending her a sex tape of him and the other girl.

Jo had come into my room that same night and told me what had happened. She'd been holding one of her mom's big bottles of wine, guzzling it like water. She hadn't been crying though. If anything, she'd looked dead. She'd told me that she wished I would've killed him, and I'd known then we were back to being okay.

"Everything's all right." I went with that, setting my temple against the glass.

"School good?"

I shrugged. "Guess so."

When I thought about school, I only thought about one thing: Bex Capone.

God, she was infuriating. The girl didn't ever stop talking. And most days, I didn't ever want to stop listening to her either—which was why she pissed me off so much. She babbled to me, laughed, smiled, questioned why I rarely talked too. Forced me out of my comfort zone when she did it. She accepted me for what I was: a good lab partner.

I'd developed a fascination with her. Nothing big, nothing like things had been with Eve either, but something I wasn't used to. Something calm and comforting. Something that made me feel too damn good. It was like when I was around her, I was an equal—not Cult Boy. Not the guy who let his life partner die. And not the guy whose father had tried to kill him either.

"And the Donahues? They good?" Simon jumped in.

"No, actually." Now *this* was something I could talk about. "*He's* never home, and his wife is usually in her room, drinking. It's not good."

Simon grunted and rubbed a hand across his jaw. I thought he'd ask more questions, but instead he sat unfazed. "And Jo?"

I glared at him. "She's still alive, isn't she?"

Another grunt, this time followed up with a long-suffering sigh. I got on his nerves as much as he got on mine. But we had each other. And that was more than I'd had for a while now.

We finished the drive without another word, pulling into a parking space by the front door ten minutes later.

"Classy-looking place." Simon shut off his truck.

"Wouldn't ask for anything else." I opened the door and got out, noting that there was only one other car in the lot besides Simon's. I'd never seen this place before. Either that, or I'd never noticed it. The Donahues didn't go this way because they considered it the bad part of town. For me, though, this place felt more like home than their place.

Bars sat on both sides of the diner. One named Vic's, the other just saying *Tavern*. The diner itself was old-looking, with duct tape on the doors and white, peeling paint. But the sign said, *The best food this side of the Mississippi River*, and I believed it.

The door jingled when we stepped inside. Simon pointed to a booth in the back, and the waitress winked at him and said she'd be right with us.

We sat across from one another, the red vinyl screeching when we got settled. Simon grabbed the menu from behind the napkin holder, handing me the other. I opened it, not really in the mood for anything Thanksgiving-related.

"I hate turkey," Simon said, sliding his glasses on. "It tastes like skunk."

I snorted. He was really the only person who could make me laugh, go figure.

"How do you know what skunk tastes like?" I asked.

He shrugged.

When the waitress came by, we told her what we wanted. Meatloaf for Simon, pancakes for me. After she left to get our drinks, Simon leaned over the table, hands folded and wearing a frown that sent a spike of nerves through my body.

"What?" I asked.

He looked down at his hands. "Noah's outta jail."

I blinked and sat up straight. "He is?"

"Yeah." He cleared his throat. "About a month ago actually. Apparently, they didn't have enough to charge him with since the others they found from Children of His Mercy all talked about him like he was a saint."

My stomach twisted into knots, and I leaned back against the booth, not sure how I was feeling. My only decent living relative—the guy who'd taken care of me and treated me a hell of a lot better than Emmanuel ever had—was out of prison, yet he hadn't once tried to contact me.

Maybe I deserved that. Maybe this was all just karma's doing.

I messed with my straw, trying to act like I didn't care. "Do you know where he is?"

Simon nodded, not meeting my eyes. "He's still messed up, after everything that happened, and I—"

"And what, *I'm* not messed up?" I curled my lip, ready

to get up and tell him to go suck a giant pile of dicks because I wasn't playing the *poor Noah* game. Just like I'd never played the *poor Simon* game either.

They didn't know real pain and suffering. They didn't live with the scars on their backs and hands like I did, constantly reminded of the hell I'd gone through and everything I'd lost.

"I didn't say that." He leaned back and folded his arms. "Let me finish before you go all bitch mode on me, kid."

"You're an asshole," I growled out.

"Never claimed to be anything but." He winked. I wanted to tear off his eyelid.

Who was I kidding though? Even if Noah wanted custody of me, I wouldn't go with him. He'd remind me too much of that night I'd lost her. It should've been that way with Simon too, but he wasn't the guy I'd known at Children of His Mercy anymore.

"Anyway, he's gone south for a while to do some digging."

"Digging?" I frowned. "For what?"

Simon blew out a slow breath, his eyes meeting mine and holding them for a long minute.

"What?" I snapped.

"I haven't been a hundred percent honest with you, kid."

My heart skipped. But before I could open my mouth and ask what the hell he was talking about, the diner doors opened and three people walked in.

Two women, dressed in jeans and crop tops.

And a girl in jeans and a sweater so long it covered her knees. Long brown hair sat over one of her shoulders in a braid, and a flash of heat filled my face and chest.

Bex. Wearing a braid.

My throat dried up.

Simon looked over his shoulder, staring. "You know them?"

"Shut up." I sunk deeper into the booth.

If she saw me, she'd say hi. And if she said hi, I'd have to say it back and then introduce her to Simon. We weren't supposed to talk outside Chemistry class, damn it. I was there to help her pass the class, and she was there to help me forget about my shit life for fifty minutes of my day—because that was all the time I'd allow myself not to think about Eve.

"I gotta piss." Head bowed, I ran to the bathroom, trying to get my shit under control. The universe was damn unfair.

Five minutes went by. I leaned back against the wall. Then ten minutes, then twenty. I slid to the floor, not thinking about how clean or dirty it was. I just...I needed to wait this out. Simon would understand. I'd text him and—

My phone buzzed, and I knew who it was before I answered.

Simon: They left.

I blew out a breath, not understanding what that sinking feeling in my gut meant. This was what I wanted. No take backs—

Simon: Food's getting cold.

I didn't text him back. Just stood, washed my hands, and left, hoping he wouldn't say nothing when I sat back down. But hope for me was about as thin as paper, and Simon didn't know how to take a hint.

"Wanna tell me who that was?" he asked, sipping his soda and wearing a smartass smirk.

"No." I poured syrup on my pancakes, then took a bite.

"Not even a name?"

I shook my head again.

"All right, then. You wanna keep your secrets, then I'll keep mine."

I stopped mid-chew and glared at him.

"Thought so." His smile grew so wide it hurt to look at. "Now, spill it."

"Asshole." But I did end up telling him, even if there wasn't nothing significant to tell. She was just a girl. Smart, snarky, funny, beautiful...

Shit.

"Was that so hard?" He grinned.

"Yes." More than he'd ever know. "Your turn."

Leaning back against the table, Simon took his time to answer. Drinking his Coke, then slurping in that annoying way when the glass was empty.

"Come on, Simon."

"Sorry." He cleared his throat and set the glass on the table. "So, you asked if I knew where Noah was."

"Yeah." I took a bite of my pancake, then picked up my glass of milk. I took a drink, set it on the table, and tried to ignore how badly my hands shook. "Where is he?"

He wiped his lips with a paper towel and sighed. "He's with your mom, kid. She's in a mental facility not too far from Children of His Mercy."

CHAPTER 37: MIDNIGHT
JANUARY 2022

IT WAS Mrs. Donahue's fortieth birthday party. Half the town was supposed to show up. And even though I didn't want to deal with it, I knew I couldn't avoid it.

Jo had said her friends were all coming over, and I wasn't lying when I said that made me feel even worse. Because Jo's *friends* meant Bex too. And if she showed, I'd be a damn mess.

That girl crawled under my skin—burrowed like an itch I wanted to scratch on a daily basis, never-ending, despite telling her she annoyed me every chance I could get. Since Thanksgiving, I'd tried to put distance between us because I didn't like how I felt when I was with her, or even when I saw her. I found myself feeling alive and ready for everything I'd sworn I'd never want again.

Regardless of my plan to keep my distance, I still saw her every time I turned a corner at that damn school. Those endless brown eyes that reminded me of chocolate —a rarity for me, even when I hadn't been at Children of His Mercy. The worst part was I'd started to notice other things I shouldn't have about her. Like the only time she ever smiled was when it was at me.

Out of everything, that messed me up the most.

I stepped out into the hallway, dressed in pair of black pants and a white button-down shirt with a red tie. The whole thing choked me and made me feel like I was back in that brown wool uniform I was forced to wear at Children of His Mercy. Mrs. Donahue had told me I needed to make a good impression on tonight's guests because apparently, they all thought I was a bad influence on the town after what I'd done to Jo's ex.

I didn't care what people thought of me. I was eighteen now. An adult. The only reason I hadn't left this place yet was because of Simon and what he'd told me about my mom. Apparently, she was getting better every day and that much closer to being a mom again. It sucked I couldn't go see her. But Simon had told me it was for the best.

There was an end in sight. I just couldn't see it clear enough yet.

"Wow, looking sharp." Jo walked out of her room at the same time as I did, her lips painted red, wearing a tiny red dress that didn't cover up much. She looked nothing like Eve—but also everything like her at the same time.

"Thanks," I said, running a hand along the back of my neck.

"Your tie's crooked," she said, stepping closer. She straightened it for me, her palm running down the center when she finished.

I cleared my throat, not liking her touch. It didn't feel right.

The doorbell rang. "Sounds like people are starting to show," she said.

I swallowed hard, nervous at the thought.

"You know, Eve hated this kind of stuff too."

I stiffened.

Jo looked down the long stairs as she continued to talk. "She'd usually stay in her room all night and watch TV." She rolled her eyes and laughed a little. "Mom would get so pissed about it. She didn't understand why she couldn't be more like me. Social and outgoing..." She shook her head and looked at me again.

This was the first time Jo had casually talked about her twin, and the pain in her voice was like a knife in my gut.

"Jo..." I whispered when she finished. "I-I'm sorry I couldn't save her."

She looked up at me, sniffled a little, then smiled, even as a tear fell down her cheek. "My sister didn't want to be saved. Not after our brother died." A shrug. "She made her choice, and we weren't it. No need to apologize when her own family couldn't do anything for her."

I shut my eyes and let my shoulders sag. "She loved you."

"I wish I believed that."

"Why don't you?" I looked at her again, eyes narrowing. "She talked about you a lot, said she missed you."

Jo reached her hand up and touched my face, wiped a stray tear from my cheek with her thumb that I didn't even know was there. Her palm was as soft as Eve's, but at the same time it felt all wrong again. Her vibe, her smile, even her smell was off.

I swallowed and took a step back, needing distance again.

She frowned at me and let her hand fall to her side. "Don't beat yourself up any more than you already have,

Midnight. Just *live* for her instead of living in regret. It'll kill you if you stay buried in the past. Trust me."

I nodded in agreement, though I didn't necessarily agree. What I did with my grief and regrets wasn't anyone's business.

Our eyes held for a little too long. There was something different about Jo tonight. Something softer yet more conniving at the same time. I didn't like the way it made me feel, how she looked at me. Like there were bugs crawling all over my skin, burrowing.

"We should get downstairs," I said.

Ignoring me, she stepped closer again, taking my hand in hers and setting it against her chest—a spot without material. Wide eyes searched mine, and I realized right away what was happening. We weren't sharing grief here. Jo was trying to manipulate me for something. And it took literally thirty seconds for me to figure out what that was when she started to talk.

"Let's go somewhere tonight. You and me. I know you see me and think of me as my sister, but I can be better for you than she ever was."

I held my breath, body stiff.

The ends of our shoes touched at the same time a flair of wild filled her eyes. I tried to pull my hand away, but she shook her head. "You like me. I like you. We can help each other feel better in a lot of ways, Midnight."

I started to shake my head, but a voice interrupted from the top of the stairs.

"Jo!" Mrs. Donahue called from the bottom step. "Your friends are here, sweetie."

Unfazed, it seemed, she looked me in the eyes and smiled with teeth as she said, "Okay, Mom. We'll be down soon."

I snapped my hand back but said nothing. If I did, I was pretty sure it'd cause a war.

She was really going there with me. Her sister's life partner—the one I'd taken a blood oath with... Jo was trying to get me to be to her what I'd been to Eve.

Jaw set, I turned away and started down the stairs, feeling her stare on my back the entire time. I had to get away—far away. Now I had two people to avoid, and that shit wasn't cool.

"That's not a no," she said behind me, laughing, like everything was one big joke. Maybe to her it was. But to me, she'd just crossed a line.

BEX WASN'T at the party. Not that I was looking for her. If anything, I was trying to lie as low as possible, if only so I didn't have to see or deal with Jo and whatever was going on with her.

By the time everyone had left, it was three in the morning. Mrs. Donahue was long passed out somewhere in her room, and I hadn't seen her husband for an hour—probably because he'd slid out the back door with a girl who didn't look much older than I was. I was really starting to hate that man.

Because I couldn't sleep—mostly due to the fact that Jo and her friends were still up and being loud as hell—I decided to be helpful in the kitchen. I stacked dishes and crap into the sink. Food sat out untouched and uncovered, like everyone was willing to let it rot for nothing. Coming from the way I'd lived with my mom, that only pissed me off.

"We have a crew coming in tomorrow to do all that," Mrs. Donahue said from behind me. "Just leave it."

I looked right, finding her standing there in a robe as she stared out the door I'd seen her husband leave out of. She was smoking a cigarette too—something I'd never seen her do before.

She turned just in time to catch me looking, her lips flattening out. For a second, I thought she was gonna yell at me. But she didn't.

"You did a good job tonight, Midnight."

My face grew hot from her compliment. I'd actually done nothing tonight, other than stay in a corner and talk to people who occasionally came up to me thinking I was part of the help. Nobody knew who I was or even really looked at me, so I didn't see why she'd freaked out about me needing to make an impression.

"My mom's the one who lives in Georgia," she said out of the blue, taking a seat at one of the breakfast bar tables. "She's who we sent Evie to live with."

Evie.

She'd called her Evie.

"I didn't want her to go, but her father insisted on it. Saying we couldn't get past our grief of losing Luke with her around, always begging for attention."

Locking my jaw, I stared at the sink. So Eve getting sent away had been Mr. Donahue's fault, then. I was starting to hate that man more and more.

"She was my sweet girl. So smart and kind. It's no surprise she went to God after everything, seeing as how her own family couldn't support her through things."

My throat burned when I swallowed. Slowly, so as not to draw attention to myself, I turned and faced her, arms folded with my hip against the countertop. But Mrs. Donahue wasn't there—at least not in the emotional sense. She stared down at her burning cigarette, lost in her head.

"I'm the one who called the FBI, you know. Simon, in particular. He and I grew up together."

I blinked. She'd known Simon. She was the reason he'd gone in. Why the hell hadn't he told me?

"He was always so charming and willing to get people to do what he wanted them to. So it was no surprise he'd been able to be a big shot within a month of being at that...*place*."

"Children of His Mercy."

She looked up at me but said nothing in response.

I winced.

She curled her upper lift, glaring at me. "She was with him five months before you got there. Did you know that?"

"I...didn't know." She'd never told me. I'd always assumed she'd gotten there around the same time I did.

"That man brainwashed her. Tricked her into thinking he had a miracle cure for grief. Not even my own mother could find fault in the situation when the two of them started spending so much time together."

"W-who?" I managed.

"T-that leader, Emmanuel. He poisoned her, promised her things that her own family couldn't, and then..."

She screamed and took her arm, shoving everything off the counter with it. It was like she'd exploded—sobbing, crying, taking out everything she could find with her. Glass smashed against the wall, and plates of food followed, sliding down cupboard doors too. The floor was covered with liquid, and she slipped the second she stood up, landing on her back with a cry.

"Mrs. Donahue." I rushed after her at the same time Jo, Carson, and Gia all appeared in the kitchen entry. "You're bleeding." Her hands were covered in blood, soaking her robe and the floor.

I reached for a towel, trying to help, but she pulled her leg back and kicked me in the shins. "Don't touch me," she screamed. "It's your fault she's not here. You're the reason it didn't work out. Simon told me all about what happened between you and her. If you hadn't showed up and ruined everything she'd be here tonight, with me."

"Mom," Jo jumped in, rushing her. "Stop it."

My eyes grew wide as I hovered over her. Something sharp stabbed me in the gut at the same time. I looked at her, feeling gazes on me—Jo's, Carson's, Gia's. But when Mrs. Donahue's eyes met mine again, I felt like dying.

"I…" I backed away. "I'm so sorry."

"Midnight," Jo said. "Hey, she's not feeling good right now. She doesn't mean—"

"Shut up, Jo," her mom said, glaring at me. "You know it's true, but you're too sucked into him like she was to think otherwise."

My gaze shot to Jo, whose face was red and covered with tears. Ignoring me, she bent down beside her mom and said, "Okay, Mommy. I believe you. You're right."

Seconds later, Mrs. Donahue focused her crazed eyes on Jo, mouth making a wide O. "Evie?" she cried out, wrapping her arms around her daughter's waist and pulling her to her chest. "Evie, I'm so glad you're home. I missed you so much, sweetie. Are you hungry? I can fix you that cheese soup you love so much."

My throat closed off.

Blood. So much blood. On hands and on the back of Jo's dress, her skin…

Glass and tears and pain.

Slowly, I walked toward the entryway as calm and as quietly as I could, passing Gia and Carson, ignoring their words. I was too numb to care. The truth was right there in black and white for everyone to see, always had been. Mrs. Donahue was the only one who'd admitted it first.

It *was* my fault that Eve was dead.

And it always would be.

CHAPTER 38: MIDNIGHT

JANUARY 2022

THREE DAYS after the Mrs. Donahue's birthday party was when everything else in my life started to fall apart. Noah had stopped replying to Simon's calls about my mom. And when he called the facility she was staying at, they said there was no record of a Cora or April Turner staying there. Nobody there had even fit her description either. Apparently, the majority of the patients they saw were people my age.

That meant only one thing: Noah had lied to Simon. Noah, who I'd once trusted with my life. My own uncle.

"You there, kid?" Simon said on the other end of the line.

I blew out a breath. "Yeah. I'm here."

"All right, well. I'll figure this out, don't stress. Got guys looking all over for them."

Too late is what I wanted to say but didn't. I *was* stressed. I was worried and anxious. Wondering too, what was next for me. Because if Simon and my mom and my uncle wanted nothing to do with me, then I really was on my own.

We said goodbye after that. I didn't bother mentioning everything that'd gone down here. How, after her breakdown, Mrs. Donahue had spent most of her time in her room, and that the only person allowed in there was Jo. Mr. Donahue had moved out of the main house and into what he'd called the mother-in-law quarters—a small miniature like house that sat in their yard about fifteen feet from the main house. Said he planned to stay there until his *wife* got her shit together. I doubted that'd be anytime soon, especially when he was a lot of the problem, if I had to guess.

My only saving grace right now was the one thing I'd been trying to avoid. The girl with the chocolate eyes and the smart mouth.

Goddamn Bex Capone. I wished she would've let me be miserable.

Shaking my head, I swiped a set of car keys and left through the garage, not bothering to ask permission. If I went to see her, or even sat outside of her house, it'd be creepy as hell. But I gave myself permission to at least drive by. Check on her. Make sure she was safe—because that's what I did. Technically that was probably stalking, but I was already messed up as is, so adding a little more shade to my name wasn't a big deal. Or so I told myself.

"I am definitely going to hell for this too."

In the garage there were four cars in total, and I stood behind each one, frowning. I didn't know which one these keys belonged to because they were all Audis, just different colors. I clicked the unlock button, and it brought me to a white one. It's what Jo drove. I slid inside and started it right up. I didn't have my license, but whenever he showed up to visit, Simon took me out and had started teaching me. He'd called me a natural.

When I started to back out of the garage, a body filled

my rearview mirror. I slammed on the brakes, yelling, "Shit!"

Jo rounded the car on the passenger side and opened the door.

"Drive," was all she said to me when she got in.

"What are you doing?"

"I said, *drive!*"

With a heavy sigh, I took off, upset I couldn't go to Bex's place but knowing it was also for the better. If she saw me, I'd have a whole lot of explaining to do.

I took the back roads out of town and headed to the Donahue barn. Jo hadn't had a party there since July, but she'd said that was going to change come this fall. Apparently, her mom had a decorating crew who'd been remodeling the inside over the last month or so. It was obvious she hadn't been a part of it, though, because I didn't think I ever saw her leave the house.

"You think that's a good idea?" I asked, damn well knowing it wasn't.

"What, to have a party?"

I nodded.

"Hell yeah." She laughed. "Just as long as you won't be there it'll be awesome."

I bit the inside of my cheek to keep myself in check. She didn't mean what she'd said. And even if she had, it didn't matter. Because I wouldn't go. Didn't want to go in the first place.

Unless Bex would be there.

"Shit," I muttered under my breath, parking down the hill from the barn, staring up at the dark shadows of it, and knowing full well I'd go if she made an appearance.

Jo turned to me with lifted brows. "What?"

"Nothing." I shook my head.

She snorted under her breath and said, "Whatever. Fuck life, right? It's not worth it." Then with a wink, she jumped out and ran up the hill toward the barn, the headlights of the car guiding her way.

My stomach sank as I watched her. She held her arms out like she was flying through the night, and from inside, even with the heater on, I could hear her cackle like a witch. She didn't use the steps. Nothing Jo did was ever easy or conventional. If it had been snowing, I was almost betting she would've face-planted.

Unlike her, I took the stairs, reaching the front doors a minute later. I pulled the handle, surprised it was open, and stepped into the dark barn. I couldn't find her right away, so I started to look around, jumping in place when the heaters kicked on. I didn't see the point of warming this place up. We weren't gonna be here long.

"Jo?" I called out, flinching when it echoed.

A spotlight flickered on with a pop seconds later, focusing on the stage. Or should I say on *Jo*, who stood there...in nothing but her bra and underwear.

"Jesus, Jo." I looked away.

"I've been waiting until tonight to do this," she said. "Hell, I've been waiting months for you to notice me enough to do this."

I stepped back, eyes on the floor. "What are you talking about?"

She jumped off the stage and stalked toward me. From the corner of my eye, I saw her bra fall to the floor. I gulped, and backed away even more, only stopping when I ran into a table.

"It's no surprise we're both a little messed up in the head, right? After going through what we did."

I said nothing. Moved nowhere. I squeezed my eyes shut and tried not to listen. But she was too close. Too loud. And the more she pressed against me, the colder I felt.

"And two messed up people should be together, don't you think?"

I pulled in a long breath, holding it until I felt dizzy. She hadn't said that. She didn't *want that*. She didn't want me or this or us—because two wrongs didn't make a right.

"Get your clothes on." My voice was as cold as my chest.

"You want me though. I know you do. I felt it on New Year's, and I feel it now. We belong together."

"No." I gritted my teeth.

She slid her hands into the front pocket of my hoodie, then stood on her tiptoes to whisper into my ear, "You want me like you wanted Eve. Maybe more."

I gritted my teeth. "Stop it."

"I read the papers about what happened, you know." Through my hoodie pocket, she ran her knuckles up and down my stomach. "I found them in my dad's office. They'd never been opened and were sealed shut with a sticker labeled *FBI*. Funny, huh? That my dad hadn't even bothered to look inside."

"Jo," I warned again.

She pulled her hands out from my sweatshirt and slid them up and under my sweatshirt, scraping nails across my bare skin at the same time. "You were supposed to have sex with her, have a baby with her, but you didn't. Why is that?"

I stared out a window from over her shoulder, silent.

She slid her hands to my jeans and popped the button. "Was she not pretty enough for you? Or was it because she was a virgin?" She went for my zipper next, taking her time.

I was frozen there, feeling like I was having an out-of-body experience.

She tucked a hand into my boxers and pressed her lips to my neck as she said, "I'm not a virgin though. Which means if you're scared of hurting me, don't be. I can take it. I can be what you need, Midnight. I can be what my sister was never good enough to be."

"I said stop it." I grabbed her wrist and yanked her hand out of my pants, then rushed around her to the stage where her clothes were, eyes and nose hot with the need to cry.

I wasn't normal, damn it. Any guy would have been with Eve. Any guy wouldn't have cared about where they were or who was in charge of them. Any guy would've given her what she'd wanted, especially if it'd meant keeping her alive. The same went with Jo. A beautiful look-alike to Eve, offering herself up to me.

Yet the thought of ever touching her disgusted me.

I swiped up Jo's clothes and tossed them at her from across the room. They landed ten feet or so short, but still. "You're not Eve. You never will be Eve. And if anyone deserved to go to that place it wasn't her. It was you."

Jo laughed—head tilted back, chin to the sky, laughed. She took her time and approached her clothes but didn't even bother to pick them up or put them on. Instead, she threw them back at me and said, "Screw you, Cult Boy. You obviously have a limp dick and were too afraid to show her. Which is why she died. Why *you* let her die."

Without getting dressed, she flipped me the finger, turned, and left the barn.

———

I CAUGHT a bus about a five-minute walk from the property. Somewhere along the way, Jo had taken the keys, then decided to leave me there alone. It didn't piss me off, honestly. It worried me. She seemed more messed up than I was for once. Not to mention I'd said one of the worse things ever to her. If something happened to her, I'd...

I shook my head, walking down the short lane leading to the Donahue house. Instead of heading inside, I decided to go to go see Mr. Donahue. He was the only person left in this house who didn't hate me—I didn't think—and I had to talk to someone about this.

"Come in," he called from the other side of the door when I'd finished knocking.

I opened it, holding my breath, not knowing what or who I'd find inside. He didn't keep his life a secret from anyone anymore, it seemed.

I stepped in and wiped my feet on a rug, before deciding to take them off altogether. "Mr. Donahue? It's me, Midnight."

"In here, son."

I flinched, hating when he called me that—probably just as much as I'd hated when Emmanuel had done it. But this wasn't about me right now.

I found him in his living room, feet kicked up on a coffee table, drinking something bubbly and clear from a short glass.

When he saw me, he patted the couch next to him. "Come. Sit."

I did, despite my nerves. Even after living in his house for a while, I didn't fully trust this guy. Eve hadn't specifically said much about her father to me, but that didn't mean much because she'd barely talked about anyone, other than her brother, Luke, and occasionally her sister.

I stuffed my hands inside my hoodie pocket and approached the couch. "Um, I can't stay long. But I just wanted to talk to you about Jo."

"Sure, sure. What's going on with her?" He looked at his glass. "You want one?"

"Uh, no. Thanks." I licked my dry lips and stared at my hand scars when I sat.

"All right, what's up with my princess, hmm?"

"She and I went on a drive a while ago." I swallowed. "To the barn actually."

"That's fine. You can go there anytime you'd like. Our world is your world. Even after what happened there in July —which wasn't your fault. You were just protecting her. It's understandable after everything you went through."

He was missing the point, though I didn't say so. If I went off on him about how shitty of a dad I thought he was, then there was no way he'd listen to me.

"She was acting strange, sir. I think she might hurt herself."

Silence filled the air. He didn't breathe. Didn't drink. Didn't even move. I waited a second to look at him, but only because I wasn't gonna sit there forever.

I just wished I hadn't.

He stared at me with twisted lips before he spoke. "Look. She's upset, yeah. But Jo's nothing like Luke or Evie. She's built differently and able to withstand everything life throws at her. She's like me." He leaned back against the couch and set his ankle on one of his knees.

"But I'm still worried she's gonna—"

"Let me guess." He smirked. "She was talking bad about her life tonight, correct?"

I nodded.

"And did she, at some point, take her clothes off as well?"

My skin grew cold, but I still said nothing.

He winked again, waving me off. "She does that. It's an attention-seeking thing. She even did it with one of my employees. Someone who'd taken an interest in her."

His employee. As in a guy he worked with, who was probably five years older than her at least.

"Only problem was he was stupid enough to fall for it. Then she told me, and I had to fire the young man." He *tsked*. "Shame too. He was one of the best computer programmers I had." He stared at the TV finishing his second glass of—I looked at the bottle—scotch.

A knock sounded on the door then. He pulled at his tie, loosening it, then rolled up the sleeves of his dress shirt before patting my knee. I stared at him, my mouth practically on the floor.

"Hate to cut this short, but I've got a friend coming over."

I gritted my teeth. He smiled wider. "Trust me, son, when I say you'll understand what it's like someday, you will." Then he walked to the door and opened it up to reveal the same woman I'd seen him leave with the night of New Year's.

And I'd thought my family life was dysfunctional.

When he said goodbye, I ignored him and took off toward the house, not stopping until I hit the garage first. It was open. And when I saw all four cars in there, I sighed in relief, though not for long. I needed to see her, make sure she was okay—that she was alive and breathing, most of all. It didn't take me long to track her down thankfully.

Just outside the window of the living room, I saw her,

head on her mom's lap. Mrs. Donahue was running her fingers through her hair, and the two of them were laughing and pointing at the TV. It was the perfect mother-daughter moment, yet the view killed me all the same because Eve, goddamn it, should've been there too.

CHAPTER 39: BEX

FEBRUARY 2022

FOR THE FIRST time in my life, I'm taking a bus to school. Not because I think it'll be some joyous trip with my lovely peers but because Midnight rides it every morning, and I want to prove to him how I am, in fact, in this thing on all fronts. Granted, we haven't exactly declared what we are. Nor have we talked about what happens when we actually get to school.

I haven't thought about what I'm going to say when we see Jo, but I know I can't go on not telling her how I feel. She can hate him all she wants, but I'm unable to. Because I know him. And I'm pretty sure I'm falling in love with him too.

I smile when I spot him in the last row on the left. His head's against the glass window and his eyes are shut. He looks like a little boy, lost in a dream, and I don't want to wake him. Still, I'm on a soon-to-be moving bus with two to-go cups of hot chocolate, so... yeah. He kinda doesn't have a choice.

"Good morning, sunshine." I plop down onto the seat beside him, grinning.

His eyes widen at the sight of me, and he immediately sits up straight, rubbing the heels of his hands against his eyes. "W-What are you doing here?"

I hand him one of the cups and shrug. "Hanging out with this really cute dude who's been sleeping in my bed recently."

Midnight gives me a crooked smile, the kind he pairs unknowingly with his infamous pink blush.

"You know where I can find him?" I tip my head to one side as I lean back against the hard seat.

He takes one of the cups of hot chocolate from my hands and sips instead of answering. No surprise there. But the blush on his cheeks is now covering his neck too.

"There's extra whipped cream inside." I point to the top. When he stares back at me, I giggle because there's a line of it on his upper lip. I reach into my book bag and pull out a tissue, not asking as I reach to wipe it off.

The second I touch his mouth, though, he wraps his free hand around my wrist and stops me.

I cringe. "Did I cross another line?"

He licks his lips, trailing his tongue across the white foam. I shiver at the view, wishing I could've done it for him. Then instead of answering me, he leans in and presses his lips to mine—slow and careful like he fears I'll go *poof* in the air.

It's a brief kiss—lingering but sweet. It's also one of those perfect kisses I'll remember for the rest of my life because this feels like a beginning. Something new that I didn't ever think I'd want, let alone find.

When he pulls back, I can't help but sigh as I stare at his mouth. "Let's skip school and make out in my bed all day."

He bows his head and laughs so softly I almost don't hear it.

Score one for this loser.

A few sips of his hot chocolate later and his fingers slide between mine. I watch as his thumb strokes the surface, and it's the first time, I realize, we can just be together like this.

If this is what it's like to truly be in a relationship, or even if this is just some sort of prequel, I can see the appeal because I feel like I'm soaring.

"Why'd you go quiet?" he whispers.

I lay my head on his shoulder and close my eyes. "Just thinking about things."

"What things?" He presses his lips against the top of my head.

"Like Jo and how mad she's going to be when she sees us together," I say.

"We don't have to tell her."

I kick my feet back and forth in front of me. "I hate keeping secrets from people. Hate it even more when people keep secrets from me."

Midnight sighs.

"What?" I lift my head from his shoulder to look at him.

"I don't know if we should tell her. Can we just...wait?"

My stomach sinks into my toes. And the flutters I felt are all nosediving into my feet. Still, who am I to argue with him about something so silly.

"If that's what you want," I say. "Or maybe I'll tell her separately or something."

He looks the other way.

"Midnight?"

He still doesn't speak. Or look at me, for that matter. And suddenly all the promises of possibilities slide away completely until there's only ash left.

"Fine. We won't tell her at all." Just the thought leaves me cold inside. Angry too. "But you at least have to tell me why she hates you."

"It's complicate—"

"No." I give my head a fast shake, annoyed now. "It's not complicated at all, actually. You tell me, I say nothing about knowing—unless it's hugely life altering or something."

He blows out a breath, staying quiet. And for the first time since knowing him and what he's like, his silence and non-answers are kind of pissing me off.

Needing space, I scoot away from him, let go of his hand too. He looks down at his empty fingers, flexing them, but not once does he look at me. Not even when I start to speak.

"Why won't you talk to me about your present but will tell me everything about your past? Like, I don't even know where you live or who you live with, when you've been spending the night at my house, in my bed for days."

"Bex," he says, covering his face with both hands. "I can't—"

"You can, damn it." I huff. "It's words, Midnight. Say them."

"Fine." He throws his hands up in the air, voice growing louder. "You wanna know where I live? It's with Jo and her whole entire fucked-up family."

I blink, thinking I heard him wrong.

"And you wanna know why I live there? It's because Jo's sister was *Eve*."

The bus stops then, slamming our bodies forward against the seat in front of us. Everyone around us has gone quiet, and there are way too many lingering eyes for my comfort. Still, the only thing I can do is stare at him.

Breathe. Then keep staring, until my mouth finally decides to start working again.

"Jo doesn't have any siblings," I say.

He drops his head back against the seat. "She does, Bex. Or she did, I should say."

"Did?"

"Not only is Eve dead but their brother too. He died in a car accident. Eve tried to kill herself because she thought it was her fault. And because her parents are a bunch of losers, they sent her away to live with her religious grandma in Georgia because they couldn't deal with it. *That's* where she met Emmanuel. And that's why she was at Children of His Mercy."

I cover my mouth, speaking through my fingers. "No. Jo would've told...me..."

The more I think about it, the more I realize his truth is actually the truth. Jo has told me next to nothing about her family. I've never been to her house either. Never met her parents, never rode in her car, never even talked about anything remotely close to her family.

"Why didn't you say anything?" I whisper, struggling to stay calm.

He bites the inside of his cheek and looks out the window. "Just go, Bex. I'm not going to school today."

"Fine." I reach for his hand. "W-we can ditch together, then go somewhere to talk about things and—"

"Leave. Please. I wanna be alone." He jerks his hand back and turns away from me, staring out the window.

I swallow down my immediate guilt, realizing I have nothing to feel guilty about. It's not fair for me to be ignored when I've put him first for over a month now.

"Look. I don't care what Jo says. I don't even care why she's mad at you either. She is not my sister or my keeper. And I'm going inside, right now, to tell her, you got me?"

Midnight stays silent. Doesn't move and refuses to look my way still.

"The silent game, huh? That's all I get?" I laugh at the same time the tears start to fall. Shaking my head, I stand with my bookbag still on my shoulders, lingering only long enough to say, "Whatever. I'm getting to the bottom of this. Then you and I are going to meet at the pond later and talk it through because that's what people do in relationships. They co-mmun-i-cate."

People start to get off, one after another. Whispers fly off the walls of the bus like messenger birds. My stomach churns because his silence is beating me up inside. And the longer I stand there, looking like a fool, the angrier I get.

Turning, I start my way down the aisle, chin high. Someone asks me if I'm okay—I've never seen them in my life—but just those words send more tears streaming down my face. It isn't until I reach the door do I finally hear him speak.

"I wanted to tell you, Bex," he says just loud enough for me to hear. "But I'm their dirty little secret."

I'm the last person on the bus, other than the driver, but everyone's looking back at me from the ground like I'm the keeper of all life's secrets, not just Midnight's.

"I'm the replacement son," he continues. "The reason for their daughter's death too. I'm the last-place trophy they never fucking asked for."

I press my lips together so hard I wind up biting them with my teeth. But instead of waiting for him or even turning around to offer the comfort I'm dying to give, I step off the bus and head straight to the doors of school, not stopping until I hit the third floor.

Sweat drips down my temples and rage burns in my body like a wildfire. When I spot Jo at her locker, waiting like she always does with Gia and Carson, I don't stop to think about what to say. It just spills out of me like a waterfall.

"You," I hiss, getting in her face and backing her against the lockers. "I trusted you."

Her eyes widen. For a second, she looks shocked, but it doesn't last long. Jo is not the type of person you want to go against, no matter your social status.

"He told you, didn't he?" She throws her head back and groans. "What an asshole. You should've stayed away from him. He's no good, Bex."

"At least he had the guts to be honest with me."

Her face pales. And a crowd forms around us. Carson says something, Gia too, but I've got them blocked out as I stare back at the girl who'd once called me her future bestie.

"He's also the reason she's dead, you know."

I'm not going to let her tell me some false version of the truth when I heard it straight from him. I may be pissed at the both of them, but Midnight spoke up first, which means I trust him more than her right now.

"No, Jo. Eve *chose* to go there with that man. She picked her fate because your family wouldn't help her."

"Shut up," she hisses, pushing me back by the shoulders.

My chest heaves in and out the more I speak. "You were supposed to be my best friend," I whisper, deciding it's not worth it to scream anymore. I'm so tired. Of everything and anything and everyone. "Why didn't you say anything, huh? About Eve a-and your broth—"

"Don't talk about him." She shoves me back, pushing me so hard I fall. My tailbone cracks the second I hit the floor, and a scream lodges itself inside my throat. All the air rushes from my lungs and the world around me is spinning.

"Jo," Carson gets in front of her. "That's enough."

Gia crouches down beside me, her sad eyes searching my face. "You okay, sweetie?"

Ignoring her and using the adrenaline I have left in me I look around the two of them until I'm locking eyes with Jo again.

"You were supposed to be my best friend, Jo."

Tears stream down her cheeks as she stares at me, but she's wearing a smile too. "Funny you should mention that because I've been rethinking things. I mean, squares break all the time. And you were just a temporary, if not boring, corner of ours."

I blink. My face numbs too. Gia grabs my hands, somehow getting me to my feet, though I don't really feel like I'm standing because I'm in so much pain.

"Don't listen to her right now," she whispers. "She's just got a lot going on at home."

"Home, as in the place she lives at with Midnight?"

Gia cringes but manages a small nod.

"Thought so." I bite my lip to keep the sobs lodged inside my throat. I'm so done crying and feeling like shit. It's why when the ache in my ass turns into a deep throb, to the point where I feel like wigging out, I take Gia's hand in mine and say, "Walk me to the nurse, okay? I think my ass is broken."

CHAPTER 40: BEX

MARCH 2022

I'M LAID up on the couch because my ass—or more specifically my tailbone—is majorly bruised, not broken. Go me.

When the nurses asked me what happened, I told them I'd fallen. And when my mom got there, I told her the same, along with the doctors and anyone else who asked that same question. Telling everyone that Jo pushed me would only cause a whole mess of other issues that I didn't wanna deal with it. Plus, deep down, I don't think it was intentional on her end. If that makes me a pushover, so be it.

All that matters now is that Dad would be proud of me for pushing until I got the whole story I needed.

The truth is, though, it isn't just my ass that's broken but my heart too. Shattered into a million pieces, buried somewhere deep inside of me to the point where I don't know how to go about putting it back together.

This is why I steered clear of friends and dudes in the past. For a fact, I know my past self is saying, *Told you so.*

I don't even have the energy to flip her off.

I haven't heard from Midnight in three days. No more coming in through my window, no more sleeping in my bed. No texts. No phone calls—not that he's a big phone person at all, but still. The only people from school who managed to even care that I'm hurt were Gia and Carson. They even showed up with balloons and cake. On the cake was a triangle.

We don't need her to make a shape, Gia said.

I'd cried like a baby.

Later, when I asked if Jo was okay—because I couldn't hate her completely no matter how much I should have—Carson told me she'd gotten suspended from school for ten days. When I asked why, they'd said it's because she turned herself in five minutes after I left the school.

Why would she do that? I asked.

Gia replied with a shrug and a small smile. *Because that's what friends do.*

I took that with a grain of salt and passed out five minutes after they left. The pain pills were badass because not only did they help me sleep but they also helped me forget the pain inside and out.

Now, two days later, Mom and I are down on the couch together, sharing popcorn and binging romantic dramadies. Mom's all up in her feels and crying about someone's death when the doorbell rings.

"Who's that?" I reach over and pause it.

She sniffs and wipes her nose with the back of her shirt sleeve, then picks up her phone. "No idea." She pockets it and gets up to answer.

When I turn to look, a blast of cold wind shoots through the room, matching my crap mood when I see who it is. Her *friend.* Sam's his name, I think. In one hand he's holding a bouquet of flowers and in the other a bottle of wine. I can't hear what they're saying exactly, but Mom's actions speak louder than words when she hugs him.

Gross. If she's going to date again, then she can do so much better than this dude.

Ignoring their PDA, I go back to stuffing my mouth with popcorn, praying this will be some quick hello-and-goodbye situation.

But my mom's, apparently, got other plans. "You care if Sam joins us?" she asks, coming to stand behind the couch.

I look at her, dead-faced, and her smiles morphs into a frown.

Make him leave, I try my hand at telecommunication, though I'm pretty sure it fails because she mouths, *Stop it right now.*

Whatever.

"How about some wine in the kitchen?" Sam jumps in, his grin wide as he stares between us. "Then I'll leave you lovely ladies alone to finish the show-a-thon."

I snort under my breath as I face the TV again, wondering where this dude even came from if he doesn't know the proper term for movie-watching.

"I could use a glass for sure," Mom pipes in. "Plus I need to put these in water before they wilt."

I roll my eyes. All that worry over the cheap bouquet that probably cost five bucks. Mom must not remember what it's like to be properly wooed by a dude, and I feel bad how she seems to be setting the bar so low with this one.

Once they're in the kitchen, I turn off the movie and settle on the ten o'clock news for a bit, mostly for the weather report. Another snowstorm is supposed to be coming sometime tomorrow, and the thought has my snow-loving heart leaping…until I remember my injury…and the last time it snowed. More specifically, who I'd been with.

Stupid Midnight and his ocean-blue eyes and the way he kisses me when it's cold but keeps sad secrets at the same time. Even though nothing he hid was really any of my business, I still feel like I've been led astray by the two people in my life I trusted the most.

"Ugh."

I flip through the cable channels, not even able to watch the snow report without feeling like I'm going to burst into tears. Instead, I settle on an old cartoon, instantly thrown back in time five or so years when Dad and I used to "hunker down," as he called it, and have Saturday marathons of them when we had nothing else to do.

God, I miss him that man. He'd have the perfect advice for me on how to handle my current situation. Granted, it's an odd one, what with the lies and the cults and his wife's crappy new boyfriend.

I'm zoned out for a while, so much so that I don't notice how quiet it's become in the kitchen until I do. I frown and sit up, as much as my bruised butt will let me, trying to see what's going on. Like I conjured their return, they walk in, clinging to each other. Or more so Mom clinging to Sam. Her eyes are the first thing I notice—how glassy and red they seem. Still, she smiles at me, and I wonder if the quiet was actually them getting it on or something. Not that this old dude could break my mom's back or nothing.

Just the thought has bile forming in my throat.

"You good?" I ask her, ignoring how Sam's arm is

wrapped around her back. More specifically how his hand is grazing the side of her right boob.

"Perfect," she grins lazily, sitting down beside me.

"Your mom's a lightweight," Sam says.

A bite of unease slides its way into my chest from his words. Mom is *not* a lightweight.

I lift the blanket off my lap and allow him to settle my mom next to me. She snuggles close and it's barely seconds later when I hear her start to snore.

My chest grows cold, and I glare at Sam who, instead of leaving, is sitting on the recliner across from us.

"What're we watching?" he asks.

I shut off the TV and frown at him. "Why are you still here?"

He kicks his feet out, smiling as he says, "Because your mom invited me to stay."

"But she's sleeping now, so..."

He shrugs. "I hope you know that I care deeply for your mom."

I laugh a little, though it's more of an annoyed scoff. "Yeah, sure."

He folds his hands on his lap and shakes his head. "The head of every man is Christ, the head of a wife is her husband, and the head of Christ is God."

I blink, wondering if I need to clear out my ears. "Um, sure, buddy. Whatever you say."

"Sweet child. Non-traditionalism in women steers them down the path of unrighteousness, don't you know that?"

"Dude, I don't know what you're talking about, nor do I want to know. I'm tired, I don't know you, and I think you need to leave."

"Your tongue is sharp." He sighs and puts the recliner down. "That will be tough to break."

I try to sit up, but the pain in my ass is getting worse. I look at the clock, realizing I'm an hour late for my pain meds—no wonder.

"Have you ever found the love of Christ before, Bexley?"

"That's not my name." I flinch, maneuvering to the other hip.

"It's beautiful though. And it means luck as well, which I've found quite a lot of recently."

"Yeah, dude. You gotta go. You're in the wrong house because I'm pretty sure my mom's an atheist."

He doesn't move. Instead, he says, "He who is mighty and follows His path shall live a blessed life free of pain."

"I asked you to leave."

Something crawls around inside my stomach. Nerves, fear...something else I can't place. Even still, I can't stop looking at the guy now that he's sitting across from me, mostly because there's something familiar about him I didn't notice before. It's his eyes actually. The color is unique, and I've only ever seen it on one person before.

Until now.

"No," I whisper, feeling my face grow cold at the same time. He's supposed to be dead. Midnight watched his car burn.

"Leave my house," I say again, with more bite than fight. "I'm going to call the police."

Flectere si nequeo superos, Acheronta movebo," he says.

I don't know the words, but I'm pretty sure I know the language.

Latin.

My hands shake when I pull the phone out from under the blanket. As fast as I can, I turn on my screen and start to punch in *nine-one-one.*

"If you're trying to call my son, I'm afraid he won't

answer. He's gone this weekend with Brother Simon." He presses his lips together and studies my phone, one eyebrow lifted higher than the other. "At least I'm assuming that's who you're trying to call from beneath your blanket. Though I could be wrong."

"You *are* wrong." The phone rings, and soon I hear the operator.

"Nine-one-one. What's your emergency?"

Before I can scream the word *help*, he swipes it from my hands and throws it against the wall. Pieces scatter on the floor, glass too.

"You are a stupid lamb," he tells me. "Far more stupid than Eve ever was."

"Screw you," I say.

Even knowing I'm stuck here I won't go down without a fight. This man has murdered people. Abused Midnight so terribly I can't think straight. And if I'm next on his hit list, I won't let him think he's won until he has.

"Bless you, Bexley. This would be so much easier if you just submit to me." Ocean eyes twinkle down at me as he carefully picks up my blanket and sets it over my mom. It's her that he stares at while he speaks this time. "It truly is a shame that my last sacrifice didn't work. But such is the word of Christ and his calling." Slowly, he runs a hand down my mother's face with his knuckles.

I slap his hand away and lie on top of her. "Stay away from her. Don't look at her. Don't touch her. Don't even try to talk to her."

"Oh, sweet, sweet lamb." He crouches down in front of me, sets one hand on my knee. "It's not your mom that I want but you. My son's truest love."

"I'll kill you. And if I don't, Midnight will."

He shuts his eyes and shakes his head, like he's ashamed.

"I know how he sneaks into your window at night," he says. "I watch him from the window when he watches you sleep. Have now for several days. But then he stopped coming, and I got worried that perhaps he's regretted his choice. But when the Lord himself came to me in a dream and told me I was to find you, I knew his love didn't matter in the grand scheme of things."

"You're sick." I spit in his face, wrap my arms around my mom even more. She's breathing. Her chest rises and falls. But she's trapped in her sleep, and I can't get her out.

Please, Mom. I need you. Please wake up.

Sighing, he wipes at the wet mark near his eye with a finger and tsks. "It's a shame you don't have her sweet demeanor."

"Go to hell, you son of a bitch."

He grabs me by the back of the hair, and my scalp burns. I cry out, clawing his wrists, but he's too strong for me. And the more I try to hurt him, the worse the pain gets.

"You do not talk to your Prophet that way, understood?"

I kick him and start to scream. "You're a murderer. What you did to Midnight..."

He slaps me across the cheek, and I fall headfirst onto the ground. I groan, seeing stars when I close my eyes. The spinning causes vomit to pool in my throat.

"I am the reason that you will be accepted through the gates when it's time to meet your maker one day." He sets his foot on the back of my head and applies pressure. "But for now, you have a bigger purpose."

My front tooth cracks, and blood pools inside my

mouth. I gasp, unable to breathe through the pain, no longer able to tell if I'm alive or dead.

The last thing I hear before he picks me up and puts me over his shoulder is, "Now. Be a good little lamb and obey me, Bexley. Because to be the chosen one of such a joyous occasion is a blessing that will grant you eternal life with Him."

CHAPTER 41: MIDNIGHT
MARCH 2022

"THANKS FOR LETTING ME COME," I say to Simon as we drive south down the highway toward Springfield in his truck.

"Sure. Sorry it's not for better reasons though, kid."

I shrug, knowing what he means.

This road trip should've been happening because he found my mom or Noah, not because he's invited me to come meet his girlfriend and spend the weekend with them. I'd needed some space and time away from things to try to figure out what to do next. When I said this to him on the phone a couple days ago, he told me he'd be there to get me Friday.

And here we are.

Problem is we're an hour outside of Altoona and I already can't breathe. Three days has been bad enough without seeing or talking to Bex. But sliding into a different town altogether, one where I can't even drive by her house, might kill me.

Between that and the fact that Jo hurt her, I'm a mess.

Which means only one thing. I don't just like this girl. I love her.

But telling her this when she's so angry at me isn't fair. It'd be like bartering. Giving her promises without being clear about what's been going on during the ten months I've lived here. I also feel guilty as hell. Not necessarily *because* I love her but because I still don't feel like I deserve to be happy.

"You wanna talk about it?" Simon asks.

"Talk about what?"

"Women." He shrugs. "I don't got a lot of experience with them, but I think I'm doing all right."

"No, thanks."

"You might feel better if you do."

"You're not my therapist," I say.

"No. But I'm the closest thing you got to a dad, right? And you're the closest thing I've ever had to a son too."

I press my lips together, not liking the feeling his words cause. It's squishy and gross and...fuck. It's happiness. Simon isn't a happy guy. Neither am I. It's what makes this guardianship work.

"She made you soft." I point to the girl in the picture. The one that's back on his rearview mirror.

The side of his mouth curls, but he doesn't deny it.

"I hate you," I say, rubbing a hand over my mouth.

"You love *her*, though, don't you?" He huffs. "The pushy, annoying girl from the diner you told me about."

My jaw flexes, but I can't deny it. Bex is the only thing in my life that has made me feel worth again. And keeping her with me feels like I'm forcing my bad memories on her too, which is why this is so damn hard to accept what she's giving me—even if she doesn't know what that is yet.

"Yeah. Thought so, kid."

Fifteen more minutes pass. Simon turns up the radio, blasts something country through the speakers. I didn't know he liked that kind of music. Hell, I don't know much of anything about him outside of what we went through and what we're doing now.

"Do you have to know someone to love them, you think?" I ask.

"Nope."

"Really?"

"'Course not. You ever heard of love at first sight?"

"That's fairytale shit."

He laughs. "I thought so too."

I squirm in the seat, my nerves itching, a weird need to spill everything piling up in my throat.

"She doesn't know me," I say. "Except for everything in my past and about what happened."

"You told her all that?"

I nod.

"That's a big step, kid."

"But I didn't tell her anything about where I live or who I live with. That's wrong, so I don't blame her for being mad at me."

"Did she say it was wrong?"

"In a way, I think."

"You think."

I shrug.

He clicks his tongue against the roof of his mouth. "Tell me. Did she say the words *stay away* or *I want nothing to do with you?*"

"No. She pretty much said the opposite."

"There you go."

I wince, knowing he's right. Knowing how unfair it was for Bex that she never learned the truth until it was guilted out of me. And Simon is right. She wasn't pushing me away. Not like I was her.

"You loved Eve." He shrugs. "But were you *in* love with her?"

I don't hesitate. "No. Not like it is with Bex." The love for Eve was comforting, protective and scary at the same time. But the way I feel for Bex is…easy. Warm. Not scary, and something that makes me smile and feel alive. Like I told her before, when I'm with her, I can breathe.

"Look, kid, you've got this heart in you. It's big and tough. Makes you wanna take on everyone else's problems instead of finding solutions for your own. That's why you're struggling with this. Because Eve's family is hurting and you can't do a damn thing to fix it, even though that isn't your responsibility. Plus, the dad's a fucking dickhead."

I jerk my head to look at him. "You know about what's going with him?"

"Of course I do." He scoffs. "Why the hell do you think I've been working so hard to find your mom?"

"I'm eighteen now," I say. "I should be able to be on my own."

"Nah. Age is a number, nothing more. You still need a support system. A family."

I do. But admitting it is embarrassing.

"I couldn't take you before because my life was too busy. But things are changing and dying down. And since I can't find your mom or Noah, I wouldn't mind it if you…"

My phone rings. I pull it out to shut it off because I'm invested in whatever he's about to say. But then I see who's calling.

"Who's that?" Simon asks, his phone ringing at the same time.

Ignoring him, I answer the phone. "Jo? Everything okay?"

"Midnight," she sobs from the other end of the line. I put her on speaker just in time to hear her say, "Y-you need to come home. Something's happened."

———

SIMON SPED the entire way back to Altoona, alternating between calls to his fellow agents and his girlfriend, and the local police. Meanwhile, I was barely holding it together.

I don't know what happened. I came over to apologize. But when I got here, her mom was on the couch and she wouldn't wake up and Bex is gone, and there's blood on the floor... I'd heard enough to understand. Bex been taken, but since her mom was passed out or drugged, we don't know by who.

By the time we pull into Bex's driveway, I'm shaking like a leaf. The truck's barely stopped along the street before I open the door and jump out. Simon cusses at me, saying I won't be any good to anyone if I'm dead or holed up in the hospital with a broken back.

Police are lined up the outside of duplex. Black cars with tinted windows too, just like that night outside of the Children of His Mercy gates. I push through them all, despite yells of protest, and the second I step inside I run to Jo, who's sitting beside an older woman with chocolate eyes that match Bex's. Beside her is some other woman—the one I saw with Bex at the diner on Thanksgiving. These two have to be Bex's mom and the Martha lady she'd mentioned.

The woman, who I'm assuming is Bex's mom, climbs to her feet when she sees me. Jo stands with her, as does the other lady. I flinch at the view, ready for a hand slap or yells. Instead, I get tears and the rush of her small body as she collides against me with a sob.

I shut my eyes, hugging her back.

"You're him," she whispers. "You're Midnight."

My throat swells, and I try like hell not to cry. I pull away, helping her sit back down. Jo cross over to me, her eyes as red as a flame.

"What happened?" I ask.

Her bottom lip starts to shake. But before she can say anything, the front door opens and in walks Mrs. Donahue and Simon.

"Mama," Jo cries at the sight of her, running across the room to leap into her arms.

I frown, looking to Bex's mom again. "What happened?"

"I didn't know. Sam brought wine, and the next thing I know, I wake up, alone, and find pieces of my daughter's hair, her tooth, and blood all over my floor."

My chest floods with panic, and I look at Simon, who's standing next to me. "Who's Sam?" I say, holding my breath, wondering the worst.

"Midnight." Simon sets his hand on my shoulder. Next to him stands a dude in a suit. "This is Agent Sharp. He's been on the working with me on this case since I first arrived at Children of His Mercy. We discovered that Emmanuel has been using a fake name for months now. He's been staying here in town months now."

My body freezes, the words thick in my mouth. "What does that have to do with anything?"

Neither of the men speak.

"Simon," I growl. "Tell me what the hell that means."

I look up when I hear it, the whimper—familiar, pained—and my knees immediately buckle when I see who else is with Jo and Mrs. Donahue.

"Eve?"

I hold my breath, thinking this is a dream. Because there's no way Eve's in Bex's house right now. She's not staring at me, not reaching for her mom's hand, and definitely not laying her head on Jo's shoulder. It's almost like they knew she was coming. Like they'd seen her before this.

But that can't be right.

"W-what the hell's going on?" I back away, grabbing the ends of my hair and pulling until my scalp throbs.

"Midnight," Simon whispers. "I'm so sorry, kid. I didn't know up until five minutes ago. She arrived an hour after we left town."

I turn to him, finding pain in his eyes that doesn't match with Simon's normal emotions. I shake my head, my own tears falling, because if Eve is alive and here in Bex's house, then Bex is...

"No." I slide down the wall and land on my ass, shaking my head until I'm dizzy. Green eyes stare down at me, wet and broken like I remember them, but not even the sight of Eve's face can take the fear away.

"No," I say again, looking up at Simon. "Tell me he doesn't have her. Tell me, damn it."

"I'm sorry." Simon bows his head.

"H-he's dead," I yell. "He died. *She* died." I point to Eve.

Simon crouches down in front of me. "We thought so too, Midnight. But the bodies weren't in the car that night."

"No," I hiss out the word. "You're lying. That's...

that's not Eve. Eve died. Emmanuel too. I watched them. We *all* watched them go down that hill and—"

Simon touches my shoulder. "He and Eve never got into that car."

"But I saw her—"

"Did you though?"

I open my mouth to say yes, realizing a second later that I never actually did see them.

"No." I cover my mouth, shake my head too. "How?" I asked looking specifically at Eve this time. "Tell me how, damn it."

"There were people hiding, they helped us..." She sniffled, burying her face against her Mom's chest. "I'm sorry, Midnight. I'm so, so sorry."

"This is *your* fault," I said, rushing Simon, grabbing him by the front of his shirt and shaking. "You knew. You. *Knew.* All this god damn time!"

Another FBI agent came at me from my left, but Simon held a hand up to stop him, his gaze never leaving mine. "I did it because I had to. I knew you'd never stop looking for her if you knew. Bringing you back here was the safest and only option we had while we looked for them."

"Fuck you," I said, shoving him back.

He barely budged, tall and bulky, everything I wasn't because I was *weak*. And weak people didn't know things, couldn't help people because they'd inevitably screw up.

Not this time, though. Not when my entire world was riding on finding the one person who really and truly mattered to me. Bex didn't view me as weak. She believed in me. She gave me a reason to keep going and now I was going to save her if it was the last thing I ever did.

Ignoring everyone's gaze, I turn back to Eve. "Where is he?" I hiss. "Where's Emmanuel, damn it!"

Tears stream down her face—her pale face that looks exactly like it did that night. I should be hugging her, thanking God she's alive, but all I feel is rage that she's alive and Bex is gone.

"Midnight," is all she says.

"It's time for us to go," Mr. Donahue says, urging his family out the door.

"Why are you not with him?" I yell as they walk out, rushing the door, face on fire with rage. "Why are you not in that car? You're supposed to be dead, and Bex is supposed to be here and alive and with me!"

"That's enough." A hand grabs my elbow from behind, nails digging into skin. I turn, expecting to see Simon, but it's Bex's mom instead. "My daughter would *never* forgive you for speaking to that poor girl like that."

Mrs. Capone glares at me through her tears, black makeup streaming down her cheeks. She's strong. A hell of a stronger than I am. And I hate myself for it.

My shoulders slump. She's right. This isn't Eve's fault. And Bex would call me out on how I treated her in a heartbeat. But everything hurts knowing that Emmanuel could have her right now. Knowing that she's in danger because of me.

"I know where they are," Eve says. "Emmanuel and your friend."

I look outside, finding her just on the other side of the door frame. She's the last to leave, but her family is behind her, chins lifted high and ready to protect in a moment's notice.

With careful steps, Eve comes forward again, three feet apart from me. She wipes her eyes and lifts her chin. "I know where Emmanuel likely took her, I mean."

"What?" I blink. "How?"

She looks at her hands, which she twists in front of her waist as she speaks. "When Emmanuel realized I wasn't the one you loved anymore, he...he started ignoring me. Treating me like an ill-fated prisoner. I didn't eat. I was barely given anything to drink."

"God, Eve. I-I didn't know."

She shrugs and meets my gaze. "It's okay, I got out."

"How?" I ask.

"It doesn't matter," she says. "Not anymore."

"It does matter." Simon says as he moves in beside me. In his hands, he's holding a small black book. "But for now, just tell us where she is so we can help Bex."

Eve flinches when she sees him, but doesn't back down either. Simon is a reminder of bad times, and Eve probably needs to adjust to the fact that he's on our side, just like I had to do. Still, I don't have the patience to reassure her when I'm barely holding it together.

In the end, whatever fear she had is swept away thankfully because when she looks at him again, the fear in her eyes is gone. "She's likely inside the Reckoning Room at Children of His Mercy."

I shake my head. "They burned that place down."

The smell of piss.

Numb hands.

Crying, grown men.

Blackness.

"I saw that building burn too," Simon tells her. "That's impossible."

"Only part of it did," Eve tells us, her voice shaky. "Emmanuel rebuilt it."

"On his own?" Simon motions for others to come closer, handing out an address on several pieces of paper.

He tells them to call the local authorities surrounding that Missouri location.

"No. Not on his own." Eve looks at me again, a single tear sliding down her cheek. "Noah was with him. And so was Midnight's mom."

CHAPTER 42: BEX

MARCH 2022

IT'S dark by the time we get to wherever we're going.
I'm so dizzy I can't see straight. Not just from pain but
because I've been riding in a trunk for six hours straight
—maybe longer. Maybe less. Time means nothing when
you're riding the line between living and dying.

For a long time, I tried to punch out the lights like I'd
learned when it came to kidnappings, but with my tailbone so jacked up and my ankles tied together, along
with my wrists, that movement was almost impossible.

The trunk lid is lifted. It's so dark out, I can't see the
faces of the men hovering over me. One has to be that
Emmanuel freak, but the other is unfamiliar.

"Brother, why?" the new one whispers, probably
thinking I'm asleep. I play that pretend game well. I'll get
more details if I do.

"Because she is the answer."

"But she's—"

"That's enough, Noah. I won't tolerate your second-
guessing again."

Noah. As in Midnight's uncle?

My bottom lip threatens to shake, but I manage, somehow, to keep it together.

"Apologies. It is not in my realm to question your judgment, Prophet."

They speak in another language then. Latin, if I had to guess. The words are short and they bounce off the men like Ping-Pong balls. A minute later, I'm lifted into someone's arms, and the pain is so bad, I can't help but cry out.

"She's hurt?" the other man, Noah, says.

"She's alive," Emmanuel says. "That's the important part. Unfortunately, she wasn't as accepting as I would have liked her to be so decisions were made."

Footsteps crunch over what sounds like gravel, or maybe snow, the shadow of Emmanuel slipping off into the night. When I inhale, it's spicy cologne and BO that I smell, with the faint smell of oil lingering in the air too.

"Rest, sweet lamb," Noah says. "You will feel better soon."

My shoulders start to shake, and only then do I lose it. Blubbering tears that are so loud they echo through the night.

"Keep her quiet," Emmanuel yells from ahead.

The guy, Noah—the one Midnight had trusted so fiercely—places his hand over my mouth and nose. "Shhh. Everything is as it should be," he says.

I blink, looking up at him from his arms, tears spilling, ears ringing. Not even the sound of a beating human heart against the side of my face can take it away. "Please," I whisper, sliding his hand off my mouth, "don't do this, please. It will kill Midnight."

He clears his throat but stays quiet, his hair long and falling over the sides of his face.

"Noah," I try. "He told me he loves you. You're the only one he ever trusted."

His hold on me slips just a little, and I wonder if I'm getting under his skin.

"He's alive because of you and Simon. You two are good men—"

"Shut up," he hisses at me, eyes narrowing. "Just shut. Up. Please."

Seconds later, I'm brought into a lit room, then dropped on top of a floor made of bricks. I cry out, rolling onto my hip, the pain so bad I can't breathe.

This can't be how I die, damn it.

A door slams shut and is soon locked from the sound of the click. I puke so hard, it covers the floor, popcorn kernels sticking to the roof of my mouth, cheek, and hair. I can't move. Moving hurts.

I let myself cry for a while, thinking of my mom. My dad. And lastly, Midnight. I wonder if he knows yet. I hope Mom's okay. If they come here, I worry that what's about to happen to me may happen to them too.

I cry again, softer now. Throat burning, eyes swollen... Then seconds before sleep takes over, a hand settles around mine.

"You need to keep your eyes open, okay?" a woman whispers.

I blink staring back at a beautiful, black-haired woman who's crouched over me. She smiles just the slightest, but it's crooked and sad and... "Midnight," I whisper.

"No, honey. I'm his mom. April Turner."

I TRIED to keep my eyes open. But as the night went on and the room grew colder, I found it harder to do so.

Midnight's mom was calm and sweet, nothing like I thought she'd be. She even sang—something in another language, but still, it eased the pain in my heart, if only for a little while.

When my voice was gone from the amount of crying, I simply held on to her hand, and her mine, as we waited for whatever was supposed to happen to us.

"He was such a good little boy," Midnight's mom whispers now. I hear the smile in her words. She's playing with my hair, and my head's on her lap. "He has his father's eyes, yes. But everything else is him. Not me. Not Emmanuel. Not even Noah. It's like he developed into his own person, and I knew when we were running all those years that he was a son I would love eternally, even knowing who he was half of."

I couldn't agree more.

"He took care of me," she says.

"He does that," I manage.

She clears her throat. "I tried to give him the life he deserved, away from all of this."

I want to tell her she did to make her feel better. But every time I think of the story he told me, how she jumped out that window and left him the way she did, I freeze up and imagine all the ways she could've done better.

Instead, I comfort her with my truth.

"I love him," I say, having never said it out loud before. "I love him like I've never loved another person."

"I imagine he loves you very much too," she whispers back to me. "It's why you're here. Emmanuel believes you are to be his now."

"I'd rather die," I whisper.

"I too, feel that way."

Shivers rack my body from her words, my love of cold weather quickly fading. I can't see anything in the dark. Midnight's words run through my mind, and I'm thinking of the night he told me about nearly freezing to death, in a room that could very well be like this one. But I refuse to believe that I'm about to live through the same events.

"How did Noah and Simon save him but you wound up back here?" I ask.

"*They* didn't bring me here. Emmanuel did. He found me. He always does. And the only way he would let me live is if Noah agreed to help him fix this place, then bring you back here as a replacement for Eve."

I swallow a hard lump in my throat. "What do you mean a replacement for Eve?"

"Meaning, you are the rightful lamb, not her. The one my son loves so truly and unconditionally."

I gasp, trying to push away her last words.

Rightful. Lamb. Not Eve. Me.

"Then where's Eve?" I finally ask, holding my breath.

"Likely back home. At least I'm hoping so. Though Emmanuel thinks otherwise."

"W-what do you mean?"

She sighs. "Noah drugged her one morning, said he found her lifeless body right here—" She pats the brick floor next to me. "—suicide he'd called it. Emmanuel came in, took one look at her, and insisted Noah get rid of the body. He had no more use for her once he'd realized you were the one my son loved."

"But she's alive? After all these months?"

April nods. "Noah took her sleeping body somewhere that day, I'm not sure where though. He never told me."

My first thought is how happy Midnight will be when

he finds this out. Maybe he can move on and live his life guilt-free now. If I don't make it through this, then at least I'll know they now have each other. But then I realize what this means for me, and the panic shoots through my veins like a shot of liquid adrenaline.

"I-I can't be here," I whisper struggling to get up, but Midnight's Mom holds me down with an arm across my chest. "I want my mom. I need her. Please."

"Shhh," she says, brushing hair from my eyes, her voice I found comforting minutes before, not sends goosebumps across my skin. "It won't be long now."

"Won't be long for what?" I whisper, shaking.

"You'll see, little lamb."

———

I WAKE up on cold concrete, inhaling something bitter. A light shines through a few cracks of the roof. My legs are bounded together still, my hands, though, are now tied behind my back instead of in front of me. I try to move, but everything hurts, and all I can do is cry.

But then I hear it.

Bex.

My name. The familiar voice.

Bex.

I blink, managing to look down at my feet, the world spinning when I see who it is. "Dad?"

I reach for him, my eyes too dry for tears. He smiles at me, waves, and calls my name once more. I try to get up, to go to him, but my body won't move, the ropes are too tight around my wrist and ankles. Plus, I'm too weak.

Seconds later, he disappears and I'm too exhausted to care one way or another. If this is my fate, then I'm hoping to fall asleep before death takes me under its wings.

"Mrs. Turner?" I turn my head, wondering where she is.

When I finally see her, I discover right away why she's not answering me. Bloody wrists; wide, lifeless eyes...

Dead. She's dead.

"Oh, god." I puke again, though there's nothing left in my system. "Help," I whimper, unmoving. "Please. Someone help me."

"*Multi autem sunt vocati pauci vero electi*," a voice fills the air. Dark and heavy. Clearer, unlike it'd been with my dad. "Many are called, and few are chosen."

When I turn my head toward his voice on the right, I see another body beside me instead. Eyes shut, blood falling from the corner of his parted lips, dripping like it's going in slow motion.

Another dead body.

A man.

Noah.

"You have quite the influence over so many." That voice pulls at me from ahead once more. I inhale a deep breath when I finally turn and make out his features by my feet.

Eyes like Midnight's, rimmed with pure evil.

Emmanuel. There's no doubt in my mind this is him.

"You son of a bitch," I whisper. If I yell, I'll cry. And if I cry, I'll be as weak as he probably thinks I am.

"I'm not the enemy," he says. "I am the Prophet. It's fair time for you to learn that my new little lamb." He shoves Noah out of the way with his foot, before crouching down beside me. "I'm going to take care of you. You'll learn to love me like you did my son. And you will be the person Eve was meant to be before she decided to abandon her cause. My real life partner."

"I will never, ever be that girl," I tell him, eyes narrowed into slits.

He *tsks* and runs the back of his hands down my cheek. "God's plans say otherwise, I'm afraid."

Before I can think about fighting back, he stands, walks to my other side, and grabs Midnight's mom's legs within seconds. He drags her away, arms above her head with blood trailing from her wrists at the same time. Somehow, her head tips back as she's moved, and though she's dead, her eyes still land on me.

A stifled sob slides up my throat at the view. This feels like a dream—a nightmare gone wrong that I won't be waking up from.

Within seconds. Emmanuel does the same with Noah's body, dragging him across the room by the legs as well. When I turn my head to follow, I watch as his lifeless body is thrown over the top of Midnight's mom like nothing—a bean bag flopping, a towel being tossed into a dirty hamper. Like farm animals ready to be slaughtered.

Seconds later, the telltale sound of a match strike fills the air. One, then two, until the room is filled with the smell of burning human skin and smoke.

Emmanuel speaks more words in Latin, then raises his hands and face to the sky. He's smiling, from what I can tell, and the view has the tears in my eyes falling faster than before.

The putrid smell of burning flesh starts to choke me, to the point where I have to look away and hold my breath. Just when I think things can't get any worse, Emmanuel moves to stand above me again, legs straddled on either side of my stomach, dark hair falling over his forehead.

"You should be so very delighted that I'm here," he says, head tipped to one side

I shake my head, watching with wide eyes. "N-no, please."

"Quiet down now. All will be at peace for you soon."

Seconds later he pulls something from his pants pocket. A rag, or towel. Thick and heavy. Wet. It drips onto my face, the smell making me gag.

"*Iesus namque verus paschalis est agnus, qui in sacrificium pro nobis ultro se obtulit, novum aeternumque efficiens testamentum,*" he says.

"No, no, please. Plea..."

"Hush, now." He shoves the rag into my mouth then ties it around my head. "All is well, my lamb."

My eyes widen. The rancid taste of fuel fills my mouth and throat. He hums like he's done this before. I'm guessing he has. Moments later, when he's checked the bindings around my ankles and wrists, he rolls me to the side, tells me to hold my breath, that it'll be easier on me if I do. Even still, the gasoline soaks my tongue and pools in my cheek.

Emmanuel moves, speaking prayers. I can't see him, but I feel him watching me, smell the flesh of burning bodies growing stronger and stronger by the second.

"When they are ash, we will make haste," he calls out from behind me. "For now, this must be the way."

My eyelids grow heavy and swollen from tears. Minutes passed, or maybe hours, I'm not sure. The only thing I want to do is sleep.

So, I do.

I shut my eyes, I keep them closed, and I imagine I'm home in Chicago with my mom and dad in our tiny apartment. We're watching movies, eating popcorn, and living our lives how we were meant to be living them.

But then my dad soon morphs into someone else.

It's Midnight. He's smiling. Until he's not.

He's holding my hand. Kissing my head. Calling my name.

He cries. Sobs, really. Holding my hands between both of his, until he morphs back into my dad once more.

A loud crash fills the air. I gasp behind the towel, choking on gasoline.

"FBI, put your hands up!"

One gun sounds. Then another, and another…

Dizziness washes over me. I blink, finding shoes. Lots and lots of shoes.

"Dad?" I say, coughing and gagging, untied, unbounded, the rag in my mouth removed.

"Come on, kid. I've got you," he says.

Then I'm lifted into my father's arms and carried away, lost in my mind, maybe for forever.

CHAPTER 43: MIDNIGHT

MARCH 2022

THE HOSPITAL ROOM SMELLS. Too sterile, like bleach. When Bex wakes up, she won't like it. I need to get her a candle. Something that smells like hot chocolate. So, I send a quick text to Simon, begging for him to check the gift shop.

Simon: Seriously, kid? I've already gotten her a dozen flowers.

Me: She hates flowers because they wilt and die

Simon: Wow. That's…weird as hell.

I look at Bex, saying out loud, "Yeah. I know."

I'm gonna need to leave as soon as Bex's mom shows up. Apparently, hospital policy only allows one visitor, no matter the situation. Still, it's gonna feel like teeth being ripped from my gums when I finally have to go. If I had it my way, I'd never leave her side again.

Seeing her there, lying on that ground in that same room I nearly died in myself, wrecked me. I'll never get over it—ever. I won't forgive myself either for bringing her into my dangerous world. But we're safe now.

Emmanuel is dead. There is no more Children of His Mercy.

I should feel relief. Happiness even. But all I feel is a stabbing in my chest that might never go away. At least not until Bex tells me she's okay.

A small moan fills the air. I shoot up and off my chair, rushing to Bex's side. Her head rocks back and forth. Over and over she says, *Dad, Dad.*

"Hey, shh, shh. It's okay. I got you."

Her pretty lips part and so do her eyelids. And then, after twenty-four hours of straight hell, she's looking at me.

"You're okay," I tell her.

She coughs and coughs, wincing a little. I reach over and grab her oxygen mask, sliding it over her head and onto her face. The fuel in her lungs may have damaged them, but the doctors can't be sure. It's a waiting game now, they'd told me.

"You need more pain medicine?" I ask.

She nods.

"All right. Just sleep." Then I bend over, kiss her forehead, and press the button that will have her passing out in seconds.

The next time she wakes up, her face is flushed, and her eyes are a little wider. She takes her oxygen mask off her mouth and nose and looks at me.

"My dad was there," she tells me. "He saved me."

I sit on the end of her bed, holding her hand as she talks.

"He picked me up, Midnight. He carried me out of there."

Instead of telling her it was Simon, I let it go.

"I'm happy for you," I say. Because if seeing her dad in her disillusioned state makes her heal a little faster, then who am I to break her heart by saying it wasn't him?

"Is Mom here?" She tries to sit up but winces, so I help her, placing a pillow behind her back like the nurses explained earlier.

"She's on her way. The second she gets here, she'll come see you. Promise." I want to stay with her. Hold her hand and kiss her and apologize a million times over. But she needs her mom.

"I met your mom," she whispers.

I shut my eyes and hold my breath.

My mom.

Goddamn her.

If only she would've held out, waited just a little longer, then I could've saved her. But I'm hoping, at least, that she's at peace finally.

"She seemed kind, Midnight. And she loved you so much."

I blow out the breath I've been holding, needing air. I've been so focused on getting Bex awake that I haven't had time to process everything that happened. How my mom had slit her wrists. Sometime along the way, Noah had probably come back to check on them, then shot himself in the head, according to Simon. I don't know. I didn't ask for many details. There wasn't a point.

The pain of losing Mom, and maybe even Noah, will probably come later. But for now, I'd rather be numb to everything I lost and enjoy the things that I'd been able to keep.

"Eve's alive," I tell her, bringing her hands to my mouth. I kissed each finger, vowing never to let her go again, if I didn't have to.

"I know." Bex coughs some more, eyes shutting. I reach for the oxygen mask, but she shakes her head.

"Midnight," she manages, reaching for my face. I bend over enough that she can touch it. "I'm so happy for you. Now that she's here again, you two can be together."

My face grows cold. "What?"

She smiles softly. "You love her. You two have a real second chance to be together—"

"No." I shake my head. "No, Bex. That's...no. I *don't* love her."

She frowns.

"I mean I do, but what I feel for her is..."

"Is what?" she asks.

"It's like rain. It doesn't last but an hour or two. Then it dries up."

Her eyebrows pull together, and I laugh.

"My love for you though..." I bend over, kissing the inside of her wrist. "It's like the snow. It stays around. It's gorgeous for a while but then gets dirty until you dig deeper and find another beautiful and untouched layer." I shrug.

"You hate the snow, Midnight." She squints at me.

"Not anymore." I lean even closer, kissing her lips, lingering with my forehead against hers when we break apart.

We stay like that for a few minutes, eyes shut, breathing each other in...until someone knocks at the door.

I groan.

Bex smiles.

And we share a second that's only for us. I try to tell her with my eyes what I can't seem to say right with my mouth, until she surprises me and says it first.

"I love you."

I blink, leaning back to see her clearly as I ask, "You do?"

"Yeah," she mumbles, closing her eyes. "It's baffling."

I kiss the top of her head this time, smiling at her sarcasm. I'm getting better at understanding it. "I'm pretty messed up."

"Hmm," she whispers. "But you're hot at least."

"And you're feeling those meds." I can't help but smile.

Ignoring me, she asks, "Well?"

I lean back to look at her fully. "Well, what?"

"Do you love me?" She blinks. "Or is this doomed?"

I shut my eyes, blowing out a deep, terrified breath. Not because I don't feel the same way but because I feel so much more, and it's terrifying.

"Not doomed," I whisper. "Never. Because the love I feel for you is forever, Bex."

"Hmm." With her eyes close, she smiles wide it's almost smug. "That's what I thought."

And just like that, I know we're gonna be okay. Because love is messy like the snow...yet it lasts longer than any other season.

EPILOGUE: BEX
MAY 2022

I CAN'T STOP SWEATING. It's pouring down my neck, into my graduation gown, between my boobs, even into the back of my underwear. If I have to take one more picture pretending to smile when I feel like I'm on fire, I'll scream.

"Look at you two," Mom says, posing her phone every way imaginable. "Adorable little lovers."

"Mom, seriously?"

"What? I was young once." She winks, then heads over to show Martha the photos she just took.

My face heats for reasons beyond just the hot sun and her verbal diarrhea. Because as of last night, that *lovers* thing rings a little truer than Mom probably knows. I'd like to explain it, the secrets of sex at eighteen, but some things are meant to be vaulted forever.

I look up at Midnight. He's smiling at me, our shared secret shining in his eyes too.

"Awww," Simon says, taking a picture of his own before pocketing his phone and tugging his girlfriend against his side. He kisses her cheek, and she nearly swoons.

"Don't you have somewhere to be?" Midnight asks, wrapping an arm around my waist.

"Yeah, yeah." Simon waves him away. "Be ready on Sunday when I get back though, all right? I don't like waiting." Simon looks at me with smiling eyes. "And congratulations again on graduating, Bex. You did good, kid."

I smile back and wave goodbye.

Midnight flips him off but walks to him regardless, saying, "Give me a minute."

"Of course," I say, watching him walk off seconds later.

He laughs at something Simon says when he approaches him. My throat burns at the view, the sadness that is already building inside of me. I don't want him to move away, to another town three hours from me. But he's getting what he deserves—finally. Stability in the form of a man who wants to be his father. Simon is legally adopting him, despite the fact that he's already eighteen.

At least it won't be forever that we're apart, seeing as how I got accepted to a college just fifteen minutes from where he's going to be living. It's only going to be a month of separation before I move down there into my dorm, but since everything has happened, he's been my consistent—aside from my mom—and losing that will be hard.

It's necessary though. I probably need to regroup and learn how to be alone again.

What happened to me wasn't cut and dry. It was a complicated, scary ass mess of time. I don't want to remember it or talk about it—and I didn't for a good six weeks. But then Midnight reminded me of something I'd once said to him. How it was better to talk about issues than shoving them away.

So, I'd done that with him.

Now I'll have to do it alone before tackling a life that stems beyond high school and Altoona.

"Hey, you!" Gia runs at me from the side, surprising me. She wraps both arms around my waist and sets her chin on my shoulder. Carson does the same, but it's less aggressive.

"You going to the party tonight at the barn?" Gia asks after mom takes a few pictures of the three of us in our caps and gowns.

"I don't think so," I finally say. "But give Jo my best, would you?"

They nod in unison, smiles sad as they say their goodbyes. Hands clasped, they head toward their families, bypassing them seconds later to wrap their arms around Jo. She sees me over Carson's shoulder and gives me a small smile. I do the same, adding a wave, though it feels forced and strange. Nothing like it used to be.

The two of us made up. We hugged it out. Jo swore she'd never lie again, but as time passed, she stopped calling. And I did the same. I heard she's going to a school somewhere in Wisconsin in the fall. Small and private. Maybe our paths will cross again—even if they don't necessarily intertwine. Her parents got divorced too, with their dad leaving them the money, the barn, and their house. According to Midnight, it was the best thing that could've ever happened.

"Do you want to talk to her before we go?" Midnight slides in beside me a few minutes later. His fingers lace through mine as he nudges his chin toward Jo and her family.

I shake my head. "Do you want to talk to Eve?"

"No." He turns to me. "You're the only thing I need right now."

The two of them spent several hours together while I was in the hospital, just talking things over—the good and the bad. Both agreed that their feelings never stemmed past the walls of Children of His Mercy. I think they'll always share a bond, but it's different than what Midnight and I have.

I wrap my arms around his neck and say, "Awww. Look at you being all sweet and relationship-y."

He groans but picks me up anyway, swinging me in a circle and making me dizzy with happiness and love and all the ooshy-gushy stuff I never thought I'd want to feel. When he sets me down, I lean into him, not only because I'm dizzy but because I love being close to him. And from the way his body is constantly wrapping around mine, I'm pretty sure he feels the same.

"You ready?" Mom asks. She's taking us to dinner. Buying me a celebratory graduation feast. Then she has to work all night, which I don't mind because I think I'd like a repeat of the night before with Midnight.

"Yep," I say before looking up at Midnight. "Are you ready?"

He smiles at me, both sides of his lips curled up. It's one of those rare smiles I only every see a few times a month. But damn if it doesn't take my breath away.

"Yeah."

"Good." I stand on my tiptoes when my mom and Martha turn away, whispering in his ear, "And later, if you want, I can teach you how to play my favorite childhood game."

"Twister."

He frowns. "Are you sure you can handle that?"

"The doctor says I'm cleared, remember? That my lungs are—" I kiss my fingers. "Chef's kiss."

"If you're sure..."

"So sure." I wink.

He shakes his head.

"What?" I grip the front of his shirt, holding tight. "You afraid I'll beat you?"

"No. I'm afraid you'll be let down when I beat *you*."

I tip my head back and laugh, the wind in my hair, the sun on my face as I say, "Yeah, right. I'm a badass."

He buries his face against the side of my neck and wraps both arms around my waist, squeezing me close as he says, "You sure as hell are."

ACKNOWLEDGMENTS

When I sat down to write *Midnight and Bex* I had no idea how much this story would affect me. For a long time after I finished, I was in a dark place and it took a village to get me out. That village is my family.

To Chris, my husband. I can't count the number of nights you'd come home from a long day at work, only to jump into chef mode so the kids could eat. So *I* could eat too. I know my writing life isn't ideal to you and this family sometimes, but you never deter me from giving up, and for that I can't say thank you enough. You are quite literally my happily ever after.

To Emma and Bella. I know it's annoying when Mom says she'll be done writing in ten minutes and it turns into a half hour instead, but without your little nudges, I probably wouldn't take breaks at all. So, thank you for forcing me to get off the computer after five hours straight. You remind me that it's necessary to take breaks in life. That without lunch, I can't function. And those five mile a day drives for energy drinks? I wouldn't change them for the world. Without our little jaunts and our time together, I wouldn't be able to focus. Spending time with you two makes everything wrong in life feel right again. I love you both so much.

To Kelsey. I won't get mushy with you because, well...I know you don't like it. But every day I thank God for you. I know life is crap sometimes, but you're my oldest, wisest, and strongest child, but I grow more and more proud of the woman you've become with every passing second. Whatever you decide to do in life, wherever you go, I want you to know that I will always be ten steps behind you, ready to have your back...even when you want to handle things on your own. It's what moms do. I love you. With everything I have in me.

To Mom and Dad. They say 2020 and 2021 were rough years. And they were. But 2022 hasn't been the best for you both either so far. I want you two to know that I wouldn't be where I am right now without you. That every day I spend not doing my laundry is one day spent writing with the brain and creative juices you both blessed me with. Someday I'll make my riches and hire that maid. Love you two so very much.

To my agent, Jem. You're an absolute queen. I don't know what I did without you before, but whatever it was doesn't compare. You're not only my number one fan, but the reason I'm able to do what I do. Thank you for everything, for being a friend too. Your time and your endless patience when it comes to my anxiety never goes unnoticed.

Jessica Calla! You get my dedication. You also GET me. Sisters, friends, besties, bff...you know I'd be lost without ya.

To my Hype Squad. (or so the young-uns call it) Jen Griswel and Noelle Strader. Our DMs give me life. Your cheerleading makes me believe I'm not so bad at this writing thing. And without you both, I'd pretty much fall flat on my face with every new book. Love you two. Let's make Nashville happen! (sooner or later)

To the team and Wise Wolf. Thank you for allowing me to write what's in my heart. I know it's not always on brand for the genre, but I do what I do because you allow me to, and I will always be grateful for this opportunity you've given me.

And finally…

To my readers. The ones who've stuck around from the beginning, no matter what genre I write in. I do this for you. And though you're few and far between, I want to say thank you for keeping me going.

A LOOK AT: THE LIARS BENEATH

A romantically dark YA romantic suspense set in the backdrop of Iowa's suspenseful farmlands.

After a tragic accident ends her best friend's life, 17-year-old Becca Thompson succumbs to grief the only way she knows how: by wallowing in it. She's a fragment of the person she once was—far too broken to enjoy the summer before her senior year. But when Ben McCain, her best friend's older brother, returns home, Becca must face her new reality head on.

She isn't interested in Ben's games, especially since he abandoned his sister during the months leading up to her death. But when he begs for her help in uncovering the truth about what really happened the night of his sister's death, Becca finds herself agreeing, hoping to clear up rumors swirling in the wake of her best friend's accident.

An unhinged ex-boyfriend, secret bucket lists, and garage parties in the place Becca calls home soon lead her to the answers she's so desperate to unveil. But nobody is being honest, not even Ben. And the closer Becca gets to the truth—and to Ben—the more danger seems to surround her.

Clearing her best friend's name was all she wanted to do, but Becca is quickly realizing that the truth she craves might be uglier than the lies her best friend kept.

AVAILABLE NOW

ABOUT THE AUTHOR

Heather Van Fleet is a Midwestern-born author with a love of all things spontaneous, like road trips. She enjoys TV shows that leave her questioning her morals and book boyfriends. As a graduate of Black Hawk College, Heather took her degree in early childhood development, tossed it into the garbage, and is now living the dream of writing young adult novels sprinkled with suspense and lots of kissing. She's currently living out her own version of a happily ever after with her high-school-sweetheart-turned-husband, their three hugely feminist daughters, and two fur babies with bad attitudes. When she's not being a mom or writing books, you can find her drinking way too many energy drinks or crashing out on her sofa with a romance novel of some sort.